DESPERATION REEF

T. JEFFERSON PARKER

DESPERATION REEF

TOR PUBLISHING GROUP
NEW YORK

FORGE

DESPERATION REEF

A Forge Book
Published by Tom Doherty Associates / Tor Publishing Group
120 Broadway
New York, NY 10271

www.torpublishinggroup.com

The Library of Congress Cataloging-in-Publication Data is available upon request.

ISBN 978-1-250-90788-2 (hardcover)
ISBN 978-1-250-90789-9 (ebook)

Our books may be purchased in bulk for promotional, educational, or business use. Please contact your local bookseller or the Macmillan Corporate and Premium Sales Department at 1-800-221-7945, extension 5442, or by email at MacmillanSpecialMarkets@macmillan.com.

First Edition: 2024

Printed in the United States of America

0 9 8 7 6 5 4 3 2 1

FOR MARY ANN PARKER WELBORN—

SEEKER, SWIMMER, SISTER, FRIEND.

LONG MAY YOU PLAN.

DESPERATION REEF

1

Hear Jen scream.

Jen Stonebreaker, that is, hollering over the whine of her jet ski, towing her husband into a wave taller than a four-story building.

"For you, John—it's all *yours*!"

She's twenty-one years old, stout and well-muscled, with a cute face, a freckled nose, and an inverted bowl of thick orange hair she's had since she was ten.

She's a versatile young woman, too—the high school swim, water polo, and surf team captain. The class valedictorian. A former Miss Laguna Beach. With a UC Irvine degree in creative journalism from the School of Humanities, honors, of course.

Right now, though, Jen is bucking an eight-hundred-pound jet ski on the rising shoulder of a fifty-foot wave, her surf-star husband, John, trailing a hundred feet behind her on his signature orange and black "gun" surfboard, rope handle tied to the rescue sled, which skitters and slaps behind her.

Welcome to Mavericks, a winter break in the cold waters just south of San Francisco, with occasionally gigantic waves, sometimes beautifully formed, but always potentially lethal. These things charge in and hit Mavericks' shallow reef like monsters from the deep. A surfer can't just paddle into one; he or she has to be towed in by a jet ski or a helicopter. One of the scariest breaks on Earth. Ask any of the very few people who ride places like this. Not only the jagged, shallow rocks, but sharks, too, and water so cold you can barely feel your feet through neoprene boots.

Mavericks has taken the lives of professional, skilled, big-wave riders.

Riders not unlike the Stonebreakers, Jen now gunning her jet ski across the rising wave, looking for smooth water to deliver John into the steepening face of it, where he will toss the rope and—if all goes well and the gods are smiling—drop onto this wall and try to stay on his board, well ahead of the breaking barrel that, if it gets its chance, will crush him to the rocky bottom like a bathtub toy.

He throws aside the tow rope.

Jen guns her two-hundred-fifty horses, roaring and smoking, up and over the wave's huge back, and lands momentarily beyond its reach, the rescue sled bobbing behind her.

She's got a good angle to watch John and help him if he wipes out.

She feels the tremendous tonnage of water trying to suck her back onto the wave and over the falls.

Thinks: Nope.

Throttles hard and away.

Steadies herself on the bucking machine, off to the side and safely out of the way of the monsters, where she can watch John do his thing.

The next wave lumbers in—she's always startled by how fast they are—and she sees John astride his big board, racing down the smooth blue face of his wave, legs staunch but vibrating, feet locked in the thick rubber straps glued to his board. He carves out ahead of the lip then rises, backing up into the barrel, casually trailing a hand on the cylinder as he streams along just ahead of the crushing lip—John's signature move; he's one of the few guys who does this daredevil-in-the-barrel thing, looking cool on a fifty-footer. He's twenty-six years old, one of the top ten big-wave riders in the world.

Jen hears the barrel roaring closed behind him. Like a freight train or a stretched-out thunderclap.

Jen smiles.

Jen and John. John and Jen.

Look at him, she thinks. This is it. This is why we do it. Nothing we'll ever do will match it. Not love. Not sex. Not being a mother or a father. Not seeing God. Not mountains of money. Nothing. Nothing can touch this speed, this perilous grace, this joy, this high.

Then it all goes wrong.

The thick lip lunges forward like a leopard, taking him by the head and off his board.

The sharp orange-and-black gun hangs in the air above him, the leash still fastened to John's ankle, then the fins catch and the board spears past John, missing him by inches.

He's lifted high above the ribs of the wave, then pitched over the falls, pulled down by his board, into the raging impact zone.

Jen checks the next wave—well *fuck,* it's bigger than this one—then steers the jet ski closer to the wall of whitewater that owns her husband.

A bright red rescue helicopter swoops down, close enough to tear foam off the crest of that wave.

Two rescue skis cut wide semicircles around the impact zone, their drivers looking for a way in.

And two more of the tow ski drivers, bucking the chop in search of John.

The seconds zip by but John doesn't surface. His broken board launches from the whitewater, just two halves hinged by fiberglass. No leash attached. Which, in spite of John's quick-release coupling, could mean the absolute worst for him—the damned leash is still fastened to his ankle, virtually unbreakable, easily caught on the sharp reef boulders lurking just feet below the surface.

Jen watches for any flash of shape or color, his black trunks, his orange helmet—anything that's not whitewater, swirling sand, and rocks. *Anything . . .*

She knows with the wave closing fast behind her it's time to plunge into the mayhem.

Feels the monster pull of it drawing her up.

Circling tightly, checking the rescue sled, getting ready to go in, she pauses one fraction of a second and thinks—among darker thoughts: I love you more than anything in the world . . .

And in that split second, the next wave lifts her from behind and Jen feels the terrible vertigo of a coming fall while clinging to an eight-hundred-pound personal watercraft.

Her personal deathtrap.

She cranks the ski throttle full open, digs a hard U-turn into the face of the wave. Jumps the lip and flies over.

She's midair again on the smoking contraption. Below her, no John in sight. Just his shattered board bouncing in the foam on its way to shore.

She lands behind the wave and speeds a wide arc to something like safety. Rooster-tails to near where John went down. Can't get all that close.

She's lost precious time. Precious seconds. A lot of them.

She grinds through the whitewater as best she can, crisscrossing the worst of it. A surge of heavy foam catches the jet ski broadside and flips it.

She keeps hold, lets another wall of whitewater crash over her before she can find the handles, right the beast, and continue searching her blinding world of foam and spray.

Smacked by the chop and wind, she clamps her teeth and grimaces to draw air instead of brine.

In shallower water, she searches the rocks below. Hears the scream of the other watercrafts around her, voices calling out. The big-wave people mostly look out for each other; they're loose-knit and competitive but most of them will lose contests and *miss waves* to help someone in trouble—even of his own making, even some reckless trust-funder wannabe big-wave king with his own helicopter to tow him in and pro videographers to make him famous.

It's what watermen and waterwomen do.

Jen keeps waiting to feel him behind her, climbing aboard the rescue sled. She knows it's possible: John has trained himself to hold his breath for up to three minutes underwater.

But not being pounded like this . . .

As the minutes pass, hope and fear fight like dogs inside her—a battle that will guide the rest of her life.

We are small and brief.

We are the human passion to stay alive, made simple.

She helps work John's body out of the rocks.

TWENTY-FIVE YEARS LATER

2

Looking Back—

WHO WAS JOHN STONEBREAKER AND WHAT WENT WRONG AT MAVERICKS?

A big-wave surfing contest left one of the world's premier professional surfers
dead. But who was he and why did he die?

BY JEN STONEBREAKER

Part one of a special series for *Surf Tribe Magazine*

They filmed the deadly 1999 Monsters of Mavericks, and they wrote
about it and talked about it, but they never got deep into the barrel of
what happened, and why.

How could they? Fifteen dead in Columbine. War in Kosovo. Bill
Clinton impeached. Y2K, when the world's computers would crash and
the economy along with them.

The world was a busy place then, but crazy surfers riding giant waves
weren't exactly a crucial part of it.

That day, there was a shifting cast of fifty or so people near or in the
water for the spectacle of a freakishly large northwest swell: contestants
and their tow partners, boatloads of reporters, photographers, videographers, and a famous novelist, all trying to do their jobs but keep out

of the impact zone, where the waves break; also rescue teams, and three contest "officials" in a helicopter circling overhead.

There were a few hundred spectators up on the cliffs above Ross Point, using binoculars and giant-lensed cameras for a view of the action.

The day was cold and bright, and the visibility excellent except for the impact zone, which was a churning cauldron of whitewater overhung with a dense cloud of sea spray.

So, there are many accounts of the same sequence of events, many points of view of how and why what happened, happened. Much video and many pictures.

There is some truth in most of them. So why should I add another voice, twenty-five years later?

I've taken questions from various media, but never answered beyond what was asked, never gone into detail.

From the beginning there was a lot of speculation, some by investigators and reporters, some by family and friends, some by strangers and opportunists telling half-truths and lies in those early days of the Internet.

Why not write about all this until now? After all, I learned how to do this in college. How to put words down. It's much easier than riding a fifty-foot wave. Or raising two sons. It isn't rocket science, to write a firsthand report of an event you were a part of.

But my husband's death was too sudden and too unlikely for me—his twenty-one-year-old wife—to understand at that time.

I did not understand.

I understood his broken bones and fractured skull and the seawater in his lungs, and the leash caught on the rocks and still strapped to his ankle.

But I did not understand the *why* of it.

I'm forty-six, and that is what I am hoping to do now.

John Stonebreaker was my new, five-doors-down neighbor when I was twelve. His big family had just moved onto our street, Alta Laguna

Boulevard, in Laguna's Top of the World neighborhood. He was seventeen and the second oldest of the Stonebreaker kids.

We Byrnes were a longtime Laguna family. My grandparents owned a restaurant on Coast Highway that I eventually inherited, redesigned, renamed the Barrel, and still operate today. My dad became Laguna's chief of police. He was a tough cop but a cuddly bear at home. He believed—still does—that a cop should serve and protect. An oath he took very seriously. He believed that Laguna's citizens and her thousands of summer visitors were his responsibility. His flock. My mother—an Olympic swimmer in the Montreal summer games of 1976—was a Laguna Beach High School girls' PE teacher, and coach of the swim, water polo, and surf teams. She believed that an athlete should win. And a coach should make that happen. Trophies, medals, ribbons, scholarships. Win or stay home.

Don and Eve Byrne, née Braxton.

Mom was my inspiration and my belief.

Dad was my idol.

I was their only child.

John Stonebreaker at seventeen was thin, blond-haired, and blue eyed. A little dip-shouldered (the left) which made him seem casual and unconcerned with his appearance.

I first saw him on a hot July evening, wheeling a trash can from his house to the curb. He had just moved in. He seemed purposeful and focused, fitting that trash can flush with the curb, making a few small adjustments to get it right.

That night I asked Mom and Dad about the new family, trying to press them for information without spilling my curiosity about the boy.

Mom told me the Stonebreakers came up from San Clemente. They were renting here. The dad was a preacher who had just opened his own church in Laguna Niguel, in a storefront that used to be a donut shop. Mrs. Stonebreaker was going to be a counselor at the high school, so we'll be working together, Mom had said.

"They have four kids and they all surf at the San Onofre Surf Club.

Even the preacher. They've got some Irish in them, like us. Or so says Marilyn Stonebreaker. Nice woman. Pretty and sweet."

The next day I saw John surfing Rockpile, north of Main Beach.

I was on the beach with my best friend, Belle Becket, pressing our boogie board leashes tight around our skinny, twelve-year-old ankles.

John rode the wave like he took out the trash, measured and confident, as if there was one perfect way to do it, and he knew that way.

This was back in 1990, when short-board, quick and nimble surfing had long taken over the Beach Boys days of nose-riding. But on one wave John went retro, sidled forward, and rode with his toes on the nose of his board. Not easy on a short, fast, fish-style wave rider.

I loved his grace, his nonchalance, his cool.

John Stonebreaker didn't just look cool, he *was* cool—the body and form of it.

I'm going to be that someday, I told myself. *I'm going to be him.*

I still see that boy and that wave in my mind's eye, as clearly as if it had happened just this morning.

We watched him awhile, and rode a few of those nasty Rockpile waves on our body boards. When we were done we headed straight to the Thalia Surf Shop, where I gave up my boogie board and a twenty-dollar down payment on a used twin-fin Infinity that the shop owner said was the right size and shape for Laguna. Eighty-five bucks.

Belle got a surfboard, too, a new Town & Country made in Hawaii that cost her dermatologist dad a small fortune.

We surfed all the next morning at Rockpile.

Rough stuff. Didn't catch a wave. Stand-up surfing isn't boogie boarding, not that we thought it would be.

Didn't see John Stonebreaker until almost a week later, when I cruised past his house again on my skateboard and saw him in the garage, doing I knew not what under strong lights.

I hopped off, flipped my board into my hand, and walked back.

Squeezing in between the cars in the driveway—an old hippie van and a newer VW Westphalia—I stood just outside the entrance.

John was taller than he looked from shore the week before. He was dressed in red surf trunks with a baggy, white, long-sleeved T-shirt. He had a tool in both hands, bearing down on a white surfboard blank on sawhorses.

"Hey, I'm Jen Byrne. I saw you surf. I'd like to join your team."

"There's no team."

"When there is one. I'm learning."

He straightened and looked at me, goggles and face misted with foam dust, hair tucked into a Dodgers cap, knees and feet knotted from hours on surfboards.

"Paddle hard and don't take off too early."

"I've got a six-two Infinity."

Another blue-eyed once-over. "Sounds about right."

"I'll be the best female surfer in Laguna someday. Soon."

"I've seen a few okay ones. Only been here a few weeks, though."

"How long have you been surfing?"

"Since I was ten. The San Onofre waves are a lot easier than these beach breaks here in Laguna. Slower, more wave."

"Is that going to be your board?"

"If it comes out right."

"What color?"

"Haven't decided."

"What kind of waves is it for?"

He looked at me thoughtfully. "Bigger. Blacks. Huntington. Malibu and Rincon."

"I don't know those."

"All six of us pile into the vans. Takes two, for the bodies and the boards. Well, back to work, Jan."

"Jen."

He nodded and turned to his blank.

Five years later Belle and I were the best chick surfers in Laguna. John was already away from home a lot, surfing the big waves of Steamer Lane and Ocean Beach, and a much-rumored break just south of San

Francisco, Mavericks. Of the four Stonebreaker surfer kids at Top of the World, John was the most driven and skilled, and his parents were able to give him a worldly surfing education. Summers in Hawaii. A week in Fiji. A month in Australia. I got a few postcards. Thumbtacked them to my wall, over the *Surfer Magazine* covers.

In those five years, Mike Stonebreaker's Hillview Chapel in Laguna Niguel had taken off, gradually then suddenly. As a high school teen busy with watersports and grades, I was only vaguely aware of John's dad's growing new church.

Then, suddenly, no more donut shopfront.

Pastor Mike and his new Hillview Chapel were everywhere, in full-page ads for Sunday services in the *Los Angeles Times,* the *Orange County Register,* and the several small papers published in Laguna Beach. Posters in shop windows, too, billboards on Interstate 5 and the big inland boulevards in Santa Ana and Huntington Beach, and on Coast Highway from San Clemente all the way north to the LA county line.

Pastor Mike was everywhere you looked.

The ads and the posters and billboards all used the same graphic: Mike Stonebreaker in a white robe, arms raised, his back to you as a bright white light washed toward him like a wave from the sky. There was darkness all around the light and the man. I thought it was dramatic but overblown.

Not long after I befriended the Stonebreaker girls—Kate and Robin—Mike and Marilyn took me under their generous wings. They had room in their vans for an only child, her surfboard, wetsuit, and a duffel for food and water, a towel, tubes of sunscreen, and a wide-toothed comb to get through her sun-and-salt-blasted copper helmet of hair.

John and his older brother Raymond pretty much ignored us girls, all three of us at least five years younger. Which, when you're twenty-two, is a lot. Especially if the women your own age are more than a little interested.

On the Stonebreaker family caravans, I'd find a way to get seated in the old hippie van, which John always drove, and I'd watch him secretly. From the right angle, I could see his eyes and part of his face in the rearview mirror. I never got more than a quick glance back. Even though he was sitting just a few feet from me, shoulders hunched over the big steering wheel in the slow, straining van, John always seemed to be miles away. Already there, I thought, in the barrel.

In the lineup at Blacks or Salt Creek or Trestles, I'd position myself medium distance to John, so I could study his technique and just basically gawk at how beautifully he handled these—now, to him—little waves.

I don't remember John saying more than just a few sentences to me over those five years, mostly surfing pointers, weather and swell forecasts, tides and wind. He didn't say much to his girlfriends either, as I observed.

On my eighteenth birthday we had an island-themed party in the backyard. Dad manned the barbecue for burgers and hot dogs; Mom made a couple of giant salads and a pot of fettuccini steeped in olive and truffle oil.

Forty or so people showed up on that chilly winter Sunday afternoon, mostly my friends and their parents. They came early and stayed late. Belle got a little more than tipsy and Raymond drove her home.

John showed up well after dark, red-eyed from the ocean, and dressed in bright orange shorts and a blue-and-orange hibiscus-blossom Aloha shirt. He raised a hand to Dad at the barbecue, who raised a hand back.

John seemed preoccupied when he wished me happy birthday but ate mightily, as surfers do.

"For you, Jen—it's all *yours!*" he said, and handed me a little wooden box.

I was collecting his empty paper plates for the trash can. Set them down and took the box. It felt empty, but inside, wrapped in a cutting from the Sunday *LA Times* funny page, was a pair of earrings—irregular pieces of sea glass strung with copper wire.

"I found it," he said. "The glass, not the wire."

I held them up to the nearest tiki torch: pale greens, soft browns, sanded clears. Even a cobalt blue, all glowing roughly in the light.

"I like them, John. Beautiful."

"It's just broken beer bottles," he said, almost apologetically. "Jen, I'm leaving before dark tomorrow for Imperial Beach, down on the border. South swell ten seconds, strong, and a rising tide. It's going to be big and fast. Just you and me. Interested?"

So much in that question.

"You can do it. I've been watching you."

I knew my answer but didn't know what words to use.

"I talked to your dad and he's okay with us going just ourselves."

John's face was serious and beveled in the torchlight. Another picture of him I'll carry forever.

I felt like I was midair, letting go of one trapeze and reaching for another.

"What time?"

"I'll come get you at five."

3

Jen's son Casey speeds across Desperation Reef off San Diego, headed home for Laguna, *Moondance* riding high, slicing through the gently rolling swell. Desperation Reef is Casey's prime tuna spot this time of year, though it's also popular with the charter fishermen.

Today, he's got his bluefin tuna in the ice hold, a one-hundred-pounder, dragged, drained, filleted, and ready for the pricey sashimi specials at his mother's restaurant.

Mae, a chocolate Labrador, sits on a bench in the cabin beside Casey, facing the sea, tongue trailing, an aging, curious dog without a mean bone in her body.

White clouds seem fixed in the blue October sky and the surface of the sea is dark and supple.

Casey is a big man at twenty-four, all muscle and bushy yellow hair, built much like John Stonebreaker, the father he never met. He's got the same knee knobs and foot bumps, the same pale blue eyes under dark brows. Without sunglasses, the only parts of Casey's face not tanned to darkness are the strips of skin between his eyes and his ears. He's wearing a pendant he had made of sterling silver—a sharp-tailed "gun" surfboard with an oval orange Spessartite garnet embedded lengthwise on the deck. It's the orange of his father's signature big-wave guns, and the orange of his mother's hair.

He sees the commercial trawler bobbing out ahead of him and by the time he gets closer something looks, well, wrong. Pulls near enough for binoculars, throttles down and banks to a sweeping stop. *Moondance,* an angler's dream at thirty-two feet, sleek and powerful, rides the swells high and lightly.

Casey two-hands the Leicas, rolling with his boat, keeping the trawler in his field of vision as best he can. It's a shabby thing, predominately blue with red trim, outriggers swaying empty and no fishing lines out that Casey can see. A rust-stained hull. A ragged black sunscreen flapping over the stern deck.

Two men and a woman stand hard at work at tables heaped high with fish, some big. Black rubber boots and aprons. Blades flashing. Seabirds wheel and dive. A shirtless, muscled guy in red shorts and a flat-brimmed black cowboy hat with silver coins on its band leans against the stern railing, and trains his binoculars on Casey.

"What do you think of that, Mae?"

Mae's native curiosity has already kicked in and she steadies herself on all fours, attentive to the trawler and, of course, the birds.

Casey gets his phone from the steering wheel cabinet, unzips the sandwich bag and pulls it out. Goes to video, reverses the direction, and holds the phone at arm's length.

Casey is Casey's favorite subject, star, and director.

So he checks his look: very tan. Hasn't shaved in a couple of days. Got on the big straw, high-domed Stetson that he wears all the time—fishing or not—which makes him look, at six foot two, tall indeed and not a little funny in his board shorts and shearling boots and the brazenly colored T-shirts he personally designs for his fledgling surf-clothing company, CaseyWear.

In other words, perfect.

Unmistakably Casey Stonebreaker, number ten big-wave surfer and currently number eighteen on the World Surf Tour.

He gives himself and his followers his right-hand shaka—the universal surfers' hang-loose sign that his brother, Brock, says is idiotic and is always trying to get him to stop flashing.

"Here are Mae and I on our way home from Desperation Reef. We got one of the best bluefin tuna I've ever caught, best sushi on Earth, all ready for dinner specials tonight at the Barrel in Laguna Beach. You all know the Barrel. Reservations, please!"

Casey gives himself his coolest smile, then kneels down and gets video of him kissing Mae on the nose. She wipes her tongue up his stubbly cheek. Casey switches the camera direction back to normal, stands and points it at the vessel.

"And what do we find here on this beautiful sea off the California coast? Well, at least four people—three men and a girl—on a commercial fishing vessel, cleaning their catch. See, they've got some big ones up on the tables. But why does this look wrong to me? Because the fish look like sharks, that's why. I'm not so sure these people are playing by the rules out here. Maybe Fish and Wildlife—hi, Craig, hi, Charmaine—would like some video and a CF number. Maybe my brothers and sisters at the Shark Stewards—hi, Booker, hi, Trish!—would like some video, too. So Mae and I are going in for a closer look."

From a hundred feet away it's clear to Casey that these model citizens are finning sharks. Not legal, not humane, but very profitable. Black Hat still has his binoculars on him and the cleaning crew is really hustling now, slicing the fins—dorsal, sides, and tail—off the club-stunned sharks, sweeping the bloody-edged silver-blue-black triangles into a bait well and heaving the finless sharks back into the ocean.

Moondance rocks on the chop while Casey shoots video. He notes his GPU location.

"Oh fudge!" he narrates as he resumes shooting. "See this! Those fish will either bleed to death or get eaten by their cousins. Man, there's threshers and blues and leopards and even a baby great white! See this baby Jaws! And you know where all the fins end up? In soup! In restaurants from California all the way to China! A whole shark sliced up and thrown out to die. Shark fins are the most valuable thing in the sea except for sunken treasure. Shark-finning is illegal and ugly, brothers and sisters. See this! This is a sin against nature!"

The swell rolls *Moondance* closer to the trawler, *Empress II,* and Casey gets its CF numbers. Black Hat lowers his binoculars, raises a hand, and flips Casey off. Mae thumps her tail on the padded bench back.

Pulling broadside to the trawler, Casey keeps shooting.

"Good afternoon!"

"Fuck you and die!" shouts Black Hat.

"How much do you get for a pound of thresher fin?"

"No sharks. No fins. This is all legal. License paid."

"Well, that's quite a fantasy, Mr. Hat. What port are you out of?"

"Don't you take video."

He's Asian looking, but it's hard to tell with the hat shading his face. Young, ripped chest like he works out.

The finners keep slicing away and throwing mutilated sharks overboard, barely looking up.

"How can you do that to living things for money?" Casey asks. And considers the dark parallels between what they're all doing out here. I'm fishing, too, he notes.

"Feed family," says Black Hat. "Buy American dream. No video. No Fish and Wildlifes to come after us."

Casey has more than enough video to post. He can edit it down and shoot a sign-off later at home. Post tonight after dinner, PST, a perfect time here, though not so perfect for the East Coast. He lowers his phone, takes another clip of Mae's trusting face. He's got, like, tons of posts across his platforms, containing more videos of Mae, probably, than any other creature than himself.

"This is majorly uncool," he says. "You should think about what you're doing," he says. "There are other ways to make a living out here. She's generous, this ocean."

"Shut up. Go."

"I'll report you to Fish and Wildlife and the Shark Stewards if I see you out here again."

The finners are still cutting and dropping the bloody black fish into the deep blue water. Pink contrails descend. The finners are laughing now, looking down at Casey. One waves a knife at him.

Casey sets his phone back in the steering cabinet, guns *Moondance* into a wide one-eighty, and away.

He's only half an hour from the Oceanside Harbor boat launch—it's much faster to trailer *Moondance* from Laguna to Oceanside to fish Desperation Reef—when he sees the ratty blue-and-red trawler lurching at a good pace toward him from the south.

Empress II flies a red-smeared white flag and through his Leicas Casey sees Black Hat waving. He slows and turns *Moondance* toward the craft.

Comes to a rest within shouting distance.

"We talk!" Black Hat yells.

Casey nudges the throttle, eases *Moondance* a little closer.

"Don't post video!"

"I will if I see you finning again."

"We make a living. We are legal."

"Come on, bud—you know it's against the law."

"If you show or post or tell Fish and Wildlifes, it would be bad for my family. And for you."

"I don't groove on threats."

Suddenly two boats appear from the west. Bigger than *Moondance*, and coming fast. They converge, Mae sitting up alertly and Casey retrieving his phone, reading trouble.

"Oh fudge, Mae, we have a situation."

He emails the shark-finning video to himself as the vessels decelerate, lunging deeply—a dark green Luhrs and a Bayliner. He furtively trades out his good phone for his cheap backup burner.

The two boats then post up a little behind him, one to port and the other starboard. No names, no numbers. With big *Empress II* at the apex, they've got Casey in a bobbing triangle. *Moondance* rocks steeply in the wakes.

Casey sees three people on each newly arrived boat. Men and women both. The ones on the Luhrs look Asian but it's hard to tell with the ball caps and bandanas and gaiters. Aboard the Bayliner are a husky Latino or maybe Middle Eastern guy, a lanky Black man, and a wiry red-headed white dude with both arms sleeved in tattoos. Casey can't guess what nationality the women are.

From the Luhrs, a female voice cuts through the rattle of Casey's idling engine:

"Hands up, surf dude!"

Most of the crew on the Bayliner and the Luhrs draw handguns and point them at Casey.

Whose guts drop and knees freeze. Hates guns. He got robbed once in Todos Santos, Baja, at gunpoint, and to his humiliation, peed. These pirate pistols look big and rusted. His brother, Brock, has much better guns than these, Casey thinks. He has no defenses except the flare gun, stowed back in the cabin. And two long fillet knives, sharp as razors, secured under the lid of the bait well, a gaff and a fish billy. None of them a match for guns. And there's no way he could stab somebody or stick them with that gaff anyhow.

Suddenly, with a muffled thud, a gangplank drops from the green Luhrs onto the sturdy gunwale of *Moondance*.

It's a well-padded thing, surfboard-wide, with filthy carpet fragments nailed through soft foam to a long flexing beam, down which strides a black-haired woman in black cargo pants, a black windbreaker, and a handgun holstered to her hip.

She's aboard *Moondance* before Casey can get to the gangplank and pitch her into the sea. He doesn't even try, believing her comrades might just shoot him. Mae approaches the woman, mouth open and tail wagging.

Up closer, Pistol Girl looks younger and bigger than she did coming down the plank. She's got a yellow muff around her neck, pulled up over her nose, fierce dark eyes and fair skin, black nylon pants rolled above her knees, bare feet.

She spreads her legs for balance and holds out her hand.

"Give me the phone, Stonebreaker."

"You weren't joking about no video," Casey says.

"I don't joke."

Casey holds up his burner but doesn't break eye contact with her. Then backhands the phone into the ocean. Laughing and hooting, the pirates empty their pistols at the doomed device. The fusillade sends geysers of whitewater into the air, and spiraling tubes of bubbles down through the blue.

Mae tries to head past him for a better look but Casey hooks a hand through her collar, falls on top of her, and pins her to the deck.

Hoots and laughter.

"Maybe you already posted," the young woman says, squinting down at him.

"Maybe."

"Stand up and act brave."

He does.

Her eyes are almost black above the yellow gaiter. They study him. "I came into the Barrel bar. Not long ago. Left you a big tip."

"Thanks so much."

"You don't remember."

It's hard for Casey to see this pirate chick in the laid-back and up-scale Barrel. He orders Mae to stay, and unhooks his fingers from her collar.

"You owe me big money for that phone," he says, exaggerating its value. Feels guilty. Casey hates to lie. Even to a shark finner.

"Maybe I'll come to the Barrel again and pay up," she says.

"If you do, I'll make you a Barrel Bomber so strong they'll have to carry you out."

"Why?"

"Payback for torturing sharks."

"I don't fin. Others fin. Illegal but very profitable. I can't talk them out of it. I fish tuna, like you do."

She lifts the hatch of the cold well, looks at his catch, nods. Gives Casey a dark-eyed stare and drops the lid.

"I'm more in the business side of things," she says. "Marketing and sales for King Jim Seafoods. I do the books. Graduate of UCLA. I am Bette, with an *e* at the end."

"Okay."

Gives Casey another long look. "Hmph. You think you're superior. I know who you are, Casey Stonebreaker. From all your socials. A surf star. Big waves. Pretty in magazines. Great abs."

He doesn't know what to say to this.

"I'm going to reverse out of here and head home. Tell your people not to shoot me."

"Don't file a police report. I am serious. Maybe I'll get you a new phone."

"You should."

"*Zai Jian*, Stonebreaker."

Casey surfed a river mouth in China once, a promotional gig that paid him a few thousand dollars. Memorized maybe ten words.

"*Zai Jian*," he says.

The crewmen and -women point their rusty weapons at Casey as Bette strides back up the gangplank.

4

In the lull before the Barrel happy hour, Casey sits at his bar with Mae at his feet, editing and posting his pirate video across all his platforms. He does a more thorough introduction right here at the bar, with his phone up on a tripod. Makes sure his hair is perfect and there's no food between his teeth. The art directors for his advertising shoots always want that messy Casey Stonebreaker hair and the killer smile. Pecs and buns for sure. He'd rather look brooding and serious, as a daredevil big-wave rider should, but, hey, whatever pays the bills, Casey believes: Basically, he's a happy dude, so why not smile?

He sends private messages to his friends at Shark Stewards and California Fish and Wildlife. They will make life miserable for the crew of *Empress II* if they can find her. Pretty big "if," Casey knows: even Coast Guard cutters and copters can only do so much reconnaissance of a functionally infinite ocean.

The shark-finning clips are gruesome and saddening. All that pain and death of living things so men get their dicks up, Casey thinks. The CF numbers on *Empress II* are clear, though probably counterfeit. Hits and follows and likes are pouring in.

He also sends video to Craig Lockabie at CFW whose Special Operations Unit makes busts on Southern California's open ocean, harbors, and marinas. They used to surf against each other in contests up and down the coast.

Craig—BOLO for nine armed, shark-finning pirates down around Desperation Reef. Throw the book at 'em, brah.

Lockabie calls right back, gets the GPU coordinates where Casey spotted *Empress II,* tells Casey he'll hit Desperation Reef and the rest of San Clemente Island tomorrow. Casey hears him keyboarding in his suspect descriptions.

"We've heard of *Empress II* and the finning, Casey. You're our second witness. Appreciate the tip."

"They're armed to their teeth," says Casey, picturing the bullets zipping into the water as his phone sank into approximately a hundred and fifty feet of ocean. He's still nervy about that. Actually, more like creeped out and jittery. Funny, he thinks now, that his first fear when the shooting started was for innocent, curious Mae.

"I've only got one cruiser and two patrol boats," says Lockabie. "But we'll do what we can."

"Good luck, brah."

"You might want to stay off that water until we round up these people."

"No chance of that! The Barrel needs its catch of the day." But even as Casey says this, he feels a tug of dread about being back on the water after having outed these pirates on his socials. His guts feel bunched up. He could borrow a gun from Brock but he hasn't fired one since he was a boy—a BB gun.

"Casey. I have a serious question now."

"My man."

"How are you looking for the Monsters of Mavericks?"

"Top shape and ready. I surfed Todos Santos on that freak south last month. Forty feet but basically blown-out mush-burgers. I'll do good at Mavericks if the waves show up."

"And Jen and Brock?"

"Can't speak for Brock. He's been pretty busy saving the world.

Mom's ready, though. She's a monster on that jet ski of hers. And her surfing looks real good."

"She's, what, forty?"

"Forty-six. Tons of training though. Great shape."

A pause.

"Good luck to you all."

"We will need waves."

"December's the month," says Lockabie.

It's another evening crush at the Barrel.

His mom is in a red sleeveless dress and white sneakers, greeting guests, checking in at tables, bustling between the kitchen and the bar and the front desk. Beyond the second-floor deck, the Pacific advances to shore in small waves that fizzle to whitewater.

From his bar, Casey can see the life-sized bronze sculpture of his father standing in the lobby, one arm around his sharp-nosed gun surfboard.

Inside the Barrel, the surfboards on the walls—each one with a history and a plaque—shimmer in the lights. The big-screen surfing videos provide nonstop rides, drop-ins, bottom turns, and wipeouts on some of the biggest waves ever ridden.

The videos are paeans to chaos: a yellow helicopter hovers over an impact zone at the Jaws break on Maui, marking a flailing, board-less surfer while a wave towers behind the chopper. Jet skis swing surfers into rising fifty-foot waves at Nazaré in Portugal, then speed for the exits and into the sky. Helmeted, buoyancy-vested men are pitched from four-story heights into mountains of whitewater at Mavericks. Boards spiral and shoot and break into pieces like breadsticks.

Casey likes the photographs better, especially the older ones:

Dewey Weber at Makaha.

Greg Noll at Pipeline.

Margo Oberg at Sunset.

Jeff Clark and Jay Moriarity at Mavericks.

Mark Foo at Sunset.

Laird Hamilton at Jaws.

Mike Parsons at Cortes Bank.

John Stonebreaker at Mavericks.

John Stonebreaker at Teahupo'o.

Maya Gabeira at Todos Santos.

Jen Stonebreaker at Mavericks.

Garrett McNamara at Nazaré.

Casey has met most of them: his human pantheon, almost gods.

Casey looks up for a moment at the picture of his father dropping into a fifty-foot wave at Mavericks twenty-five Decembers ago. He's beautiful in the air, arms up, legs extended, feet locked into the straps on the deck of his orange-and-black board. Of course Casey wasn't even born yet but he knows his dad made that wave, got massive points for it. His father looks confident, firm in his destiny. Or is it fate? God's will? These are large considerations, and not yet settled in Casey Stonebreaker's twenty-four-year-old mind. He's looked at this picture thousands of times. Sometimes it's a celebration, sometimes a headstone, knowing what happened just a day later.

"Nail those pirates, Craig," says Casey. "They must have killed fifty sharks today. Beautiful threshers and blues, everything. Even a baby white. Threw them all back in to die."

"She's a big ocean out there, Casey."

Casey knows that the CDFW is understaffed and outgunned. They always say that. Realizes with a little chill how defenseless he and Mae really are out there.

Not to mention the sharks, and Craig Lockabie.

Casey enjoys his last peaceful pre–happy hour minutes. He tells Jen about "Bette" and the shark finners. Soon the Barrel bar will be stuffed with drinkers. Locals and tourists. Loud, but good people. All cocktails half price, including their signature Scorpions and Lapu-Lapu triples, with jalapeño skewers and miniature umbrellas. These cocktails are messy and time-consuming to mix, but crowd-pleasers just the same.

So, before all that cuts loose, he checks his mail for word from his twin brother, Brock, last posting from Florida in the deadly and massively destructive aftermath of still another category-four hurricane.

Sure enough, Brock and his Go Dogs are in Fort Myers, performing their so-called "rescue mission" in the wake of the storm.

Casey watches the NBC video of Brock, his wife, Mahina, and two other women—all clad in Day-Glo green and black Go Dogs rain suits with the snarling dachshund stenciled front and back. They're helping drenched and bedraggled citizens into a school bus. The rain slants in; palm trees reach out like they're trying to grab someone. The refugees from the storm have rolling luggage and bulging plastic bags, children by the hand and babies in strollers.

He calls Brock:

"Brah, looks like you're beating back hell in Florida."

Brock answers:

"It's evacuation at this point. Eighty-six confirmed dead. The school districts are supplying the buses. We're getting people to higher ground, which in this part of the world is far, far away. You should be here. The Go Dogs need drivers. We need muscle and energy."

"I'm fishing for Mom and training for the Monsters."

"You're a selfish, vain striver, Casey."

Casey takes this one on the chin, same as he has his whole life with Brock. "I caught a hundred-pound bluefin for the Barrel today. Caught some shark finners, too."

"I saw that *Surf Tribe* underwear ad last week and you looked like a dolt."

"It's just work, brah. The modeling."

"Get off your ass and help! It's not what the world can do for you."

"Only God gives and takes."

"That bullshit again," says Brock. "Look, Casey, I'll be in California tomorrow. The Feather Fire in Ukiah. Twenty thousand acres and zero percent containment. Come on up, help me out."

Casey is again amazed by his brother's ferocious energy and drive. Leave a Florida hurricane and fight a California wildfire the next day?

"When we get those people safe, you and I can surf," Brock says. "Get ready for the Monsters."

"Are you even going to show up for it?"

"You know I hate contests, but I like the money," says Brock. "That's all I want . . . keep the rescue missions financed . . ."

Brock continues on but the connection falters, then corrects.

"I'm worried about Momster surfing Mavericks," says Casey. "She hasn't ridden big waves since before we were born."

"Or done much towing with the jet ski," says Brock.

"Right. Is Mahina going to tow you?"

"Hell, yes," snaps Brock. "She's the best. Look, Case, I'm stoked that Mom is towing you. Just remember—she hasn't done it since we went big-wave pro. Six years."

"But she's working out real hard now," says Casey. "Every day. Especially on the jet ski. You're the one who has to get yourself ready, Brock. You gotta be ready to surf Mavericks, or you know . . ."

A beat of silence, then: "Well, Casey, Dad was ready, but there's that jealous God of yours again—giving and taking for his own entertainment."

"Yeah, there He is," says Casey. "But I love you, Brock, and the unbelieving demons inside you."

"You're messed up, man. See you at the Feather Fire. You should help this miserable world for once, instead of only yourself."

Casey pictures Brock, his minutes-younger twin brother—lanky, dark dreadlocks, inked to the max—in every visible way Casey's opposite.

Casey worries about him. Always has. Worries about the body that Brock drives to physical extremes in order to ride immense waves. And the angry heart that Brock so eagerly displays. The fights he picks, the scars he wears, and the weapons he collects. The way he thinks he can save the world, one disaster at a time. Playing God instead of worshipping Him.

"There's bad karma at Mavericks, Brock. Pray to God for protection. Valley of death and all like that."

"I dread your God, Casey. Just shut up."

5

Beneath a billowing gray sky pocked with red embers, Brock Stone-breaker and his wife and his Go Dogs—in a motley battalion of pick-ups, utility vehicles, and vans—have encamped within the eye-burning haze that chokes the Feather Fire evacuation center on the Mendocino College soccer field.

The hills surrounding them are limned in wind-driven flames that launch embers into the sky like fireworks.

The fire was zero percent contained when Brock, Mahina, and the Go Dogs got here two hours ago, and it's zero percent contained now.

The Go Dogs are the activist wing of Brock's Breath of Life Rescue Mission in Aguanga, California, a sprawling, state-licensed and accredited house of worship. The buildings and acreage are gifts from the Random Access Foundation, run by a young Silicon Valley billionaire and her husband. The foundation continues to make modest monthly contributions, mostly earmarked for the Go Dogs rescue operations in the US and in Mexico.

Now sheriffs, police, and an alphabet soup of fire department vehicles prowl the perimeter field with their headlights and searchlights, as if looking for something more to do than keep their eye on the flaming, not-very-distant, timber-studded, tinder-dry hills around them.

Brock drips sweat. The tattoos all over his sinewy body are black, slick, and island themed. Got his first one at age twelve, much to his mother's annoyance, which was half the point. The other half was he liked sea turtles like the ones they'd see surfing on Maui. He's dark-skinned for a man of his ancestry—some Black Irish way back, his mother told him—*your great-grandfather Devon Byrne had that, and blue eyes like yours.* Brock's dreads are short and tightly woven. He's stripped to the waist because of the record-busting October heat wave, and he's drawing foul breaths through one of the two hundred cheap "tactical" gas masks donated to the Dogs by a manufacturer down in Orange County.

He's handing off forty-bottle flats of donated water to thirsty evacuees, many of whom have lost their homes or are losing them this very moment, losing almost everything they love, basically—houses and horses and dogs and gardens—as they tear open the bottles of fresh warm water for their children first, then themselves, quaffing then pouring it onto their upturned, smoke-blackened faces to quench the ember stings and the fires in their terrified eyes.

These are people who have lost it all, Brock thinks. And there will be no regaining what is gone. Only substitution.

He leans into the back of his flagship Go Dogs van, an old black Econoline with the goofy-looking dachshund emblazoned on the sides in Day-Glo green.

Mahina, whose name means "moon" in her native language, is all the way inside, hefting the flats into Brock's waiting hands two at a time. She's Hawaiian big, strong and imposing. When they first met, Brock had to really work to beat her at arm wrestling, and she was a stronger, more buoyant, and better swimmer than him. Good surfer, too. She looks like a post-apocalyptic Pacific Island warrior with her hair up in a tight bun, her XXL Day-Glo green and black Go Dogs T-shirt, the gas mask, and goggles. She posts and blogs like crazy for the Breath of Life Rescue Mission. Doesn't say much out loud, but when she does, her words count.

"We need more water," she mouths from within the mask.

"Another run to Ukiah," says Brock. Their third run of the day.

"Thank the gods for Ukiah," she says.

Ukiah and its roads have so far been spared by a change of wind direction. The Feather Fire—the experts were saying, like so many of the new "super fires"—was so big and so hot it was making its own weather. One expert said the change of wind was a miracle. Another said that the super fires were spawned by the megadrought, which was caused by global warming, which was caused by greenhouse gases.

"The gods have nothing to do with it," says Brock, who does not believe that a god—and certainly not some cabal of them—in any way intervenes on behalf of the human beings of Earth. He's always berating his brother for Casey's self-promoting, Christian notions of divine intervention through prayer. Much better in Brock's mind is Mahina's worship of nature—gods who openly help and sometimes destroy their mortals.

The Breath of Life is what Brock would pray to if he prayed at all.

Instead, he worships actions, forged by the heat of the real.

Forged in the absolute belief that people can change the world.

You can just watch, Brock says in his "sermons." Or you can act. Join the battle.

That's the foundation of the Breath of Life Rescue Mission, and of every angry sermon and call to action that Brock has issued from his pulpit on the Aguanga compound over the last year. And ranted from his media platforms.

God(s) or not, in Brock's mind, the Red Cross simply made it to Ukiah because they made it to Ukiah, and—with typical NGO caution—wouldn't risk getting close enough to the danger to give away their ample supplies of water, food, clothing, blankets, diapers, pet food, battery-powered lanterns, generators, coffee and coffee makers, generators, motel vouchers, and, oddly, twelve pallets of canned beets! There are twenty-four twelve-ounce cans per plastic-wrapped bundle. Though none have pull tops, and not one manual can opener is in sight.

Which is the kind of thing that drives Brock Stonebreaker crazy—always has—when people get ninety percent of the job done but don't close it off with the final ten. Then blame it on a god's will, or a rule or a law, or a forecast, or a tarot reading, or global fucking warming.

Which is why he created the Go Dogs, and why he only accepts people who will not hesitate to go that last ten percent, or more, to get it done. And called them the Go Dogs because a dog understands that last ten percent without ever being taught it, or even bothering to think about it.

You see. You go. You do it until it's done.

You take off on that wave and you are committed.

On a huge wave, the last ten percent is fear. Brock dwells on that a lot in his rants. Fear is hesitation and hesitation is death on a sixty-foot wave.

Hell, thinks Brock: a twenty-foot wave. He saw a boyhood friend killed by a wicked-thick eighteen-foot demon at Sunset Beach on Oahu.

A friend.

Brock was a teenager himself then, and he'd gotten Glenn to shore as fast as he could and CPR'd him until the paramedics came running across the beach with their boxes and stretcher, and they let Brock ride in the back of the truck to the hospital under colors and a loudly optimistic siren.

Brock had prayed to God in that bumpy, wailing truck, just like his grandpa—Pastor Mike Stonebreaker—had taught him to.

Pressing his forehead to Glenn's bouncing chest, praying hard and clear and rationally, offering all he had, making a hundred promises if He would just keep Glenn's heart beating.

Well, He didn't.

Which is another reason Brock created the Go Dogs within his

Breath of Life Rescue Mission. To help people who are too bad off to help themselves.

Brock wasn't going to be fooled twice.

By 2 a.m., the Go Dogs have given up every last water bottle, food stuff, bar of soap, tube of toothpaste, and family-sized tent—thirty of them— donated by a Go Dogs friend who owns a chain of outdoor/camping/ fishing/hunting stores in Costa Mesa. The tents are high quality and expensive, waterproof, fire resistant, and quick to set up.

Now—just after two in the morning—Brock helps a family of five drive the final stakes into the soccer stadium grass. Mahina circles them, shooting video for the Go Dogs website and Brock's social media, to which he posts with great volume and profanity. Mahina writes some of the less heated dispatches under the Brock Stonebreaker/Go Dogs handle.

The tent-building dad drives his last spike with an angry swing; his wife sits on the ground with her back to the tent, wrapped in a clean new blanket, nursing her baby.

Exhausted Brock sits on his butt beside Mahina and they look out through the drifting smoke to the hills sparking in the near distance, and to the mountains farther out glowing red with flames and rocket- ing embers. He's been up for thirty-six hours. His eyes are burning but looking out to the little village of tents pitched on the soccer field, he feels his heart beating steady and strong.

6

Two hours later they make Ukiah, where they load the ash-encrusted Go Dogs Econoline with more Red Cross survival provisions, and find gas.

Mahina squeegees the filthy windshield while Brock tries to post a call for reinforcements on his heavily attended socials. His phone has only two bars out here, but he writes anyway, his orders as separate posts, like bullets:

> Come on you lazy people, JOIN the GO DOGS here in Mendocino County where the Feather Fire is 100% NOT CONTAINED!

> Everything is burning! ALL ANIMALS HUMAN AND OTHERWISE MUST HELP! Bring food and water! Bring your motor homes and trailers if you have them.

> All you soft-bodied techies, you Bay Area libs, charge up your Teslas and GET HERE NOW!

> All you tough outdoorsmen and women, you survivalist and 2A dimbulbs, you mountain people, you survivalists-GET HERE NOW!

He and Mahina watch the ash-caked screen as Brock's posts are slowly, one-at-a-time delivered.

On their way back up the highway to the evacuation center they stop at a checkpoint, where a hefty, bearded man in a black Right Fight T-shirt, a matching trucker's hat, and an AR-15 slung over his shoulder comes to Brock's window.

Brock knows him: Kasper Aamon—former Laguna Beach High School jock, former member in Brock's grandfather's Hillview Chapel, founder of Right Fight—a group of violent, anti-immigrant haters masquerading as conservatives. They've been having an extended, on-line, obscenity-ridden "debate" lately, Kasper claiming that Brock's church was a "godless slum/front for a devil-worshipping surfer and a tax-dodging tech billionaire."

Brock can't reconcile Kasper, the skinny, ectomorphic high school football player who always seemed so focused on his game, with this hate-fueled thug he is now. Can't quite believe that his body size and type have evolved so dramatically. Pastor Mike told Brock years ago that his prodigal black sheep Kasper would return to his fold someday. Because people can change. And they do.

Of course, both Brock's and Aamon's followers flooded the message chains, accelerating the heated arguments. There's so much shit flying Brock can't even keep up with it. Mahina has taken over most of the postings as well as getting out the weekly Breath of Life videos of Brock's rambling, sometimes hours-long sermons, which he calls "rants."

Aamon shines a flashlight into Brock's weary eyes. Brock rolls down his window to a blast of hot wind. There's a big white Tahoe with an after-market light bar squatting partially across both lanes of the high-way, bringing drivers to a stop.

"I heard you heathens would be up here, agitating," he says.

"Glad you're following us, Kasper," says Brock. "Man, that's one fucked-up hat you have on."

With a quick glance, Brock sees Mahina with her phone up, taking pictures of the man.

"Hey, wahine, why don't you put that camera down?" Kasper Aamon chortles then breaks into a smile. "Yo, fighters! Look what came up in the net. Weird Brock Stonebreaker, our favorite preacher!"

Brock sees other Right Fighters approaching his van in the smoky darkness. There's one at Mahina's window now, eyes curiously wide, his light beam refracting through the glass. A woman behind him. Two more men join the first guy, and in the sideview mirror Brock sees another woman stopping to read the Go Dogs emblem and steadying herself against the wind. All variously armed, all wearing black Right Fight T-shirts with blue stars and red stripes, and the trucker hats that make their heads look huge.

Aamon gives Brock a sidelong stare. "The man with the church who doesn't even believe in God."

"Not in past gods, Aamon. But they've got a new one out now. We call it the Breath of Life. I've explained this to you before."

"We've made it simple," says Mahina. "The Breath of Life is a god."

"'Zat right? Then what's this new god stand for?"

"Life," says Brock.

Aamon looks puzzled and affronted at the same time. "Ain't that kind of circular? Can't you be more specific?"

"Look around you."

Aamon shakes his head. "What horseshit. Out of the vehicle, you little demon," he says.

"Nope."

"What's inside?" Aamon asks, shifting the flashlight from Brock's face to the back of the van.

"Provisions for the fire victims."

"They turned us away at the evacuation center because we're armed. We carry open, which, as you might know, is now legal in most parts of California."

"We leave our guns in our cars," says Brock. "So we can get people food and water and shelter. Help them, instead of just strutting around, playing Army man, like you fools. What good are you really doing?"

"I'm going to ask you, again, to step out of the vehicle."

"Same answer."

Kasper Aamon's eyes bug as he shifts his light beam to Mahina, who has set down the phone and hefted her pistol-gripped, combat 12-gauge from the darkness at her feet. She goes nowhere without it. The man at her window springs away and Aamon takes a step back, too, trying to unsling his tightly strapped gun.

Brock swings open the van door, catching Aamon just right and knocking him to the asphalt. Then he stomps the gas and slams the door.

Engine whining under him, Brock doesn't think these people will actually open fire on him, but his heart is racing and he hunches down behind the wheel in anticipation of small arms fire, his right hand on Mahina's big shoulder, trying to scrunch her down, too, but she wrenches herself away and points her shotgun out the window.

"No!" yells Brock. "Mahina, *no!*"

She drops the gun back into the darkness.

There's a tense few seconds as the Ford's engine screams and up-shifts, and the flats of water and soft drinks behind them topple and crash to the floor. Mahina mutters lowly to herself.

Brock waits for the bullets to slam into them, but by the time he realizes that nobody's shooting, he's around a bend and temporarily out of range.

One problem solved, but the next question is—will Right Fight come after them?

They've gone less than a mile when Brock sees in the sideview mirror not one, but three sets of headlights aligned behind him, running three abreast and gaining easily on the old van.

Mahina has taken up her phone again, holding it out the window to document their pursuers.

A red, searchlight-festooned Suburban pulls up on Brock's side, as an old two-tone white-and-aqua Chevy pickup appears just a few feet from Mahina's open window.

Brock can't go right or left without hitting one of them, and when he looks up the straight, narrow highway ahead of him he sees distant headlights topping a rise. The pines that line the highway thrash, and a cloud of ash paints his windshield. Brock can hardly see. He hits the wipers, which help little. The trucks on either side of him are honking now, and the red Suburban has its remote rooftop floodlights trained on his face.

Brock squints and glances left a split second, just enough time to see the face of burly Kasper Aamon.

"Brakes, babe! Hold on!"

Mahina tries to work her big body down into the seat.

Brock presses his foot down, hard and steady, but not too hard; the old van's brakes were never terrific and the antilock system is weak.

The tires bite and the Econoline hunches down. Brock feels the rear end shimmy, meaning crazy swerves if he pushes any harder.

Both vehicles roar past as Mahina shoots them on her phone, the drivers screaming and laughing as they merge into the right lane.

He lightens the pressure then reapplies force and the van slows back into control. As Brock stays to the right of his lane, the oncoming cars honk and speed past.

Up ahead Brock sees the Red Suburban and the two-tone Chevy at a northbound pullout, awaiting him.

He hits the accelerator and barrels past them anyway, both he and Mahina flipping them off as horns and "Born in the USA" wail from the pickup. Brock hates it when idiots misunderstand this song.

Mahina rolls up her window, lifts the shotgun to her lap, and goes to work on her phone.

A half mile farther up the road, Brock watches in his sideview mirror as the Suburban and the Chevy bounce onto the highway and head back toward Ukiah.

7

The following day, alone in the ocean at first light, Jen glides into a glittering Brooks Street wave.

She's standing up on her paddleboard, guiding herself across the glassy shoulder, wielding her paddle as a rudder. The daily stand-up paddleboard session is one of her training tools—a fun way to build the muscle mass, cardio strength, and endurance when the waves aren't big. Of course, there are also daily weights to be lifted in her garage gym; a two-mile run and a mile ocean swim most afternoons; high-speed, bone-crunching, open-ocean sprints in the jet ski three times a week—the rougher the sea the better; and her daily breath-holding sessions in the high school pool, where, as a celebrated alumnus, Jen is welcome pretty much anytime she wants. At yesterday's pool session, Jen held her breath for one minute and thirty-four seconds before pushing off hard from the deep-end bottom, breaking the surface with a full-body gasp, her eyes bursting with stars. That's enough time to survive the legendary back-to-back hold-downs at Mavericks, Jen knows—so long as the waves that have sent you to the rocky bottom haven't first crushed the air from your body or snapped your neck. It's a lot different in a pool than in a furious ocean trying to kill you, John used to say, and he always focused hard on his breath training.

Thus, at forty-six years old Jen is not in the best shape of her life, but near it. Her running and swimming speeds aren't quite what they were twenty-five years ago, and she's not as limber, and her knees creak when she gets out of bed in the dark every morning to hit Brooks Street. But her jet ski skills and underwater breath control are better.

The biggest question is, how good is she at riding enormous, fast, lethal waves in fifty-degree water over jagged rocks?

Well, Jen knows she's not quite as good as she was back then, in the thick of it with John.

But this coming December, less than two months from now, she'll be ready to surf the Monsters of Mavericks, women's division.

And to tow Casey. And Brock, if he wants her to. Though Brock's wife, Mahina, wants that honor and, as his wife, Jen knows she deserves it. And she knows Mahina is good, but good enough? No room for error, she thinks, and all that.

A blunt fear eddies inside Jen as she considers towing either or both of her sons in the waves that killed their father. But they've trained hard and they're ranked among the top twenty big-wave riders in the world.

This fear is part of the larger fear of riding those waves herself. After witnessing what Mavericks did to John, she has lived and relived and dreamed what they can do to you.

Just the idea of being on the water at Mavericks again terrifies her. More than the towing in and the riding of the waves. The wild soul of nature lives there, without conscience or remorse.

Her husband taught her how to face it.

And for John, she's going to complete the journey she began with him.

Now, Jen's thoughts boomerang back here to Brooks Street, and she drops into another nice right, a smooth five-footer with a steep, smooth shoulder to work with. She banks the big heavy SUP off the upper face, dragging her paddle along the ribs of the barrel as she heads for the bottom turn. Then straightens and rises up the face, her bowl of orange hair matching her paddleboard and wetsuit—orange and black, John's colors for his wetsuits and big-wave guns—and then she's inside this gin-clear barrel, and her colors quiver and fragment within it. This would be a beautiful sight for an onlooker but there is none at first light.

Just Jen Stonebreaker, here alone. Alone since John made his early earthly exit.

She had ridden her first big waves with John when she was eighteen and he was twenty-three. The waves inspired a primal fear in both of them, a fear that kept them respectful, alert and—until that day—alive.

Jen had towed John into a Mavericks monster on her jet ski for the first time two months after her eighteenth birthday.

Married him on the beach at Sleepy Hollow in Laguna six months later.

Partnered with him in big-wave contests all over the world: Jen towing John into the men's heats, and John towing her into the women's. Winning a little prize money. Sponsorships. Earning some respect. Even as middle-class haoles from small-wave, big-money Laguna Beach. Even from the Hawaiians on the big-wave tour.

Jen buried her husband up in Newport Beach when she was twenty-one.

Gave birth to his sons, Casey and Brock, nine months later.

Not a day goes by that Jen doesn't think of him, usually not an hour.

Mostly, she thinks of how she failed him.

In the privacy of her Laguna Canyon home, and her office in the Barrel, she talks to John. Answers for him in a voice that even sounds a little like his.

John had meant almost everything to her. She gave herself to him, heart and body, and there was practically nothing that she wouldn't do for him. Practically nothing she *hadn't* done for him.

Loved him and listened to him; cooked his meals and did his laundry; handled the money and paid the bills; endured his hangovers and his surprising, petty violence. Saved his life one brooding evening at Todos Santos with a jet ski and a rescue sled.

Their dizzying, smoky hours of pleasure in the little cottage on Victory Walk.

Not an endless summer at all. A brief one, but crammed with life.

But since that day at Mavericks twenty-five years ago—excepting the careful, focused raising of her two sons—Jen Stonebreaker has felt few moments of joy. Her life since John's death has been over two decades of dedication to motherhood and the Barrel. Two decades of thinking she might try to ride the big waves that terrify her.

She hasn't ridden a big wave since that day, but that's about to change.

During her waking hours, she can imagine those monsters, can see herself making that drop, carving that turn, riding the thing with her own particular strength and grace. Yeah, babe, she thinks: you can still do that.

But in her dreams, she feels the enormous mountains, lifting her higher and higher, carrying her toward land faster and faster, then heaving her toward the world of rocks and whitewater so far below. From up there, she sees the pale sharks gliding over the reef. Sees John's body, leashed to the rocks, surging peacefully back and forth like kelp.

The wave takes her down and down and down.

She wakes up, gasping, heart pounding, sweating out the vodka and Xanax that bear her off to sleep every night.

And she thinks about the Monsters of Mavericks coming soon, regretting that she agreed to compete in a big-wave contest for the first time in twenty-five years.

In spite of the terrible fear.

Because of her terrible fear.

Fear of the waves, fear of failing John on her jet ski, fear of the casual, supernatural power of Mavericks.

She's going to beat that fear.

She *has* to beat it.

The Monsters of Mavericks is not a dream.

Next, Jen rides a few more of these little Brooks Street waves, then heads out to sea, paddling fast, reaching with her arms but pulling with her core, legs tense for balance.

She paddles a tiring half mile through the now choppy Pacific, building strength and endurance, then heads back and rides a few more waves before most of the local surfers have even waxed their boards.

Which is when she sees a shiny red Cigarette boat slashing toward her in the distance. She can see it coming a long way off, perched up on her paddleboard as she is.

It closes fast on Jen, circling her. The wake is fast and high but she knows her SUP like she knows her own body, and she uses her legs and the big curved head of the paddle to stay on the bucking board. She knows that boaters don't always realize how strong the wakes of their vessels can be, how easily they will knock around a lone individual astride a buoyant SUP. But these guys know exactly how disabling their wake is—that's pretty much the whole point.

The two men stand in their rocking race boat, watching Jen from above their low, built-for-speed windshield. The sleek vessel is called *Dragon*. Her engine cuts out with a hoarse cough.

"Jen Stonebreaker!" the captain shouts.

He's Chinese by the look of him, big and wide-shouldered in a black-and-white Kings hockey warm-up jacket. He shifts his Kings hockey team cap bill forward.

"Your son Casey is spreading lies about King Jim Seafood. On TikTok and Facebook. He has contacted law enforcement. I am King Jim and we are strictly legit!"

"Take it up with him."

"He's stubborn. He lied about posting the video of the sharks. Said he would not, then he did. Last night. Everyone is talking now, asking questions. My daughter Bette is being hated and harassed. She is very smart girl and innocent of all crimes. King Jim Seafood is not criminals."

Bette, Jen thinks—Casey's shark-finning butcher on the high seas. She easily traces the events leading to this surprise confrontation: Bette's recognition of surf celebrity Casey yesterday; Bette's and her father's Internet search of the Laguna Stonebreakers and the Barrel, through which they would learn of Jen Stonebreaker's entry into the Monsters of Mavericks, her impressive training, which includes this early morning surf-paddling at Brooks, followed by her half-mile out-and-backs in the Pacific. Hell, the *Laguna Beach Independent* and *Los Angeles Times* have run pictures of her doing that!

Alone here at sea with nothing but a board to cling to, a ripple of worry goes through her.

The copilot is thin, and half a head shorter than King Jim. Black hair to his shoulders. A white Polo windbreaker over a navy sweater and white pants. Their clothes look new, or at least clean. In their sleek red Cigarette boat, they look like an advertisement, though Jen is not sure for what.

"You tell Casey Stonebreaker he should take down the video and give apology," the captain calls out. His voice is strong and clear. "You tell Casey to say the video was taken in international waters. You tell Casey to say the shark-fin video was taken two years ago. You tell Casey leave Bette alone!"

"A little late for that, don't you think?"

"Better late."

"We like your restaurant!" Polo yells. Voice sharp, a smile. "Like very much!"

Jen hasn't seen these guys in the Barrel that she can remember. Not that she necessarily would. Her restaurant has a big Chinese clientele, fish and seafood lovers, big parties from Taiwan, mostly, recommended by friends and relatives, big on the half-price happy hour cocktails and the Barrel catch of the day.

"What do you pay for rent at the Barrel?" asks Polo.

"It's mine."

"In her family a long time!" calls out the captain. "Your website is very good with the history. And the photographs. Are you going to surf the Monsters of Mavericks?"

"Yes, I am."

"Oh, that's a scary place to surf. How much money if you win?"

"Fifty thousand dollars."

"To risk your life?" asks King Jim.

To beat your fear, Jen thinks, but says nothing.

"You could get more than that as a magazine model," says Polo with a knowing smile. "Like your son."

"I did that for a while. It got old. So did I."

"You make Casey to take down the posts," says the King.

"No. Shark-finning sucks and you guys should know better. Put it in soup so guys can get it up? Pathetic, gentlemen."

"We'll come to your restaurant."

"Is that a promise or a threat?"

"Never make a threat. We want to open a restaurant in Laguna. Chinese seafood and fish. All fresh. A modern place, hip. More hip than Barrel. More *now*."

"Good luck."

"Laguna has money. It needs good restaurant," says Polo.

"Sure. Laguna can use another good restaurant. Gentlemen—please go slow on your exit, would you? I'm heading home."

Jen digs in her paddle for an eastward tack and starts off through the choppy water.

Then, something really bugging her, she angrily swings her board around to face *Dragon*.

"Leave my son alone."

"Leave my daughter alone!" yells the King. "You make Casey Stonebreaker follow my orders!"

"He won't," Jen yells back. "He's brave and good and always does what's right." Admittedly, though, Casey can be a bit self-righteous. For twenty-four.

"But maybe he stupid, too," says Polo. "Makes trouble for everyone for no good reason."

"Mutilating wild animals is a good reason for trouble," she says.

"You kill fish for your restaurant," says the King. "Big money. Same thing."

"We use the whole fish. Sashimi, soup, sauces—everything but the skin and guts. The gulls get those."

"You make Casey take down the videos," says the King. "All platforms. Don't let him be a fool. Maybe good things happen."

"I'm not afraid of you," she says, turning away again and paddling for shore.

Well, maybe I am, she admits, with regards to Casey and his idealism. He's no match for shark-finning pirates on the high seas. Right now her knees feel brittle and her heart beats hard.

She's plenty angry, too.

She isn't afraid of bad men, threats, heights, sharks, fists, guns, car accidents, wildfires, or viruses. In fact, Jen Stonebreaker is afraid of only one thing: the big waves she'll be riding at Mavericks, and hauling Casey—and maybe Brock—into. Dragging her beloved sons into the waves that killed their dad.

By this notion she is privately, unabashedly terrified.

8

The next morning Casey hooks a 102-pound bluefin tuna—the largest and most delicious tuna in the world—on Desperation Reef. The reef is a not-so-secret hot spot for sportfishermen, and the prized bluefin hit it hard in summer and fall. Just a few hundred yards outside Desperation Reef lies San Clemente Island, owned by the Navy and used as an amphibious training base and bomb/rocket/missile proving ground. Not even the wild goats are welcome. Occasionally, Navy patrol boats will stop Casey, board *Moondance,* check his bait and refrigerated holds. They're pretty cool guys, Casey has found, and some of them recognize him from the surf journals and the many YouTube videos of him riding gigantic waves around the world.

Today, this tuna fights him so long and hard, dragging *Moondance* across the heavy chop, that the anglers on the nearby charter, *Buenisima,* cheer and hoot as Casey finally completes his gaff-free landing of the beautiful, scintillating silver-blue missile.

Paws on the gunwale, Mae barks for most of this grueling forty-minute battle, the tuna sounding and taking line off Casey's Penn reel in heated screams. She only barks at big fish.

Breathing heavily, Casey finally tail-ropes the tuna to a stern cleat, and sets the engine low to drag the fish slowly east, cooling the tuna's internal temperature after its hard battle. Casey watches it through dark blue water shot with pipes of sunlight, the fish losing strength, gills slowing. Casey knows something of how it feels, having held the very last of his breath on long hold-downs by huge waves.

The swell is too heavy and the chop too high for cleaning the fish at sea, so Casey lowers his catch to the ice blocks in the hold, and hightails *Moondance* to Oceanside Harbor.

Where, an hour and fifteen minutes later, he ties off his boat and clomps up the launch ramp, leaving Mae to guard the catch, per usual. Casey gets his keys from the waders' pouch, then climbs into the truck and backs the trailer down the ramp.

The truck cab is warm in the early afternoon sun, and Casey feels the post-adrenal peace that comes from a big fish well hunted, well fought, and well caught. He feels dreamy but clear-headed. He still understands that he's killed this animal for nourishment and profit. And he knows that he will someday be killed against his will as well. He doesn't romanticize himself enough to believe that he'll end up killed and eaten by something further up the food chain. This fish has become a victim in a way that he—the human Stonebreaker—will almost certainly not be. Which in Casey's mind means he and the fish were put on Earth for different purposes. He doesn't believe that the fish has a soul like his. A different kind of soul—maybe. What they do have in common though, is creation by, and eventually absorption by, the same God. Thus, sharing relation, even brotherhood.

Casey knows the Barrel will turn this fish into food for people, and approximately ten thousand dollars of revenue for the restaurant's owners and workers. Bluefin tuna—*kuro maguro* in Japanese—is not only the world's largest and most delicious tuna fish, it's the most expensive by far. Casey as a child was astonished to be told by his mother that a bluefin tuna weighing 489 pounds had been recently caught and sold for $1.8 million in Japan's Tsukiji fish market. In that instant young Casey—a good Laguna shore angler for bass and halibut—decided to hunt *kuro maguro* in his own backyard ocean, which was getting to be a real possibility down off San Clemente Island and its nearby Desperation Reef. Catch a fish. Make a million dollars.

When he backs down the ramp Casey swings his right arm over his seat back and turns for a full view of his target.

Moondance is fast to her ties, but Mae is not keeping vigil atop the ice-cooled hold as usual.

Which of course happens occasionally, sociable Lab that Mae is.

Casey cleans the magnificent fish at one of the marina basins, drawing a crowd.

"Come to the Barrel in Laguna, people," he tells them. "This'll be some of the best sashimi you've ever had."

"My dad caught one bigger," says a boy.

"Your dad is a great fisherman," says Casey.

"I saw you surf giant waves on YouTube. You didn't look scared."

"I'm not scared. I'm hardcore, brah. Core doesn't scare."

By the time he's gotten the slabs on ice and locked the big Yeti cooler in the king cab, Mae is still MIA.

She's not at any of the cleaning stations, or hanging around the fish market, or begging for food off the patio diners at the Harbor Café, as she sometimes does.

Not casing birds at the Bait Barge.

Or begging from tourists at the parking lot Clapping Circle, where Casey positions himself, and claps and hears not a clap but a squeaking sound like a dolphin. Since he was a kid, Casey has been drawn to this mystery, as is almost everyone. He's tried for years to link this audio anomaly to God himself but hasn't found a way. Why *should* God turn a clap into dolphin speak? Still in the Clapping Circle, Casey calls out Mae's name, loudly.

No Mae.

Lynda, who runs the mini-mart, tells Casey she saw Mae trotting along with that chick from the *Empress II* and some of her crew. They had bags of deli food.

Casey's gut drops to his feet.

"Headed into parking lot eleven," she says.

Casey sees no sign of Mae, or Bette, on or about parking lot eleven, or any of the others, or the river, or the beach. He cups both hands to his face and yells out. A pit bull tugs on its leash and looks at him, ears perked.

Nerves bristling and his heart loping, Casey gets his binoculars from *Moondance* and makes the rounds again, hitting every place he's seen Mae.

He covers Oceanside Harbor in long strides, stopping to glass the scores of boats moored in the marina, the half-day morning anglers disembarking *Lucky 7,* and the afternoon anglers boarding the *Orca.*

No Mae.

Some rough-looking hombres landing at a tie-up dock, but no Bette.

Fudge, man. Casey feels his pulse speeding up. He might be core and fearless on waves, as he bragged to the kid, but not when it comes to Mae hanging out with sharp-knifed finners.

Lieutenant Tim Kopf at the Coast Guard station is a buzz-cut guards-man in a spanking-white uniform. The diss at the harbor is Tim never leaves his office because his shirt will get dirty, but Casey has always found him polite and helpful. The gleaming cutter *Point Tamarack* sits at berth.

Kopf tells Casey he hasn't seen Mae today, or *Empress II* since last week. The big ugly trawler moves around a lot, he says. Here today, gone tomorrow.

"But I did see some of her crew here this morning," he says. "Early, coming through lot eleven."

"Bette?"

"Yeah, Bette Wu."

"Toward the marina, or from it?" Casey asks.

"Toward the marina," says the lieutenant.

Arriving early, thinks Casey, and departing at lunch, with Mae in tow?

"Why not arrest her, Tim? Or call the sheriffs? You saw my posts."

"On the seas it's up to Fish and Wildlife. Coast Guard has bigger fish to fry. But those videos of yours sure got everybody's attention. I didn't expect those people to show their faces around here for a while. They're probably lying low off San Clemente Island, or maybe they went home."

"Where's she berthed, *Empress II*?" Casey asks, his impatience and his spirits both rising.

"My whole point, Casey, I don't know. But she's supplying restaurants up and down the coast. Why?"

"Because she shows up here the same time Mae disappears, that's why. She threatened me that day."

The ugly thought that some people kidnap dogs for ransom descends on Casey like a cold wave. Mostly those funny-looking Hollywood dogs, but why not a beautiful Lab like Mae? He reminds himself that Mae has a locator chip. That she has a tag with his phone number on it. And he reminds himself that Mae will follow almost anyone who offers her food.

Tim Kopf gives him a look. "She'll turn up. Try the beach again, around the trash containers. And FYI—San Diego County Sheriffs did us some background on two of Bette Wu's associates. One for felony assault, the other for smuggling marijuana out of Mexico and guns in. Ask for Detective Bob Temple and tell him we talked."

Casey uses the good *Tamarack* Wi-Fi to post pictures of Mae on all his socials, describing her disappearance from Oceanside Harbor.

Sees that his shark-finning videos are collecting lots of hits. Pushing viral. Subscriptions up.

Casey walks the harbor again, calling for Mae, sweeping through wide vistas with the Leicas. The docks, the restaurants, the parking lots. Another pass along the beach and the San Luis Rey River. He's getting hoarse and angry.

There's plenty of dogs: another chocolate Labrador down by the river, which from this distance looks almost like Mae, sending a futile bolt of hope through him; a big German shepherd practically dragging a young woman along the river path; two flouncy Lhasa apsos crisscrossing in front of their heavyset human; a Parsons terrier with his leash trailing, shrieking and tearing after a gull that hops twice, then climbs the onshore breeze on bright white wings.

Mae's just flat-out gone.

Gol'-dang.

God, help me find her.

Back at his truck Casey calls the Oceanside Animal Shelter, which directs him to a link on the county website, which has no female brown Labs. He finally gets a body at the shelter, but no dogs have been admitted today. He sends pictures of Mae to the shelter, the Oceanside Police, San Diego Sheriffs, his buddy Craig at California Fish and Wildlife, Lieutenant Tim at the Coast Guard, and posts another round to his tens of thousands of friends, surfers, followers, critics, and visitors to his platforms. In return Casey's getting lots of false sightings that don't help a bit, and lots of speculation that maybe Mae's disappearance from Oceanside Harbor has something to do with the shark finners Casey has shamed.

Detective Bob Temple of San Diego Sheriffs recognizes Casey and calls back that he loves how Casey surfs those big ones. Admits that he started surfing San Onofre when he was eight, with his dad and mom and sister. Still surfing, he says, although at fifty-two he's kind of slowing down.

He listens to Casey's missing-dog story, tells Casey that Bette Wu and her crew are fish pirates, raiding coastal San Diego and Orange County fisheries with a fleet of older vessels and a couple of sleek red Cigarettes. They ignore limits and size and seasonal restrictions. Sell to restaurants from Imperial Beach all the way to San Francisco. They've been caught with dope and guns. Their mother ship is *Empress II*.

"I know," Casey says impatiently, "but where can I find Bette Wu and *Empress II*?"

A beat then, while Bob Temple decides whether or not to give up Sheriff Department information to a Laguna surfer who's a virtual stranger.

"Slip 41-B, Pier 32 Marina, National City."

9

Casey glasses *Empress II* at her slip at the National City Marina. Through the Leicas, he sees a man half reclining on a chaise lounge, smoking. Casey thinks he was one of the gunners aboard the Luhrs that day, but he's not sure. *Empress II*'s tables and nets have been stowed, but she's still just a peeling blue-and-red commercial trawler berthed way out at the end of a crowded landing, as if trying to hide within the gleaming motor yachts and elegant sailboats. Her boarding ramp is down.

Casey wonders how Bette Wu and her multinational, occasionally felonious crew can afford this big vessel, its slip fee here in National City, and the green Luhrs, the white Bayliner, and the swanky *Dragon* his mom told him about, all by supplying fish and shark fins to Southern California restaurants.

Just not feelin' it, he thinks. Maybe they're in some other business, too?

He stops at the ramp gate and the smoking man stands up. He's short, with ropy arms and a scrawny torso. Filipino, Casey guesses.

"I came to get my dog," says Casey.

"No dog."

"Everybody at the harbor saw Bette stealing her."

"No Bette. Not here."

"Where, then?"

Smoker flips his cigarette butt into the bay and shakes his head.

"Fine, then," says Casey. "Permission to come aboard requested. So I can look for Mae."

"No. No dog here. No Bette here. Out selling to restaurants. All legal and good money so you go now."

Casey throws the latch and knees open the ramp gate and Smoker meets him halfway up, crouching into a boxer's stance, fists up. Casey— six feet, two inches tall, two hundred and twenty pounds of youthful muscle, plus years of immense waves pounding him around like a pool toy, years of gym workouts, and some truly evil Hapkido training with Brock—springs in and pushes Smoker hard, but not too hard, over the railing and into the bay.

"Sorry, sir. I'll be just a minute!"

Which is less than it takes him to check belowdecks for Mae, or Bette, or whoever else might be aboard this fish-reeking, cigarette-smoke-steeped trawler. He scribbles his number onto a Tsingtao coaster.

"Mae! Mae!"

But no Mae, and back on deck Casey sees Smoker, fully drenched and lurching up the ramp toward the boarding gate.

"Tell Bette she owes me a chocolate Lab named Mae."

"You should take down video. Going viral. Bad for business."

"Soon as I get my dog back. And I want enough money for a good phone. You tell her that."

He presses the coaster into the man's cold wet hand. "I'm sorry if I hurt you. But I do expect her call."

He's at the Barrel an hour later, still midafternoon, transferring his hundred-plus-pound tuna fish from his cooler to the walk-in refrigerator in the restaurant kitchen.

In the Barrel's third-story office/apartment, Casey showers quickly, balancing his phone on the aluminum shower top, just out of spray distance.

When he's done he posts another round of Mae pictures on all his socials, pleads for sightings, be-on-the-lookout fors, any clues no matter how tenuous as to where she might be. His Mae posts are going viral on more than one platform but the false sightings are everywhere and useless.

He sends out another CaseyGram with pictures of Mae and pleas for help.

Someone has seen something! he writes.

But what if Bette Wu doesn't call?

His Woodland Street home is a small 1950s cottage surrounded by walls of purple bougainvillea, and yellow, red, and white hibiscus. Some of the blossoms are already folding in for the night.

He takes his laptop to the bistro table in his backyard, profuse with bird-of-paradise, potted plumeria, succulents, and a fragrant center-yard tangerine tree now heavy with fruit.

An hour later he's removed his posts, blogs, and videos from every platform he uses. Goes through his accounts once more, to make sure. But he wonders what real good this is going to do for Bette Wu and her fellow pirates, considering how many thousands of them have already viewed, forwarded, liked, forwarded again, around the Internet, around the world. Hasn't the damage been done?

While he's at it he checks his brother Brock's Breath of Life Rescue Mission feed, reads another vitriolic exchange between Brock and Kasper Aamon, the founder of Right Fight.

> Brother Brock Stonebreaker, it was great to see you up in Mendocino.
>
> My pleasure, Aamon-you looked more intelligent than you do on Fox.
>
> You look like the same slimy dude who bores his congregation at the Breath of Life Rescue Mission for hours on end. I know that because some of my Right Fighters live practically right next door to you. They tell me it's a squalid pit, your alleged church. A slum. A black hole, a barrio.

Why don't you come by, slip a couple grand into the collection plate sometime?

So you can give it away to the pathetic, pregnant, drug-addicted minorities you love so much?

Sure! Be happy to.

You're a sick donkey, Brother Brock. A waste of white skin. Just look at you, with your plantation hair and your ink and your fat wahine wife.

Careful now, Kasper—your stupidity is showing through, again.

I think we should meet face-to-face again, Brock. Maybe clear the air a little.

I'd rather step on a rattlesnake. Don't waste my time. I could be helping someone who needs it.

Like you helped tie off those disease-riddled junkies shooting up in the drug cafes in San Francisco? I saw the video. That's the kind of help you mean?

Kasper, lose the hate for people you don't even know. Then find someone to care about, other than yourself.

Back at the Barrel he preps the bar for happy hour. His two barbacks, Dylan and Diego, are already there, tending to the bottles and glasses, coolers, ice machines, building the garnishes from tiny umbrellas, nasturtium petals, and cubed melon.

Phone in his pocket, ring tone and vibrate turned up high, he chats with some local regulars—Janice, Aurora, Gaye, and Tessie. They're pretty, reliably thirsty, cheerful. Not his type for a relationship but he likes them, and their attention.

Tessie recently bought one of his signature model surfboards at Hobie Sports here in town and he feels guilty for avoiding a promised lesson on the lavishly beautiful, expensive tri-fin. He feels her sincere, happy interest in him but he's never been one to take something offered without genuine reciprocity, which he does not feel—has rarely felt—in a woman.

He can hardly keep up the small talk, waiting on word about Mae from Bette Wu.

Who walks into the bar just before happy hour with two male associates, hangs a silver clutch on the back of the barstool, and sits down in front of Casey.

At least he thinks it's her.

This Bette is dressed in a seafoam-green leather pantsuit and matching rhinestone-studded sneakers. No blouse required. No pistol on her hip. Pearls around her neck. Hair up and lipstick on.

The men wear dark suits, solid-colored shirts and ties, and take stools on either side of her. They frown.

Casey's locals have gone silent, four faces trained down the bar on Bette with full attention.

Jen passes by, menus clutched to her chest, followed by two customers. A sharp look at Bette Wu, then a questioning glance at Casey.

"Stonebreaker, make me a French 75," Bette says. "Then we'll talk. Beers for my crew. Kingstar if you have it. Tsingtao if you don't."

"You're talking different now," says Casey.

A look from her, possibly dismissive.

He makes and serves her the drink, Tsingtao for the men. Glances at Tessie and friends, isn't sure what expression to offer. Bette lifts her drink to them, and sips.

One of the cocktail waitresses down the bar hoists a Scorpion-loaded tray to her shoulder, spikes Casey another order to fill near the far cash register.

Bette Wu relocates to a stool in front of it and sets down her drink.

Casey looks at her, not certain that this Bette was the Bette on *Empress II*.

"I want Mae back and twelve hundred for a phone," he says.

"I don't have Mae."

"People at Oceanside Harbor saw you with her."

"But I can tell you where she is when you take the videos down."

"They're down."

"Good. But I will only direct you to her and the money when I see the proof. You post a lot. And all those YouTubes. I want it down. All of it. Every pixel."

"I just told you they're down. You better not hurt her."

"I don't have her."

"God loves Mae and He'll protect her."

"I think that's funny."

"Some people think everything's funny."

Bette Wu drinks half of her French 75, sets the glass down, and fixes her skeptical brown eyes on Casey.

"You look like Bette from the *Empress II*," he says. "But you don't talk like her."

"I'm Bette Wu. A fisher, actor, businesswoman, and graduate of UCLA. Business, with a minor in film."

"I think *that's* funny."

"I was brought up on Hong Kong crime and action movies. Now I play my heroines in real life. Helps beat the boredom on the boat. I will make a pirate movie someday. A big hit. Have you seen the Chinese film *The Pirate*?"

He shakes his head. "I want my dog."

"I'll check your platforms and see if you're lying or not. And when I'm satisfied, I will call."

She smiles at Casey, then strides out of the bar, trailed by her escorts, who drop money on the counter and hustle to catch up.

Casey gets his mom and his barback to handle the rest of happy hour, and races up the outside stairs to the third-floor Barrel apartment/office to double ensure all his shark-finning posts and pictures and videos are in fact down. He can't lose Mae on a technicality.

Five minutes later, he's back on duty on the bar.

When his phone rings he almost fumbles a Lapu-Lapu on its way to a customer, then yanks out the device—vibrating ecstatically and playing the first notes of a Jack Johnson song.

"We have small wrinkle," says Bette.

When he hears her pirate talk his heart speeds up in a bad way.

"There better not be!" blurts Casey, as adrenaline and anger burst through him. "It's all down. Every clip, picture, post, and word."

"We ask twenty-five thousand dollars to give back Mae. Twenty. Five. Thousand. Jacksons only. If you call police, Mae goes overboard at sea. Or maybe smuggle to a buyer far away."

Casey feels his deepest fear for Mae landing on him like an avalanche. "I'll get the money."

"Call me tomorrow at this number at noon exactly. From your home in Laguna Beach. If you don't, your dog will disappear."

She gives him a number, which he writes on a Barrel napkin and slips into his wallet.

"Miss Wu, the second commandment says to love your neighbor as yourself. But I don't love you. I'm closer to not liking you at all."

"I'll cry myself to sleep."

Casey's ear gets two kisses; then Bette rings off.

He calls Brock, who answers with an obscenity, sirens in the background.

"Mae got dognapped by pirates and they want twenty-five thousand dollars or they'll throw her overboard. I'm calling them at noon tomorrow."

Silence as the sirens whine. Casey can't believe his own words: Would they really do that? The idea makes him queasy. Jelly kneed. Helpless. Like he's being stranded in a leaking dinghy while Mae dogpaddles for some distant shore.

"Do you have the money, Case?"

"I can get it."

"Mahina and I will be there tomorrow morning by six thirty."

"I'm praying this works out," says Casey.

"Prayer won't do you one bit of good, brother."

"No guns."

"Don't argue," says Brock. "Don't speak. See you soon."

10

Casey distractedly fills drink orders and tries to yak with his customers while checking his balances. His thoughts are spinning and he can't slow them down. Tessie and Aurora have stayed late. Tessie asks after Mae, who is often on her pad in the Barrel lobby, leashed to the ankle of the bronze statue of Casey's dad.

"She's at home, resting," he says. "Worn out from the fishing today."

Tessie looks at him doubtfully. "You okay tonight, Case?"

"Worn out, too, I guess. That was a big fish."

"I'm ready for that surfing lesson whenever you are!"

"You got it, Tess. Maybe next week."

Keeping track on the back of a bar check, he logs in the $648 in his checking account down at Wells Fargo, easily gettable in the morning. It's mostly from tips and his small bartender's hourly.

There's another account with various sponsorship and endorsement money in it, about $4,000.

And $10,000 in CDs he opened with signing bonuses from a hip young clothing company and a start-up watchmaker. It will cost him an early withdrawal penalty of who knows what, but he *thinks* he can get most of that money tomorrow because the bank manager likes him.

Subtotaling $14,648, exactly $10,352 short.

"Fudge," Casey mutters.

He's got $1,500 in a savings account. And about a thousand in undeclared tips safe under the towels in a bathroom cabinet at home.

He adds it all up and writes the new $171,480 total excitedly, then takes a breath of deep relief. Checks his addition to find he's slipped in an extra zero so the correct amount should be $17,148.

Still almost $8,000 to go.

Fudge *me*.

He knows what his tax returns say about gross income—just under $35,000—annually, for his last few years at the Barrel.

Also knows he has plenty of new sponsor merch but it's not like the pirates are going to want surfboards, XL wetsuits, trunks, beach shorts, T-shirts, hoodies, leather flip-flops, surf-inspired jewelry made of shells, beads, and sea glass. Certainly not organic sunscreen, Day-Glo nose-coats, CBD lip-savers, or blocks of scented surfboard wax. Maybe the Seiko Waterman watches, he thinks. He's already given most of them to friends, but he's got six of them with different-colored dials, still in their boxes, worth five hundred bucks a throw, though technically he's not allowed to sell them.

"Casey! Another margarita! And a couple of Bohemias!"

A bank loan?

Or maybe money from Mom or Brock?

But Casey knows that Brock's funding for the Breath of Life Rescue Mission isn't steady, and he's got Mahina depending on him. Plus, Brock blows money like crazy, getting the Go Dogs to the latest disaster with generous donations, but many of the life-saving supplies are covered by his always meager personal funds.

His mom has eight grand, though how much she can put her hands on, quickly, he doesn't know. The idea of borrowing from your mom at age twenty-four doesn't seem right.

Makes Casey feel like the dumbass that Brock and everybody else have always told him he is.

Later, after locking the Barrel doors for the night, he joins his mother on the outside deck for their customary vodka rocks.

It's the only alcohol he drinks. One vodka with Mom, per night. Doesn't love the woozy booze buzz; never has. He honors this ritual for her, though. She has her single drink with him, but Casey knows she drinks more at home, later, to help her sleep. He isn't sure how much she drinks but he knows she's up before dawn for her miles of paddling, swimming, running, weight lifting, breath exercises in the high school pool. All in preparation for the Monsters of Mavericks in a few short weeks. Then there's her fourteen-hour days here at the Barrel, noon to 2 A.M. Six days straight and one day off.

His mother has always run on some inner fuel that Casey has never clearly understood. At times it seems desperate. He thinks it has to do with his father. Maybe with her near worship of him. And maybe to do with some things between them. Secrets. Regrets. Things unsaid. Maybe to do with trying to fill the immense hole that's been in her for as long as he, Casey, has been alive. The same hole in him.

His just a different shape and size.

Now, from the deck, Jen can see the Brooks Street break she'll be paddle-surfing just a few hours from now, the hotel lights on the beach, the shining low-tide boulders, the moonlight wobbling on the water.

The waves are small, just a puny west swell, the water temp down to the high fifties. But nothing like the cold Mavericks had been—and will be, she thinks—remembering the bone-deep shock that gripped her there as she powered the jet ski in search of John, her body numbed not just by the water but compressed and constricted by four millimeters of neoprene head to toe. Hard to feel her toes and fingers. Ears aching.

Then the sudden recognition: John under the ice-cold water, leashed to a boulder like an infant by his cord.

Yes, so much to fear there. So much to fear at the Monsters.

Enough. Think "do." Think "strong."

"I'll have the money by ten tomorrow," she says. "Does it matter what kind of bills?"

"Twenties. Thanks, Mom. I'll pay you back really fast."

So Casey, she thinks. So good and sweet and sometimes naïve. "I know you will."

It makes her almost sick, thinking what might happen to Mae. Those men out in the water today looked strong and dangerous.

"I keep thinking I should call the FBI," he says. "They won't let me pay the ransom but they'll help me set the dognappers up, then try to nail them. At least they do that with people. But what if it doesn't go perfect? What if the pirates smell the sting and Mae ends up dumped? To hide evidence? The feds flub up kidnappings all the time. I just can't take that risk. Am I being stupid?"

"I urge you to call the police, Casey."

Jen locks eyes with her beautiful son.

"No, Mom. They'd just mess things up. I called Brock instead."

A bolt of fear hits her. "The pirates could end up with the money, *and* Mae," she says.

Immediately regretting it.

Jen has spent the last twenty-five years not allowing herself to fear small things. Small things like Bette Wu, or her father the Kings fan, or his leering sidekick, Polo. Not allowing herself to be afraid of anything. So she hates it when second-rate fears come drifting over the terrifying pit that is Mavericks. Hates to infect Casey and Brock with them. And herself, too.

"But I don't think they will," she says, overriding her last unnecessary, fearful sentence. "So stick to your plan with your brother, Case. We'll get Mae back. I'll do anything you need. I can help you pack up the money, drive you to the dropoff, keep an eye out for anything going wrong. I'm not afraid of these people."

Casey taps his empty glass on the table. "They'll want me alone, probably."

"I'll hang back," she says.

"Brock's on his way."

"The three of us will get her back, Case. We'll be drinking toasts after work tomorrow night, Mae asleep on somebody's feet like she always is. I'm feeling it. We're going to own this thing, just like those waves at Mavericks."

For twenty-five years, it's been pure Jen Stonebreaker to encourage her sons to face what she's afraid of. So long as *they're* not.

And just a few weeks from now, to tow Casey into the deadly heart of her own fear. Can she save him from John's fate?

Of course I can, she thinks: that's the whole point of the Monsters. To beat what I'm afraid of. To slaughter the fear.

She won't let Casey sense it.

"I told Brock and Mahina not to bring guns," he says.

Always the pacifist, Jen thinks. Always the peacemaker, the good, the fair, the God-fearing.

"And?"

"He said don't worry."

But worried she is, knowing that Brock's heart will always beat with anger, no matter how many churches he founds, or "sermons" he gives or disaster victims he helps out.

Jen sighs, says nothing more on this topic.

Almost noon, sheltered by the flowering walls in his fragrant backyard in Laguna Canyon, Casey zips the last thousand-dollar bundle of bills into his backpack, takes pictures and video.

"Heavier than I thought."

"Two-point-six pounds," says Brock, just back from gassing up the Go Dogs Econoline.

"Don't tell me how you know that," says Jen.

"My colorful past," he says.

Mahina hefts the backpack by its handle, nods. "Feels like power."

Casey gets the Barrel bar napkin from his wallet and a pen from his shorts pocket, then sits and dials Bette Wu. He's on speaker so everyone can hear.

"Bette Wu. Yes?"

Casey says his full name, quietly, then listens and writes.

She gives him the slip number for *Empress II* in the National City Marina.

"Let me guess," says Bette. "You are on the speaker with your mother and brother and his wife."

"Yes, I am. Is Mae alright?"

"Yes, and hello, everybody! I have read so much about all of you. A family of celebrity American surfers!"

Brock leans into the phone and whispers a profane curse.

"I recognize that voice and 'tude, Brother Brock! I love the Breath of Life Rescue Mission. People need anger. And comedy."

Jen crowds close: "Don't hurt Mae, you conniving bitch."

"Mae's fine, Jen. No worries! But there is now another small wrinkle."

"No more of those," says Casey.

"Very easy and simple, though," says Bette. "Jen, we have business to discuss. So you come with Casey to deliver the money. See? Easy wrinkle! Casey, Jen, and the money. In Casey's truck. We see any police, any car that is not your truck—then Mae goes overboard. We see Brock or Mahina, or the Go Dogs van, then maybe Mae runs away and we can't find her. We find guns or phones on you . . . well, you know what happens. Okey dokey?"

Casey pictures Bette from last night in his bar. He's never felt real anger before, at least nothing like this. Bette Wu has more wickedness in her than anyone he's ever met. His first brush with evil. She seems to be made of it. To enjoy it.

"Mae misses you so much," she says. "We will be watching for you, Casey and Jen!"

She rings off.

11

Casey steers his pickup out of Laguna Canyon toward the toll road, headed south for San Diego, Jen beside him, the cash-stuffed pack on the cab's back floor.

Over the Pier 32 National City Marina, skies are blue, and a brisk breeze pings the lanyards and halyards of the pleasure yachts.

Empress II sits heavy and workmanlike in slip 41-B, with her fading blue and red paint, well-used outriggers, and her tag lines swaying loosely in the wind. The coiffed motor yachts seem to ignore her.

Casey hoists the pack and strolls toward the vessel, his mother beside him. He's dressed as he almost always dresses, and it's perfect for the role of ocean-bound young adventurer that he's now suggesting: tan corduroy board shorts, flip-flops, a black hoodie with Day-Glo orange draw cords, and wide-temple sunglasses.

Jen's got on shorts, a T-shirt, a windbreaker, ankle-high trekking shoes, her orange bowl of hair partially contained in a black-and-green paisley bandana.

Casey sees Bette Wu standing atop the hold, phone to her ear. Mae stands beside her, tail wagging, her aging eyes recognizing Casey at this distance. Casey feels his eyes tearing up, feels like his heart is trying to get out and run to her.

Smoker, whom Casey had jettisoned just yesterday, a cigarette in his mouth and a pistol in his waistband, holds open the lower boarding gate with a bored stare. Casey starts up the ramp, Jen behind him. He looks up to see Mae propped up on the gunwale, looking down at him, smiling between barks with that big open smile Labs get.

Now aboard, Casey kneels and gets a mauling from Mae, kissing her forehead and kneading her ear joints. Mae howls emotionally. Jen kneels too and just about gets knocked over.

Bette, dressed in snug black tactical garb and red mid-ankle Air Jordans, leads them down a short steel gangway and into the cigarette-smoke- and incense-infused galley. The ship seems bigger than Casey remembers from his initial search for Mae. There's a row of portholes along the port and starboard sides, the thick plexiglass bearing the scars of years. Through which Casey sees the gently swaying blue-green bay, a ketch coming into its slip, the marina ships bobbing at dock. Hears the *Empress II* generators moaning away, their vibrations coming through his flip-flops. Keeping their catch frozen, he thinks, and their lights on.

Seated at the head of a heavily shellacked table is the Kings fan his mother described—Bette's alleged father. To his right sits a handsome Latino in a trim suit, a leather briefcase open on the table just a short reach away. Casey notes the black grip of a stainless-steel pistol peeking out from under the fastener file folders, and a yellow legal pad bristling with handwriting.

Bette pulls out a chair and sits to the left of her father, who is hatless now, but again clad in black-and-white Kings hockey team warm-ups, with a jungle of gold around his thick neck.

He offers a half smile, nodding to Jen and Casey. "As you know, I am Jimmy Wu, Bette's father. I have many interests. Such as King Jim Seafood. All the very best seafood, always fresh. I am famous in seafood distribution in Southern California. I have big social following. I have YouTube. I have ads on TV late at night. My colorful trucks are all over the place. This is my attorney, Octavio Benitez. Mergers and acquisitions. Octavio."

Benitez rises as Jimmy completes the introductions, but sits without shaking Casey's offered hand. "A pleasure to meet you both."

They sit and Benitez fixes first Jen, then Casey, with dark, amused eyes.

"I know of your many accomplishments and awards and medals. I saw you, Mrs. Stonebreaker, announcing the Olympic water polo competition on TV not long ago. Very insightful commentary."

"Why thank you."

"Mr. Stonebreaker, I've followed your big-wave conquests through the streaming coverage of the Monsters of Mavericks . . . what is it now, canceled three of the last five years?"

"No," says Casey. "Two of the last ten. They say climate change is making the waves bigger now. The next Monsters could be more like when Dad died. Huge."

Jen's heart drops at this, but the lawyer smirks.

"Casey, I saw video of you as a seventeen-year-old, in your first big-wave competition at Mavericks."

"I didn't exactly tear it up."

"But you survived."

"You don't get a lot of points for survival," says Casey, reaching down to pet Mae, who has laid down on his feet. Casey feels her warmth on his skin. "You have to bring more than survival to the ride. You need a special thing to win."

"Yes!" says Jimmy Wu. "You need style, and cool, and the attitude that you own the wave and it does not own you. If your legs are shaking, or your eyes are wide, you don't win points!"

Casey remembers his first big waves, not so much the fear itself, but his fear of fear, of choking. He didn't choke but his legs trembled on the bottom turns and when he looked at the footage the next day he was surprised and embarrassed by his expressions: wide-eyed dread, grim determination, nerve-jangled relief as he flew like a trapeze artist over the tops of the waves, kicking out, then falling down into the marginal safety of a furious ocean between waves.

"And I am also aware of your wonderful Barrel restaurant, Mrs. Stonebreaker," says the lawyer. "But I get ahead. Mr. Wu, you should count the money."

"Bette?"

"Danilo!" Bette calls out.

Smoker comes in, takes the backpack from Casey, and sets it on the far end of the table. Zips it open, then retreats to lean against the kitchen bulkhead, one foot up against the peeling white steel, pistol in place behind his waistband.

Bette goes to the pack, unbands and counts each thousand-dollar pack with careful patience, setting the completed stacks aside and apart.

She looks up at Casey after each one. ". . . nine hundred eighty, eight thousand."

A few minutes later she announces, "Money's all here. I didn't think Stonebreaker would cheat us. He is much too good and innocent."

Casey breaks eye contact with her for lack of an apt response. He can't tell if she's being complimentary or contemptuous. Doesn't really care. Notes that her father gives Bette a hostile stare.

He stands, looks at the lawyer, then at the briefcase in which the gun waits, then to the table with his and his mom's $25,000 in it. Lawyers, guns, and money, he thinks. He was singing that song in the shower just a few days ago, scrubbing down with a stiff brush and strong soap, trying to get the smell of bluefin tuna fish off his hands.

Through one of the portholes, Casey sees the green Luhrs and the white Bayliner that corralled him a few days ago now approaching just two hundred feet off the trawler's starboard flank.

"I'm gonna, like, take my dog and go," he says. "I'll be honest. I think you people suck. You broke nature's law by slaughtering those sharks for their fins. For your dang soups. But you take Mae and threaten to let her drown? Then steal twenty-five thousand of ours for ransom? Even greedy, small-minded people like you should be ashamed of that.

But you're not. You don't know anything. You are toys in the devil's hands."

"You're not a moron," says Bette. "You don't really think we'd hurt your dog, do you?"

"You said you would."

"You are naïve. That's ridiculous. To you, we're just evil Chinese who brought the plague to the world. And communism."

"You're pirates who threatened to kill my dog. Come on, Mae. Mom—we're leaving now."

"Sit down, Casey," says Bette. "My father has a very interesting offer for you."

Danilo steps away from the bulkhead, crossing his hands before him, spreading his feet.

Casey sits and Jen follows suit. Mae stands, tail wagging, looking toward the galley exit.

"An offer for what?" asks Jen.

Jimmy Wu purses his lips and glances at Benitez. Then back at Jen. "Okay, now you listen. Simple offer. We supply restaurants but we want a restaurant where there is much money. We want to buy the Barrel in Laguna. It is, very actually, the best restaurant location in Laguna Beach, and Laguna Beach is the best coastal city in California. This is very true and factual. My partners back home are very wealthy businessmen and hungry to invest in a very championship location. Mr. Benitez expert in dining and hospitality. He is a graduate of Harvard Law School. He has written the contract for you to sell to us. We keep the name the Barrel. You still manage the Barrel. Casey is still the bartender and assistant manager. You both get a big salary from me—more than what we estimate you declared to IRS last year. Very generous."

Benitez takes a file from his briefcase and opens it, thumbing the metal clasp at the top.

"Ninety-six thousand dollars annually for Jen Stonebreaker. Sixty-eight for Casey, with raises determined by the Wu family. Hourly staff and contractors will get what they're getting now, and whatever increases they have been promised in writing."

"How much for my restaurant?" asks Jen.

Jimmy smiles. "It brings me pleasure to offer two million dollars. One half is cash, in the bait tank, fifty feet away from you right now. It is bundled and, of course, we have a good scale. The other half will be wire-transferred from First Taiwan Bank into whatever secure and private account you wish. Swiss, I would suggest, or Grand Cayman. And, if you sign right now, we return to you the twenty-five thousand for your idiot dog. Quite a nice payday for you!"

Jen does not smile back. "Two million? That's what a small *house* costs in Laguna. The Barrel lot alone is worth three times that. The structure adds another two million, and the established business even more. My answer is no. And if you came up with ten million dollars I'd still say no. Twenty million I'd say no again. The Barrel is my life. My family. I'd set it on fire before I'd sell it to you."

"Jen Stonebreaker! We think so much alike!" says Wu with a jolly smile. "Oh, funny, funny, when I say Barrel and you say fire!"

Casey meets the incredulous look on his mother's face with one of his own.

They stand again, as if helping each other up with their locked eyes. Mae heads for the galley door as before.

Casey looks at the piles of money on the table, thinks about the gun in the lawyer's briefcase, and Danilo's gun, and he can't imagine how he can get his money out of here without getting himself and his mother and maybe Mae shot.

Through a rusty porthole he sees that the Luhrs and the Bayliner have eased closer. Through another he sees two red Cigarette boats, *Dragon* and *Bushmaster*. Remembers Lieutenant Tim's description of the pirate fleet. The speedboats are center consoles, and Casey sees two men in each, standing and focused on *Empress II*.

Jimmy smiles, as if he's hearing Casey's anxious thoughts.

Benitez collects another folder from his briefcase and offers it to Jen.

"You should sign this offer now," he says pleasantly. "Casey is your witness. I will notarize. The offer is fair and reasonable in this current real estate market. You will not lose the Barrel or your history there. You will still be a part of it, and it of you. You will gain two million dollars and who knows? Retire? Open another restaurant? Somewhere other than Laguna Beach, of course."

"Go to hell, counselor."

"Many years from now, I hope. Casey?"

Casey shakes his head and backs toward the door. He senses Danilo's movement behind him.

"No, thank you. No."

"Ask your mother to sign this," says the lawyer. "You can then leave here with good money for an aging restaurant, a wonderful dog, and your twenty-five thousand in ransom—a gift from the Wu family. Bette would also like to give you an additional twelve hundred dollars for a new phone. To replace the one you threw into the ocean."

"Never," snaps Jen, striding toward the exit behind Mae and ahead of her son. Stops and turns. "You people don't scare me one bit. If I see you anywhere near the Barrel I'll set *you* on fire."

Before following his mother out, Casey hesitates and studies Bette Wu. "God forgives you."

"I don't care, but thanks for putting in a good word for me."

Casey can't tell if Bette is scowling or amused. He senses in her face something beyond the wickedness that surrounded her on *Moondance* and had just minutes ago seemed so obvious here. Now there's something more, something alien and difficult to know. Something not him.

"Casey, you are a beautiful, weak man," says Bette Wu. "Be strong about our offer. You and I would be partners. We can discuss details and I can point out the many benefits of partnership with us."

"Nothing to discuss or point out," says Casey.

"You're missing a great opportunity."

"To be swindled. I'm not stupid, you know."

Bette gives him an assessing look. "You're very smart, in fact. So, two million. Think. And good luck at Mavericks. I think you will win."

"I think my brother will."

Suddenly, through the galley door stumbles a small man in white Polo warm-ups, his long black hair wrapped around one of Brock Stonebreaker's big knuckled, tattooed fists. Brock's other hand holds a big pistol firmly to the man's temple. Brock's dreadlocks sprout from his head, dark little stacks. Casey thinks he looks kind of evil but knows he's not.

"The lawyer's got a gun, Brock!" Jen yells.

Danilo draws his pistol but Brock already has his gun trained on the man's chest. Danilo drops his sidearm and looks at Brock with frank hatred. Then raises his hands.

Polo struggles but Brock clenches the knot of black hair and the man yelps.

A big Asian woman barges in next, hands apparently tied behind her, the even bigger Mahina with the pistol-grip, short-barreled scattergun inches from her back.

Brock and Mahina point their guns deliberately and patiently at Jimmy, Bette, Danilo, and Benitez.

"Be calm, everybody," says Brock. "Lawyer man, you go for that briefcase, they'll have to clean your brains off the bulkhead."

Mahina plunks down her shotgun near the money, gives her captive a baleful glare, then palms big handfuls of cash back into the pack and zips it shut.

"This money is not yours," she says, Brock covering her, pistol in one hand and Polo's hair still clenched in the other.

"These people think they can steal the Barrel from us," says Jen. "For two million dollars."

"Cute," says Brock. "Where's that two million going to come from? Not shark-finning."

Wu's smile is gone, replaced by a stony, affronted glare. Casey can tell that Wu wants respect, wants to be seen as dangerous.

Wu raises his hands and gets up from the table. In his Kings warm-ups and heavy gold, he moves purposefully across the galley to the life-jacket stowage cabinets. They're well-marked with images of life vests, and text in English.

Facing his audience, Wu gestures to the nearest drawer.

"Behind this lock? New precursor for fentanyl, headed to Mexico. Very hard to get. Norfentanyl. Four-AP, and 1-boc-4-AP. Over six million dollars in there. Every cartel wants this. They bid up price."

"Fresh from China," says Brock.

"The best," says Jimmy Wu. "And these."

He signals another cabinet with his upturned palm. Casts a theatrical frown at Jen and opens it. Fog billows into the dank galley but Casey can't make out what's inside.

"Frozen shark fins," Wu says. "More valuable than lobster or crab. Make happy boys and girls."

Wu's frown upshifts to a smile, and he won't shut up:

"In other boats we have grass for San Francisco, Colombian cocaine for San Diego, NATO seven-six-two and five-five-six ammunition for Los Mochis. We have ghost guns, no serial number, private made in California. We have best bluefin tuna for Los Angeles, and fresh shark fins for the restaurants. And cash! So much you can't believe. More in LA and San Diego. This is how the money comes to us. We can buy the Barrel easy, you bet! And my partners in Taiwan have much more!"

An odd moment of silence then as Bette Wu stares at Jen, and Polo finally stops struggling.

Casey sees men on the decks of the Luhrs and the Bayliner looking down on them. Same guys who shot up his phone. Guns scare him like a sixty-foot wave never could.

In the middle distance, the Cigarettes lurch like bulls in a chute.

He wonders where his God is right now, why He isn't down here acting on behalf of the upright against the soldiers of Satan.

"Pirates, smugglers, shark finners, lawyers—you really are a fun crew," says Brock. "Let's do this again sometime."

Brock underhands the backpack to Casey, and marches Polo to the door, followed by Mahina and her captive, then Jen and Casey.

All the while he's got his gun on Wu, Danilo, or Benitez, alternately. Waits for his family to clear the galley, then releases the hostage and backpedals up the gangway to the deck.

Soon as Casey's back in his truck and moving, Jen calls 911 and describes what she's just seen at slip 41-B in the National City Marina.

In the rearview mirror Casey sees Bette, Jimmy, Benitez, and their outmaneuvered crew milling around on the deck of *Empress II,* apparently without a plan.

Jimmy shakes a fist, gold chains glinting in the bright San Diego sun.

Casey falls in behind his mother's VW Beetle, top down, and follows it to the freeway, Brock driving and Mahina waving a big brown paw at him, her profuse, black island hair blowing in the wind.

12

Looking Back—

WHO WAS JOHN STONEBREAKER AND WHAT WENT WRONG AT MAVERICKS?

A big-wave surfing contest left one of the world's premier professional surfers dead. Who was he and why did he die?

BY JEN STONEBREAKER

Part two of a special series for *Surf Tribe Magazine*

No more little surfer-girl crushes on John Stonebreaker. No more "Beach Blanket Bingo."

No more gazing at him from five houses away at Top of the World, no more spying on him in the hippie van.

John Stonebreaker pulled me into his world that day at Imperial Beach like a riptide that has you before you know it, and you can't really fight it until it lets you go.

The stats:

Five to seven feet.

Slight offshores.

Top-to-bottom barrels, over fast.

Short shoulders and hard crashes.

By the time we got out of the water at nine o'clock, I was so cold and weak I could barely get my wetsuit off. I stood there for a while with the neoprene pulled down to my waist and a black sweatshirt on, letting the sun thaw my skin and muscles.

I looked beyond the metal border fence to Tijuana, its shanties climbing the steep hills, smoke rising, the smell of burning trash, just a half-mile distant across the river.

I crashed butt first onto a towel in the slightly warm sand, still half-clad in my wetsuit, a hoodie zipped tight, hugging my knees, my hands brine-soaked and wrinkled, eyes closed and heart slowing. The sun warmed my eyelids and I saw the ornery, orange-burnished waves I'd just tried to surf in all their speed and sudden caprice. I missed at least a dozen, just couldn't paddle fast enough. Quickly fell off a dozen more—they were much steeper and faster than I'd been riding up in Orange County. Crashed another ten or twelve times on the bottom turns—my legs weren't strong enough. I caught four short, fast waves that I couldn't outrace, and ended in nasty wipeouts. But what I saw most clearly on the orange-tinted big screen in my head were the three barrels I got into, and belched out of, with what seemed like the velocity of a motorcycle. These beautiful, ribbed, roaring cylinders held me close, then set me free.

And those moments you know why you do this and you believe that there is no other thing on Earth so personal and so good.

It was my introduction to big surf—yes, sir, yes, ma'am—please accept my wipeouts as bows and curtsies.

"You did good out there," said John.

I stayed in my burnished orange world, eyes closed. Saw a five-foot section opening up for me like a gift, looked down to see my feet on the board and the leg-throbbing bottom snap to beat that crashing lip. Saw from the corner of my vision the collapsing wall of whitewater that took me out by surprise.

"Thanks, John."

"You took a beating, too."

"Nothing broken or cut."

"Imperial's a devil and you handled it."

"I got to get stronger."

"All your swim and polo training is great. You just need more waves. And bigger ones. You feel it, don't you?"

"What."

Some time went by as John thought. I felt the sun easing into my muscles and bones. Sleep knocked.

"How important this is. How it doesn't matter but it means everything."

"What exact everything does it mean, John?"

"Freedom. That if you go fast enough, time stops. The barrel is the moment but the moment is eternal. And you are free. Dad says that surfing can lead to God. I say, surfing *is* God."

I opened my eyes and looked up at him. Saw that same older-than-his-years expression he had in the tiki light the night before. Saw the same boy's glitter in his eyes. The child in his man's body.

"That's a bit much for me to believe, preacher son. But we never went to church, so what do I know?"

"I want someone to do this with, Jen. Don't say anything. Just think about it. It would be our world. Our strength."

"To ride waves?"

"Big waves. The biggest you can. There are these computerized programs that forecast waves all over the Earth. They crunch the wind and storm power and direction, the swell size and frequency, factor in bottoms and tides. They're discovering big waves—enormous waves—that nobody knew about. The old Hawaiians say you can't catch a wave over thirty feet by paddling into it. There's talk about jet skis and fast boats and helicopters. That's where I want to be. That's what I want to ride. Dad's got his church, and huge waves are going to be mine. I want a partner. Don't say anything, Jen. I'm asking you not to say anything."

"Are you asking me to be that partner?"

"Damn, I told you not to say anything."

"It's a pretty important question, John. I just turned eighteen. I'm kicking butt in all my sports and hauling down a four-point-two GPA. I'm looking good for the Creative Journalism Department at UC Irvine. I have a little tiny bit of talent. A life and a future. The world's going on out there, John. They caught the Unabomber. That spooky bin Laden has *declared war* on America! I'm not so sure that surfing gigantic waves is the way I want to spend my time. Medium waves, maybe. Part of life, you know, but not a religion."

"You wouldn't lose anything. You'd get a bigger life. Think about it, Jen."

"Why me?"

"You're the best chick I know."

"What about all your twenty-and-more-year-olds? They've got more to offer than I do."

"You surf better than any of them. I see you at twenty-two, and thirty-two and forty-two and, based on today, you'll still have them all beat. You've got something rare, Jen Byrne. You got all your mom's fight and win, win, win. And your dad's big heart. He really *cares* about the people needing protection. You're a tough package to beat."

I was still sitting upright, feet on the blanket and arms resting on my knees.

"Well, John, I thought I was going surfing today. Not getting buried in a life plan."

"I know what I want. For now, we'll surf together every chance we get. There's this place called Cortes Bank a hundred miles off San Diego. It breaks on an undersea mountain range just below the surface! They say they're the biggest rideable waves discovered so far. Only a few people even know about it. I've seen the secret pictures."

"Secret pictures of waves? That's funny."

"It's not funny at all. They're obviously huge. We just can't tell how huge because there's only a distant buoy to compare them to. Could be fifty feet. Could be eighty. As partners, we'll be there. Our life will be the biggest waves on Earth. The biggest we can handle. See the whole world! I've got decent pay and flex hours with UPS, and free rent at home when I'm not on the road surfing. I know you, Jen Byrne. And you know me. I can tell by the way you look at me that you know exactly who I am."

"You're blowing my mind, John."

"We can do it."

"I can think about it."

"If you're in for Cortes Bank, we're headed out Friday evening. I'm fixing some straps to my gun to hold me on. Gonna be rough and cold. But you won't miss a day of school. You can stay on that honor roll. Pick you up at six."

That smile of his. That face. The boy in the man, the man in the boy.

I was roiling with an eighteen-year-old's emotions, suddenly too dense to untangle and name. I knew that life, in the form of John Stone-breaker, had offered me a path. But it felt like looking down into the Grand Canyon when I was ten, and getting that queasy clench in my gut as my breath caught and my head went light.

I wanted no part of that canyon.

And wasn't sure I wanted John's path. But I didn't want him on it without me.

13

Jen makes her two o'clock with Dr. Penelope Parker, a Berkeley-educated psychiatrist whom Jen has been seeing for almost twenty years.

In Dr. Parker's ocean-view office on Park Avenue, they have talked about Jen, the girl, the water polo and surf teams' captain, class valedictorian, and Miss Laguna. Jen, the just-off-the-podium Montreal Games freestyler, backstroker, and butterflyer. Talked much about Jen and John, surfing the world together in love, crazy love that Jen has called the best hours of her life. Talked big-wave competition, big-wave fame, her need to win, a gift from Mom, her need to protect and serve, a gift from Dad. Talked of her striving to love John perfectly. Of John's death. Of Jen, the sudden, grieving widow at twenty-one. Of Prozac, vodka, and Xanax. Being a mom, raising her sons, and them leaving home. The sadness. The failed men since John—her pretty boys of summer, dead to her eyes. Jen the published journalist, loneliness and aloneness, Mom and Dad aging. Quitting big waves after John died, surfing small waves only until the boys turned pro. And they've talked of riding big waves again—soon, just a few weeks away now, depending on this winter's storms—in the Monsters of Mavericks.

Penelope knows her as well as her family does.

"How was your week?" asks the doctor.

"Hairy," says Jen. "Casey and I got into a scrape with pirates down in San Diego. Pirates, if you can believe that. Worse. They made my skin crawl."

"I've read about them. Poachers and smugglers, into all sorts of illegal things. Difficult to catch out on the high seas. Underfunded agencies and overlapping jurisdictions."

"They dognapped Casey's Labrador, Mae. We got her back."

A beat then, because Penelope Parker knows by now when Jen is evading.

"You'd rather not talk about it?"

"Not really."

"You certainly know our frontal attack by now, Jen."

"I do."

"Then I'll pivot: Did the pirate encounter leave you afraid?"

"No. I'm not afraid of anything but big waves with me or my sons on them. The pirates threatened to burn down the Barrel."

"Have you filed a police report?"

"Yesterday. A sergeant, Bickle, said he can't do much but step up patrol. He calls it increased visibility. Which means an extra pass or two per shift. He doesn't think it's anything but a wild threat. These people claim to be into some ugly stuff. They bragged about all the contraband they buy and sell. The cops recommended private security but I've already got that. I'm going to move into the apartment over the Barrel. It's a good-sized two-bedroom. Brock and Mahina are moving in, too. Which means Stonebreakers at the Barrel twenty-four, seven. Plus Casey, who's in the bar almost every day. You can see the restaurant from the back deck of the apartment. I've got a three-fifty-seven Magnum that Brock gave me for my fortieth and taught me to shoot. Kicks like a mule. I go to the range once a month. I don't think I'd have the courage to ever use it."

Silence but for the cars heading up and down Park and the thrum of Coast Highway.

"I don't recommend you living at the Barrel with a gun, Jen. You know all the stats on gun owners."

"It's not my gun I'm worried about."

Penelope adjusts herself on her big leather wing chair, scribbles in her notebook. She's tall, with a pleasant face, a bushy brown ponytail, big hands and feet. Twenty-something years older than Jen, and old-school regarding laptops or tablets. Today's reading glasses are blue.

"I don't recommend you living at the Barrel. Let the police handle the pirates."

"I did hear you the first time, Doctor."

"I'm here to help my patients lead fuller, happier lives. Which does not include gunplay and death by firearms."

"I do appreciate that. I'd be careful. Can we talk about the Monsters? As I told you last month, I've begun having the dreams again. Almost every night. Very vivid and believable."

"Describe your most recent."

"The one where I drop in and make the wave and the lip crashes into my back. I don't see it coming. I'm on my board, down at the bottom, and there's fifty feet of water behind me, over me; I don't see it, either. I think I'm going to make that bottom turn, then I'm flat down on the rocks holding on like John did and everything looks infrared, then I wake up. Sweaty and hot and my heart beating fast."

The scratch of pen on paper.

"One of your three near-death scenarios."

Jen adds nothing to that.

"We can increase the Xanax and suppress the dreams. Though I don't recommend it."

"It actually seems to be encouraging them lately."

"Then we can decrease, or stop that medication altogether and see what happens. Try another mild sedative. Even an over-the-counter sleeping aid."

"That backfired years ago."

"And you've been having these same three dreams since the very year we began therapy."

"You sound accusatory," says Jen. "I don't control my dreams."

"Not an accusation. Rather, I'd like to suggest a new modality for reducing the emotional negativity of the dream, or even finding a pathway for allowing these dreams to help you."

Jen feels a jab of impatience. "Doctor, I respect your judgment very much, but *that* backfired before, too."

"We can consider a just-approved anti-anxiety medication. Stronger than the Xanax."

"I don't want the heavy stuff."

"The recent literature is promising."

And now, along with the impatience, disappointment.

"Am I that big a nutcase?"

"Just frightened," says the doctor.

"Nothing scares me but those waves and these dreams. But okay. I'll think about it."

"There's another attack we can try, not involving medications at all."

"Lay it on me," says Jen.

"Maybe you should reconsider. Don't surf the Monsters. Don't tow in Casey on your jet. With that adjustment, I think there's a very good chance that those dreams will recede again, as they did for so many years. Before your decision to compete."

"I don't look on them as a warning."

"Maybe you should. They are damaging your emotional strength, and could hinder your performance in the contest."

"So just quit? Isn't that, like, a ruptured appendix infecting my stomach, and you remove the stomach? You know me better than that, Doctor Parker."

"Consider it."

"You don't understand, I have to beat the fear of the big waves. Not just avoid them. I have to get back on the horses that threw me. And threw John. And might throw my boys. I'm tired of running and hiding, Doctor. I need to confront the past. I need to find my courage. I need to win. I need to finally beat these fucking monsters."

"But, Jen, fear is one of the many things that keeps us alive. It has helped through the ages. It allows courage but discourages death. Allows fight and flight. We wouldn't be here without it. You told me that John respected those potentially deadly waves. That he was always prepared and always cautious."

"But he was never afraid of them!"

"Do you think, possibly, that he should have been?"

Because I had his back, Jen thinks. That was my character and my love and my calling. Protect and serve. She looks at the tissue box on the end table beside her, decides not to, just lets the damned tears roll down her freckled cheeks.

"Jen, after John's death, you experienced these fearful dreams over *years*. But you gave up the alcohol and didn't require the sedatives. You listened to your subconscious, and you decided to stay away from things that can harm you. Or worse. Now, you've chosen to ignore yourself by entering the contest that killed John. The dreams are back, and you are depending on alcohol and Xanax for sleep again. What's taking you back to Mavericks? Why now?"

"Six months ago I decided to tell the truth about John and myself and what happened. Tell all. The truth, from start to finish."

"Was there an inciting incident? Some moment or event?"

"No. Just twenty-five years of evasion and silence. On my part. I need to tell, Doctor. I need to write it down."

A long pause from the doctor, pen poised over the notebook.

"You've been telling me the truth for twenty years, haven't you?"

"Mostly. But I mean publicly. For the world. To write it."

"Well, I read your first installment in the *Surf Tribe Magazine*. It was touching and beautifully sad. I learned a lot I didn't know about you and John. I'm sure the writing is cathartic for you. And I encourage you to continue the series."

"I think I'm done, Penelope."

"I suppose that's between you and your editor. But it's absolutely your decision to make."

Another long beat, then Jen snatches a tissue from the box and wipes her face.

"We have four minutes."

"I think I'm done with this, I mean. You have helped me so much. I love you, Dr. Parker. Thank you."

The doctor looks over her blue glasses at Jen, writes something in her notebook, then sets the readers on her table and stands.

They meet halfway across the Persian rug and hug a long time. Jen can feel their heartbeats.

"I think we should continue here together for a few more sessions," says the doctor. "I think you should discontinue the Xanax and really put your foot down on the alcohol."

In Jen's silence, the doctor considers her with pursed lips and sympathetic eyes.

"These narratives that you've been piecing together with me over the years, Jen," says Dr. Parker. "Are they complete? Is there more?"

"There's more. That's what I'm writing. I'm so tired of falling. I'm ready to fly, Penelope."

"You don't seem ready to fly at all. More like a young bird, crouched on the lip of its nest, terrified."

"I'm going to make those waves at Mavericks. I'm going to help my boys survive and compete. If I dream at night, so be it. Well, thank you again."

"I'm disappointed. But I'll be reading every word you write. I know you'll find your way. I'll leave this two o'clock open for a few weeks, in case you change your mind. And remember—sometimes fear is a friend, and caution a teacher. Tell your whole truth, Jen Stonebreaker. Confess it to the world and yourself. And for heaven's sake, don't move into the Barrel upstairs and try to guard the place with a gun."

Jen feels like she's been punched in the stomach by Mike Tyson.

Confess it . . .

Nods and hugs Dr. Parker again, then breaks free and walks out.

Heart pounding, stomach aching, knees uncertain.

14

Jen tracks Belle Becket to the beach behind the Laguna Hotel. Belle moves her business around a bit. This is Jen's monthly three o'clock and she's as faithful to it as she's been to Dr. Parker—until ten minutes ago.

Belle sits at her flimsy card table in the shade of the old hotel, just outside the roped-off section of beach reserved for guests. A small yellow batik tablecloth is held down at all four corners and in the middle by big abalone shells brimming with smaller shells. Sea-glass necklaces and earrings dangle from driftwood hangers. Jen thinks of John every time she sees sea glass. Just one of those memories in the legions of memories that don't go away.

Belle's sign is written in her small, graceful calligraphic hand, on a brown paper Ralphs bag inverted over a shadeless brass lampstand with no cord:

PACIFIC VIBRATIONS

PSYCHIC INTERPRETATION

FORTUNES TOLD

TWO DOLLARS SHORT

FIVE DOLLARS LONG

"Hey, hey, Belle!"

"Jen?"

A good sign, thinks Jen, because Belle doesn't always remember her.

Belle gets up, plants her bare feet on the sand, and gives Jen a brief hug. Brief is okay with Jen because Belle doesn't bathe often. She does try to keep her limited wardrobe clean. Dries her clothes over the painted psychedelic sea wall running south along the cliff from here, a depiction of John Stonebreaker riding a bright, melodramatically perfect wave meant to be Brooks Street. Jen remembers the day she first saw it completed, fresh and psychedelically vibrant. Laguna commissions mural art all over the city, often inspired by or dedicated to local heroes. She stops for a moment, as always, feeling the familiar longing and regret.

Jen sits facing her long-ago best friend and the glittering Main Beach breakers beyond.

Belle's wearing an old-fashioned hippie tie-dye dress, and of course a sea-glass necklace and earrings. Her dark brown hair is long, tangled, and stiff with sea salt. Gray eyes. Her face is dark and lined, her mouth a nest of wrinkles and ruined teeth.

"You look worried, Jen."

"I just fired Dr. Parker."

"Maybe it was time."

"Apparently."

Jen introduced Belle Becket to her shrink almost twenty years ago, when Belle began hitting the crack, living in flops, then the downtown alleys, then in the Laguna Canyon brush, really letting go. Belle had seen the psychiatrist, irregularly, for a year, on Jen's dime, then vanished from Laguna without a word. Five years later she was back, panhandling on the Main Beach boardwalk, scrounging food from the Coast Highway cafes and fast-food joints and dumpsters, marginally cleaning herself up in the tourist rinse-off showers.

Belle Becket, an incorrigible beauty, a once loyal—if troubled—friend, a hot surfer, had returned home a hollowed shell.

Not unlike the scoured abalone halves on the table here, Jen thinks, lifting an all-green sea-glass bracelet from one. She gets five twenties from the wallet in her shoulder bag, sets them in the mason jar.

"Short or long?" The standard opening.

"Do what you do, Belle. Look at me and tell me what you see."

To Jen, the most surprising part of this arrangement—this crust of a friendship going back to when Jen and Belle were ten years old, in fourth grade together at Top of the World Elementary—is that they still understand each other, still get what makes the other tick.

She wonders how fifteen-plus years of silence, Belle's mental illness, and brief monthly visits have allowed them to know each other this well. Or, Jen thinks now, as she has thought many times before: Is it just each other's limits we know so well?

Perhaps not surprisingly, Belle Becket is a very good fortune-teller. She can read a mood in a second, and creep into the future on it.

She moves the lamp for room and takes Jen's hands in her rough and dirty ones. Stares at Jen with her dark, heavily made-up racoon-style eyes.

"I see your waves, of course. Always waves."

"The Monsters of Mavericks is coming up."

"I feel something different is happening inside you. Your mind is cluttered and your blood is unsettled. Does this have to do with the contest?"

"Yeah. I'm competing for the first time since John."

"Oh, girl. When did you decide this?"

"Six months ago."

"Why?"

"I'm trying to whup the fear. About what happened. There's anger, too. And regret. They're all mixed up and stormy."

"Like those big waves."

Silence then, Belle's rough hands warm on Jen's on the table in the sun.

"I see a picture now," says Belle. "A still picture of a future day. Dark mountains of water. A gray sky with rain. I see you on a large wave. Your orange-and-black wetsuit and helmet. Your orange-and-black board. You have just let go of the tow rope and Casey is speeding away on the jet ski. You must see this picture often—"

"Almost every night. I don't know what happens. If I make the wave or not."

"You will make the wave if you can see it happen. You will ride that wave only if you let it break in your mind."

"Will I wipe out on the rocks?"

"Show us. Close your eyes, Jen. Open yourself to this dream, this day that hasn't happened yet. It is real. Be there. Let Casey tow you. Watch it happen. Give me a film, Jen, not a picture. *See.*"

"I see black. Nothing beyond."

"You don't want to see beyond. Let the black go."

For a long moment Jen can't free the wave from its black wrapper.

But then, the black wave turns into blue-green ocean, with a sleek speedboat bobbing at rest.

"Jen, what is this? Something disturbing happened on the water. Not far from here. Recently, but not a wave."

Jen pictures Jimmy Wu and Polo in their gleaming Cigarette boat.

"Pirates," she says. "They threatened to kill Casey's dog. They threatened to burn down the Barrel."

"They will not kill Casey's dog," whispers Belle. "They will try to burn down the Barrel. I see the Barrel bar now, just as you do. A woman argues with Casey. I don't think they know each other."

"Bette Wu."

"Yes, Bette. I saw this Bette Wu on the beach here in Laguna," says Belle. "Below Heisler Park. Posing in fashion clothes. Reclining on the rocks. Sleek like a seal, glossy black hair."

"When?"

"I don't know, Jen. But you know me, and you know my cosmic reality—tomorrow, yesterday, today—all the same."

Jen opens her eyes and Belle does likewise. Her racoon eyes are sloppily drawn and the exhaustion Jen sees in them always follows a psychic excursion into their pasts, presents, and futures.

"I know this is hard work for you," says Jen. She pulls her hand from Belle's, patting the sun-wrinkled skin lightly.

"It's always been," says Belle. "Other people's emotions and thoughts get mixed into my own. It frightens me when I can't tell them apart. Even someone I've never met. But especially someone I've known so well and so long, who has powerful vibrations. Your past haunts and confuses me."

"Have you ever been betrayed, Belle?"

Belle studies Jen sidelong and hard, a suspicious racoon.

"Never. I've felt love and loyalty from my friends and family all my life. They've been angry and afraid of me. Ashamed and confused. But they never betrayed me. Have you been?"

"No, the same."

Belle points a jagged-nailed forefinger into the air between them. "I see your words here in the space between us—'no, the same.' They're bright, lemon yellow. They wobble and fade. This is the color of a lie."

Which Jen continues. "If I was betrayed I didn't know it."

"So much happens to us that we never see. Or admit to seeing."

Jen holds Belle's gaze again, detects a lack of sanity in her flat gray eyes, her botched makeup, her mane of filthy hair. Replaces all that with the memory of the beautiful girl she'd known and loved and hugged and argued and rode waves with. Nothing kicks you harder than time, she thinks.

"*There* I am," says Belle. "As you see me."

Another long look shared, eye to eye.

"Jen? I don't see your latest friend. Mark."

Which of course brings Mark to Jen's mind, duly intercepted by Belle.

"Ah," she says. "Where has he been?"

"We didn't work out."

"Why? You were so interested in him the last time we talked."

"He's a little too loose and a little too young. NMR."

"No man required, hmmm. After all these years, that's where we end up. Your mom and dad good?"

"Dad's retired. Playing golf and kind of bored. Mom's still hyperactive, running the girls' watersports programs at the high school."

"I always loved those two."

"And yours?"

"They're still in Montana when it's warm. Dad's thinking of selling his practice and retiring."

Jen comes around the little table and hugs Belle. Wonders for the millionth time if this is really good for either of them.

"I'll see you later, Belle."

"But which me will you see?"

Belle's old joke from when they were kids.

At home on Castle Rock, Jen changes into a one-piece swimsuit and warms up for her hour of breath-control training in the high school pool.

Stands for a moment at a window and looks across the rain-greened, unspoiled hills, Laguna Canyon Road a winding black ribbon bustling with cars, the blue sky holding wispy clouds.

Loves this canyon. Loves these beaches. Loves this city.

In the kitchen she pours the last half of her black pepper vodka down the sink.

In the upstairs bathroom she flushes the Xanax pills down the drain.

Minutes later she's in the LBHS pool with weights on her ankles and in her hands, running in slow motion across the bottom as hard as she can toward the far deck.

15

Still flush with adrenaline from beating down on King Jim and his pirates, Brock stalks a sidewalk in downtown San Diego, pulling a wheeled cart of naloxone, clanking oxygen cylinders, and bottled water. He's posted to all his Rescue Mission followers, and is hoping to get a little participation here. He's got on a black-and-green Go Dogs T-shirt with the snarling dachshund mascot, and cargo shorts loaded with granola bars and vitamin packets. He and Mahina are looking for anyone struggling to breathe.

He knows there will be some customers, just up ahead in the shadows of the towering Central Library. There are Right Fighters and cops around, giving Brock hard looks and occasional nods of recognition.

One of the Right Fighters waves at them.

"Guns on the left, clowns to the right," says Mahina.

It's late afternoon and the streets around the library are crowded with tents and strung tarps and shopping carts stuffed with clothes and blankets and random items from boom boxes to swim fins, a beaten guitar, boxed wine, donated greens wilting in plastic bags, dog kibble, a trike, an American flag on a tilting pole. People everywhere, tucked into the shadows, some moving and others still as statues on this breezeless day. A dog, a parrot atop a tent, a pet rat on a man's shoulder.

Just behind him, Mahina tugs a cooler filled with chopped, chilled pineapple and watermelon.

"You, bro, you're looking puny to me," Brock says, kneeling next to a heavyset man in a wheelchair.

"Hard to breathe, got 'can?"

"You don't get Narcan yet," says Mahina, offering him a cube of watermelon. "You just dose?"

"No, no, this morning."

"Narcan'll keep you alive but mess up your brain. You're not overdosing. You need air, man. Oxygen. Breath of Life."

Brock gets the pulse oximeter onto the guy's cuss finger. The guy is sweating but his cheeks are cold.

He and Mahina have trained sixteen hours to do this. They pay for the oxygen cylinders, naloxone, food, and water out of the unsteady Breath of Life Rescue Mission bank account.

"You're all over the place, man," Brock says.

"The 'can keeps me high."

Mahina has the cylinder out, and she fixes the breathing mask to the top. Brock takes off the oximeter and holds down the big man's arms as his wife presses the mask to his face and toggles open the valve.

The big man inhales deeply, then again. Brock and Mahina lock eyes briefly and he sees not just compassion in her but forbearance—the same things he feels.

Sometimes he hugs these sufferers; sometimes he wants to slap them silly.

"You just breathe in big, mister," Mahina says. "Take in the breath. Take in the life."

Brock notes that one of the Right Fighters is videoing him from across the trashy, fast-food-wrapper-strewn street. Mahina walks toward them, her own phone brandished like the weapon it is.

"You a Jesus nut?" he warbles through the mask.

"I'm a life nut. I want you alive. I want you alive enough to get up and help these beat-up souls around you."

"I gots Petey to take care of. My dog. He's got a soul, too."

"You bet," says Brock. "I'm going to let go your arms now, so don't be thrashing around. I'm going to get you some cold fruit and water. Keep breathing, bro."

Brock and Mahina's next client is face up on the sidewalk on a sleeping bag, and she's completely stopped breathing.

In seconds, Brock has the Narcan out and sprays the full four-milliliter dose into one nostril.

All Brock and Mahina can do is wait two minutes before administering a second dose, but they know that every second of not breathing means brain cells dying off fast. They've heard dozens of times from friends and family that when some naloxone revivals come to and revive, they're not the same person ever again.

But just thirty seconds later this young woman gasps and tries to dig her fingernails into the sidewalk, and is soon gulping air as deeply as she can.

Mahina has the oxygen cylinder on her, mask snug and valve open.

The woman sits up, crossing her bruised and dirty legs. "Thanks. Thanks."

Breathing deeply still, she looks at Mahina then Brock with what looks like gratitude and suspicion.

"What's your name, woman?" asks Mahina.

"Gail."

Brock fetches a cold bottled water from his cart, breaks it open, and hands it to her. She brings it to her lips, hands shaking.

"It's going to get bad when the 'can wears off," says Gail.

"Don't get high again too soon," says Mahina. "You're just going to be doing this again. Unless you just overdose, up and die."

"I don't want to die."

Gail pulls on the oxygen for another three minutes. Eats some melon and pineapple and downs another bottle of water.

"Help me up?"

With both big hands, Mahina pulls her upright. Gail manages to pick up her sleeping bag.

"Thanks again."

She drags the ragged red nylon sleeping bag to the library wall, under-hands it into a blue dome tent among other dome tents and lean-tos, then waves back at them, stoops, and crawls in.

When she's inside, Brock looks at Mahina, shakes his head with weariness, and turns to see the Right Fighters shooting video of him again.

"You're saving the wrong people, Stonebreaker!" one calls out, raising his phone high.

Brock feels the anger and takes off toward them, mayhem in mind.

"Thanks for the invite, Saint Brock! We'll see you again!"

They sprint off in different directions.

Brock brakes and watches them go, heart pounding, bile rising.

16

Next afternoon Casey is on time for his *Travel & Adventure Magazine* interview and photo shoot up in Hollywood. A cover, no less. Last month it was Gal Gadot.

He's standing on a small stage in nothing but swim trunks, his back to a ceiling-high black backdrop blanched bright by a blinding forest of lights. It's hot, even with the fans turned up high to make Casey's yellow-blond hair stand up and lean back with apparent velocity.

T&A is what Casey calls this mag, aware that his *A* is part of what they're after here. The magazine contract requires one backside image to include "minimally and tastefully exposed buttocks, mutually acceptable by both parties."

"Minimally" isn't precisely spelled out, and Casey is definitely concerned about this picture, given his reputation as a privileged, vain, self-hyped pretty-boy Jesus freak who surfs big waves more for fame and money than the actual thrill of surfing. This being the general drift of the small, loose-knit, and very opinionated big-wave surfing scene—the writers, photographers, and filmmakers—and even some of the surfers themselves. There's been some ugly backstabbing that Casey doesn't dig, mostly from the tough-ass Santa Cruz guys, things like,

Casey's a Ken doll on a surfboard, Casey's a rich Laguna boy, Casey's chasing the legend of his father, John, who was surfing the Monsters of Mavericks the day he died.

Casey was surprised when he started hearing things like that, some years ago, when he first began making very big waves at Sunset, Jaws, Teahupo'o, Todos Santos, and Mavericks—and riding them pretty well for a young gun. Didn't understand why how he looked and where he came from were such negatives. It wasn't like Laird and Buzzy and some other guys didn't do some modeling to make money. You had to make it somehow. There wasn't a big-wave surfer on Earth—and might never be—who could make a decent living without sponsorships and modeling and product pitching. Heck, the biggest first-place big-wave contest purse for risking your life was, thus far, a whopping $50,000. How long could you live on that? And travel the world, chasing the biggest waves on the planet? Just the airfares and lodging were a fortune.

There have been digs on Jen, too. Not published or recorded, but rumors about what she didn't do the day her husband died, how she could have gotten to the impact zone faster, should have used a more powerful jet ski, how she once said that she was never great on a jet ski to begin with.

Of course, Casey had read every word published about that day, and seen the video and film, and talked to everybody he could find who was in the water, and not one of them would say anything about Jen Stonebreaker being in any way at fault.

But still, he's heard and overheard the rumors and innuendo, always attributed to someone who was there, someone who of course, to Casey's face, denies all. His brother, Brock, punched out a flippant photographer who'd "insulted Mom" at the annual World Surfing Awards banquet not long ago, clips viral, assault charges pressed, a no-contest plea and ten days in Los Angeles County Jail and a $15,000 medical-damages bill for Brock.

Casey's take on all this is he's got a billion followers and fans who like and respect him and his family, and he's not going to let the rumor mill distract him. It's hard to put their wishes for bad karma out of his mind, but Casey does. Sure, they sneak in once in a while but Casey turns his heroic chin the other way, just like the good book says.

Now, after changing his swim trunks once again, the makeup guy dabs Casey's crow's-feet. Then, with a wide paintbrush, retouches Casey's chest and arms with a body oil that gives him a slightly amphibious glimmer.

Well, Casey thinks, *T&A* has a circulation of 842,000 in print alone, so whatever floats their boat.

Mae lies in the corner of the studio, head resting on her feet, almost hidden behind the black backdrop, keeping an eye on Casey. After the pirates, Casey takes Mae everywhere he goes. It's hot in here and she pants softly.

The magazine writer sits on a director's stool with a small tape recorder on the floor halfway between him and his subject. He's a hearty, middle-aged Australian, bearded and loud-voiced. Ian Keneally.

Casey has never done an interview and photo shoot simultaneously, and it's hard for him to field questions and take the photog's orders.

"Chin down and eyes up, Casey," she says. She's a thirty-something blonde who looks like a surfer herself. She's got a camera in one hand, another around her neck, and two more on a folding table beside her. "Get that intense, matter-of-fact look."

He gives it his best but Casey's no model or actor, and he doesn't know if he looks intense or just silly.

kerchack kerchack, kerchack kerchack

"Now wet your lips, then part them and pucker just a little. Like you're about to say 'surf's up!'"

"Okay."

kerchack kerchack

"Mr. Stonebreaker," says the writer, "can you remember the first wave you caught?"

"Yeah, sure! I was five and Mom took me out at Old Man's at San Onofre. Seven tries. Put me on a long board. This cherry eight-six Hobie—"

"Again, Casey," says the photographer. "Part your lips and go ahead, just say it like a surfer would, say, 'surf's up!'"

Casey does as he's told, which isn't difficult. He's spoken fluent surf since he was six—the slurred vowels and schwas, and his slack sibilants combining for cool nonchalance. The exuberance and the slang. It's the only language he knows, having grown up with Jen, Jen's surfer mom, Eve, and the Stonebreakers.

kerchack kerchack

"Nice, Casey, now look up and to your left, like you're seeing a jet high in the sky. Don't squint! Look amazed."

Casey tries amazed. Tries not to squint against the ferocious lights.

kerchack

"So you're at Old Man's on the longboard, then what?" asks the writer with a terse glance at the photographer as she changes cameras.

"Mom had me lay flat and stand up a few times. Then she pushed me into a wave and told me to stand up when I felt it take me. I fell six times. Hit the board twice. Gnarly. Then on the seventh try I stood up for, like, twenty feet. Awesome and a half. I was stoked. Forever. It was like—"

"Terrific, Casey! Now turn away from me and face the screen. Put your hands on your hips, you know, like you're standing on the beach, looking out at the waves. Relax your waist, and cock one hip."

"Which one?"

"Up to you, Case!"

Casey strikes this pose.

kerchack kerchack kerchack

"Mr. Stonebreaker!" calls out the writer. "What was your first big wave? I mean, over ten feet!"

"Hanalei Bay on Kauai. I was thirteen. It was fifteen feet, totally double-overhead. Victory at sea to a kid! I fell on the takeoff and it held me under, like, bad. Mom and Brock were there. Saw stars when I finally made it up."

"Were you terrified?"

"No way. I couldn't wait to go again. Got my breath, paddled hard through the incoming. Finally caught one and rode it. Massive. Mom and Brock watched. Kicked out and landed good. Epic. Life changer. Never forget. Ever."

"I'm impressed you could ride Hanalei that young," says the writer. "And Mavericks at nineteen. And Cortes Bank at twenty-one."

"Dad did."

"It just seems like one day you're in Laguna riding five feet at Brooks, next day you're surfing fifteen feet in Hawaii."

"Mom took us all over the world for big waves," says Casey. "Spent every penny for big waves. Summers and holidays mostly. Especially Christmas break, because that's when the big swells hit. Brock and me haven't had Christmas at home the last five years."

"Casey!" shouts out the photographer, stepping in closer. "Now, keep watching those imaginary waves up there on the screen, but loosen the ties on those cool trunks of yours."

Over his shoulder, Casey thanks her for the compliment on his trunks, made by his struggling beachwear line, CaseyWear.

"Now, Casey, reach back with your right hand and place your thumb between the waistband and your waist. Yeah, good—now put your fingers in the pocket and spread them out, like you're trying to find something in there. Now, with your thumb still hooked over the waistband, lower the trunks an inch down your right side. Keep those fingers spread—you're searching for your car key in the pocket. Or maybe some ChapStick. Yes, good bun work!"

kerchack kerchack kerchack

"Now pull down a little harder, Case, give me another inch of skin. It looks great, by the way, you were smart to do the tanning back there. Good, tan, oiled, and glittering muscle."

kerchack kerchack kerchack kerchack

Casey shakes his head slowly and smiles at the black backdrop, holds his pose, thumb on his trunks, fingers in his rear pocket, as it hits him that this is one of the funniest but most uncool things he's ever done. He listens to the camera motor drive, firing away like it can't get enough. It's some kind of rad joke, he thinks, to tan and oil your butt for a picture. He decides to post about this. Make a little fun of himself. God knows what the Santa Cruz boys will say. Maybe post when the story comes out in *T&A*.

"Do you ever get tired of being handled like a piece of meat in some of these photo shoots?" asks the writer.

"Not really," Casey says over his shoulder. "The people are always nice, and if it's for an ad, it pays really good. But I do wonder what God thinks."

"What do you think *He* thinks?"

"He must see vanity under the sun, and striving after mammon. Maybe some not-cool sacrilege and coveting, too, in how people think when they see the pictures. Nothing super heavy, though."

"So far as pictures go, Casey," says the photographer, "these will be pretty tame. I don't think God would mind one little bit. He's got bigger fish to fry, this world being what it is."

"Gnardical," says Casey.

"What's that mean?" she asks.

"Gnarly and radical together. Gnardical."

"You mean God and frying fish?"

"Exactly."

Half an hour later the photog says it's a wrap.

"Thanks, Casey. You're great to work with. And I have hellos to you from Bette Wu. We went to school together at UCLA. I shot her in Laguna a few days ago. Bette lit up when I told her we'd be working together. Says she knows you."

Casey doesn't know what to say to that, goes with nothing.

"Oh, and don't miss that billboard right out front on Sunset."

17

With the photo shoot done, Casey puts his shirt and jeans and flip-flops back on, then pulls up a director's chair in front of the writer. The stage is dark and the fans turned to low.

He talks and talks.

Interviews are easy now. He used to get excited and wig out talking about surfing and lose his train of thought, but at twenty-four he's so used to talking about himself—how he does what he does, and what's the biggest wave, scariest break, most dangerous wipeout, most terror-struck moment in the water he's ever experienced—that he can answer without really thinking. He knows what a sound bite is.

But sometimes, an interviewer wants to get the really choice, heavy-duty stuff, which is what this writer asks now:

"So, Mr. Stonebreaker, why do you ride waves so big they can easily kill you? Give the *why* of it."

This isn't a simple answer, but Casey doesn't have to think about it.

"I feel God when I'm on a big wave. He's closest to me then. I'm His creation and He loves me."

A moment of silence while the writer nods and looks down at his tape recorder.

"What about the rest of the time?"

"Oh, for reals, man. But not as strong. I went to the interactive van Gogh a couple of years ago, and felt God there. Yeah. In every one of those pixels."

Keneally clears his throat.

"Where do you think Jesus Christ fits into all this?"

"He's a part of everything, like we all are."

"Even the wicked?"

"Maybe less so them," says Casey. "I'm not sure how it all works."

Mae seems to have sensed that things might be winding down here. Aging and slow, she lumbers to Casey's side and lies beside his chair.

He leans over and scratches behind one ear, runs his finger along her graying muzzle.

"Good luck at the Monsters of Mavericks," says the writer.

"Thanks, man. I'll be ready."

"Some of the contest people up in Half Moon Bay say all the contestants have a chance, but don't say you're a contender. Your brother, but not you. Thoughts on that?"

Which hurts Casey's feelings, on top of his rep as a privileged, semi-talented, money-mad, pretty-boy action doll.

"I hope Brock wins," he says.

"Instead of you?"

"Heck yeah."

"When does he find time to surf and train, with all those rescue missions he does—the fires and floods and hurricanes, or taking those vaccines to people who couldn't leave their homes or tents or encampments?"

"Brock has the energy of ten men," says Casey. "And doesn't even train that much for contests," says Casey. "He's a total natural."

Casey thinks of Brock robbing the Wu pirates at gunpoint just days ago. Robbing the pirates *back*. It's no wonder that Brock thinks he's in a good enough place to win at Mavericks. He also thinks he's invented a new God to replace the old, burnt-out, useless ones. Brock is Brock because he *believes*: the Breath of Life! Go Dogs! Get off your asses and help! It's not what the world can do for you.

While I tan my butt for a T&A *cover story.*

"Thanks for your time, Casey Stonebreaker. Lots of good stuff to work with here. Don't miss that great billboard right out front."

When the writer leaves, Casey stays in the director's chair, posts some pictures of himself and Mae here in the now-empty studio. Dashes off a quick CaseyGram on how he thinks his brother will win the Monsters if they get the waves this year. He gets a lot of responses to that post, most of his followers saying, no, "YOU'RE GOING TO WIN IT!"

He loves his fans. The confidence they bring him. The trust he tries very hard to deserve.

He's also always liked being an underdog. Makes him feel hyper-depressurized, like nothing can go wrong. Well, in the case of sixty-foot waves, like *less* can go wrong.

Casey walks outside to a sunset on Sunset, the lessening orange light of LA holding the world in its glow, the boulevard already dark, head-lights on.

He stops on his way to the parking garage, looks up at the bottom-lit clouds and the blue-gray sky. Sees himself on a towering digital bill-board wearing a collegiate-looking Dream Coast cowl-neck sweater.

Mae pulls at her leash and whines softly.

"Pretty man, isn't he?" someone asks from just behind his right shoulder.

"Whatever."

Turns to Bette Wu, in a white linen suit and white pumps, fedora, and purse. Every time he sees her she looks taller, and in this light her skin is perfect and she's pretty. Wicked pretty, Casey knows. Mae wags her tail and smells her shoes.

"Woah. Not you again."

"Take a walk?"

"What exactly *do* you want? You guys aren't planning to burn down the Barrel while we stand here, are you?"

"Don't be so dramatic."

"That's what your dad said."

"He'll say anything to get a reaction. Inside, he's an insecure child."

"He's a criminal, too."

Casey keeps abreast of fast-walking Bette, but puts plenty of distance between them. Her perfume is tropical with cinnamon, and fully stoke-worthy. Two big Teslas and a Rivian truck go by so quietly that Casey can hear his flip-flops on the sidewalk.

"Exactly what I want is for you to be able, someday, to trust me, Casey."

"I'll never do that."

"Let me reintroduce myself. I am Bette Elizabeth Wu. My father and mother named me after Bette Davis and Elizabeth Taylor because they love old American movies. I am twenty-seven. I am smart and loyal to my family and my crew and anyone I choose. Such as you. I want you to be my partner. I want us to run the Barrel under King Wu ownership. I want you to talk your wonderful mother into selling to us. Not two million like before. That's an insult. Now, four million. *Four million.* And higher salaries for you and Jen and all the employees, from the top down, as my father said. Profit-sharing plans. We want a contemporary redesign. No more surfboards and the endless wave videos that all look the same. No more tikis and lame specialty drinks. Something sleek and elegant, a California-Asia fusion that will define the future. A more creative menu, built around the best sustainable fish and seafood we can get. Farm-to-table California crops. And today's music! No more ukuleles and pedal steel guitars! Your mother is a great woman and a great restaurateur, but she's old. No more Beach Boys. No Jan and Dean."

Casey tries to picture all this, his head swimming with images brought forth by Bette Wu.

"Why not just open your own restaurant?"

"*Location.* The Barrel sits on the best restaurant location on Coast

Highway in Laguna Beach. There is none better, and the Wu family wants to have the best."

"Would you play Jack Johnson music?"

"Okay, Casey. Sure. For you. Are you leaning into this now?"

"No. Leaning pretty far away."

"Lots of money for your family. Some control and income from the restaurant."

"Mom can prove even four million isn't anywhere near what the Barrel is worth."

"Four million is lots of money for your family. As a friend and partner, I can show you how to invest your share. I'm good at business and finance. And you wouldn't have to go out fishing alone for the daily catch. You could retire and surf all day."

"I like fishing. But us together as partners is totally never going to happen, Bette. You stole the best dog I've ever had. You tried to extort money for her life. You tried to steal my mom's restaurant."

"You can still play with your hot surf babes."

"They're good, honest friends. And I don't play with them."

"Maybe you should. Those ones lined up at your bar sure looked ready."

Casey shrugs.

"I want you to convince Jen to sell. It will be a new foundation for us all."

Casey's brain feels crowded and directionless, like a raft full of refugees without paddles. So much ocean. He tries to consider things one at a time, and he's good that way—one thing at a time—but there's too many here right now.

They come to the traffic light at Horn, cross Sunset, and reverse course.

A long silence as they walk side-by-side but apart back toward the parking garage.

"We can stay just like this," says Bette Wu. "Together but separate. Partners in a thriving, beautiful, very profitable business."

"No. No, thank you. Partners is never gonna happen."

"Well, damn, I tried."

Bette stops him, pulls him to her by his shirt collar, and kisses his left ear. Lip-clamps and shakes it gently before letting go and stepping back.

Then reaches up and snaps his earlobe with a lacquered middle fingernail. *Snick!*

And walks away, hand up, finger raised.

18

Late that night, wired on coffee and NoDoz, Brock and Mahina leave sleeping Casey in the apartment above the Barrel, then head out for their church in Aguanga.

He drives pretty much as fast as the old Go Dogs Econoline will go to retrieve the supplies they might need if crazy Jimmy Wu tries to burn down the Barrel. Mahina naps with her head against the window, her crown of dark hair for a pillow.

Brock thought that Laguna Police sergeant Bickle was a nice guy, but awfully damned nonchalant for a cop, and no expert at threat assessment.

One of the things Brock learned years ago, in the messy business of illegal grass, is that you take threats at full face value. Just ask the seven Laotians recently murdered on a big grow not a mile from Aguanga. Sheriff investigators still have no firm motive nor suspects but Brock does: New Generation cartel soldiers from Tijuana suggesting that the poor, overworked, if not enslaved, Laotians vacate the greater Anza Valley dope industry and get back to cleaning rooms and washing dishes in LA and San Diego. What those Laotians needed was proaction, Brock reasons. Proaction, like, yesterday, dude. *Do it now!* Which goes against his laid-back surf upbringing—courtesy of his mother and his grandpa, the pastor Mike Stonebreaker.

And something else he learned, in Ukraine—alongside some of the Go Dogs' finest—was that fools and showoffs like Jimmy Wu are dangerous, especially when armed and in charge. He'd seen the volunteer mercenaries outside Kyiv, swaggering and self-assured to the point of foolhardiness, even martyrdom.

And, from his aging Belfast relatives, Brock had absorbed the bloody tales of his forebearers and noted the important fact that families were the fiercest but also the most vulnerable fighting units on Earth. There was just no stopping them once they joined the battle, not until every last one of them was gone. Then you have the sons and daughters. And theirs. Irish, Chinese, Californian, Brock realized—it didn't matter.

Now Highway 371 leads him higher in elevation, and in his headlight beams the rolling grasslands give way to boulder-strewn hills bristling with manzanita, wild buckwheat, and mallow. Brock saw a mountain lion right about here at the old Bergman Museum just last month, standing on the highway shoulder, looking at him steadily as he sped by.

Just past the tiny village of Aguanga—really just a US Post Office and a small market run by a soft-spoken Cahuilla Indian named Bill—Brock brakes, hits his brights, and follows a well-kept dirt road that descends along a creek, through sycamores and high cottonwoods shivering in the quarter moonlight.

"Not as beautiful as O'ahu," says Mahina, straightening in her seat.

Brock comes to the gate, locked by a chain of heavy padlocks to which Mahina, Jen, Casey, and Mike and Marilyn Stonebreaker have keys. As do most of the Go Dogs, and the Breath of Life Rescue Mission elders.

Brock locks the gate behind him and drives onward, the Econoline's rear tires skittering on the hard gravel.

The Breath of Life Rescue Mission compound is a mile in, past a cattail-ringed lake, built into the feet of the steep hills. Most of it went up in the fifties.

The chapel is cinderblock, charmless but huge. It's got small windows, an aluminum roof, and a cavernous fireplace inside.

The ranch house and some of the outbuildings are white plaster, with terracotta barrel roofing, deep-set windows framed with Spanish tiles, and heavy wooden doors.

The redwood barn and stucco guest cottages are in decent repair, recently stripped and repainted in Go Dog bright green, with matte black trim. The buildings would be a shock to the locals, but they're invisible from the highway and to the few, very distant, neighbors.

Brock could care less. When you see it, the Breath of Life Rescue Mission should wake your lazy ass up, is how Brock thinks of the jarring green-and-black color scheme.

Brock parks and steps out, hears the frogs down in the pond, and smells the fresh scent of sage. Sees the dark thicket of manzanita down by the creek. Loves this land. Checks that moon again. A quarter. Stands there for a moment, a grown man in shorts and a dumbass dachshund logo T-shirt, with tattoos of waves and suns and moons and fish and birds all over him—"Mom" inked on one shoulder and "Mahina" on the other—arms raised as he listens to his wife climbing the front porch steps, unlocking the security screen door, and banging into their home.

The house is a small two-bedroom built in 1915 by locals. River rock walls, heavily cemented, a newish aluminum roof. Vaguely Craftsman in design, with a peaked front porch under the roof extension and staunch beam caissons.

Brock and Mahina have furnished it in secondhand, mostly Pacific Island furniture—bamboo and rattan, bright floral padding, a glass tabletop on coconut-tree stumps, Hawaiian carvings of turtles and fish. White bamboo bookshelves. Masks. A humble tiki bar.

Inside, Mahina hands him a very cold Bohemia. They touch bottles and sip.

"We did good work today, Brock. We maybe saved Gail's life."

He nods. Imagines the sidewalks of tents and tarps, the slow-motion citizens eyeing them suspiciously, caught in squalor.

"And we got Mae back," she says. "What do we need from here, for the Barrel?"

"Fire extinguishers, guns, and night-vision goggles."

"Are you worried?"

"Yes."

"That's why you're still alive."

Brock looks through the windows facing east. Hidden down there are twenty-six trailers, some small and some large, most of them older. Last he checked, there were eighty-seven people housed there, including twelve children—six home-schooled and six who catch the bus at the Aguanga post office for the public schools in Anza Valley.

The Breath of Life Rescue Mission charges no rent, and supplies the electricity, propane, and water pumped in at some expense by the county. Random Access Foundation, which bought and donated the property four years back, chips in a little every month.

All the Breath of Life Rescue Mission asks of its once-homeless citizens is that they help each other as they help themselves, keep up the grounds and pick up after their dogs, obey state and county laws, attend Breath of Life services on Friday mornings when possible, help clear the brush, level the ground and pour the cement pads needed for more trailers. No recreational drugs except for marijuana.

Brock sets his empty bottle on the kitchen counter and looks out the window. Considers the faint shapes of new trailer pads being cleared, which is tough work in the tall, dense, iron-tough manzanita that thrives throughout the church property.

Back outside, they load the gear they'll need if Jimmy Wu and his rough crew actually try to burn down the Barrel.

Brock sees a minivan parked across the big parking area in front of the big cinderblock church. He notes the crippled slouch of the van, and a stuffed, tarp-clenched luggage rack on top.

They crunch across the lot toward the church, pale in the moonlight. Brock likes the stout, secular, no-nonsense air of the church. No meddlesome gods there. It's the opposite of spiritual. It's functional: serving as chapel, schoolhouse, meeting room, kitchen and dining hall, concert theater and auditorium, and a half-court basketball venue when it rains. Plus an indestructible concrete floor, and a fireplace big enough to keep the whole thing almost warm on the cold, high-desert nights.

It was built in the 1950s by a San Diego utopian cult as a meeting hall, complete with a steel-reinforced basement bomb shelter. There have been various owners, squatters, and vandals since then. The entire property was purchased then gifted to the Breath of Life church just after Brock and Mahina founded it. Brock was just twenty-two, Mahina thirty. The gift was an unpublicized donation.

Brock and Mahina and their scant new "congregation" reroofed the building, cleaned out the massive stone fireplace, broomed away the lizards and field mice, rebuilt and refurnished the industrial-sized kitchen, bought enough folding chairs for a small army, and set up a good PA system so Brock could be heard.

Now, the congregation varies on any given Friday morning between ten and seventy worshippers. Brock chose Fridays for worship to distance the Breath of Life from the other churches, gods, and saints.

But he's not at all sure this hasn't hurt attendance, given that lots of people work on Fridays.

His very first Friday morning congregation?

One: Juana Flores, a young Cahuilla Indian woman who was living in one of the caves in the rough hills behind the compound, selling her handmade baskets and carved wild gourds from a blanket on the shoulder of Highway 371.

Juana listened to Brock haranguing about this Breath of Life, this new god that he had discovered after being rag-dolled underwater so long at Nazaré that Mahina had to mouth-to-mouth him back to consciousness, and, when Brock came to, there was his god: Breath. Life. Breath of Life.

From Mahina.

Brock had talked on and on about that day.

Breath of Life, show us what to do.

He explained to Juana that the Breath of Life was stronger, angrier, but more generous than the old, jealous, self-inflated gods of the past.

Brock admitted to having a temper, alright, because anger gets things done, and never turn the other cheek. Life is a fight. The Breath of Life has just one fundamental, nonnegotiable law: Give it up for your brothers and sisters. Love and protect and serve each other, especially those short on love and without protection. People like you, Juana. Find them and help them. Make them better. Breathe life into them just as Mahina breathed life back into me. The Breath of Life is awesome.

Juana dozed through the sermon in the back row, ate half the box of donuts, and drank a lot of coffee.

Now Brock and Mahina go through the always-open door of their church. The lights are on inside, and the smell of woodsmoke fills the big, chilly room.

In the big river-rock fireplace burns a modest fire, with a ragged human family of four arrayed on lumpy Salvation Army chairs before it. There are fast-food bags and empty wrappers on one of the long, burn-scarred vinyl tables.

"I'm Brock and this is Mahina."

The man stands but doesn't straighten, giving Brock a long, worried scan, trying to take in Brock's fierce face and spikey, dark brown dreads, his tattooed legs, the flame climbing up his throat framed by the hoodie. He regards Mahina blinkingly.

"We're not going to steal anything," he says. "Just saw the sign on the highway and we're about down to our last. We're the Kupchiks. Stan and Angela. On our way back to Tulsa. I was a car mechanic when the back went out, and we can't live here on comp and food stamps. Sorry to just bomb in."

"We'll get you fixed up."

"The boy tested positive this afternoon. The new respiratory thing they got out now, not the Covid, thank God."

"Thank the Breath," says Mahina.

"There's bunks through that door," says Brock. "Clean up in the morning. There's a trailer you can have in a couple of days."

"Oh, man, really? Thank you."

"Thank the Breath of Life, brah. Take it in."

Mr. Kupchik looks from Brock to Mahina then back to Brock again, skepticism brimming. "Yes, I will try. I've never been a believer in that kind of thing myself."

"You don't have to believe to help yourself and others. You just have to act."

Brock thinks of the Kasper Aamon message that came to him early today on one of his right-wing, out-there socials:

"Brother Brock, you're not a Go Dog, you're a sick dog! Taking care of all those useless pukes at your church. It's not a church, it's a slum of sin. You're no brother of mine, you're just a jester giving the rest of us something to laugh at."

"We want to help ourselves," says Stan Kupchik. "We really do."

As forecasted, the Santa Ana winds come hard and fast as Brock and Mahina head back for Laguna on Highway 371. The boxy Econoline takes the gusts on its rear flank. This high-pressure front from the Great Basin is pressing the dry air across the deserts, where it picks up warmth, then surges through the passes, howling all the way to the Pacific. Which is where Brock likes to be during a Santa Ana—on his board, bobbing in the Pacific—where the waves stand up hollow and glittering, the wind back-spraying his face at Brooks or Blacks or Malibu or Mavericks.

Breath of Life, for sure.

19

Casey, sleeping as always like the dead, suddenly wakes up to a loud *bop!*

Sounds like one of those M-80s he used to buy in Ensenada as a kid. Or maybe a gun.

It's 3:17 in the morning by the apartment clock. He feels the covers for Mae then remembers she's with his mom.

Gets his white robe with black lettering on the back—"Muhammad Ali"—over his boxers, and the checked red-and-white slip-on sneakers. Heads out the front door to see the first-floor kitchen side entrance of the Barrel on fire. It's a Santa Ana wind-blown orange demon, devouring the redwood siding in a widening circle.

He gets the fire extinguisher and a set of restaurant keys from the apartment, slips his phone into the robe pocket, and hustles down the stairs, past the Barrel's ocean-front deck toward the fire. But another explosion rattles the night, blowing a hole in the deck from underneath, plank splinters shooting up next to a four-top with its umbrella collapsed for the night. Flames jump through the hole, leaning seaward in the offshore wind, chewing at the umbrella fabric. Casey stops right there, not sure if he should dial 911, or leap the banister and climb the

deck railing to engage this new threat, or haul butt to the ground floor and fight the kitchen-wall fire, which has grown substantially.

He jumps the banister, drops six feet to the entryway pavers, lands heavy but balanced, like dropping in on a twelve-foot wave at Makaha. Runs to the burning kitchen side entrance, dials 911, drops the phone into his robe pocket—they use GPS to find the caller, don't they?—yanks the extinguisher pin and triggers the white, pressured retardant into the fire.

Swings the device in a big circle, clockwise, trying to corral the swooshing, growing flames, and he hears another explosion to his right—on the north side of the building, then a fourth from the west, between Casey and the beach.

Still spraying, Casey turns reflexively when an engine revs high behind him on almost-empty Coast Highway. Sees a black Mercedes Sprinter van screeching away from the curb right out front of the Barrel, headed south on Coast Highway. It has some kind of decal or emblem on the side but he can't make out what. A white oval with a dark something and hot orange writing on it.

He really wants to know where that damned thing is going in such a hurry while his restaurant burns, but he can't abandon his post.

Turns back to the flames, circling them tighter and tighter, the foam converting them into rising tendrils of eye-burning smoke. The wind helps, blowing the retardant directly into the diminishing fire.

Which is finally out, but so is the home-sized, compact extinguisher.

A smoke alarm wails inside the restaurant.

Casey keys open the restaurant front-entrance door, knows the nearest fire extinguisher is behind the welcome/cash register desk, a curving mahogany beauty just steps away.

He dials 911 again and hangs on forever, letting the burglar alarm deactivation time run out. *Finally:*

"Fire at the Barrel in Laguna! Coast Highway! Fire at the Barrel!"

The burglar alarms join the smoke alarms in a harmonic chaos as Casey grabs the front-desk extinguisher.

He climbs the stairs four at a time to the second-story deck, jumps the banister, and scales the deck railing, almost drops the extinguisher

but gathers it back like a nearly fumbled football and brakes just short of the flaming gap in the deck.

This extinguisher is twice the size of the first and its pink foam throttles the lapping flames, then shuts them down. The wind lashes at his back. Casey is not stoked by how big the burned-out hole is. Sirens now, and the station is barely half a mile away. But he fully can't believe it when another explosion rips away, somewhere down near the front entrance.

This is like hell, he thinks.

When the deck fire is mostly out he unlocks the door to the restaurant proper, flies down the stairs, across the dining room, past his bar and into the lobby, which is swirling with flames. Through one of the big picture windows he sees the beautiful outside waiting-area benches made by John Seeman burning, too, and the palm trees in the planters, and the privacy fence, and the wave-shaped wooden pedestal on which stands the bronze statue of his father.

Where I just was, Casey thinks: Are they firebombing us?

In the lobby heat Casey plants his feet and fires away with the extinguisher. He can't get too close because of the heat, and he can't find a good target—it's all burning—the walls and the fantastic Wyland whale paintings, and the awesome sculptures by Nick Hernandez, even the old barn hardwood floors.

Did they put, like, napalm in the bombs?

He snatches another extinguisher from the kitchen and lets go with it in the dining room, hoping to save the vintage surfboards and the hand-tooled chairs and tables from Taxco and the massively poetic Barbour and Severson photographs, but he can't keep up with the fire's advance and the second extinguisher coughs and dies and he can't get back into the kitchen, which has really gone up, so by the time he returns from the utility closet by the restroom with another cylinder there's hardly anything in the dining room that isn't burning.

He's light in the head and his hair and Muhammad Ali bathrobe are taking on tiny embers, and fudge if that doesn't hurt.

He retreats past the restrooms to the rear emergency exit, shoulders through the door and into the Santa Anas howling in his face.

When he rounds the building, a Laguna Fire Department engine has already claimed the prime Coast Highway parking slots right out front, and the firefighters are arching water high over the sidewalk and the embankment and onto the Barrel. A fire truck, its red flank throbbing, settles longwise—half onto the curb and half off—and its search lights illuminate the throbbing, windblown water cascading through the dark sky, into the face of the restaurant and the third-floor apartment and its roof.

Casey just stands there for a moment, feels the heat of the Barrel's wooden walls and the warm fury of the Santa Ana wind blasting down the canyon to the sea. Embers rise and fall through the smoky night. Brushes tiny sparks off his robe.

Help us, God.

Calls his mom, who's heading in on Laguna Canyon Road, traffic already backing up in both directions. If she can't get onto Coast Highway she'll use the Art Festival parking lot and run to the Barrel.

Calls Brock.

But the call drops just as two Laguna Beach patrolmen order him off the property, and when Casey hesitates, they each take an arm and guide him to the steps leading down to the sidewalk.

"Okay, man," he says, shrugging them off. "I'm going."

"Sorry, Casey," one says. "You're in danger here."

Casey joins the growing batch of spectators cordoned off behind a police barricade. Sees the helicopter tilting in from the east, another circling high.

The wind funnels down from the mountains, pushing Brock and Mahina southwest down Laguna Canyon Road as if they're hurrying him to the Barrel.

Short of Coast Highway, just past the Art Festival grounds, the traffic has come to a stop. He sees flashing lights up ahead and cops turning the cars around. Ahead of him, drivers pick their moments to U-turn back out of the canyon.

He waits a full minute without moving, gets a faint whiff of the same sickening smell he breathed for three straight days at the Feather Fire evacuation center in Mendocino.

Sees the faint orange smoke rising south and west of here, the sparks rising in the black sky like campfire embers.

Brock feels that familiar anger crawling up through him. Knows he shouldn't have left Casey alone in the apartment.

Knows he should have truly *listened* to that sick fuck Jimmy Wu and his smarmy, know-it-all daughter making their lame moves on Casey and Mom. Turning Mom's fire comment into a not-so-veiled threat.

You knew. You let your guard down.

Santa Anas, he thinks: best time to set a fire if you want things to burn fast. Ask any arsonist. They do it all the time.

He gets a break in the oncoming cars, cranks a U-turn and floors it back to Broadway, tells the uniform he's Brock Stonebreaker, a licensed pastor, lies that he lives right up here on Third Street, kids at home, please let me through, and incredibly the young cadet lets him through.

He screams up the Third Street hill, tires smoking, zigs and zags Bent to Park to Short to Wilson, then down Thalia toward Coast Highway.

He can see orange flames atop the Barrel, leaning back, a rippling, wind-blown wall. Silver rivers fraying in the wind. The second-floor apartment windows belch fire and the roof spits whirling dervishes from between the tiles.

"Brock, this is most very evil."

He parks in someone's driveway on Thalia, runs down the middle of the street in his flip-flops and swim trunks and the Go Dogs shirt for Coast Highway, Mahina just steps behind him.

Hits Coast Highway and looks north, where the Barrel burns before him like an enormous bush.

Bottom to top.

All sides.

Flames bent west with the wind.

He gets to the barricade but the cops won't let him through this time.

He sees his mom, Casey, and Mae standing in mute shock, their faces burnished by the flames.

20

Looking Back—

WHO WAS JOHN STONEBREAKER AND WHAT WENT WRONG AT MAVERICKS?

By Jen Stonebreaker

Part three of a special series for *Surf Tribe Magazine*

Remember "Adios," the Linda Ronstadt song about running away from home when she was seventeen to be with some man on the California coast?

That was me but I had a year on Linda.

I said yes to Cortes Bank.

Which John said was the biggest surfable wave on Earth.

Said it was rough and cold out there.

Rough and cold indeed.

We arrived near Cortes Bank at sunrise, after a punishing journey in a small cabin cruiser, the twenty-two-foot *Skipjack,* the sky dark with clouds, a biting, six-knot wind out of the northwest.

The boat bobbed like a toy on the swells mounding and passing under us. A few hundred feet from us, the peak of the undersea mountain unleashed the waves in a succession of enormous peaks breaking right. Out on Cortes Bank you're a hundred miles from shore. There's no land in sight, nothing to gauge the size of the waves, or the boat you're on, or even your own speck of a body struggling for balance on the wet deck.

Watching and hearing the waves breaking, I remembered the stories and lore that had surrounded the Cortes Bank for centuries: accounts of when this now-submerged mountain range was an island stretching north toward Catalina, where warriors and fishermen had drowned when their canoes capsized; and later of the wooden galleons and trading ships that had wrecked and sunk with all onboard, of sharks large enough to swallow a man whole, of yard-long lobsters hugging the rocks just below the surface, of compasses sent awhirl and radios jammed by atmospheric anomalies that seemed to arrive on the backs of the monstrous surf.

Nobody onboard *Skipjack*—there were only five of us—had ever ridden a wave there.

John and I wrestled the jet ski off its home-welded rack and into the heaving sea. He jumped in and climbed on and started it up with a burst of white noxious smoke. Revved the engine against the roar of a wave breaking fifty yards away, a plume of white tearing off its crest as the lip curled over and the face stood upright.

Thirty feet? Forty?

The seasick photographer shot.

The captain kept his pitching boat from being pulled into the waves.

Randy Payne—who had read the centuries-old charts and ship's logs, and volumes of Navy archives and diaries to pinpoint the location of once mythical Cortes Bank—jumped into this cauldron with a rigid smile and his eight-foot gun, and paddled to the ski. I watched him, bobbing on his board like a praying mantis blown into a rushing river, praying the shark stories weren't true.

John eased the jet ski into place and threw Randy the handled nylon waterski rope.

They were off in a bark of engine and a billow of smoke, semicircling away from the break. They came to a stop, below and well to the left of the incoming peaks. I could see them through the smoky wave spray, watching the set, and hear their voices yelling back and forth.

Then John eased his jet ski onto the forming shoulder of a giant, turning to see Randy, who threw the rope and dropped onto the face of a wave that looked to be six times his height.

We three witnesses stood mute, silenced by fear, and by a fierce, almost paralyzing hope as Randy bounced down the wave, his legs bent at the knees, his feet locked into straps improvised from wetsuit neoprene fastened to the board's deck with plastic bolt sleeves and fiberglass.

He rode a smaller wave, then, after a blue-lipped cup of instant coffee back on board, during which he tried to explain through chattering teeth what it had all felt like, Randy looked at John.

"Your turn."

John's first wave was the size of Randy's, but choppier in the growing wind. Randy towed him in flawlessly.

John dropped into the thing, all his cool gone, nothing but survival on his mind. Crouched, arms out, feet locked into his homemade straps. He was too far away for me to see his expression but I guessed it was one I'd never seen.

He caught two more before the wind came up hard and the lumbering behemoths of Cortes Bank were blown out and unrideable.

When I helped get him back aboard, his face was pale and almost expressionless but his blue eyes brimmed with light.

"He was there, Jen. He was there."

On that rough run back to land I tried to knead the cold from his back and shoulders. We hardly said a thing.

Hours later, by the time we got into his truck in San Diego and cranked up the heater, I looked at myself from above and saw an eighteen-year-old girl in the front seat of a pickup truck, leaning uncomfortably over the center console to put her hand on the shoulder of the young man driving.

But when I looked inside me, I saw that he was mine and his journey was mine. We were us, one wave at a time. Maybe for a week. Maybe for years.

He had seen what he was looking for, and so had I.

I graduated from high school with a 4.35 GPA and gave the graduation valedictory, became Miss Laguna Beach in a pageant, and in the fall started the creative journalism program at UC Irvine.

Getting the grades was tough, but Mom pushed me through to the finish line. She taught me to read early, and I did have a knack for writing, starting with printing, then the cursive script that I tried to make perfect and beautiful.

I entered the Miss Laguna pageant on a dare from one of my good friends, Ronna Dean, who said she'd do it if I did. For the talent part of the program, I played Mom's slick video of me at surfing contests, several of which I won. Ronna, a beautiful honey-blond California girl all the way—daughter of a US Mail carrier and a waitress at the Ranch & Sea—finger-picked her guitar and gave a sassy, sexy rendition of "Wild Horses."

After the pageant at the Women's Club, there was a big party, vegetarian food and soft drinks. Ronna snuck in some schnapps, which we shared in the bathroom, but she seemed upset, and drank most of it, fast. I suspected she wanted to win that pageant, but she wouldn't admit to being that un-hip until years later. She was second runner-up and became part of my "court."

I thought being Miss Anything would be silly and a little demeaning, but when I did my civic duties—attending art festivals and ribbon cuttings, greeting visitors, spending a Memorial Day dedication at the Sandpiper nightclub, which was owned by two veteran brothers and their mom—I saw how good and alone most people were, how much they longed to belong.

I did all those long, boring Rotary lunches, but loved their motto: Service Beyond Self. Reminded me of Dad's police motto, to protect and serve. He took that oath very seriously. I had no formal oath as

Miss Laguna, other than an agreement to comport myself "with good cheer, high morals, and a willingness to help the less fortunate."

So when the Rotary gave out scholarship money for high school grads based on need and not grades, I was proud to be one of the presenters.

I didn't mind being looked at as an object of beauty. There were some touches and hugs and kisses that were not quite appropriate. Nothing flagrant. I warned them off, though. After years of bikinis and boys, I understood how hard it was for some of them *not* to stare at my body. I saw to it that my swimsuit for the competition, and later, my formal gowns and casual wear, were modest. I really was the girl next door.

Ronna and I drifted apart when I started college. She took up with the drug crowd and left town—allegedly for Hollywood—without saying goodbye.

Three years later she was back in my life.

But, to be honest here—as a journalist and a person—the world I cared about wasn't mine: it was John's, and I spent every minute I could with him.

When I said I'd run away with him at eighteen, it wasn't literal but it was true. But after Cortes Bank, I was all in for him, all about being with him, surfing with him, even though I was physically anchored to Laguna, and UCI. Everything I did that wasn't with or about John Stonebreaker was an interruption.

I was on his team, like I had asked John to be, in his garage when I was a girl.

Just another young girl in love.

I gave up my virginity to him later that year, at about the time my Miss Laguna days were to end. I felt duty-bound to complete my reign as a virgin, but happily failed.

Unsurprisingly John was some years ahead of me on that count. With how many women and how many times, I didn't ask and didn't want to know. He never referred to a relationship, never said a name, never alluded to anything he'd done along those lines. Never got a call that I overheard, or an email or a card I wasn't supposed to see. He turned a lot of heads, though—both genders. John was recognizably, preposterously handsome, of course, and a growing celebrity in the world of surfing. Everywhere we went—from California, then around the world back to California—John was noticed. And usually recognized. He did a magazine spread for Ralph Lauren in *Esquire*. People stared at him, many of them sensing celebrity, though they couldn't place him.

I was his loyal girl, his sidekick, and, at nineteen years old, his wife. Early, for sure, but it felt natural and right. We were married at Waimea Falls Park, then caravanned with family and friends up to Sunset Beach, which had caught a small December swell breaking six to eight feet, good shoulders, very shapely. Honeymooned all of December on the North Shore and hustled home for the winter quarter at UCI. That was where I rode my first waves over twelve feet, beautifully shaped freight trains of speed and power, the sheer weight of them enough to break boards and bones.

Married and happy. Fueled by waves and love.

Sex from the sublime to the comedic, the urgent to the languid. Frantic seconds. Long hours.

And waves. Weekends we surfed California: Blacks, Cortes Bank on the rare days it would break for us, Salt Creek, the Santa Ana River Jetty, Huntington Beach, Malibu, Rincon, Hollister Ranch, and Mavericks. Mavericks, of course. Anytime a winter swell lined up and we had a couple of days off from my classes and John's part-time UPS work at the Anaheim hub, we'd drive all Friday night to Half Moon Bay in the Westphalia and find ourselves, teeth chattering, in the dawn darkness of the scariest break in the world. A writer once described Mavericks as "a portal to the dark side." And on mornings like that, with fifty-foot crushers lining up to hit the reef, so much fog you could hardly see them until they were towering over you, it seemed to be the dark side indeed.

John towed me into an eighteen-foot Mavericks wave on my twentieth birthday. It was a lumbering, uneven thing but the face was smooth and after my drop, it sectioned beautifully. I rode it well but wiped out badly.

Managed to get back onto my board and ride out of the impact zone on my belly, until the whitewater pushed me into a soft valley that seemed unconcerned by the fury around it. I breathed very hard for a very long time. Then paddled back into the lineup and took the tow rope from John again.

That wave didn't change my life; it gave me focus. It gave me what *I* wanted. Not John and Mike Stonebreaker's God, but something bigger: freedom. Freedom through velocity. Skidding along behind the jet ski before dropping into that wave, I looked out at the distant hills and the Pillar Point Marina filled with matchstick boats, and the houses of Princeton-by-the-Sea, small as Monopoly pieces. After my first Mavericks tow-in, I didn't want just waves anymore; I wanted *big* waves. To give me freedom, speed, and release. To let me ride them, these gigantic stallions stampeding in from the depths from miles away.

I *wasn't* John anymore.

As I had wanted to be, from the first time I saw him surfing Rockpile when I was twelve.

Three years later things were different.

By then, John and I had seen much of the world on terrifying, beautiful days at Mavericks, Jaws, Teahupo'o, Cortes Bank, Todos Santos, Nazaré.

In spite of spotty attendance at UCI, my writing was good, and I was on track for early graduation and honors. I'd managed to publish some surfing articles in the *LA Times,* the *Orange County Register,* and the *Daily Pilot*. I had full-time offers from two of them.

We'd moved into a rental on Castle Rock, high above Laguna Canyon Road, a house built on caissons so when you walked in, you were standing in the sky. Little cars and houses below, like looking down from a giant wave.

I was absolutely faithful to my birth control, but guess what?

I miscarried.

Felt some little spirit inside leave me for parts unknown. Really hurt. Empty and disappointed though I didn't want a baby yet.

Picked myself up and got back in the water, every day, surfing hard. Writing hard, too, getting it all down. Surfing and sadness, putting my heartbreak into words that I could sell.

I'd become the ninth-ranked female big-wave surfer in the world, out of ten.

John was fourth of fifty.

We were tight, emotionally and physically.

By fall, the Monsters of Mavericks was just weeks away.

I could feel that big swell out there, headed for Half Moon Bay, building speed. The same as I'd felt that baby trying to land inside me.

21

Three days after the burning of the Barrel, Brock and Casey cruise King Jim Seafood in the Port of Long Beach in Casey's pickup, surfboards bagged in the bed.

The main reason they're here is to case King Jim Seafood with an eye for action.

An eye for an eye, Brock calls it. But Casey's not so sure.

Jimmy Wu's HQ is a low brick building huddled among others in a small business park beneath towering container ships, and rows of terminal cranes swinging containers through the sky to the docks and trucks below. The port is in constant motion, a heaving jungle of steel and concrete, chain link and railroad tracks. Skinny palms sway.

"What a place for smugglers," says Brock. "A port that handles the entire Pacific Ocean and every country near it. And once the goods are here, thousands of trucks and trains to the rest of the Western Hemisphere. After that, you refill your containers with what the Eastern Hemisphere needs, crane them onto those freighters, and send them back."

"Like they could have done to Mae," says Casey. "Bette Wu is a liar. She said they wouldn't have done that. Then she comes up to LA and tries to buy the Barrel out from under Mom and chats me up while they, like, burn it down. I could slap her for that. Not literally, I mean."

Brock marvels, again, at his minutes-older brother's gullibility and general innocence. A trusting heart is a liability on Earth, Brock believes. And very strongly does *not* believe in turning the other cheek, and most of the other Bible babble that the world—led by ministers like grandpa Pastor Mike Stonebreaker who, bless his heart—takes as, well, the gospel truth. Don't tell the victims of fire, flood, cold, heat, starvation, war, betrayal, and disease to turn their cheeks. Help them not to turn their cheeks. Help them fight back. Help them win.

"I shouldn't have conked in Mom's apartment, Brock. It's my bad and I own it. It was two o'clock by the time I locked the Barrel and went upstairs. I had some tea but still fell asleep."

"You did what you could, Casey. You fought. You've got the burns that prove it."

Brock looks at his brother's face and arms, the backs of his hands. Small, painful, slow-to-heal burns.

"I can't believe they put the fire bombs in Amazon Prime boxes," says Casey. "With the logos and the black tape with the smiling whatever it is on them. You know, that squiggly, wormy thing? I guess it's supposed to be a smile but it reminds me of an axolotl. The Japanese love axolotls. They have whole stores dedicated to axolotls. I did a Seiko shoot in Tokyo and went in one."

"It was smart and simple," says Brock. "A driver and a delivery guy in those matching golf shirts. A black Sprinter that any shipper might use. Easy to rent. Amazon boxes that everybody's used to seeing. Delivered to the Barrel on a late, dark night, long after it's closed and empty. Boxes filled with plastic bottles of gasoline, gunpowder, and cell signal detonators."

"But I might have recognized the delivery guy from the security tape. Even with his cap pulled down low. He looked like one of the shark finners that was on the *Empress II*."

"Might doesn't count, Casey."

Brock—with his teenage experience growing and smuggling pot in Riverside and Laguna, and later, his months as a volunteer fighter in Ukraine—is impressed by Jimmy Wu's crafty arson.

"Then they set them off by phone," he says. "Waited a minute to enjoy the show. That's when you saw them scream off."

"Sergeant Bickle said it was one of the ballsiest arsons he'd ever seen," says Casey.

Brock agrees. "Nobody can ID them from the security video, including you, Case. It's what security video almost always is—too fucked up to tell anything for sure. Smeared and jerky and useless."

"Like me, falling asleep at Mom's."

"Let it go, bro. Fight again."

Casey parks his truck in a cracked and weed-sprung parking zone, as far from King Jim Seafood as he can get.

Brock raises his Nikon binoculars, and Casey the trusty Leicas he uses to spot fish from *Moondance*.

To Casey, King Jim Seafood looks quiet today. There are no lights on behind the security screen door or wrought-iron window rods, no cars parked out front. Beyond the King Jim building, huge blue cranes lower Maersk and Hanjin and Cosco containers to the docks.

"It would be hard to burn down a brick building," says Casey. "Wouldn't it?"

"Right. They've got iron window screens so you can't throw anything through. You'd need to get inside and use a lot of accelerant. But you'd probably get caught. Look at all the people here on this dock, twenty-four, seven. More law enforcement and fire and rescue than you can count. A pro could pull it off. Maybe."

"They have pro arsonists now?"

"They always have. They're generally insane."

"Rad you know all this stuff."

"Most of it's just common sense."

"You sure you want to do this?"

"Kick their asses out of business like they did to us? You bet I do. If you're not up for it, Case, okay. Stay in Laguna and let me handle it. In my world, no one does what these people did to Mom and doesn't pay a whopping price."

"That other-cheek thing you're always haranguing about."

"That very thing."

"I don't agree with the philosophy behind this," says Casey. "It's, like, revenge for material things. But in this case, because of Mom, I'm going to bend my rules."

"Thank you."

"But it seems like we need a better way to do this."

"Give me your thoughts, Casey."

"Well, if the purpose is to put the Wus out of business like they did to us, and their brick building is a fortress in plain sight, then maybe we should go after something else. Like, what they *use* for business. Same as they went after the Barrel. How about their boats? The *Empress II,* the red Cigarettes, the Luhrs, and the Bayliner?"

Casey lowers his binoculars to find Brock staring at him point-blank. "What."

"I like it, Casey. But the Wu boats aren't worth what the Barrel was, especially with Mom being way underinsured."

"Might be enough to run them out of business, Brock."

"I want more."

"You maybe should consult your Breath of Life God on that."

"It's nothing to do with God, Casey. It's a thing in the human heart."

"You can't remask justice into vengeance and call it justice."

"'Remask' isn't a fucking word, Casey. Maybe you'd be singing a different song if they'd dropped Mae into the Pacific."

"You're not saying I love Mae more than Momster, are you?"

"You're so dumb."

"I know."

"I'm saying stand up for your family."

"And don't ask what people can do for me?" asks Casey. He's paraphrasing his brother's paraphrase of John F. Kennedy from last week's

Breath of Life sermon. Kasper Aamon had gone viral by saying that Kennedy was a dark-state socialist president shot down by his own operatives, and that Brock was a "lice-ridden dope fiend running a fake church."

"Exactly, Casey. Stand up for your family and anyone else who needs help."

"See, there's that old-fashioned Bible stuff sneaking in past your defense," Casey says.

"Grandpa's fault. I can't help it sometimes."

Casey smiles. He likes it when Brock drops his hard-guy act and shows that he's, like, good.

"After all, Gramps inspired you to start a new church with a new God."

"He *made* me start a new church."

Both brothers raise their binoculars when a windowless white Sprinter parks out front of King Jim. It's got the King Jim Seafood logo along the sides: a stylized, bright red lobster with a bib around its neck, eyes bulging, pinchers raised, clamping a fork and knife.

"That's not the logo I saw," says Casey.

"No," says Brock. "You wouldn't send out fire-starters in one of the company vans."

Casey watches the driver and one passenger spill out. The driver is the big woman Mahina strong-armed aboard *Empress II,* when they all went to get Mae. The passenger is Polo—Jimmy Wu's sidekick from the Cigarette boat—dressed in a red warm-up suit with the King Jim lobster logo on the back.

"Darren Fang," says Brock.

"How do you know who he is?" asks Casey. Who knows how Brock knows things? Casey figures the Go Dogs must have an intelligence network of some kind. Something coded in their messages, maybe.

Brock ignores the question.

Darren stops and looks in their direction. Casey hopes the noses of their surfboards don't catch his eye. Apparently not, as Fang swings open the back of the Sprinter, bounces a hand truck to the pavement, and loads on four big boxes with "Frozen Meat—Refrigerate Upon Arrival" stickers on each side. They look heavy.

"Meat and dry ice," says Brock.

"Shark fins, man."

The brothers watch as the door opens and Fang reverses the hand truck to pull it inside. The big woman scans the lot and follows him in, and the metal security door slams shut with a clang.

Against his own will, Casey pictures Bette Wu in the Sunset Boulevard sunset, feels that evil tongue of hers in his ear, smells the tropical-cinnamon perfume coming off her. Sees Mae smelling her white pumps.

He pushes those thoughts back into the empty room in his mind, closes the door. Temptation is sneaky.

"Casey, exactly how many King Jim pirates did you see that first day, when Bette Wu boarded your ship with a gun and the two boats came up and blasted your phone?"

"Nine. Not counting hands belowdecks, or sailors behind blackout glass in the consoles."

"Add at least three," says Brock. "Then, there's Jimmy himself, and Darren Fang, and the woman there, and Danilo and the lawyer who packs."

"And two more on the second red Cigarette when Jimmy and Fang threatened Mom off Laguna," says Casey, lowering his binoculars to count on his fingers. "So that's nineteen, minimum. And five ships. What are you thinking, Brock, like, we're going to need a bigger boat?"

"No," snaps Brock. "*More* boats. We've got *Moondance*, and Mom's old panga in her garage. Three of my local Go Dogs are deep-sea fishermen with some really sweet watercraft. We take down King Jim and his fleet, one vessel at a time."

"We don't kill anybody, do we?"

"No. We wreck their livelihood, like they wrecked Mom's."

"Maybe we should just call the police."

"You'll recall that we already have, Casey. And look what good it did. No arrests, no suspects, no witnesses. Just hearsay from us, useless security video, and a ten-million-dollar restaurant that's burnt to shit and underinsured."

"Yeah, but—"

"Are you in or not, Casey? You don't have to be, but answer me, right now."

Casey tries to balance the enormous weights shifting around inside him. Like Mavericks is mounding up in there, he thinks. He knows his innocent mother has been greatly wronged, that her life has been badly damaged. As if she hasn't had enough suffering, with Dad. But what will destroying a bunch of boats do to make Mom better? Isn't the point to make her better? Or is the point to bring justice into a violent world of fire, narcotics, guns, and bloody, finned sharks? With *more* violence?

"I don't want to kill anybody."

"We'll try not to."

"I'm serious, Brock. You can't kill people for burning down a restaurant. Even Mom's."

"I agree."

Casey lets the binoculars dangle around his neck, looks at the track marks of fire sparks on his suntanned skin.

Brock does, too.

"I don't believe this is right," Casey says. "You forgive and turn the other cheek. I'm still not exactly sure *where* you turn it or why, but count me out, bro. I hope you out-pirate the pirates, though. Could be epic."

"I'll count you out, Case. You're not cut out for that kind of thing."

"Makes me sound like a grommet."

"To each according to his abilities," says Brock. "You showed plenty of balls trying to save the Barrel."

A beat. "Yeah. Tried."

The second reason they're sitting here in front of King Jim Seafood is because friends have invited them to the Hollister Ranch—just under two hours north of here—which has picked up an October swell with some real heft to it. They need fine-tuning before the Monsters.

That, and they need a break from the stinking rubble of their restaurant.

Jen has declined today's surf getaway invite, however, to continue the labor of salvaging what is salvageable from her beloved Barrel.

She's got help from her mother, father, and Pastor Mike, but Casey feels guilty leaving her to it; Brock is too amped up on vengeance to care what his mom thinks.

22

Hollister Ranch is a private fourteen thousand acres for a select few millionaires and billionaires who have homes on hundred-acre parcels, and sole land access to some of the best waves in California. James Cameron. Jackson Browne. Yvon Chouinard.

Casey and Brock have met them and they're all nice guys if you ask Casey. They're creative, liberal, and corporately responsible. Jackson writes great songs. He and Yvon surf. Brock's not a fan.

The ranch break at Cojo Point, an hour and a half north of LA, is picture-perfect that afternoon—four to seven feet, big-shouldered, and uncrowded.

"Extraglassive," says Casey.

"That's not a word, either, Casey."

"Should be."

Casey and Brock carve it up on their small-wave boards, making things look easy. The locals watch and cheer—which, Casey knows, without the Stonebreaker brothers' surf pedigree and celebrity—wouldn't happen in a million years.

Casey makes the drops with muscular precision, slashes the bottom turns up and off the lips, rides the barrels until the crests eat him alive, stays invisible in the white chaos, then comes charging out like the six-foot-two, two-hundred-and-twenty-pound sculpture he is, all corded neck and shoulders, water-resistant and built for strength.

He gets caught inside on a bigger set, which lets him watch Brock full frontal, Brock at his casual best, rising and stalling deep into the tubes, then blasting out with a spit of spray, with one hand patting the faces lightly, casually, like the pictures of their dad. Unlike Casey and their dad, Brock is rangy, flexible, and ropelike. Darker skin, and the brown dreads. He has the reflexes of a boxer, and the tattoos swirling over his body gives him—Casey thinks—unintended menace. But he's not a menace. He's too busy helping people in need.

Watching his brother shredding a fast Cojo Point right, Casey prays, asking that he win the Monsters.

Him—Brock.

They surf four hours, well past sunset, hit Lance and Teresa Blacketer's for barbecued steaks, potatoes, asparagus, and wedge salads, key lime pie, and Pacifico.

Lance is a venture capitalist headquartered in Palo Alto; Teresa an intellectual property attorney specializing in AI, based in San Francisco. They're the ones who got Random Access Foundation interested in Brock's church.

Casey declines the beer, doesn't like the foggy alcohol buzz. Declines the grass, too.

With the kids in bed, Lance, Teresa, and Brock do their share of both beer and dope, nursing little waterpipe bowls of powerful indica. The stuff is expensive, Casey knows. Brock has these island connections through Mahina.

So Casey masks up against the secondhand smoke, like during Covid. Brock just shakes his head.

They talk about the Monsters and check the online BetUS Sports-book World Surfing League contest odds. The surfers' names come up on the big screen, with soft-focus, slow-motion waves breaking in the background. They're handicapped like thoroughbreds, which we kind of are, thinks Casey, especially us big-wave dudes. We're like specialized muscle masses trained to do just one thing. We work hard and sleep a lot. He wonders if, like a horse, he'll be put out to pasture someday, hopefully at Main Beach in Laguna where he can loll around in the sand like a sea lion, catching rays and croaking for handouts. He wonders if the potent herb is getting through his KN95.

Casey is among the favorites, paying even to win at 2–2.

Brock the same.

Jack Briggs from Hawaii is favored to win.

Mike Schwaner from Australia right behind him, favored to place.

Astonishingly—though not surprisingly, after the way he handled Mavericks *and* Jaws *and* Nazaré last year—nineteen-year-old Thomas Tyler from Santa Cruz is picked to show, and he'll pay out 2–5 if he wins.

Casey thinks it's weird to bet on surfers but some people will bet on anything. If he had money, he'd bet on Brock. But he'd still surf like heck because God will be with him on every ride.

Brock and Lance get into a rambling discussion about the way time changes when you're in the barrel of a wave. The bigger the wave, the slower time gets.

"And you know," Brock says, "when you're locked in way deep, and you're going real fast, and you look out to that big lip closing down, but opening up ahead of you all at once, and you feel like you're going backwards? Well, you *are* going backwards in time because the future and the past have collided, and time has stopped."

"So true, man," says Lance.

"Which is why every time I come out of a wave I feel younger," says Brock. "I *am* younger. I've stood still with time."

"I know exactly how that feels," says Teresa. "Like if you catch enough barrels you could live a long time. Maybe forever."

Casey says good night early, just past midnight, his muscles heavy from four hours of surfing in cold water.

Posts a quick report on the Hollister Ranch surf today, and wishes for a good night to all. And a selfie in which he looks tired but happy.

He's only been sleeping an hour when he dreams that the bedroom door is opening and someone is coming in. Then he hears the voice and sees the faint light outlining the guest room door.

"Hi, Casey, it's me, Alyssa."

"Oh wow, hi."

"I'm the older girl."

"Sure, yeah."

"Sorry to wake you up but I wanted to talk to you."

Casey sits up in the bed, leans his back against the headboard, pulls the bedspread close. Funny, he was dreaming of a girl, well, a woman— Tessie from the Barrel, actually. Now this.

"Talk about what?"

Silence, then the door closing quietly on the light.

"I watch your videos and listen to your *Surf Nation* podcasts. I follow and like you all over the place, get your blogs and those extra cool CaseyGrams you do. Mom and Dad know."

"I'm stoked, Alyssa."

"But I have these dreams about you all the time. Mom and Dad *don't* know that."

She sits on the foot of the bed. Casey tries to draw the cover tighter.

"So, I was wondering if you'd like me to get into bed with you."

Surprised as he is by this, Casey doesn't hesitate.

"No, Alyssa—I don't think so. You're too young."

"I'm seventeen and it's not illegal if I consent. Which I do."

"I mean, you know, that's still awful young."

"You're only twenty-four. It's up to me and you. Consensual."

"I don't think it's right."

"I'd like a second opinion on that."

"From who?"

She laughs softly. "No, silly. Is me being too young some weird sexual deal you have?"

"It doesn't feel weird."

"Is something else about me not right?"

"No, but you don't know me. What if I was like, fully aggro, or a chick hater?"

"Casey—it's obvious that you're not. So far as age—women are just more mature than men. Every guy I know at school thinks I'm hot. You wouldn't believe the expressions they get, the things they say. Such goofy boys. Maybe you think I'd turn out to be a rotten tomato."

"No, really, no. You've always been real sweet."

"You've hardly looked at me. Over a lot of years!"

Casey feels cornered. Like he's being checked by a better chess player.

"I'm looking at you now," he says. "And I can see you're a high-quality girl."

Which of course doesn't come out like he wanted; makes things worse. What if Lance or Teresa had heard *that* from the hallway? Fudge, they could call the police, couldn't they?

Casey's afraid he's about to do something stupid, then realizes he already has by letting her close the door and get onto his bed.

The next few seconds of silence seem like an hour.

"So," she says, standing.

Casey feels relief as her weight lifts, then quick fear that she'll come over and kiss him or something.

"I'm really sorry if I made you uncomfortable," she says. "You're a dream I always wanted to have."

"I'm sorry if I let you down."

"Night then, Casey Stonebreaker."

"Good night, Alyssa."

"You're the most beautiful man and surfer I know."

Casey's trying to form a polite and humble reply when the weak hall light sections into the room, then is gone.

At sunrise, Casey and Brock are back in the lineup at Cojo Point at Hollister Ranch.

The silver-gray waves are head-high and smooth as glass.

The locals aren't as welcoming as they were the day before. No nods or words, no problem dropping in late on the brothers, forcing them off the waves.

Casey is sitting outside between sets, chewing on an errant fingernail, when Brock paddles over and climbs astride his board.

"I had a dream last night," he says. "It was weird and when I woke up I'd learned something from it."

"Maybe it was all that good weed."

"It was me as a lion in a big room. Like a banquet room in a hotel. And there were people there, too, wearing animal skins. Giraffes and buffalo and zebras. But mostly it was other lions, like me. They all had black tails but mine was red. I knew it was up to me to get justice for my pride. Some of these other lions had set a fire in our cave. Burned everything we had. They were watching me at the big table, loading up a plate of meat.

"Then you walked in. A white tiger. Bigger and stronger than any of us lions. They started circling you and we started circling them and they fully outnumbered us. One of them snapped at you but I saw he was afraid to touch you. He backed away, then slunk to an exit door. Bumped into a tray of empty plates and glasses on a stand, knocked it over and dodged out. The other lions snarled at you but backed away, too. Headed for the exits. End of dream. I woke up in a sweat. Realized you were right about the pirates who burned out the Barrel. I'm not going after them, Casey. I'm not going proactive, which is my nature. I'm going reactive, which is yours. I'm going to turn this stubbly cheek of mine the other way. Wait to see what they do next. If anything. I think they'll be like the lions in the dream. I'll let vengeance be the Lord's. As you suggest."

Casey wonders if he's hearing right. Can't remember a time when he's had a disagreement with Brock and Brock has come around to his point of view. Trusted his judgment. Believed in him.

"Cool, Brock. I think you're doing the right thing."

"Thanks for being my big brother sometimes."

"You make me feel smart."

Brock is smiling, his dark face dripping seawater, his stubby locs catching the early light.

23

Jen stands in the reeking lobby of the Barrel, Mae sitting at her feet.

She's looking at a $400,000 replacement rebuild, of which $150,000 is covered by insurance. She hasn't upped her policy since remodeling the Barrel eighteen years ago. Her bank is considering the loan. Her annual personal income is $10,000 from freelance magazine and newspaper writing, and occasional consulting work for television.

She's got $75,000 in her savings account.

She draws a $75,000 yearly salary from the Barrel.

There's a lot of demo to be done. Jen's remodel was conventional construction—wood frame, Sheetrock, and expensive redwood siding. The wood flooring, walnut dark and streaked with blond—Jen always loved how it greeted her in the morning, buffed up clean the night before—has been destroyed. The raised foundation is still good.

Adding to those costs is the fact that the furniture, art, lighting, plumbing, electrical, sound system, ovens, stoves, warmers, and appliances were all high-grade commercial and expensive. Much of it has been damaged thoroughly by flame and smoke, some of it irreplaceable. The surfboard collection is almost totaled. The paintings are ruined.

The high-end projection screens on which the surf videos played are now melted around the edges.

Laguna Beach fire trucks had gotten there less than twelve minutes after Casey's first 911 call. But four crude fire bombs—casually staged as deliveries just outside the lobby, the back door, the side kitchen entrance, and the upstairs apartment deck—had already exploded, accelerant and high winds spreading the flames rapidly. Remote fuses, the arson investigator said.

His team found a fifth bomb under the north floor of the dining room—placed through a crawl space under the raised foundation. The access screen had been snipped off. No north-wall security cameras because of the inaccessible sandstone drop-off and chain-link fence heavy with mandevilla. The flames ate up through the framing timbers and into the room, swiftly.

According to Jen's contractor, she's looking at spring of next year. Which means a five-month wait, *if* the City of Laguna Planning and Building Department and the California Coastal Commission sign off promptly, and the supply chains hold. He says the price of his materials have doubled in two years and the union wages he pays are out of sight.

Mae follows her into the dining room where Jen kneels and touches one of the classic Hawaiian redwood surfboards that caught flame and finally came crashing down from its ceiling mounts. It's a hundred years old and badly burned. Most of the other boards were made of foam and fiberglass, which of course ignites viciously and melts when swarmed by flames. Some are John's. Some belonged to the greats: Kahanamoku, Noll, Weber, Dora, Young, Nuuhiwa, Lopez, Andersen, Tomson, Irons, Slater, Clark, Bethany, Parsons, Laird, McNamara. There are twenty-six of them, Jen knows—one for each year of John's life. Some of which, blackened and disfigured, are still hanging on the walls.

She stands, pats Mae's soft round head, feels like crying or kicking Jimmy Wu hard as she can in the nuts, but she's not much of a crier and Jimmy's a bit out of range.

Since the Barrel burned up and cooled down Jen has thrown herself into the cleanup—and into her training for the Monsters of Mavericks—with her usual ferocious energy.

And now, with a $175,000 shortfall for rebuilding her love and livelihood, she's even *more* inspired to win the Monsters.

Which is a long shot, she knows, at forty-six, and not having ridden big waves in twenty-five years, according to the Surfline.com rankings and the surf contest handicappers on BetUS Sportsbook.

Not that she isn't training *and* working her ass off: in between her sunrise stand-up paddleboarding, surfing whichever SoCal break is going off best, weight lifting, and striding underwater along the bottom of LBHS pool with dumbbells in her hands and weights on her ankles—Jen still reports to work exactly as she has for eighteen years.

But now she's demolishing the ruins rather than running the most popular restaurant in Laguna Beach. She's got help from Mom and Dad and Pastor Mike, from Casey and Brock when they're not surfing—god bless them—but they're still not done yanking out the now-toxic drywall. Or scrubbing the smoke stains off the flame-scorched ovens and stainless walls and backboard in the kitchen. All this and more, instead of making sure that Casey's catch of the day is being properly prepared, greeting and seating her friends and loyal local customers, tweaking the menu, touching up the paint, polishing the now destroyed floors, making sure the surfboards and framed photos and paintings are one hundred percent dust free and glittering like jewels in the sunlight shooting through windows.

The smell is awful but face masks make her dizzy. People out on the sidewalk stop and stare at her through the opaque plastic sheeting hung to keep the curious out and the ash and stink in. Every ten minutes she takes Mae around back to the deck facing the Pacific, lets the dependable onshore wind fill their lungs.

Her task today is to scour the ash, extinguisher stains, and carbonized burns off the life-sized bronze statue of John in what was once the lobby. She has to tend to every inch of him, faithfully rendered by the artist: face, neck, chest, those beautiful arms, the six-pack stomach, the butt inside the surf trunks, his thighs, calves, knees, and knobby feet. The statue doesn't feel or smell human, doesn't sound anything like a person when Jen accidentally bangs it with the handle of her brush, or pings the bronze with the wedding ring that she's never stopped wearing. There's still something painful and intimate about touching this statue. Makes her wish she could touch the real, living him; reminds her that she never will.

Mae seems to sense this, watching Jen fretfully, forehead furrowed.

Scrubbing away at her bronze husband's forehead, Jen is reminded again—for what, the ten thousandth time?—that her hardwired instinct to protect and serve had failed most spectacularly in John's death. If ever there was a test, that was it. Her cop father understands this better than her coach/athlete mother.

As she works on John's eye with a toothbrush and cleaning paste, whispering, "I won't hurt you, John, I won't hurt you," Jen thinks of those nights just after his drowning, sitting up late with Mom and Dad in their hillside house in South Laguna, staring at the fire but talking little.

What was left to say?

She had failed to protect and serve the love of her life.

And now, the Barrel.

Drifting back from this memory, Jen becomes aware of something behind her—just a slight change in the light coming off John's face.

Mae sits up.

"Jen Stonebreaker?"

She doesn't recognize the voice but when she turns she knows the face: Timothy Stanton Orchard, the man who set Laguna ablaze thirty-plus years ago, starting a fire in Laguna Canyon on a hot night of howling Santa Ana wind. Gasoline and a fireplace lighter. The wind blew the flames across the hills and into town. Spread north and south when they hit the city. Four-hundred-something homes destroyed, sixteen thousand acres. And, miraculously, no deaths. She was twelve. Orchard was arrested by her father. It half broke his heart that he had let his citizens be served and protected so poorly.

Mae is on the man—a potential treat giver—looking up at him hope-fully.

"Mr. Orchard."

"I heard about your tragedy. It smells like, well . . . they all smell dif-ferent."

"What could you possibly want?"

She steps off the stool and looks into Tim Orchard's calm blue eyes. He's mid-fifties now, she knows. Short and lithe, thinning brown hair. Chinos and running shoes and a button-down white shirt tucked in tight. A harmless-looking man. She had written about him for *West Coast Monthly* when he was released from Atascadero State Hospital ten years go. One of those reentry stories people hate. What the edi-tor wanted. Jen wasn't sympathetic but was at least somewhat positive about his chances, based mostly on stats and studies from the state's attorney general. Got some heated mail. Talked to him for hours at his halfway house. Neighbors with signs, going bonkers. I'm absolutely, one hundred percent rehabilitated, he said. Took my therapy, take my meds. A very sorry and very changed man, he said. Demons banished. Showed her his positive discharge letters from the doctors and coun-selors and hospital staff. Even one from a fellow patient whose life he had saved with CPR. Nursed a crow back from a cat attack and made a pet of him. Orchard had asked his original arresting officer, Sergeant Don Byrne, for a letter of recommendation because the policeman had always treated him courteously, and told him once that people can change for the better. Her father had declined. Orchard says he's hop-ing to be a paramedic someday but knows he's a long shot. Wanting to volunteer now. Maybe with the disabled. Maybe become a caregiver. Hoping to undo some of the bad he's done.

He's got the same harmless, apologetic face today as he had back then. Same thin, almost ready to smile lips.

"I'm up in LA county now."

"What do you want?"

"To help you put things back together."

"I've got help."

"How's your father?"

"He's fine."

"Treasure him. My father is still alive but we haven't talked for thirty-four years. Roger Orchard. The third."

"And what are you doing these days, Tim?"

"Volunteer landscaping and maintenance at my church."

"Quite a switch from burning sixteen thousand acres and four hundred houses."

Orchard nods and looks at the floor. Toes the ashes that settle back down no matter how many times Jen uses the shop vac on them.

"I can't tell you how sorry I am," he says, looking up at her. "I didn't know, until you interviewed me and published the story, how much you loved the place I destroyed. Its people and its uniqueness. Its waves and quaintness. I realize I burned much of what you loved. So, when I heard about your restaurant being ruined by arsonists, I thought I'd offer to help you. You must be very busy getting ready for the Monsters of Mavericks."

Jen gets that weird, dark unease that she always gets from weird, dark people who know who she is, and what she does, mostly by following her online. Garden-variety pervs and stalkers.

"I am a fan of big-wave surfing," he says.

"Who's favored at the Monsters?"

Orchard shrugs. "Your sons? I'm not that big a fan, actually."

"Why are you here?"

Orchard toes the ashes again. "It really smells strong. I used to go back to my fires when it was safe. Smell them. Relive the excitement."

"Get out."

"I'll try to explain. I was never a sane or normal or good person. I was what I was and now I am what I am. So, when something like this happens to someone who is all those things I'm not, I have to imagine what they're feeling. And thinking. And wanting. Beyond getting your restaurant open again."

"Well, fuck, Orchard. Exactly what do you imagine I'm feeling and thinking and wanting beyond that?"

"Revenge."

"Okay. Sure. I wish a lightning bolt would hit each person responsible for this. They wouldn't die but it would hurt like hell and burn the letter *A* onto their chests."

"That's a good one."

"Thanks for dropping by, Orchard. Now beat it."

"I think something more balanced would be better. Something equivalent and appropriate. Such as the destruction of the King Jim Seafood headquarters in Long Beach."

"What do you know about King Jim Seafood?"

"I saw Casey's videos and photos before he took them down. It wasn't hard to ID Bette Wu, who has a DUI police record and brags about her activities on the platforms. She's the daughter of Jimmy Wu, owner of King Jim. I've studied their building. Brick and steel security screening are difficult. You have to get inside. You need a probable reason to be inside. Massive accelerants and explosive. But I see how to do it."

Jen can't believe what she's hearing. Stares at Tim Orchard with what feels like a dropped jaw. But he's real, and this is happening, and his words hang in the air, invisible but real as the ash that greeted her here this morning.

Jen allows herself an image of King Jim Seafood exploding into flames. Bricks flying, flames shooting through the roof. Enjoys it quite a lot.

"How much?" she asks.

"Time and material. This is something I want to do. You were kind to me in that magazine article. Much kinder than the neighbors. I'd feel good about doing this. For you."

"How much would time and material be?"

"Truthfully, my time is worth nothing, so two thousand dollars should cover it."

"Two thousand."

He nods and touches the floor again with a clean white athletic shoe. Looks up at her, eyes placid, forehead wrinkled with inquiry.

"No, thank you. Please get out now. *Please.*"

"Sure, I will. I was expecting you to say no. It says much more about you than a yes would."

"If you'll excuse me, Mr. Orchard."

Orchard stands backlit through the rippling plastic, the cars on Coast Highway moving behind him.

"Wait," she says. "Give me your phone number and your address."

In case I change my mind?

Orchard pulls a phone from a front pocket, works the pad with a forefinger.

"Is the Barrel number still good?" he asks.

Another creepy rush as she realizes he's got that number.

"For now."

The arsonist patiently taps away. "Okay," he says. "If you change your mind. Or maybe if you want to write about me again."

He raises a hand, then picks his way across the Barrel lobby and fades through a flap in the plastic.

Jen sits on the back deck, sun on her face, smoke stench in her nostrils, chomping down on takeout from Adolfo's.

It's Brock on her phone.

"Mom, five-plus earthquake off Baja less than an hour ago. Marlon at Surfline says Todos Santos will be going off by tomorrow morning. So, kennel Mae. Casey, Mahina, and I will pick you up at home in an hour. We'll trailer your ski, load the gear, and hit the road. Take us three hours, max."

"Oh, boy."

"This is us, Mom. Marlon says it might be crazy big. Or just crazy. Todos Santos hit sixty feet last year. You need a break, Mom. From the fire and the Barrel. And we all need a good warm-up for the Monsters. Need it badly."

"I'll be ready in an hour."

24

Todos Santos is thirty feet of chaos, and one hundred percent on.

The quake-driven waves march in fast and crowded together, like they're in a race, partially blotting out the sky as Jen looks up from the cabin of the charter boat *Magdalena*. The impact zone is a mist-shrouded valley and looks as if it's boiling.

Israel, the captain, has pulled up well away from the spectacle. Tells them in broken English he's not going to die in there.

To Jen the waves look rideable, just barely. They're rapid shape-changers, sections forming and closing out, towering A-frames offering lefts and rights that form, then suddenly collapse. Some gruesome wipeouts. Jen spots Jamie Mitchell and Jojo Roper and Greg Long out in the lineup, all expected to ride the Monsters in a few short weeks.

Casey and Brock have driven the jet skis across the deceptively glassy quarter mile from shore, and they're waiting a hundred feet from *Magdalena,* skis belching white smoke and whining with pent-up horsepower.

Jen and Mahina plop overboard one at a time with the brothers' boards, the water a cold shock on Jen's face and down her neck and chest as it cuts under her wetsuit. She paddles hard through the chop to her idling ski, trades places with Casey, who has a smile on his face as he sits on his board and fastens the leash to one ankle. Her heart pounds like a dryer with a bowling ball in it.

"Gonna do this, Mom, gonna *do* this," he says. "Thirty feet of God's love, marching in to hold us!"

"The rights are better, Case," she says, noting that the right-breaking waves are clean, but the lefts are sloppy. "Never seen waves this fast!"

She steers the jet ski in a wide semicircle, checking back to make sure Casey has the tow rope and his balance on the eight-four gun before she accelerates and pulls him into the lineup.

Waits now, bobbing on the heavy jet ski. High-fives Roper, who high-fives back. The BetUS Sportsbook has good odds and lines on him for the Monsters, she knows. Just behind Brock, who's just behind Casey, are the big, big boys—Hawaiian and Australian—and that truly miraculous Tom Tyler out of Santa Cruz.

Anybody's game, she thinks.

Will come down to wave choice, and luck.

Now Mahina cuts out front of a towering peak, towing Brock behind.

Jen watches as Mahina speeds along the forming shoulder and Brock swings high into the wave, well in front of the massive crest. Where he drops the handle, and Mahina, after looking behind at him, speeds up and over thirty feet of still-forming wave.

Brock drops into the deep blue wave as if his board were a gallows trapdoor.

The crest is thick and shifty, rudely cleaving a left and a right, but the right is where he is and Brock rockets across the face of it. Then a blast of speed into a carving bottom turn as he banks and lets the face have him, brakes against it with that reckless cool of his, letting the maw have him as if he's daring it to. Comes out of it leaning back a little, like he's bored. Rides the elegant shoulder in sweeping, beautifully composed turns.

John all the way, Jen thinks—John in his last couple of years, when his instinct guided his body and his control submitted to grace.

Brock kicks out, and Mahina glides in.

And, minutes later, when Jen tows Casey into a similar, speeding, near forty-foot wall of water, she watches her firstborn son drop powerfully down that rising face, his legs like shivering pistons, crouched, arms out and flexed, and his bull's neck clenched, and his big-jawed, heavy-browed face locked in an expression of undefeatable concentration.

John again, Jen thinks. In his early big-wave days, when surfing was survival. A battle of will over fear, of body over mind.

Casey bullies his way along, powers into the barrel and out like a man fired from a cannon.

Rides the smooth shoulder with his arms up in praise—Jen knows, always Casey and his God—then kicks out in a fists-raised victory leap, cartwheeling over the roaring wave.

Jen delivers him into another.

Mahina and Brock again.

Casey.

The waves are pushing forty feet by the time they get back to *Magdalena* for lunch.

Jen, wrapped in a blanket, still unusually cold, finishes her burrito and looks at the waves, her throat dry, her heart slamming away again, that awful, dark, 3 A.M. fear taking her over. Listens to the booms of the waves, the screams of the jet skis.

Sometimes fear is a friend, and caution a teacher, she hears Dr. Penelope Parker say.

"Mom?" asks Casey. "Ready?"

The words hurt when they leave her mouth. She feels as if a thousand eyes, both living and dead, are on her.

"You know, Case. I'm going to sit this one out. I'm not feeling it."

"Yeah, Mom," he says. "And you have to feel it because Mavericks could be fifty, sixty feet. Thicker, meaner, and colder. You have to commit. Or, you know . . . you could get hurt."

"I understand that perfectly."

She sees the looks that Casey and Brock exchange.

"This is a good decision, Mom," says Brock.

"I'll pray with you right now for help," says Casey. "He'll answer us, Mom. He always does."

"Shut up, Casey," says Brock.

Casey looks down at the spark burns on his hands. He's sitting spread-legged on the bench in his bright orange-and-black wetsuit, his thick hair matted, and Jen sees him at age six, this towheaded first-grader in a Waimea Bay T-shirt with a Batman lunch box, boarding the bus for El Morro Elementary.

Now Casey looks up and gives her a look that makes her feel like she's being forgiven. It both angers her and makes her want to cry.

"Totally right on, Mom," he says. "You don't need to surf today. Brock's right."

Jen looks out at Todos Santos Island, the curve of the bay, the blue water, black rocks, and tawny hills.

But what she sees is her husband taking off on the final wave of his life.

"I'll be ready for the Monsters," she says. "Ready to win it. And tow you in. Don't you worry about that."

That evening at the Barrel, scrubbing away at the once-beautiful stamped aluminum bar, Jen still hasn't gotten over her Todos Santos chill, and the 3 A.M. fantods that follow her everywhere.

Casey, Brock, and Mahina are helping out. Jen catches their occasional looks—the kind that people cut short when you look back. Even Mae looks concerned.

She pretends not to hear their soft, intense discussion of the freak autumn swell now forming way up in the North Pacific, spawned by an early Aleutian storm and an unusual shift in the Humboldt current. It's already very powerful, and aimed at the Bay Area coast of California. A late October or early November Monsters of Mavericks is possible.

"Man, I hope so," says Casey. "Pray to your Breath of Life that it happens."

"I don't pray," says Brock.

Mahina mutters something that Jen can't quite hear but it sounds portentous.

She's tired of living in dread. Feels exhaustion right here in front of her, curling a bony finger her way. Maybe Dr. Parker was right: she should bow out of the Monsters and battle her demons on a less deadly playing field.

Just the mention of the Monsters deepens the chill from Todos Santos, but it's even worse because she publicly *committed* to the Monsters. Months ago. With some minor fanfare from the surfing media, and from the big-wave riders she's still in touch with.

Jen bears down with the fine-grade polish pad, demolishing those stains, protecting and serving the Barrel with all her might.

Thinks of tomorrow's early paddleboard workout, followed by the weights, the breath-control training in the high school pool, maybe a visit to Belle. Then back here to her stinking former restaurant, to her ash-ridden rubber gloves, her brushes, solvents, and scratch pads, her black fingernail sludge.

She knows that swell up in the Aleutians is going to finally break at Mavericks. Knows she's supposed to ride enormous waves. Knows she's not going to let what happened to John happen to Casey. That Mahina isn't going to let it happen to Brock.

But can Casey keep it from happening to her?

She misses the vodka and knows that Ralphs, just a few blocks away, has the pepper Stoli she loves. What would a quart of *that* look like on this bar? Feel in her hand as she pours? On her lips, in her nose?

But she refuses to give in.

25

On the bridge of the elegant Chris-Craft *Cinnamon Girl,* Brock stands beside bald, gray-bearded Dane Crockett, who eases back the throttle. Brock feels the big cabin cruiser slow and settle in the bright, late afternoon.

Dane is an irrigation supply wholesaler from Riverside who admittedly joined the Go Dogs for dangerous missions, not so much to help people out but for the rush.

It's been three days since Todos Santos. All three of those days spent searching at sea.

But as of one hour ago, eureka!

Brock, Mahina, and the five-boat Go Dog flotilla have finally found and surrounded the pirates' flagship. The rust-stained, blue-and-red steel-hulled trawler *Empress II* waits at anchor just off San Clemente Island.

Brock's vengeful heart has been beating hard. His blood pressure is probably off the charts but he doesn't care. Feels liberated by lying to Casey, such that like his brother's guilt—and maybe even blood—will not be on his, Brock's, hands. Besides, he'll need something very important from Casey, down the line: his innocence.

They've had *Empress II* under watch, at a distance, easing in and keeping in touch by radio. She's unaccompanied and possibly unmanned. If there are crew aboard, Brock thinks, they'll have to swim the two hundred feet to San Clemente Island—rocky and current-blasted and forbidding as it is. The island is a bomb and artillery testing ground, for Christ's sake. A few hundred Navy guys. They'll drag the pirates ashore and ship them back to Pier 32 in National City. Maybe deport them, for all Brock knows.

The touchy part is boarding *Empress II* without getting shot, and before anyone can call in reinforcements.

Which means Brock and two of the Go Dogs on *Cinnamon Girl* will board the old trawler, which from here, through Brock's binoculars, definitely looks unattended. Almost too good to be true, but it's possible that the pirates are out on their smaller, faster crafts, patty-hopping for tuna and sharks. Where else would they be?

Brock continues his surveillance. Sees no movement anywhere on the trawler, just the nets neatly stowed and the tag lines swinging with the breeze. The swells are weak, on long intervals, and *Empress II* rides them heavily. Brock lowers his binoculars.

"Get us close, Dane," says Brock. "We'll hop these fuckers."

Mahina mutters a prayer.

Brock and his vigilantes pull balaclavas over their heads—plain colors, no Go Dog logos on these, only their eyes showing.

"We're good, hon," he says. "No one home."

Brock leans at the stern deck rail, a Smith .40 caliber autoloader jammed into the waistband of his jeans and a red plastic gas can at his feet. Go Dogs Keyshawn and Javier flank him, their weapons holstered.

When Dane gets them close, Brock hoists himself to the low stern gunwale and makes the jostling, wet jump onto *Empress II*.

Lands well and gets the rope thrown by Mahina, draws *Cinnamon Girl* tight and ties off.

Keyshawn slings the red gas can onto the trawler, then follows Javier aboard—steadied by Brock.

Pistols drawn and dangling at their sides, Brock leads them into the spacious galley, where Jimmy and Bette Wu had tried to force them into a short sale of the Barrel, and the lawyer with the gun in his briefcase had tried to broker the deal. Where the life vest stows are supposedly packed with fentanyl precursors and frozen shark fins. All locked now, he sees.

They clear the galley and the kitchen, the bridge and the foredeck, the captain's quarters and the cabins. Check the johns and the showers, the bait and cargo holds, even the cold catch holds—every place a human being might fit.

Brock starts in the captain's room, splashes the gas over the bed and desk and chairs, the little wall-mounted TV, the shelves and fridge, the tattered, braided oval rug.

Soaks the bridge, the radios, the navigation gear.

The nets and the worktables, the racks of gaffs and guns and finning knives.

The engine room.

The cabins and toilets.

Then the galley and kitchen.

Standing just outside the galley entrance, Brock tosses a lit matchbook onto the gas-soaked table at which Jimmy "King" Wu had sat and laughed and tried to rob his mother.

Flames swoosh and huff.

"You don't do that kind of shit to people," he says, the flames swirling. "The Breath of Life doesn't fucking allow it."

"Amen, Brother Brock," says Javier.

They unhitch and scramble back aboard *Cinnamon Girl*.

Cinnamon Girl and the other four Go Dogs boats—a very old retired police patrol boat from San Pedro, a Boston Whaler, two Baja-style pangas with big Yamaha outboards—bob at rest around her.

They're a quarter mile away when flames begin to dance atop the bridge and deck of *Empress II*.

Brock watches through his binoculars as Dane Crockett nimbly guides *Cinnamon Girl* northwest with the swell.

He hates to watch a seaworthy boat destroyed, but he knows he had to do this, and will have to do more to put things right. To help the victims. The needy and the bullied and abused. Ask not what people can do for you . . .

"She's going to blow any second, Brock," says Dane.

Which she does.

Empress II, an orange, firework-spitting inferno, rages on a blue-black sea.

Three days later, from *Cinnamon Girl,* Brock and Mahina glass the dark green Luhrs *Stallion* atop Pyramid Reef off San Clemente Island. The other Go Dog boats form a wavering string in the soft current.

Brock glasses a white man with red hair and a burly Mexican finning sharks in the thick morning fog. They're working at a table set up on the long Luhrs foredeck, the cabin and convertible observation platform behind them. The windows are dark and Brock can't see in.

The Go Dog boats drift off to surrounded *Stallion,* and Dane Crockett eases *Cinnamon Girl* toward the finners with his silent electric motor.

Brock's got his phone on burst mode and the shutter muted, and after a quick selfie that he'll use to open the next Breath of Life post, he points it at the men.

Who look up in surprised unison, knives in their hands. They curse, waving their blades, and Red tries to get something from the pocket of his yellow, bloody, waist-high slicker. But he suddenly sees Javier, leaning over the gunwale of his panga, now drifting motorless through the fog and silently upon him with a sawed-off shotgun.

Two knives and four hands go skyward, then Red swings back to Brock.

"You can't hide in a mask. You blew up *Empress.*"

"You burned down the Barrel," says Brock.

The big Mexican looks eagerly to the cabin but Brock sees no movement there, and the man's cagey expression seems false.

Brock reads it, too. "Dump the fins."

Red lowers his knife and his free hand to the cleaning table. "Two days of fishing, over the side? Thousands of dollars of fins?"

Brock nods at Mahina. Who fires a ten-gauge warning shot into a *Stallion* cabin window. The safety glass fragments into diamonds around a big hole.

With his knife still in hand, Red sweeps the pile of shark fins on the cleaning table into the ocean with his forearm. The Mexican does likewise.

"Empty the buckets," says Brock, filming again.

Red reaches back and hurls the long, thin-bladed knife at Brock, who sees it pinwheeling toward him through the fog. He dodges it, blood drops smacking his shirt.

Red and the Mexican empty four buckets of shark fins, cursing with each heave. Brock shoots the silvery triangles glittering through the dark, clear Pacific.

Mahina blasts the electronics cluster on the bridge with her shotgun, then the big-game rods and reels lined up along the aft flank of the cabin.

Two fruitless days later, aboard *Cinnamon Girl* and acting on a tip from one of Casey's many YouTube followers—Brock, Mahina, Dane, and the Go Dog flotilla jump *Bushmaster*. She's one of King Jim Seafood's sleek red Cigarette boats, thirteen miles off Crystal Cove near Laguna, in international waters. Where she rocks on the pale, breeze-scrubbed sea.

They glass it from an idling, near silent distance.

Darren Fang—Polo—is alone on board, downloading white boxes with "FROZEN FISH" stickers on them over the transom from a man in a white fiberglass panga with twin outboards.

Brock recognizes Danilo, the hapless gunman from the former flagship *Empress II*.

Who, feet spread, rocks in the stern, is passing up the boxes.

Thirty seconds later, Brock, Mahina, and the Dogs have surrounded them from the four cardinal points of the compass, guns drawn, cursing wildly and ordering their hands up, like furious cops.

Danilo looks up and into the short barrel of Mahina's shotgun. Drops a box and raises his hands.

Fang—now clad like his boss in a black-and-white LA Kings warm-up suit—turns a half circle, staring silently at his tormentors, then drops the box and puts his hands on his hips like he's had enough of these crazy California freaks.

As Mahina holds her 10-gauge steady on Darren Fang, Brock motions him onto *Cinnamon Girl*, then takes the man's hand and pulls him aboard.

Same for Danilo from the panga.

Dane has already boarded the Cigarette boat and cut open one of the white "FROZEN FISH" boxes. Holds up a clear plastic bag heavy with gray pills.

"Fent?" Brock asks Fang.

Who shrugs and says nothing.

Brock watches Dane as he twists open the Cigarette's fuel tank cap, then douses the entire boat from a red gas can.

Then clambers aboard the panga, unscrews the fuel line from its tank, then hefts the entire half-full thing over his head and empties it inside the bobbing panga—benches, bait and catch tanks, fore and aft decks, the center console, steering wheel, radio.

Soak it all, thinks Brock.

Dane drops the panga gas tank, throws his red gas can back to Mahina aboard *Cinnamon Girl*, who smothers it in her big arms like a rugby ball.

The Go Dogs clear out, except for *Cinnamon Girl*, piloted again by Dane, who nimbly guides his vessel to within twenty feet of the Cigarette.

Brock climbs to the crow's nest with the flare gun in one hand, and when he stands on the platform sees what an easy shot this is going to be, what with his elevation and the low-slung Cigarette wide open below him.

The flare whooshes into the sleek red speedboat, clanging and caroming off the hull and the seats, spewing pink-black flames and smoke, a thrashing demon with his tail on fire.

Sparks jump into the breeze which carries them a few yards downwind and into the panga, where the gas fumes ignite with a loud thump.

Brock raises a fist to the inferno and steadies himself on the nest rails as Dane guides *Cinnamon Girl* away from harm.

Mahina watches her husband—a dreadlocked, tattooed figure washed in orange flames—and for a second sees a vengeful ocean god. A haole devil. Or maybe a different species of otherworldly being. She believes in such things. Would like to see a sea god one day. Welcome it into her heart to dwell within her Breath of Life. But as Brock climbs down from the nest, what Mahina decides she sees is just a man answering his calling, testing his limits, fueled, and now almost immolated by, his mysterious, bewildering anger.

A gift? she thinks.

A burden?

From his father?

A moment later, Brock is still in the crow's nest, admiring his conflagration.

Dane eases *Cinnamon Girl* away from the Cigarette.

From a hundred yards out Brock watches *Bushmaster* explode, then slowly list into the sea, a gleaming, helpless former beauty.

Ten minutes later they've lowered their respective captives overboard, a hundred choppy feet from a rocky beach on San Clemente Island.

And thrown their cell phones into the ocean.

26

The next afternoon, Brock, Casey, and Mahina await San Diego Sheriff detective Bob Temple in Laguna's Marine Room, a locals hangout with good views of Coast Highway and Main Beach.

They've got a table by a window and tequila sunrises, Casey's and Mahina's virgin, and Brock's not.

"I want you to do the talking today, Casey," Brock says quietly. "All you have to do is tell the truth. You did not burn up any boats. You have a good alibi because it's true. You are innocent of this, and you know that we are, too."

"Totally," says Casey.

Of course, Casey isn't at all *totally* sure of Brock's innocence. Whether or not Brock had that big lion dream where hero Casey as a white tiger saves the day, or maybe just made it up so he—Casey—can testify to the cops about Brock's innocence. But, the fact of the matter is Casey hasn't seen or heard one shred of evidence that Brock has done anything against the Wu pirates or their boats. Except that such a thing is exactly what his brother *would* do. Dream or not.

A minute later, Temple comes in, goes to the bar, then carries a cup of coffee their way. He's long-haired and rangy, in jeans and a brown sport coat that doesn't quite hide his gun. He sits and sets a thin deck of photographs on the table.

"Thanks for meeting me on short notice," he says.

"Thanks for coming up our way," says Casey. "Must be important."

"I believe so."

Temple fans out the photos, which show *Empress II, Stallion,* the white panga, and the sleek red Cigarette boat *Bushmaster.* All are in varying states of destruction from fire and bullets.

He also snaps down four more photographs of four different boats, long-distance shots from a cell phone, Casey surmises. The crew is hard to make out, for the ski masks.

Casey catches the hard expression on the detective's face, and he's glad he doesn't have to lie to this guy. He's never been a good liar, pretty much gave up trying by the time he was twelve.

It's three days since somebody set *Empress II* ablaze, two days since they blew up the *Stallion,* and just yesterday destroyed the sleek red Cigarette *Bushmaster,* and a panga. And dumped their crewmen onto the rocky beach of San Clemente Island.

Brock glances at the pictures, then gets up and goes to a window looking out on Ocean Avenue, his back to the detective, boredom personified.

"I'm talking to all of you, Brock Stonebreaker. You might want to listen up," Temple says.

"I hear you just fine."

"Jimmy Wu told me you three—and unidentified others—took out these boats. He values them at four million dollars. Says they're all owned by King Jim Seafood of Long Beach, their family business."

"We didn't burn their boats," says Casey. "They torched the Barrel but we didn't burn the boats."

"Wu denies burning the Barrel," says Temple.

"I'm sure they did it, Detective Temple," says Casey. "But we didn't burn up their boats."

Temple looks at Casey with amusement.

"And Brock, how do you weigh in on *Empress II*?" he asks.

"I wouldn't waste a good match on that piece of shit. And I haven't seen it in over a week. None of those other boats, either."

Temple nods, consults his phone, then sets it down. "I'm sure you have tight alibis for the afternoon the *Empress II* exploded. I mean, you can lawyer up if you want, but if you give me some straight answers here we can save a lot of time. No recording. No notes."

Casey tells Temple the simple truth as alibi: he was helping his mom rebuild the Barrel.

Brock and Mahina claim to have been way out in Aguanga the last few days, and they've got half a dozen "rescue missionaries" to corroborate.

"So that's not you up in the crow's nest with the flare gun?"

Brock gives the cop a derisive shake of his head.

"Do you have another witness, Casey?" asks Temple. "Someone not family?"

"Just me and Mom and Grandma, and sometimes Grandpa Don," says Casey. "We've been there for, like, weeks. The air in the Barrel is totally foul; Mom bought some new KN95s for us but I still had a headache every day."

Temple nods, dubiously. "Did you make or receive any calls or messages while you were there?"

"Sure," says Casey. "I'm always doing that."

A beat of silence then while Casey tries to gauge how much the detective suspects his alibi, which is fundamentally true. And that of his brother and Mahina, which, technically, Casey can neither confirm nor dispute.

A tough face to read, he thinks. Cops must practice that.

"Did you shoot any pictures or video that afternoon at the Barrel?" Temple asks. "A time-and-date stamp would be nice."

"None those three days," says Casey. "But lots before. We just worked and went outside every half hour for fresh air."

Temple nods.

"Mr. Temple," says Casey. "I'd like to know if you guys are going to nail the Wus for torching the Barrel."

"Not my jurisdiction. Laguna PD is in charge of that."

"Why don't they arrest them?"

Brock gives Casey another sharp look. Casey looks down at his hands, rubs the pinpoint burn scabs.

"Casey, these people are hiding on or near the world's second largest ocean. The *Empress II* was a speck. The Cigarette boats, the Luhrs, and the Bayliner are specks. Even to choppers and search planes, specks. Laguna Police don't even have a patrol boat. Orange County Sheriffs has six single-engine patrol boats for harbor and shallow-water work. And some helicopters. A lot of Wu's organization lives up in San Gabriel. You're lucky to have found them at all, if in fact . . ."

"Exactly," says Brock. "We didn't."

"I wish I could believe your brother on that."

Casey hears the condescension in the detective's voice. Hates it. Has always hated it when people talk to him like he's a child, or a moron.

"Plus," says Temple. "There are fifty public marinas between Ensenada and San Francisco. Dry docks, too. Hell, Wu and his flotilla can stay on the high seas—if they're outside the twenty-four-mile line—only the military can touch them."

"DEA can find anybody," says Casey.

"Too busy with big-time fentanyl at the border," says Temple. "Jimmy's small-time."

"They aren't even going to *look*?" asks Casey.

"Eventually," says Temple. "You guys found *Empress II, Stallion,* and *Bushmaster.* According to Jimmy, that is."

"I told you we didn't do anything to those boats," says Casey.

"You don't have to tell him again," says Brock. "He gets it by now."

Casey knows that lots of people think he's dumb, but Brock was the first. The only people who have ever told him right to his face that he's smart are his mother and, weirdly enough, Bette Wu.

"Casey, Brock? I'd understand it if you guys blew up those boats. Because of what you say Jimmy Wu did to the Barrel. I've eaten at the Barrel. I know what a great place it was."

"We didn't blow up those boats, Detective," Casey says firmly.

"I'm just saying I could understand it, if you felt like it."

"Well, sure, I *felt* like it."

"Please shut up, Casey," says Brock.

"Let's talk again soon," says Temple. He finishes his coffee, stands, and drops a twenty on the Marine Room counter. "I'd like you three down San Diego way."

"Yeah, sure," says Casey.

"Just one of you at a time, though. Like to start with you, Casey."

"I know a good lawyer," says Brock.

Outside, Casey, Brock, and Mahina walk up Ocean toward Casey's place in Dodge City.

Casey's guts are tight and he can't figure out why he feels like he's just lied to the detective.

"Brock?" says Casey. "Did you burn those boats?"

Brock stops and sets his dark, strong hands on Casey's square shoulders.

"I already told you we wouldn't. And you just about convinced the cops that *you* didn't. Good job, Case. You are awesome."

27

A day later, Casey's shaping a board in his backyard on Woodland.

He's trying to relax, go with the flow of karma, but the heat is on and the heat wants answers.

Detective Temple grilled his mom earlier today, trying to poke holes in his alibi, she said. Then went ahead and set up an interview with Casey at the Oceanside Sheriffs' substation for tomorrow morning. No Brock this time. Casey's bringing a lawyer.

Not only that, but state Fish and Wildlife senior investigators have arrived, all the way from Sacramento.

Even Coast Guard lieutenant Kopf, who has opened his own investigation of the fire aboard *Empress II*, says that "new witnesses" have reported seeing a five- or six-boat flotilla motoring toward the old trawler just an hour before arsonists set her on fire. He's got digital images that don't show much, but he says one of the boats looks like it could be *Moondance*.

Casey feels like the whole world is after him. But he feels safe here in his backyard in Dodge City in his yellow hibiscus shorts and flip-flops, surrounded by all his bushes and plants and trees, his surfboards, and Jack Johnson on his Dot.

Casey's house is clapboard, small and uninsulated, built in the 1950s when this then-poor Laguna Canyon neighborhood was home to artists and musicians, many of them Black, and a growing cadre of weird young surfers.

The neighborhood of narrow streets and dirt walkways was nicknamed Dodge City in the late sixties for the shoot-'em-up busts of the drug dealers, artists, and surfers who congregated there for the cheap rent, plentiful drugs, and a sense of security against the invading cops, narcs, even the FBI.

Dodge was peace and love, psychedelic music and weed smoke in the air, surfboards leaned up against the houses and decks. Kids and dogs everywhere you looked.

The Brotherhood of Eternal Love founder, John Griggs, lived here, his home the unofficial BEL headquarters for their worldwide hash- and LSD-smuggling network.

Tim Leary dropped by now and then. Got himself busted here.

Casey likes the lore and vibe of Dodge. Thinks its outlaw reputation gives him street cred, even though he himself is a non-doping, barely drinking, health-food-eating, body-building, Bible-reading environmentalist. And, a semi-ashamed virgin except for the woman his friends embarrassingly rented for him at his twenty-first birthday party. He regretted it before he even did it. Apologized. What a downer. But it was hard in his always-looking-for-answers mind to say exactly why.

Casey prays at least three times a day—before getting out of bed, before his afternoon siesta, and after lights-out at night—but often prays for special requests, too.

He's a man who has never really cussed, fought, or said uncool things about people even behind their backs.

So, living in Dodge makes him feel his part in the surf-outlaw tradition that started in Hawaii and spread to California and Australia, then the world. Part of something old and wild and dangerous. Something that makes you feel like nothing else makes you feel: real, authentic surfing. Not commercialized surfing, though he does love the excitement of the contests. Here in his Dodge City living room he's got a really

cool picture of the old surf star David Nuuhiwa in Dodge in 1968—
just a couple of houses down from here—talking with BEL heavyweight
Johnny Gale, surrounded by surfboards.

Grandpa Don had stories about Dodge in the late sixties when he
was one of the Laguna cops chasing around the drug dealers and the
"general no-good-niks," as he called them.

But with affection. Casey always thought Grandpa Don was too nice
to be a cop. Too permissive. Grandpa Don let him surf when Casey
was five. Grandpa Don let him and Brock keep a baby alligator they'd
bought from a reptile store in Huntington Beach. In their extra bathroom's tub 'til Grandma said no. Let them have chocolate milk with
their meals when they visited.

For sure, Grandpa Don saw some crazy things in Dodge back then,
some funny and others not. Casey remembers hearing about the time
that Grandpa was one of the officers raiding a South Laguna home back
in '67 and one of the cops—not Grandpa Don—shot, in the back, and to
death, a suspected Brotherhood of Eternal Love drug dealer, Pete Ama-
ranthus. That name stuck in Casey's head because it seemed wondrous
and beautiful. And tragic. Pete was twenty-two. He was well-liked, and
Grandpa Don knew the family. Casey's mom told him that Grandpa
stayed up alone late the night they killed Pete, got himself drunk on
bourbon. Grandpa Don was not a drinker.

Now Casey leans down and gets his cheek against the rail of the
board, gauging the rocker it will require to handle Mavericks' four-
story waves moving as fast as freight trains. Too much upsweep in the
rocker and the board will slow, trying to displace water; too little rocker
and you dig a rail and it's wipeout time.

Down you go.

Hard.

Escorted by fifty tons of fifty-degree water, which is quite a bit harder
than warmer water. It's like the difference between hitting the surface
of a warm lake, or a frozen interstate. Then the tumble cycle and the
hold-down that just might be your last.

Mae rises from her shady spot under a brightly blooming yellow hibiscus and lumbers through the open slider into the house. Probably hears the mail lady, who always has treats.

Casey straightens and takes a moment to appreciate his dog, and another to note with gratitude all the plants and shrubs and trees on his lot, from the fruit on the tangerine tree, to the pink trumpet vine, to the purple bougainvillea smothering the old grape stake fence in scintillant violet bracts. And the birds-of-paradise with all their orange-blue plumage, the white-flowered plumeria, and the red lantana alive with butterflies and moths.

Pretty awesome.

Now from the house here comes Mae, head up and tail wagging, trotting ahead of Bette Wu as if showing her to her table.

Casey's heart bucks.

She strides midway into his little backyard, then stops and stands there, looking at him as if she's just walked onstage in scene one. Mae licks her free hand. Bette's dressed in a black knit suit with gold buttons. Black-and-gold pumps, plum lipstick and nails. Hair up, bangs down, and a brushed aluminum Halliburton briefcase in one hand.

She steps up and sets it on the blue-tiled, wave-patterned bistro table. Leans forward on both hands, right into Casey's grill. Up this close her face is the size of a billboard.

"My family had nothing to do with the Barrel," she whispers. "I swear it. And I have *proof.*"

"Jimmy made a threat that day on *Empress II.* I heard it with my own ears."

"My father is a clown. Sometimes worse. I expect to be free from him soon."

"But who else would set the fire? I got burned, you know."

She softly touches the back of his free hand. "I do know. It hurts me."

Then she straightens, looking down at him with a hard expression.

"I'll tell you exactly who set the Barrel on fire. The same people who burned our boats. Monterey 9—a criminal tong spin-off settled in Los Angeles County. They've been enemies of the Wus going back fifty years. They were ruthless then and ruthless now. We were just fishermen and -women. One of their businesses is Imperial Fresh Sea-food. They knew of our offer to buy the Barrel. They want rich Orange County to themselves. So, destroying our fleet was the next logical step toward ruining us completely. Luckily, we have a paid informant in Monterey 9."

Casey less than half believes this story, but wonders if it could be true. Remembers the black Sprinter with the logo speeding off from the Barrel. Why not Monterey 9, destroying Jimmy Wu's future assets? And maybe—just maybe—Brock and Mahina and the Go Dogs declined to torch the Wu family fleet after all. Just as Brock had said he would.

"Excuse me," he says to Bette, as he googles "Imperial Fresh Sea-food" and finds pictures of their delivery fleet. Yep, he sees: Sprinters. The same as Laguna Detective Brian Pittman's, gray, not black, and their logo is a smiling great white shark wearing a red robe, dancing on the ocean on its tail. Like Imperial Fresh is trying to out-logo King Jim, Casey thinks. What kooks.

But it's not much like the logo he saw that night.

Which he tells Bette and shows her his screen. She shrugs and fixes him with a who-gives-a-shit look.

Casey remembers the pirates that first day, bloody knives and dying sharks, their rusty guns and eagerness to use them. Like, if they'd do that, why wouldn't their enemies do likewise? Destroy assets? Like a chess game but the moves are sudden and violent, and there's lots of money at stake.

"See?" Bette says. "Mae likes me. She's forgiven my little prank. I hope you do."

"Get lost, Ms. Wu."

"Where are your manners?"

"They've left the building. So you leave, too. I get nothing but bad actions and bad karma from you."

"Not so fast, Casey. I have gifts for you and Mae. Who I would never hurt in any way."

"Yeah, well, what about throwing her overboard or smuggling her somewhere far away?"

"A joke. An ugly little joke. I apologize. And Casey?"

Again she leans into seated Casey, face to face. Up this close her eyes look like black lakes and within the scents of plumeria and tangerine he smells that smell from Sunset.

"Do not blame my family for the Barrel," says Bette. "Do not blame me."

Knowing Bette Wu as he thinks he does, everything she says sounds like a threat. Or an excuse.

But what if she's telling the truth?

She sits across from him at the bistro table. Gives him a softened expression, then looks down.

"What are you doing here?" he asks. "What do you want?"

"An Arnold Palmer, thank you."

"I'm asking you to go. Mae is asking you to go."

"But why?"

"We don't trust you."

"Someday you will."

Bette gets into her Halliburton, pulls out a colorful foil pouch, and hands a salmon-and-pumpkin treat to Mae. One of her favorites from a boutique pet store.

"I have some ideas for you," says Bette. "Please make me that drink. I'm very thirsty."

Arnold Palmers are one of Casey's favorite drinks, and fun to make. Here at home, he uses mint from his garden and lemons from his tree.

Through his kitchen window he watches Bette and Mae in the backyard, Bette giving his dog another treat from the briefcase, Mae sitting at attention with her usual food lust. Feels wrong to leave them together and alone. So he keeps an eye on both of them.

He cuts the lemons and dices the mint, his emotions writhing inside like eels. Bette Wu is his enemy. She's kidnapped his dog, tried to swindle his family, and almost certainly helped burn down his mother's restaurant. He has never felt hatred for another person but Bette Wu is near the top of his don't-like list. Maybe even *at* the top, considering the Barrel, which he swears he can smell now, gutted by fire, stronger than the mint he's using.

But part of him is attracted to her, fully against his will, but attractions don't wait for invites—they just barge in. He's especially attracted to her non-pirate side. He likes her general attitude, energy, and her blunt language. Her manner. Her poise, her clothes, her sophistication and looks. She's really pretty. And let's face it, he thinks: *I like the way she kissed my ear on Sunset Boulevard.* He thinks her mystery might be the best part of Bette Wu. Like, how can a shark-finning pirate sit out there in my backyard in a suit and feed my dog treats from a Halliburton? Who, really, actually, is this chick, anyway?

He has a brief thought of being in bed with her, or better yet, on a beach blanket just after dark in a private cove he knows near Sunset on Oahu. Such notions he has rarely followed up. When he has, they've proven disappointing, and screwed up friendships, and led to misunderstandings and frustrations.

Right now, frankly, his desires aren't bothering him, though other things are:

Such as betraying his mother with a woman whose family probably destroyed her restaurant.

Such as Mae, whom Bette has threatened to dump overboard at sea. *Jokingly?*

And the $25,000 she tried to get in ransom.

The eels writhe as he looks at her through the window.

It's hard not to be attracted to a pretty woman who has given him probably the most bitchin' compliment he's ever received from anyone except from his mom and Grandpa Don: Bette called him smart.

Still at the kitchen window, he chops and drops the mint leaves, quickly and deftly as he would in the Barrel, his domain since he was a thirteen-year-old dishwasher. He takes a bartender's pride in his drinks.

Be very careful, Casey thinks.

He sets down the glasses and sits across from her.

"This is like the Garden of Eden," says Bette. "The flowers and the smells. The tree of the knowledge of good and evil would be the tangerine. Right?"

"It's not *like* the Garden of Eden," says Casey. He's always thought his yard *is* his Eden. Always took extra good care of it to make it perfect and sinless. Tangerine juice is his favorite thing to drink in the whole world, and he's had gallons of it, right from this tree. Hard to attribute any evil to it at all.

"I was raised Christian," says Bette. "My dad is an atheist but Mom was converted by LA Methodists. So, every Sunday off to church. Bible school in summer. Such terrible boredom. At church school I tried to read Dad's action comics, but they took them away. So I'd look out the window and imagine scenes from the Chinese action movies he always watched. I loved the boat and ocean scenes the most. Casey, I think you understand more about what you see than you let on."

Casey shrugs and looks away. Lets that observation sit warmly inside. Wonders if she's just stroking him now. And why.

"Just hours ago, my father retracted his statement against you and your brother and his wife, accusing you of destroying our boats," she says. "He knows you didn't do it, but he's still furious at you for the postings. Humiliated."

"I removed them."

"But the world saw his pirates finning sharks."

"Well, that's what they were doing."

Bette sighs, cuts Casey a hard look. "Monterey 9 are violent people. Make us look like Girl Scouts. The cops are familiar with them. We've talked to Los Angeles County investigators and filed this new report."

"Well, we didn't burn your boats," says Casey, feeling the flush of truth on his cheeks. "We did not."

He's inwardly proud that this is at least partially because of him. Causing Brock's dream of him as a tiger by not condoning his brother's violence. By turning his other cheek—and Brock's, too.

"I know you didn't!" says Bette. "I *know,* Casey. From now on, let's believe each other. Maybe even trust each other, even if only a little, so we can proceed honestly."

Bette pulls a set of stapled papers from the briefcase. Smiles at Mae and gives her another dog treat. Hands the papers to Casey.

"This is a copy of our statement regarding Monterey 9, to the San

Diego and Los Angeles County Sheriffs. Jimmy has admitted his misguided assumptions about who did what to our ships. It's a peace pipe, Casey. So the Stonebreakers and the Wus can work together, not against each other."

"I doubt that, Bette," he says quietly.

She looks disappointed. "That's the first time you've used my name."

Casey wonders again if she's just stroking him. Thinks of the manipulating women he's known, or known of.

"I always thought Bette Davis was scary," he says. "Those old movies where she's the insane bad woman."

"My dad's kind of woman," says Bette. "He asked me to apologize to you for him falsely accusing you and Brock and Mahina. Do you accept?"

Casey considers this. Sees that it might well be an apology based on a convenience.

"An apology? Okay, I guess."

"Thank goodness! You can keep this copy, as a reminder, you know. Something in writing."

Casey leafs through it. Lots of names, companies, addresses, excerpted courtroom documents, police reports, several newspaper accounts focusing on a tong offshoot called Monterey 9. Also a *Los Angeles Times* story on the competitive world of fish and seafood fishermen supplying high-end Southern California restaurants. A smiling Jimmy Wu is pictured, wearing a Kings windbreaker at what appears to be a Kings game.

"I'd like to have something comparable from you, of course."

"You mean something written?"

"Yes, just saying you don't think we burned down the Barrel. Because, Casey—*we did not*."

"I'd have to talk to Mom and Brock."

"I'm asking you because you're the most reasonable."

"But they would have to agree."

"Will you try, Casey?"

"Why do you ask for this? Are the Laguna cops closing in on you for the Barrel?"

"Do not say that! Absolutely not. They've been respectful. Maybe a little frustrated that there's not one speck of evidence against us. Everything points to the Monterey 9 and Imperial Fresh Seafoods."

Casey takes a long moment to consider. Bette's tale of the Monterey 9 sounds possibly believable.

Laguna PD detective Pittman has asked about them, indicated that they are of interest to his investigation of the Barrel arson. He's already sent Casey a useless photograph of an Imperial Fresh delivery van with the dancing shark on it.

Pittman has also asked Casey about the infamous Laguna arsonist Timothy Stanton Orchard, who Casey's mom wrote an article about years ago. Shown him pictures.

But Casey hasn't even thought about—let alone seen this weirdo—in years.

"I'll talk to my family is all I can say. About something written."

"Wonderful, Casey. Totally rad, as you might say."

She pats the back of his hand lightly with hers. Which pricks his burns but also sends a zing of pleasure through him. Same as when she kissed his ear on Sunset.

"I brought something to make you respect me more," she says.

Bette gives Mae another treat, then pulls a small trophy from the Halliburton and hands it to Casey. It's a brass surfer girl on a wooden stand, a brass wave behind her. Nice little two-footer, Casey sees.

"I got third in the under-twelves at Huntington one year," she says. "The waves were big, and Bethany Hamilton gave this trophy to me."

"Sweet," says Casey.

"You can have it to put with yours."

"No, you should keep it."

He sets it back in the briefcase and he sees the hurt on her face. Remembers that Bette told him she was an actor and film school graduate, too. Out here in the cool autumn sun, Bette's face looks pale and luminescent as a pearl. And her hair black and shiny as obsidian.

"I didn't mean to hurt your feelings," says Casey.

"You can't. The other reason I came is because I want to talk to you about a business arrangement. I want to help manage you."

"Manage me?"

"Your business, your money, your happiness, your life."

"But I'm already doing that."

"Casey? Let me be honest and caring. You're not doing a very good job of it."

"In exactly what way?"

"Hear me out."

28

She gives him a hard, matter-of-fact look. He can't exactly hear her wheels turning, but he's sure they are.

From the Halliburton she gives Mae another treat, then hands Casey a sheaf of papers with a fastener at the top. It looks like the purchase offer for the Barrel that the lawyer had in his briefcase, not quite hiding his gun.

He's expecting some kind of proposal about management, but as he scans through the pages he sees copies of his contracts with sponsors and contest organizers, endorsement deals, pay schedules for modeling contracts, commission agreements with an agent for the book he's writing, a Hollywood studio option for his life's story, even his first surfboard endorsement with a small Laguna Beach surfboard maker when Casey was fourteen: Lagunatic Surfboards.

Deep in the pages, Casey sees offers and proposals he hasn't had time to deal with. Or, usually, *has* had the time, but not the energy. Business makes him sleepy.

"These are some of my deals," he says. "How did you get all this?"

"Public records, Internet searches. A good private investigator is a friend, and a sharp LA lawyer is a Wu. By marriage."

"Well, now you know what I'm worth."

"That's right, and it isn't much."

"I'd say eight thousand bucks for fourth at the Pipe Masters is pretty sweet. And the twelve grand from the Locomotive Watch company for three photo shoots. And the dough from Dream Coast Clothes and World Statement Denim and Ripley's Organic Bakery isn't bad."

"But it's not good, Casey. Your non-Barrel income adds up to an average annual twenty-five thousand dollars for the last three years. Your own CaseyWear clothing line actually loses money. Without your paycheck and tips from the Barrel, you couldn't afford to surf the world. You could barely afford to live."

"No, I'm living fine. See?"

"Have you been audited?"

Casey's not-so-dormant suspicions of Bette Wu sting him like a bee. Everything a threat. She wouldn't rat him to the IRS, would she?

"Bartenders never declare all their tips. Do you?"

Casey has always been uneasy about this, but Jen and the Barrel managers and the other waitstaff have all told him that he should only declare ten percent of his tips. Max. The Feds expect it. Tips that he works hard for, in his opinion.

"You should answer me."

"Half."

"Oh, Casey. That's so like you."

He shrugs, feels dumb. "It still keeps me in a low tax bracket. I hardly pay any taxes. I get refunds sometimes."

"Who negotiates these deals for you?"

"I do. The companies like dealing with the actual surfers."

"You bet they do!"

Casey sets the financial history of his life on the table.

"Do you own this place, Casey?"

"I rent. The owner's cool so it's two grand a month, plus utilities. My truck's paid for."

"How many miles, driving that pickup truck from here to Oceanside three mornings a week to hunt down the catch of the day?"

"Two hundred forty thousand, but I change the oil every three. Those Toyotas last forever. I told them I'd love to pitch their trucks on TV or something but they never got back."

"Who did you talk to? Some guy at a dealership?"

"The sales manager."

Bette Wu clears her throat. Then slips out from the table bench and walks over to the centerpiece tangerine tree, loaded with late October fruit. "May I?" she asks, hand raised.

"Go for it."

"You, too?"

"For sure."

"How many?"

"One."

Bette takes her time, reaching up, fingering one tangerine after another. Casey pushes his suspicions of her as far away from his brain as he can get them. Enjoys a long, beautiful minute during which she has nothing to do with shark-finning, or dognapping, or real estate hustles, or arson, or trying to snake her way into his meager fortune. For that minute, doesn't even try to derail his attention away from her.

Finally she's back, sets four perfect tangerines on the table between them, and sits.

"You don't ask for as much as you should. Because you are polite and thankful. Considerate and shy. And that's why you need me as manager. To get what you are worth."

He peels a piece of the fruit, smells that unmistakable, sweet, heavy scent. They're seedless so he eats it in two bites. His favorite, ever since he was a kid and Grandpa Mike picked him and Brock tangerines off his tree up in Bluebird Canyon. They used to collect and juice them with Jen's blender, and sell them at the pullout on Laguna Canyon Road where the tourists got traffic-jammed on their way out of town in summer. Set up their card table near Rashad, the Persian rug dealer who sold from his van, and Libby, the Protea girl. Made some good coin.

"Casey? I want you to listen to me now. There is a *very* large difference between your income and your income potential. You're tenth overall in the world in men's surfing. Ninth in big-wave surfing. You're only twenty-four. You have seven hundred thousand fans on TikTok. Fifty-five thousand followers on Facebook—I mean followers, not just likes. You're up over forty thousand on Twitter, and forty thousand subscribers to your YouTube content. Subscribers, not hits. Then, the CaseyGrams and blogs on your web page, which gets more traffic every week. And the *Surf Nation* podcasts. You are an influencer, big time."

"I know there's a way to get money for all that, but I'm not sure how. A little confusing."

"Which is why you need me. Then, there's the non-social media— your television ads and billboards—your handsome face and perfect body, your magazine covers, everywhere people look, there you are. Casey, you need Seiko, not Locomotive! You need J.Crew, not Dream Coast Clothing. You need Lucky Jeans, not World Statement Denim. You don't need Ripley's Organic Bakery, you need Dunkin' Donuts— life-sized posters of you in every store in your surf trunks drinking coffee! You need to make money on CaseyWear, not lose money. And *please,* change the name."

"What's wrong with CaseyWear?"

"It's boring and too on the nose."

He shrugs. Doesn't really mind the CaseyWear handle at all.

"Look, Casey, I took film and business, and I know people in the industry, so I know how it works. Based on my Books into Film class, you should have gotten five times that advance for your book, twenty times the biopic option. Someone has to make these people feel *lucky* to pay what you're worth—and not just in today's dollars, but *tomorrow's.* That someone is me. If you win the Monsters of Mavericks, I will renegotiate your contracts. Bring you to the table with the heavy hitters. It would move you into second place on the World Surf Tour, and first in big-wave riding. Too busy surfing and fishing to manage all this? Too shy? Too cool? I understand. That's where I come in. I'm good at this kind of thing. *Better call Bette.* I always get what I want. I'll get what you deserve, Casey. And I'll take fifteen percent of everything you earn. Not counting the Barrel, of course."

Casey's brain whizzes with all this information, speculation, and what sounds like real opportunity. Makes him want to take a siesta. The five-thousand-dollar biopic option on his unwritten *The Legend of Casey Stonebreaker* has always seemed kind of low.

"Here," says Bette.

She draws another document from the briefcase, this a much shorter, stapled Agency Agreement Form from Bette Wu and Associates, an LLC with a Long Beach address that Casey recognizes as that of King Jim Seafood.

"Please do read it. If you have questions, I have answers."

"No, Bette, I'm not going to sign this."

"But then I wouldn't be your agent."

"I still don't trust you. Mae. The Barrel. A week ago you were finning sharks and now you want to run my life."

"I was *not* finning. I have never finned a shark or been cruel to any animal except the fish I catch for food. I do other things that are illegal, but never cruel. I try to survive. Maybe I'll explain them to you someday."

Casey takes a moment to look at Bette Wu, let his thumping heart settle some.

"I'm not going to sign, Bette. I like what you say about me being better at business, and I could use some help. But I don't want you as a manager. I still don't trust you all the way, and your family not one bit."

Bette cups a cool soft hand over his. "I didn't think you would sign with me. I'm hurt that you don't trust me or believe that Monterey 9 torched your restaurant *and* our boats. I don't blame you. Maybe you'll believe me when the arrests are made and you see them on the news."

"Well, maybe then, I guess."

She gives Mae another salmon-and-pumpkin treat, then collects her papers—including Casey's copy of Jimmy Wu's statement against Monterey 9—sets them in the briefcase, and latches it.

Bette gets up from the table and looks down at Casey.

"We could be a great team," she says. "Maybe someday. Maybe I can earn your trust. Maybe you will be able to see through my bluffs and my acting and fantasies to the brave, good woman inside."

Casey stands. Walks Bette in silence to his backyard gate nearly invisible in the bougainvillea, takes Mae by her collar, and pushes open the door for Bette Wu.

"Casey, I have planted the seed of truth in you. And you have not seen the last of me."

"You can't keep showing up whenever you want."

She smiles.

He nods and closes the gate.

29

But something more than just Bette Wu is bugging Casey. It's like a little present in his head, trying to give itself to him.

At his backyard picnic table, he tries to draw the black Sprinter he saw leaving the Barrel as it burned. As he sketches in the van, the unclear logo partially resolves itself in his memory and appears on the paper: a towering, white-capped mountain. Orange script at the bottom.

Nothing to do with seafood or fish.

Meaning what?

Not King Jim?

Not Imperial Fresh?

He's pretty good with pen and paper, having spent half his K–12 classroom hours sketching waves and little stick boys and girls riding them.

He completes a decent image, based on his night-vision, fire-addled, scared-to-shit memory of that night.

Casey clickety-clacks in his flip-flops down Broadway to Forest, the Laguna Beach cop house a short half mile from his Dodge City cottage, and for the second time this week lucks into Detective Brian Pittman in his cubicle.

"Interesting," says Pittman. He's an older guy, tall and slender, with thinning white hair and the suntanned, sun-lined face of a fisherman. Casey's pretty sure that Detective Pittman grew up here in Laguna. Grandpa Don said he was cool.

"You fish for the Barrel catch-of-the-day specials, don't you?" Pittman asks.

Casey nods. Studies Detective Pittman's steady gray eyes as they look down at the Sprinter sketch.

"How far away was it?" he asks.

"Hundred and fifty feet, maybe."

"Three A.M. But the streetlights there are good."

"I wouldn't have looked if it hadn't burned rubber."

Pittman nods. "Good thing you did. The security video is pretty bad."

He considers the sketch thoughtfully. Taps on his desktop keyboard and waits. Taps and waits more. Then turns the monitor toward Casey.

Where Casey sees a black Sprinter with a decal of a dramatic snow-capped mountain on the driver's side, tiny skiers gliding down it, and the words, in vivid orange lettering at the bottom:

SIERRA SPORTS
MAMMOTH LAKES CALIFORNIA

Casey's questioning blue eyes meet Pittman's questioning gray.

"What'd you get on Google?" asks Casey.

"Zip. No such place."

"Out of business?"

"Five years ago."

"What's that mean to us?"

"It's a nice little whiff to send dogs like us down the wrong trail."

"Did you talk to that fire setter? Orchard, that Mom wrote about?"

"No," says Pittman. "He's in the wind, where he likes it."

30

Friday morning Brock stands behind the pulpit of his Breath of Life Rescue Mission and looks out at his congregation. Sparse, as it often is. Twenty-six people. Only one Go Dog is here.

Brock is wearing his standard preaching uniform: red-and-green flannel pants, a yellow pineapple Aloha shirt over a long-sleeved black T-shirt, and shearling-lined boots.

The pulpit, waist-high and curving, is from a secondhand furniture store in San Bernardino. It's got a signature Brock Stonebreaker eight-foot Day-Glo green surfboard bolted upright over the aluminum cross, the arms of which peek out on either side of the gun like rays of light.

That light signifies the Breath of Life, in fact, Brock tells his motley crowd, his voice well amplified in the big cinderblock room.

"The life in my wife's breath when she brought me back from death to life, and I was blind but later saw!"

A faint murmur rises from some of the worshippers. Most of them are seated near the enormous river-rock fireplace, in the back, on Salvation Army couches and folding metal chairs. Some doze. The fire licks their faces with orange tongues. The pots on the stove bubble with venison stew, and the chafing dishes on a long picnic table offer up the smell of bacon, eggs, and potatoes, and Brother Brock knows full well that the food is a much bigger draw here on Friday mornings than he is.

As it should be.

Now he directly addresses Mahina, standing mid-room at the video and PA control board. She's in charge of sending his sermons out live to his YouTube subscribers, who number a modest 955, Brock knows.

Hoping his Internet audience is a little more aroused than these twenty-six live wires, he reads from "The Second Coming" by Yeats, then asks his followers to join him in a silent prayer, asking the Breath of Life to shine on them and inspire them to go into the world and help those in need, wherever they might be, however sick, poor, tired, cursed, hated, cold, wet, burned, hungry, wounded, or beaten down they might be. Bring them food and water and shelter and medicine. Bring them service and protection. Bring them money and love. Bring them action and energy. Bring them the Breath of Life. Bring them *something*! Our path on Earth *is* the Earth, and all the people on it!

Brock shouts out passages from Psalms, drops the Bible to his altar.

Picks up the Talmud and reads in his forceful baritone.

Slaps down the Talmud and quotes Muhammad from the Quran.

Which he sets on the stack but the holy books topple to the floor and Brock stares down at them for a moment as if unsure what to do.

He picks them up one at a time and brushes them clean on his Aloha shirt, and sets them carefully atop the altar, squaring them off for balance.

Then Brock nods to Mahina at the console, who cues up a Scottish bagpipe dirge that fills the big room with sweet, weary notes.

Which is when Right Fight leader Kasper Aamon quietly enters the church. Even with his trucker's hat in hand and his Right Fight windbreaker, he still looks to Brock like a bearded, pot-bellied bear. He's followed by six not much smaller bears, three female and three male—same jackets, caps in hand, too. They carry holstered sidearms, some up high at the belt, some low-slung and tied off like gunslingers from another century. Three of them have carbines slung over their shoulders.

Aamon nods at Brock, moves past six folding chairs not far from him, and sits.

"Welcome, dullards! What can we offer you?"

"Peace on Earth, Brother Brock," says Aamon.

"Not on the Earth I know. But welcome to the Breath of Life Rescue Mission, Aamon."

Aamon crosses one thick leg over the other, settles back into the spindly metal chair but says nothing.

Brock has Mahina cue up another Scottish bagpipe dirge, closes his eyes, and stands still behind his pulpit, letting the full, eerie notes fill the room.

Stirred by the pipes and inspired by these intruders, Brock sermonizes on the value of helping others, friends and family, for sure, but especially people you don't even know. Whoever needs. Whoever has little or nothing. Equal-opportunity rescue. Your heart turned to action, not pity, not disgust. He thinks it's a particularly good message for the visitors, these equal-opportunity complainers who hate their brothers and sisters of this world, hate the people who were on this land before them, hate their own government.

He feels like the Boss up there, by whom Brock's endless performances—some go on for nearly three hours—are inspired. He used to sing along and play air guitar to Grandpa Stonebreaker's Springsteen CDs.

With such hideous actors as Kasper Aamon and his thick-necked henchmen and -women in his audience, this morning Brock continues on for well over three hours.

At Brother Brock's invitation, most of his congregants head for the chow, fragrant and steaming hot on the scorched commercial ten-burner range donated by his mother in the recent overhaul of the torched Barrel kitchen. He asks them to keep down the noise so he can finish.

Kasper Aamon looks up at Brock, shakes his head and smiles.

Just after noon, founding member of the Breath of Life Rescue Mission Juana Flores takes her handmade Cahuilla basket from person to person, most of whom set down their paper plates and dig into their pockets.

Brock eyes the few wadded bills as Juana sets the offering on the Day-Glo green-and-black altar.

Brock, Mahina, Go Dog Ray Acuna, and Juana give Aamon and his six disciples a tour of the compound, as requested.

The day is bright and cool and Brock can hear the quail calling from the hills as they walk past the dispensary, the schoolhouse, the smoke house, the *tortilleria,* and the food pantry. Doors are open; people mill.

"These miserable squatters just take what they want?" Kasper asks.

"What they need," says Brock.

When they come to the trailers, Aamon stops and pulls the bill of his Right Fight cap down against the early afternoon sun.

Brock nods curtly to his Breath of Life flock, some of whom are clearing brush for another trailer pad. Four young boys swordfight with surveyors' stakes. A woman tends threadbare late-autumn tomato vines. Another stands on her trailer deck, sliding burgers onto a propane grill.

"How many total parasites?"

"Fuck, Kasper, they're my congregation," says Brock.

"For a total of?"

"Eighty-seven," says Juana, with a steely patience. "A new family of four next week will make it ninety-one when the trailer is ready. Isn't that wonderful, Mr. Aamon?"

"All US citizens?"

"Almost," says Juana.

"How many different races?"

"Depends how you define race," says Brock. "We've got white, Black, Hispanic, Native Americans, Pacific Islanders, Asian, and a Maori couple. Some aren't sure."

"Show us which ones live in which trailers."

Aamon's demand hits Brock Stonebreaker hard. He's surprised that

Aamon would do something this ugly and Hitleresque. Sees that he's underestimated the hatred in the man. Sees that he should never have let Kasper onto his property, into his church.

"You're done here," says Brock. "Get your ass off the property or I'll kick it off myself. That would be nice. We could do it right here, Kasper. You and me, no guns or knives, just us."

Aamon turns to his people, then back to Brock. Steps forward, leading with his beard. Gets right up in Brock's face. Aamon has an inch and probably eighty pounds on him.

"This is what we expected," Kasper says. "We've got friends here in Riverside County. Property owners, in fact. Good people. Patriots. So settle down, boy. We just want to know who we're dealing with."

Mahina draws her phone from her bright floral dress, points it at Aamon, who slaps it away into the dirt.

Brock knocks Kasper Aamon to the ground with a vicious hook, lines up a head kick but holds it.

Aamon is on his back, mouth open, out.

And the guns are out, too, all of them pointed at Brock in his lounge pants, Aloha shirt, and sheepskin boots, his dreads bristling, his fist cocked like Ali's over Liston.

Mahina videos the Right Fighters as they surround Brock, who sees that they're eager for mayhem but not sure what to do. Like the first rioters into the Capitol, he thinks. Two kneel over their leader, a young man and a braided, dark-haired woman who pours a plastic bottle of drinking water over Aamon's bear-like face.

He gasps, sputters, and coughs. Wails in pain.

"Get out, simpletons," says Brock. "The next time you show up we won't be so friendly."

Two big men lift Kasper Aamon by his armpits. He backpedals, his bootheels kicking up gravel.

"Next time you won't know what hit you," slurs Kasper. His jaw is already swelling; a trail of blood runs from one ear.

Brock and his people and his trailer-park citizens watch the Right Fighters guide their wobbly leader past the trailers, toward the cinderblock chapel, and into the big gravel parking lot. The boys with their stake swords watch, too, two of them calling out names and threats.

A moment later Brock sees Aamon's red Suburban and another SUV raising dust down the dirt road toward the highway.

Knows they'll be back and wonders when.

And how many Go Dogs he'd need to repel them.

"He is a danger and a monster," says Mahina. "You must understand this now. No matter you drink beers with him in high school. No matter he was in your grandpa Pastor Mike's church once. And Mike told you that he is worthy of forgiveness. Kasper Aamon loves hate. You love Breath of Life. Opposite people. Protect us here, Brock. Don't let the snakes back in."

"If we don't believe a man can change, then our Mission is just a façade without meaning."

"Don't let evil win."

"We let the Breath win."

Later that day, exhausted by his three-hour sermon and his sudden violence over Kasper Aamon, Brock excuses himself from family and congregants, and makes the walk into the stout hills that shelter the eastern flank of his property.

Here, in a deep swale surrounded by manzanita and toyon, he sits cross-legged near a spring that feeds a tiny creek that trickles down toward the compound. At night this time of year, the swale is filled with the croaking of tree frogs, but now it's quiet except for the occasional cricket and the pleasant chirping of the quail coveys hidden throughout this rough country.

Except for when he's surfing a very large wave, this little spring is where Brock feels the Breath of Life at its strongest and most consistent.

A hot spot for the Breath of Life, valuable because . . .

The Breath of Life can be evasive.

The Breath of Life can be temperamental.

The Breath of Life is not always available.

He closes his eyes and lets the fall sun warm his eyelids. Lets in that burnished orange light.

The Breath of Life, he thinks: come into me again.

Time glides and thoughts dissolve, leaving him in the blackness of that three-wave hold-down at Nazaré, caught inside after a punishing wipeout. Leaving him with those three sixty-foot beasts thundering over him, and finally stomping out his consciousness.

Until Mahina breathed it back into him.

Now, when he regains his consciousness in the dream—and in the swale—it's not Mahina's voice but the ringtone on his phone that Brock hears.

It's Marlon from Surfline again, texting that the rare early season swell heaving toward Mavericks is right on time for arrival six days from now. Right now it's the purple blob on the map, denoting a potential storm-driven swell. They're calling it FreakZilla, Marlon says, and it's the biggest northwest swell he's seen since the four-trawler destructo just outside the Pillar Point Harbor breakwater twelve years ago. Which turned Mavericks into an unrideable wind-blasted blowout with waves at seventy feet. The four-trawler swell had arrived at Half Moon Bay as a twenty-four-foot, eighteen-second-interval behemoth, and right now, FreakZilla is bigger, and faster.

So it looks like the Monsters is going to happen, soon.

Over and out, brah.

Brock messages his mom and brother:

Four-trawler time. Game on.

31

Of course, Bette Wu does show up whenever she wants, in this case just after sunrise at Oceanside Harbor where Casey is backing *Moondance* down the ramp into the bay.

A dockhand aboard *Moondance* reverses her into deeper water and swings the boat toward the loading docks, where Casey and Mae can board.

Casey punches his truck up the ramp and heads for his parking spot, fully surprised by Bette, the pirate/dognapper/failed extortionist/possible arsonist/amateur actor/wannabe filmmaker and business partner, standing in his usual parking place up by the cleaning sinks and tables.

She's got a laptop cradled on one hip and a fist balled on the other. Back in her pirate uniform, he sees, the black nylon cargo pants and the windbreaker she was wearing when she boarded *Moondance,* the yellow gaiter around her neck. No gun. Barefoot again.

Casey honks her out of his way, pulls into his spot, and gets out.

"I doubt you've seen this," she says.

She sets her laptop on the cleaning table and swings open the touch screen. Scrolls down.

"Today's *Los Angeles Times*," she says. "Back in the California section."

Casey peers at the page as Bette taps a story and it fills the screen.

Reputed Gang Members Arrested
in Laguna Beach Restaurant Arson

Two alleged members of the Monterey 9 criminal organization were charged with arson yesterday in the fire that badly damaged the Barrel Restaurant in Laguna Beach ten days ago.

Glen Lee, 24, and Roy Song, 30, were arrested in their homes without incident, and booked into Los Angeles County Jail. They pled not guilty and were released on $100,000 cash bonds.

"My clients are one hundred percent innocent of this baseless charge," said Bob Gold, defense attorney for the men. "They were nowhere near Laguna Beach the night of the fire. It's ludicrous. Just another instance of anti-Asian sentiment sweeping this country."

Explosive devices with accelerants were used on a night of high Santa Ana winds, igniting fires that destroyed much of the popular restaurant.

LBFD response was quick, and damage to surrounding buildings was slight.

"We are almost done demolishing our beloved Barrel," said owner Jen Stonebreaker. "We'll be open again by summer of next year. They tried to break our hearts but they did not."

Laguna Beach Police Department detectives and Los Angeles Police Department arson investigators have been cooperating in the investigation.

"We've been working full time on this since the second the flames were put out," said Laguna PD Detective Brian Pittman.

Casey's a slow but thorough reader. He glances at Bette, who has come in close to read along, then back down to the article. She taps a long, slender finger on the names Glen Lee and Roy Song.

"Imperial Fresh Seafood—backed by Monterey 9. Just as I said."

Finishing the article, Casey feels big emotions surging up against each other inside him. Surprise. Doubt. Relief. Suspicion. Joy?

He says, "Woah, this is heavy."

"I told you we were innocent. My dad. King Jim Seafood. All of us. *Me!*"

"I still don't see why these guys would burn up the Barrel."

"To punish enemies," says Bette. "The old way of the underworld. Of gangs and tongs and blood feuds."

She kneels and hugs Mae. "*And* I would never hurt your dog. *And* our offer to buy the Barrel was honest and sincere. Low? Yes, low. But we doubled to four million. We negotiate in good faith. Generous terms for your family and all employees. You have us wrong, Casey. One huge mistake."

She draws a salmon-and-pumpkin treat from her windbreaker pocket and Mae snatches it with a snort.

Bette rises and gives him a frank look. Even barefoot, she's not a lot shorter than six-two Casey. He wonders if she played basketball for UCLA. In this damp, early morning light, her skin is smooth and moist and her black bangs hang thick above her ebony eyes. Not a scar, Casey thinks. Not a mole or a blemish.

Not that that means what you are inside.

And not a line on her face, until she smiles.

"I thought you'd be happy to know who burned your restaurant." She brushes a lock of Casey's thick blond hair off his forehead. "And maybe if I present myself better, you might let me help you with your businesses and finance. Maybe become your partner someday. Maybe become a friend."

Suddenly, Casey feels . . . empty.

Because everything he thought about Bette and her pirates, and her father, was wrong. *Probably* wrong. The pirates were shark finners, for sure. Ugly stuff. But not Bette, right? The pirates shot up his burner phone and scared the shit out of him but Bette never drew her gun, and it was right there on her hip. Yes, Bette tried to leverage Mae into their offer for the Barrel, but she never laid a finger on her. Jimmy tried to buy the Barrel cheap, but he didn't burn it up.

Empty, when what you think is true is actually not.

But he feels weirdly . . . filled up, too.

With total positivity. *Bette a friend? Who helps me figure out how to increase my "earning potential"?*

This woman isn't really a shark finner, a Mae-napper, a real-estate hustler, or arsonist? Isn't a major criminal at all? She's a choice woman who kissed my ear on Sunset and said she thinks I'm smart?

Slam the door on *her*?

Gulls keen overhead. Mae sits and looks up at them.

Bette has already shown him the LA sheriff's report filed by her father, accusing rival Imperial Fresh of torching his fleet. She has told him that she believes him, that the Stonebreakers did no such thing. Suspects the Monterey 9 of escalating their attack on the Wu family and King Jim Seafood.

Logical enough, thinks Casey, but the facts weigh heavily on him, and on his morals and honesty. They're both lying. Two big fudging lies, but can he spill his?

Out of the question, not on the table.

His guts tighten but he's keeping his secret. For now. He was against the dang King Jim boat attacks anyway but he's got his family and Brock's Go Dogs to protect.

"Your words sound good, Bette. You tempt me with how smart and beautiful you are."

She blushes slightly, a pink undercurrent swelling up beneath her perfect white skin. He wonders if she can do this on cue. The acting classes.

"I don't want to tempt. I want to help."

"But I still don't want a manager now," he says. "Signing those papers. That whole fifteen percent commission thing. No."

"Then let the whole thing go!"

"Maybe if, like . . ."

"Seriously, Casey."

She spreads her arms, hands balled tightly, then closes her eyes and opens her fists. "I let it go. There it goes. You should, too. Now."

"Okay."

Lowers her arms, opens her eyes and studies him. "I didn't know how you would react to this news. But I'm glad you don't hate me. The first step toward trust."

He pulls his phone from his shorts pocket, leaves text messages for Jen and Brock. *See the California section in today's* LA Times. *Looks like we might have made a mistake.*

Mae looks out at *Moondance* tied to the loading dock.

"I'll be seeing you, Casey."

Casey feels a nervy little rush, something forbidden but good, then:

"The bluefin are still in. Interested?"

The swell is steady and the chop is mean but by eleven thirty Casey and Bette have each caught a bluefin tuna weighing eighty-eight and eighty-three pounds, respectively.

"Glad I beat you," he says, half seriously.

"Mine will taste better," she says with a quick grin.

They drag the fish to preserve the quality of the best sashimi in the world, and an hour later clean and ice them in the cold well.

Casey watches her all he can without staring; admires her easy work with the rod and line, her strength and balance fighting the powerful fish, her wordless concentration on the task at hand, her swift, efficient knife work. Liked the way she helped him rope his fish in without the gaff, and was happy to help her do the same.

After hers, they sat panting, facing each other across the bait tank.

"You're strong and coordinated, Bette. You a baller in college?"

"Too busy."

"Being a pirate and a student?"

"Mostly student. I got bored and dropped out. Dad made me work. He was happy to have me back in the family business."

"Back?"

"Started at eleven. Cutting bait, mending nets."

"Were you happy to be back?"

"I like it okay. The ocean and the freedom and the money. Pretty good. I owe almost twenty grand in loans—not to the school, to Dad. He holds me to it. Holds me to a lot of things. But King Jim Seafood, we're together, you know? Like a family. Kind of. We got different races. Different languages and beliefs. But we work hard and we have each other's backs."

"Sounds good."

"Your hands and clothes get stinky, though. And you don't stay in bed. I get up in the dark six days a week."

"That's tough. Me, only three, maybe four. I just have one restaurant to supply, not a whole coastline full like you guys. I can sleep an hour in the late afternoon, before I bartend."

Bette gives him an indecipherable look, then a small smile. "You're a good bartender. I gave you a big tip."

"You came in because you recognized me?"

"From a magazine ad for CaseyWear. And your socials. I was with friends. You had a lot of customers at your bar that night."

"For happy hour."

"Oh come on, you handsome surfer celebrity!" Bette says, smiling. "Be truthful with yourself. And me."

A few minutes later Casey tucks into a cove on the eastern side of San Clemente Island, at least as close to the island as he can get without getting run out by Navy gunboats. Sometimes the sailors are cool; sometimes they board *Moondance* and check the hatches and holds and tanks for contraband. Once in a while he'll see the cannon and mortar shells suddenly booming on the island, or fighter jets bellowing in low, mangling the barren hills with rockets. Now and then he'll see a herd of wild goats up on the grassy flats, hundreds of chewing faces looking down at him.

Casey shares his lunch with her: two peanut butter and honey sandwiches, two nectarines, a slab of grilled tuna, two chocolate protein drinks.

They sit in the cabin, eating in silence, giving Mae bits of everything. She likes nectarines. *Moondance* bobs at anchor and the gulls badger them overhead. The fog is long gone and the day is clear, with the westerlies cool from the stern.

"You worried about them seeing you here?" he asks.

"Would not be good."

Casey sees a shadow cross her face, looks up but the sky is cloudless. "What would they do?"

"My father has a big temper. Lacks control of himself. But tries to control others. Family especially."

"Violent?"

"Sometimes. My sister no longer speaks to him. Moved to New York City to get away. My mother left him years ago."

"But not to you?"

Bette shakes her head but says nothing.

When the food is gone Mae heads for a sunny spot on deck, circles it twice, then plops down.

Another silence. Bette has her back to him, facing east toward shore.

Casey divvies up some bread crust and backhands the load to the gulls patrolling his boat. He likes having someone around but not having to talk. Bartending, you just babble for hours at a time. Enough small talk in one shift to last all week. Plus it's just hard to hear in the Barrel sometimes—anywhere, for that matter—his years in cold water and wind giving him a growing case of surfer's ear, abnormal bone growth in the ear canal.

"I want to talk to you about something important," says Bette.

So much for golden silence. "You mean right now?"

"I can help you win the Monsters of Mavericks. Listen. There's a large swell headed for Half Moon Bay. It's freaky early for the storm season."

"I know."

"I talked with the contest organizers. If the storm stays on course for Half Moon Bay, the Monsters of Mavericks will be held seven days from now. The waves will be very big. I have reserved separate rooms at the Ritz-Carlton. You need to get there days early, to see the waves and the conditions. To do media, write your CaseyGrams, and post your YouTube videos. You need to rest, mingle with the other surfers, but keep your privacy. Not be over-socialized. You need to eat well and mentally prepare. You need to relax and think about surfing and not surfing. Read your Bible. I'll drive. When we get there, you won't have to be around me in any way. I'll give you total privacy. Separate everything. We should leave the day after tomorrow. Take our time and not feel rushed."

Casey's first thought is *Woah, that sounds really good.*

His first thought and a half is of his mom and brother. Bringing Bette to the Monsters would be a major betrayal, even if they fully believed that Monterey 9 was behind the Barrel. Wouldn't it?

"My family would freak out."

"Mine, too. Let them. You know this would be good for you. I would simply be your guest, your companion, your driver, your fixer, your protector."

Casey feels the tingle of sweat on his scalp, like the outrageousness of this idea is heating him up and spilling out.

"Mom and Brock might not believe that article, Bette. They might believe it was Jimmy who did the Barrel. They'll remember what he said about fire."

"He's a show-off and a fool, Casey! You've seen him enough to get that!"

At Bette's rising voice, Mae raises her head and gives them a look. Then hoists herself from the sunny spot, lumbers over, and sits at Casey's feet.

"Yeah. I get that."

A beat while Casey tries to find a way that showing up in Half Moon Bay with Bette Wu would not infuriate Jen and Brock. Is he underestimating them? Is it his duty as a man to stand up for someone he's begun to see as innocent?

"But maybe, Stonebreaker, they'll see that we are a good combination. Maybe they'll come to believe that King Jim Seafood had nothing to do with the Barrel—as I have promised on my soul is true. Maybe—with your acceptance of my companionship—they will give me a chance. Maybe the truth will have to be enough for them. Maybe you should trust your judgment above theirs. You can show them a truth they can't see for themselves. You are twenty-four and a man of intelligence and high moral ambitions. Don't underestimate yourself."

Casey tries to think all this over in his plodding, one-fact-at-a-time way. It's the "ors" that trip him up. And the "ifs" and the "maybes." It's always taken him a long time to weigh things and set his course. Brock, it's always taken him about two seconds.

"I have good feelings for you, Stonebreaker. I know you have good feelings for me."

He looks at her, feels his blush, nods. Never could keep his emotions off his face.

"Why would you do all that for me?"

"I want you to win. I want you to become, and be recognized as, the best big-wave surfer in the world."

"I'm barely number ten, Bette."

"Not if you win the Monsters."

"I want Brock to win it."

"Fine. So long as that doesn't change the way you surf."

"No, I just surf all out. Everything I have goes into it."

"That's why you need calm and peace in Half Moon Bay. The adrenaline alone is enough to tire you. Stay inside yourself. I'll build an invisible wall around you. Only good thoughts can get in. If you want, I'll be invisible myself."

"Sounds cosmic," he says, thinking it sounds pretty good, too.

"And, Casey? I also want you to win because I've bet two thousand dollars on you. I'll be protecting my investment. You're paying out four to one. The big money is on the nineteen-year-old from—"

"Tom Tyler. Santa Cruz." Tyler is the best nineteen-year-old big-wave rider he's ever seen. Maybe *the* best, period.

"Woah. Is that BetUS, online?"

"No. It's a strip mall sports book in the San Gabriel Valley. Nails, massage, too. Don't ask where."

Casey pictures his mother's face when he walks into the restaurant where most of the surfers and their teams and friends and family meet the evening before the contest—Barbara's Fish Trap.

Walks in with Bette Wu, that is.

Now that's a painful expression, he thinks.

Brock's is even worse.

Casey stares long and appraisingly at Bette. She purses her lips, widens her eyes, and turns away like she's been caught at something. Casey's long stares have always worried people for as long as he can remember—icy blue eyes that they tell him look cold and removed between blinks, which slow down to almost none.

The cold blue eyes mean he's thinking, though, his plodding calculations proceeding within.

Bette Wu didn't dognap Mae to hurt her. Bette and her family didn't burn up the Barrel.

I want this.

I want her with me for the Monsters.

Mom? Bro?

Believe in me.

"I always stay at the Oceano in Half Moon, with Mom and Brock and Mahina," he says. "Some of my friends will be there. I leave Mae home."

"But the Ritz would give you privacy and set you apart as a celebrity surfer, not part of the pack."

"I *want* to be part of the pack. Even though some of them think I'm a spoiled Orange County brat."

"Okay, I'll book the Oceano instead."

Casey gives Bette another long, calm, blue-eyed assessment. But this time Bette shows no unease at all, just an equally delivered, analytical return of serve: a nod.

"I'll profit handsomely if you do what I know you can do. You'll take home fifty thousand grand-prize dollars if you win. By the way, my gambling instincts have always been very good."

"I'll surf good," he says.

"My father won't be happy about you and me doing business together," says Bette. "He'll hate me, temporarily. I've known for a while that I need to break away from him. From King Jim Seafood. From all of what being a part of the Wu family is. You are my harbor, Casey. My berth."

She reaches over and squeezes Casey's big warm hand with her own cool and smooth one. He feels a rare, crazy heat inside, spreading from his hand to his heart, then out to everywhere. Who'd have thought that after twenty-plus years in cold oceans his ears could burn this hot? His face? All of him?

"We share a fatal illness, Stonebreaker."

"Which one? There's lots of them."

"Time," she says.

32

WHO WAS JOHN STONEBREAKER AND WHAT WENT WRONG AT MAVERICKS?

BY JEN STONEBREAKER

Part four of a special series for *Surf Tribe Magazine*

In late December, a long-expected but devious winter swell bypassed Half Moon Bay and landed south.

Postponing the Monsters of Mavericks left fifty of us surfers huddled under tents in the rain at the Pillar Point landing, teeth chattering, all suited up but nowhere to go.

I counted twelve boats tied up and waiting in the water, ten trailered jet skis waiting to be unleashed, a bevy of photogs and videographers, writers and rescue teams. Lots of terse jokes and forced optimism. *I can feel her turning around,* John said, meaning the fugitive swell, but making me think of the miscarriage. Luckily, another storm-generated swell was forming—a potentially stronger one at this point—up on latitude 38, full of silence and possible fury.

ETA at Mavericks: twelve days.

Christmas Eve, sitting with John in his father's impressive, new

Hillview Chapel in Laguna Hills, I listened to the hymns and Christmas standards, watched the procession to the manger with real sheep and costumed shepherds, all part of Pastor Mike's quaint and scented Christmas Eve service, which drew sellout crowds every year.

I sat in the pew with my reindeer scarf still around my neck, a bit of a cold since the Mavericks false alarm, one hand on John's knee. I sang the hymn lyrics projected alongside the stained-glass windows that flanked Pastor Mike's stately mahogany and mother-of-pearl pulpit. He was in great form, expansive and filled with the inner light that looked so good through him, especially on video. When we closed our eyes in prayer and Pastor Mike thanked the Lord for His blessings and asked Him to help us use them wisely, I asked the God of whom I was skeptical to give me once again the child who visited and left me, like a ghost.

With the monster swell stalled in the Northwest Pacific, but hungry for diversion, John and I went to a New Year's Eve party out in Laguna Canyon.

The party was mostly older, drug-enthused people, everybody high and chipper, stoned on weed, dodging into rooms for the edgier stuff—you know the scene.

And it surprised me to find myself here, because I didn't know many of these people and didn't do drugs, and John didn't either. I wondered why he'd accepted the invite without talking to me. I still let him keep our social calendar in those days. And our travel, training, and finances, too. Happy to. I was surfing and writing and he was more than I could keep up with. My orbit was busy and secure. A happy Earth to his sun.

The only person I really knew was Ronna Dean, who spun me around from behind and threw her arms around me. Hadn't seen her in years.

She looked even prettier now, same golden skin and thatch of honey hair, same cagey smile and skeptical brown eyes. Dressed in a tailored black Western tux with red front yokes and plenty of rhinestones, she looked like a Nashville headliner.

She caught me up on her music in LA, mostly touring with artists I knew of—lots of work but decent money. And between tours she got time gratis from Cherokee Studio in Hollywood—best in the world, she said. Cherokee thought Ronna's bluesy, vulnerable voice was something that *everyone* should hear. Even got herself a sponsorship from Taylor Guitars, which was giving her "the most sweet-ass acoustics" she'd ever played.

"I'm going to do a short set tonight," she said. "And you, Jen? I know you're big-waving now, up for the Monsters if they can get some waves. How do you ride those things?"

"Carefully," I said.

I caught her up on the big-wave circuit, about John getting up to number five in the world on the surf tour, told her I was writing for newspapers, and helping Mom coach the girls' water sports teams at the high school. I downplayed my modest successes, aware of how hard Ronna had taken it when I won the Miss Laguna pageant. Even then I knew she was prettier, more outgoing and talented than I'd ever be. I thought I saw that smiling disappointment still in her—rock star in the making that she obviously was.

"Johnny Angel!" Ronna said, waving him over. It was a girlhood nickname we'd taken from a corny old song Mom used to like. We used to giggle at.

John looked through the weed smoke layering down from the ceiling like fog, and started his way toward us.

One of Laguna's young newspaper photographers did a slide show on the home-theater screen, focusing on the departing years' highlights and personalities. Plenty of beaches, waves, and sunsets. Warm, sun-blushed pictures of the town where I was born, the town I loved, where I went to school and learned to surf and fell in love. Was married, and intended to raise my family. Where I would scatter Mom's and Dad's ashes, and die myself someday.

My Shangri-La.

Having been tipped that John and I would be here, the photographer included some of his most recent pictures of us: John, carving up a stormy Rockpile right, daring that frothing lip to knock him off.

Me, locked in a Thousand Steps barrel, then rifling out in a blast of spray.

Me, as Miss Laguna, in my blue formal dress and gold sash, holding roses—which brought hoots and whistles from the stoned partygoers. I was embarrassed. Don't know why, because I was never embarrassed to *be* Miss Laguna. But I was surprised at how long ago that seemed, how innocent and young I looked. Three years!

Ronna took the stage after the photo show.

Voice like a fallen angel, and the guitar was a living, breathing instrument in her hands, "Romeo and Juliet" a hopeful, streetwise lament.

The overhead lights caught the sparkle in her eyes, and the amp threw her voice into the room like a handful of rough diamonds.

"Bringing Out the Elvis."

"Angel from Montgomery."

"Blue Rodeo," written and recorded by Cat Parker, a friend of ours who had passed on:

> *Come on shoot us a star*
> *Play some guitar*
> *So we can find where you are*
> *In the blue rodeo . . .*

I loved these songs. Beautiful things, straight from the heart. During that set I felt alone with her, happily trapped in a small room, the notes falling on me like stars. I wasn't worried about the child who had come to me, then left, or the swell that might or might not come, or the giant waves I'd be trying to ride, or money, or the article I was writing for the *LA Times.*

The songs took me away.

Later, John went back to the theater to watch himself in some Tahiti surfing videos he'd never seen. John loved surf movies with him as the star, as almost all surfers do. It's vanity, sure, but it's also a way of seeing yourself as you never do when riding a wave. Another adrenaline-charged moment. Another high. And a way of learning, too.

But I wasn't in the mood for enormous waves. I suspected I'd be seeing plenty of those soon enough.

So I hung around the steaming backyard swimming pool, where hired bartenders circulated through the crowd with trays, serving big-bowl "midnight margaritas" made from "secret ingredients." At midnight, we counted down and sang "Auld Lang Syne." Our singing voices were bold and a bit wobbly by then. Our hosts lit against-the-law firecrackers on the pool deck, those snaky black ones that wiggle and smoke. I took a rare hit of grass off a hookah, and moments later was high beyond my experience. Felt like my horizontal hold was gone, and I was falling facedown and bouncing up, falling facedown and bouncing up, over and over—even though I was standing still. Flashes of color, floaters of light. Fragments of conversations, the words stretching and reforming like rubber. I found it incredibly funny when people—some fully clothed and some only in their underwear or less—started jumping into the pool. Someone pushed me in, so I purged most of my air and sank to the bottom and sat there in the overheated water, legs extended like an infant, blowing bubbles and watching them burst at the silver-blue surface. My denim pantsuit felt rough as shark skin. The deep-end pool light studied me—a monster's eye. I wondered if John was enjoying his videos.

They had good towels for us New Year's Eve party animals, so I got my long down coat from a rack in the foyer, wrung out my suit in the pool-house bathroom, ran my brush through my hair, and set out to find my husband.

Later, I found out that the midnight margaritas were laced with LSD and peyote, and the hookah weed with opium, and pharmaceutical cocaine supplied by a Laguna ear, nose, and throat specialist whose daughter was on our water polo team.

Some of our core Laguna surfers were in the theater toking up, the videos done and John gone. I sat down for a minute and watched the lights and colors on the projection screen. Eavesdropped on the surfers, loose-jawed and a little slurring as surfers can be, but with that stoked hopefulness we almost always have. It's all about tomorrow. The next wave.

I went room to room, looking for John. The house was a three-story custom that climbed a steep hillside, and you could see the ocean from all the windows and the stairway landings. If I could afford a home in Laguna it would be something like this. I looked at myself in the mirror of a well-lit second-floor bathroom, and saw this almost cute chick with a pale green face and a bowl of orange hair on her head. Set one hand over the bottom of that bowl and lifted, seeing if it was attached. I leaned over and splashed some water on my face to sober up, but it sparkled musically going down the drain and I thought I heard a melody in it, so I let my face just hang there in the sink, watching the music go down.

Nobody on the third floor except behind a closed door, from which came the grunts and whimpers of Human Reproduction 101.

Muted and urgent.

A bump and a gasp.

A moan I knew.

John.

And—I realized, through a psychedelic and powerful surge of nausea—Ronna.

Of course, with my senses addled and perceptions blurred, I had to see.

So I shut myself in a catercorner hall bathroom, turned off the light, and left the door ajar.

Five minutes later John strode past, and five minutes after that, Ronna.

The longest ten minutes in sports.

I locked the door, ran the faucet, then turned and knelt on the cold tile, felt the foul surge rush out, splashing toilet water and vomit onto my face.

When the second wave of nausea ended, I rinsed in the sink, then zipped my long down coat up to my chin, and sat on the john.

Betrayed.

Hung on a noose of innocence.

One chapter concluded and another about to begin.

Over the next few days, John was as attentive and affectionate as he'd ever been, fueled by guilt and the brittle comfort that he had gotten away with something. He smiled more than usual, a sheepish, apologetic thing in which I also saw pity, which infuriated me.

I was a moody wreck but hid it. Threw myself into my weightlifting and breath-control exercises for the Monsters of Mavericks. Spent extra hours in the ocean, wrestling the jet ski through the local waves and whitewater, trying to master that eight-hundred-pound brute. Sometimes I'd head into the open sea and gun the throttle, cutting a straight line across the ocean, fast as the ski would go, pretending I was outrunning John's betrayal. Outrunning John himself. Leaving him behind in the smoky roar of the machine.

Two nights after the New Year's Eve party in the canyon, I led John into our bedroom and made love to him. It was heartbroken and powerful, and left me in tears. I wouldn't let him go and we made love again, this time long and sweetly desperate for me. He told me he was sorry though he didn't say for what.

Lying there after, I knew I'd catch that wandering spirit again, that life that had been trying to find a home inside me.

I knew it. Felt it.

Smiled as I lay there, listening to John's soft, slow breathing.

John's breath of life.

All ours.

33

This from Brawn, the latest far-right social platform that Brock figures will be out of business in a year:

> Kasper Aamon #kasperaamonrightfight
> The devil broke my jaw yesterday at the Breath of Life Rescue Mission in Aguanga, CA when I asked Brother Brock Stonebreaker how many illegals were living there. Ninety-two, and hardly a white face among them. Ugly, dark people picking the lice off each others' backs. A fake sermon by a madman with rabies. Stay away! Or...?

Brock sits at one end of a gray-and-blue plaid Salvation Army couch in the mild morning sunlight outside his Breath of Life chapel. He's got his phone out, trading punches with his enemies. Months ago, he got tired of the Right Fight and other creeps hounding him on his website and Twitter page so he dove right into the sewer with them on Brawn, where he can always find a fight if he's in the mood.

He's also got a tablet beside him, with live Mavericks cameras on Surfline.com. Right now the surf is flat, gray, no swell, just windy chop and pelicans diving into a school of anchovies. But FreakZilla—freakishly early for sure—is forming more strongly now, its speed and

width growing, but its path still open to interpretation. Brock studies the NOAA Data Center maps: impressive. Surfline is bullish on the swell hitting Half Moon Bay; NOAA cautious. Brock's gut tells him it's going to be big, very big. Possible ETA at Half Moon Bay is 120 hours: five days from now. A key reading of the Southeast Papa buoy in Oregon currently has a twenty-six-foot, nineteen-second swell. A swell that big, with a nineteen-second interval, Brock knows, means very large, once-in-a-decade surf—if it stays on course.

Storms upon storms, Brock thinks.

Mahina's at the other end of the sofa with the current weekend edition of *USA Today.*

Brock looks at Kasper Aamon's very swollen face on the Brawn feed. It looks plenty painful but Brock's heart doesn't exactly go out to Kasper. Fucking Nazis trying to hurt my people, he thinks: Kristallnacht '38.

#brockstonebreaker1

Kasper, you say such nice things about me, but you deserve what you got! You were armed, threatening, and trespassing on church property. Stay away is right. And what does "stay away!...Or?" really mean? Going to send more Right Fighters out our way? Hey, dim bulb, there's a wildfire in Flagstaff, uncontained, evacuations. Why don't you ice that jaw, join us Go Dogs and HELP! Plenty of white people there who need a hand up!

#timothy.45rightfight

You can tell from Brock Stonebreaker's YouTubes that he's an oily fool spoiling for a fight. Look at those greasy dreadlocks! If I see you in Mt. Shasta I'll break your jaw and tear out those dreads with my teeth, one filthy little bundle at a time. After that, you can crawl over and pick up your balls in the gutter.

#wardblock214

You lice pickers! Do you eat them like monkeys do?

Brock looks at Wardblock214's picture. He's a hairy, glaring guy in a plaid flannel, an iron cross pendant peeking out below his beard. Looks something like Kasper. Brock likes the Brawn graphics because they're

big, and he can clearly see the faces of his critics. Sometimes the faces match the message. But sometimes the posters look nothing like what they say.

Such as this sweet-faced blonde behind big, flame-red glasses:

#joanofdark187

Nothing worse than a false savior. The Brock Stonebreakers of the world should be excommunicated and burned at the stake. I'll pour the gas and light it myself. And shoot him on my smart phone, screaming, his nappy little locs on fire. Motherfucking traitor to his race.

#brockstonebreaker1

Joan! Bring all of your positive energy to Flagstaff! We need you! Bring water, food, clothing, blankets, camping stuff, money! If you don't have wheels, Go Dogs will pick you up!

#kittybitch

Hang the President. Eat his lips.

Brock considers Kittybitch's sullen face, her storm of red hair. Doesn't know what to say back.

He checks Arizona Wildfire, figuring it's going to take him and Mahina six and a half hours to make Flagstaff. The Go Dog Econoline is packed to the rafters with supplies, and its tank is full. The latest containment numbers are eight hundred acres, zero percent contained.

Brock watches both Kupchiks, checking the tires and changing the oil in his battered, black-and-green Go Dog van.

Closes the laptop and sets a big dark hand on Mahina's warm shoulder.

He's got the mission but he hates to leave.

Breath of Life.

Protect and serve.

"I'm going to get some Go Dogs out here while we're gone," he says.

"Kasper?" asks Mahina.

"Yeah. Kasper. I need to take better care of our people."

"It's why we are," says Mahina, setting her big paw on his. "But we might miss the Monsters."

"Flagstaff is more important. I love you," he says.

"*Aloha wau ia 'oe,* Stonebreaker."

Stan Kupchik, his body curved like a question mark, drops the heavy little hood of the Econoline and waves.

Juana Flores and a passel of children—the new Kupchiks among them—come down the road from the trailers, one of the older ones kicking a soccer ball against three determined, smaller opponents. Some are on bikes or trikes. The compound dogs bound and circle and zigzag along with them, all headed for the reservoir, led by Juana.

34

Three days later, Jen, Casey, Brock, and Mahina huddle around a table in Barbara's Fish Trap, Half Moon Bay's most popular restaurant. It's cold inside, but packed with customers, the waitstaff bustling between the tiny kitchen and the dining room.

Jen's mother and father—Eve and Don—are there. As are Pastor Mike and Marilyn Stonebreaker, who flew into Half Moon Bay just an hour ago and drove to the Ritz-Carlton.

FreakZilla is arriving tomorrow, as predicted by NOAA, Surfline, the National Weather Service, and other big-wave prophets around the globe. The heart of it, with the biggest surf, is expected for late morning the day after. There's no doubt the swell is coming. The question is how big and exactly when. NOAA says it's a thirty-foot swell, which means fifty-foot faces, with clean-up waves possibly bigger. The biggest worry now is not the waves, but the wind.

Barbara's is packed with Monsters surfers eager to compete. Jen knows at least half of them. Both the men and women wear their big-wave, cold-weather uniforms—beanies and hoodies or puffer jackets with fur, thermal shirts, flannel lounge or ski pants, and shearling boots.

Jen looks out a window toward the bay, where a firm, cold breeze drives little whitecaps toward shore. If it whips up strong and doesn't change direction, she thinks, it'll blow out the waves and it's adios, Monsters.

But none of this wave worry has rocked Jen Stonebreaker's soul as hard as the arrival of Bette Wu, now being seated by Casey, who holds out the chair opposite his mother. Bette's dressed like the surfers—in a Rasta beanie, an orange CaseyWear hoodie, snug black pants, and boots with puffs of shearling below her knees.

Before sitting, Bette waves and looks at each person around the table, then slings her purse over the seat back.

"Hi, everybody," she says. "I'm Bette Wu, Casey's friend and business associate."

Jen barely hears it, but half the crowd cheers, and there's a few hearty *whoops*. The other diners are silent, having seen Casey's videos—now taken down from his feeds—that show this Bette Wu working with shark finners, and illegal fishermen and -women, and maybe having something to do with Casey's dog disappearing. And that suspicion about her family burning down the restaurant.

Jen knows she should just get up and walk out, or maybe—just *maybe* reach across the narrow table and shake her hand. But she can't move. Just like she couldn't move her hand on the jet ski throttle for the split second she took that day twenty-five years ago, when she paused to tell John that she loved him.

Is this a waking nightmare? Is this really her naïve and beautiful son Casey, bringing a criminal into his life? Into *hers*?

She looks at him in numb disbelief. Sees the shame on his face.

Fact is: Jen doesn't view the arrests of the Monterey 9 arson suspects as a vindication of Jimmy Wu. Not by a long shot. Jimmy might not have lit up the Barrel but he definitely tried to buy it for a pittance, to extort her acceptance by threatening her son's fucking dog. And who knows—what if the Monterey 9 guys were hired by "rival" Jimmy? Or even framed by him?

And Jen sure didn't view Bette's threats against Mae as forgiven, just because Casey vouched, very emotionally, for Bette's "misunderstood intentions" and "saying things she didn't mean." Casey, god bless him, actually had *tears* in his beautiful ice-blue eyes.

Now she's his *friend*?

Not on my watch.

She stares at Casey but he won't meet her eyes. Bette gives her a humble, lips-pursed kind of look, which Jen does not answer.

Brock looks amused. He stands and nods, reaches across the table, and shakes Bette's hand. Jen takes his betrayal almost as hard as she does Casey's. A smile parts his dark, hard face and his locs sprout and glisten.

"So we meet again," says Brock.

"A lot has happened."

Jen knows she should do the same, just shake the pirate's hand, make peace long enough for her sons to fully and wholly compete with the immense, now-inevitable FreakZilla.

Pastor Mike stands and clears his throat. "May we bow our heads in a prayer of thanks, for guidance and great waves, and for the wonderful food we are about to receive?"

The spirited din of the dining room respectfully lessens as many of the customers recognize Pastor Mike from his streaming Hillview Chapel show on Hulu, his ubiquitous freeway billboards and online vids.

"Bless this food to thy service, Lord, and welcome Bette to our lives. Show us your way forward, that we may follow and learn, and make amends. Our thanks to you, Lord. Amen."

Jen hears the smattering of "amens" that follows. Could almost puke. She's way too rattled to say an amen of her own, not at all feeling thankful or like making amends with Bette Wu.

Pastor Mike sits.

The dining room noise hasn't returned since his prayer, but there's a steady buzz—customers sensing something important at hand.

Casey pulls out her chair and Bette stands. Jen is silently disgusted by this, but she can't take her eyes off of tall, beautiful Bette Wu, suddenly holding sway over her son, her *world*.

Casey, standing beside Bette with a small smile, suddenly sits.

Bette nods to him, then considers the room with a serious face, drawing them in, before focusing for a brief moment on the eight people at her table. Clears her throat and swings a strand of shining black hair back under her beanie.

Silence settles over the crowd, broken only by kitchen clamor and the sound of the waitstaff serving and clearing.

"Thank you for allowing me to be here. I love surfing even though I'm no good at it. I admire so many of you big-wave riders. You are brave and beautiful."

This gets them going again, hooting and cheering, glasses raised.

"I was born in the United States. But because my family is of Chinese ancestors, there have been hateful, racist suggestions made in news and social media, mostly from the extreme right. My socials are filled with hate. We are taunted on the streets where we live. Our old people sometimes get hit and kicked. We get blamed for disease, communism, and a bad economy. For yellow skin. These are some of the prejudices that led to rape, beatings, and murders of my ancestors, as far back as the California Gold Rush. I, my father, and some of our associates have been interviewed by the Laguna Beach Police, the LA Sheriff's Department, and the FBI. They found no evidence that anyone in my family or in King Jim Seafood is even related to the fire that destroyed Jen Stonebreaker's beautiful restaurant. On the opposite, arrests have been made and charges filed against two individuals tied to the Monterey 9 criminal organization in LA. So, I thank you from my heart for letting me sit with you tonight, and see the wonderful contest. Thank you, thank you. Casey?"

Jen watches her son stand. He's taller than Bette Wu but not by much. His face is flushed.

Bette's serious words have hushed the crowd, and the waitstaff have paused to listen. Jen stews in the relative silence. The only sounds in

Barbara's Fish Trap are the distant banging in the kitchen, the slow cars out on Capistrano Road, and the raindrops hitting the windows.

Jen dreads what her son is about to say, whatever it might be. Wishes she could cradle him in her arms and carry him away. Maybe elbow Bette in the face on their way out. By the way he looks at Bette, Jen sees that she has overrun him, body and heart.

Casey: "So now you know that Bette's family didn't burn the Barrel. I want you all to know that. Welcome her to the Monsters, maybe be, like, cool to her. She's really great."

Casey drops back into his chair like a kid who's being stared at. Looks at Jen with the same dashed expression he got when he was six and asked her if she would marry him someday and she told him no, it doesn't work that way, son.

Then comes a murmur, followed by louder "alrights" and "yeah, mans" and a strong, clear "Go, Bette!"

Who is still standing. "I don't want to go," she says. "I want to stay in this world with all of you."

She holds up a white letter-sized envelope she's taken from her purse.

"I'm almost done, really! But this is a check from my family's bank in Hong Kong, made out to Jen Stonebreaker in the amount of one-hundred and seventy-five thousand dollars. It is for restoring of the Barrel. This is a gift from the Wu family to the Stonebreakers. No conditions or obligations are attached, but we would like a small plaque somewhere in the new restaurant. Maybe near that bronze of John Stonebreaker in the lobby, acknowledging this gift from us."

As the cheers rise and the applause gets louder, Bette leans across the table and hands the check to Jen.

Who is too angry to even look at the envelope. How else could Bette know that $175,000 is her shortfall? Another facet of Casey's betrayal?

Reset, she thinks. One of Dr. Penelope Parker's favorite words.

Reset.

Say the Wus did not, in fact, set fire to my restaurant, and Bette never intended to hurt Mae.

Say the threats were ugly and idle, but empty. They were fairly vague.

But she remembers Jimmy Wu's happily ominous words that day on *Empress II*, when he thought it was so funny that she mentioned fire and her restaurant together.

The Barrel is my life. My family. I'd set it on fire before I'd sell it to you. Oh, funny, funny, I say Barrel and you say fire!

So who really brought up the idea of setting fire to her restaurant in the first place, Jen thinks now—she or Jimmy? Could she have misread his words, his cultural compass, or his quirky reactions?

But it's damned hard for her to accept all that—daughter of a cop, by nature suspicious and doubting. Her father who, come to think of it, judged Jimmy Wu a "creep" based on info from his LBPD friends.

Okay, forget about Jimmy's guilt or innocence for now, thinks Jen. Before the arson, his pirates had been publicly shamed and challenged by her son. They—and Bette—had been caught at sea, on Casey's social media vids, illegally mutilating sharks for soup.

Isn't that enough to justify her intense dislike and distrust of Bette? Especially as a sudden friend of her trusting boy?

Bette Wu's smile appears hopeful and genuine as Jen looks up at her, tears the envelope in half, and drops the pieces to the table.

35

The Oceano lobby is empty this late. Jen and Casey sit near the fire in heavy silence.

"Mahina's getting some rest," says Brock, setting down the drinks. "She's exhausted."

Brock looks exhausted, too, from three days at the Flagstaff fire. "Where's Bette?"

"She's got a room here somewhere," says Casey. "Not with me."

"Your friend and *business associate*, Casey?" asks Jen. "What are you thinking?"

Casey nods and swallows hard. Takes a sip of orange juice.

"She's really good at business, Mom. You just gotta realize she didn't burn down the Barrel. She didn't hurt Mae. She helped her nutty dad try to buy your restaurant at a really insultingly stupid price. They're big talkers, Mom. But Bette asked to come here to help me stay relaxed and not have to drive ten hours and have to deal with reservations and all that. Just concentrate on the surfing. Let it flow, man. Let it be. You'll see her different when you get to know her. But if you can't or won't, then I ask you to at least trust *me* and my judgment. At least be nice to her. She really wanted you to take that money, Mom."

"What's her cut as your business associate?" asks Brock.

"We earlier talked about fifteen percent but that's on hold for now. There's no money in this for her."

Jen listens to this, feeling as if her cheeks must be red but the rest of her face white. The red is how much she loves Casey in all his naïve goodness right now; the white is her anger at Bette for conniving her way into Casey's life. In Jen's mind, Bette is a fast-talking, sharp-dressing, *maybe* Hollywood-connected, lowlife smuggler and shark finner, no matter what she's got Casey believing.

Although, to be fair, thinks Jen, even though I don't want to be fair—Bette Wu never handled a knife in any of Casey's postings, never touched a shark.

"I like her," says Brock. "As a fan of unusual women. Trust? Hmmm . . . But I wish you'd have taken the money, Mom. That much money would put the Barrel back on the map in no time."

"She said she'll get another check if you want, Mom," says Casey.

"Absolutely not. She can't buy me. But I guess she's bought you two."

"That's harsh," says Casey. "She's a business associate and a friend. Not a slave owner."

"Heaven help you, Casey," says Jen. "With Bette Wu's hands in your pockets. And wherever else they might be."

"It's not like that, Mom."

"You're a stupido if you don't think she'll try," says Brock.

Casey slumps a little, crosses his arms, and shakes his head. Stares at the floor.

"Bette says I'm smart," he says quietly. "Not like Fredo in *The Godfather*."

"You gotta be realistic about this, bro. You gotta look things right directly in the eye. She might be a good friend and want the best for you. She's definitely hot. But she's trying to buy the Barrel. And us, too."

Casey's still staring at the floor. "She wants to manage more than just my business. My happiness and my family someday, when I have one. You know, like, the future and stuff."

"Bro," says Brock. "The best advice I can give you is to use a condom that Bette Wu hasn't poked a hole in."

Casey shrugs. "That's pretty gross, Brock. To say about her."

"He's right," says Jen.

Who wants to slap Casey's face.

Instead she comes over and hugs him and tells him she loves him, that he's going to shred this Monsters contest tomorrow, and she's going to be there to tow him in and get him to the rescue sled if he needs it, but you won't need it, because you're going to tie for first place with Brock and you'll have to split the money and saw the trophy in half and we'll put both halves in the lobby of the new Barrel by John's bronze.

John, she thinks, feeling Casey's face warm and wet with her tears.

John, whom she had promised to love and protect all those years ago, back when she truly believed she could.

Bette Wu knocks on Jen's door just after midnight.

Through the peephole, Jen bores in on the composed, pretty face.

And opens the door. "I suppose you have a gun."

Bette glances down the hallway each way. "In my purse. You should let me in."

Jen unlatches the chain and closes the door behind Bette, who takes the couch and sets her purse on the coffee table. Jen sits near the little gas fireplace, rippling with flame.

"What do you want?" she asks.

"To get you another check," Bette says.

"Don't bother. I'll tear it up, too."

"It will make your rebuild go faster, and let you use first-quality materials and labor. You can be open again by summer, bringing in money."

"You can't buy my restaurant, or me. Or Casey."

"I'm not trying to buy your restaurant or you. I feel your disgust for me. But I do want Casey. He's a generous soul. He's beautiful. He can be the most famous and well-paid surfer in the world. I'd love to help him be that."

"You don't deserve him."

"So much hate, Jen Stonebreaker. You detest me, but that's okay. I've been down that road. But—with respect—Casey no longer needs *you*. He's no longer yours. He's a grown man with a good mind, a strong heart, and a brilliant future. He needs me now, and I intend to be a part of him."

"You're just trying to cash in."

"Who wouldn't? But I'll do well when he does well. And, we should be truthful here—cashing in is only a small part of everything. We will make our own new path in history."

Bette goes to the fireplace, rubs her hands near the glass. "I could never live up here in this cold. I was born in Southern California and I hope to die there."

"Be my guest."

"I've enjoyed the articles about you and John in *Surf Tribe*. You're a good writer and your heart shows complexity. I can't wait for part five."

"Maybe next week. It'll be the last."

"You have to write about this contest, which I think Casey will win."

Jen considers Casey's chances for the thousandth time. Brock's, too. And her own.

"What do you want?"

Bette, rubbing her hands, returns to the couch.

"I want to tell you how I see Casey," she says. "It will clarify my actions."

"Clarify away, Bette."

"The first time I saw him, I saw in Casey what you saw in John Stonebreaker when you were twelve. When you saw him rolling that trash can to the sidewalk up in Top of the World. I was sitting in your bar at the Barrel."

"Not mutilating sharks off Desperation Reef?"

"I have never finned. I fish. Like Casey."

"What did you see in him, bartending at the Barrel?" Jen asks.

"A beautiful, powerful man. Composed and focused. But that was only how he looked. I wanted to know the inside of him. I came to the Barrel again but it was his night off. He was there a few nights later, but it was crowded and there was no way to talk to him, or even get close. He was surrounded by beautiful women and men. I gave up and put him out of my mind. Later he caught some of us pirates shark-finning, and posted his videos. Two days after that, I went to the Barrel early, before happy hour, and he was there."

"After kidnapping Mae."

"I borrowed Mae. She followed me for the treat in my hand. I would never have hurt her. I was able to talk to Casey. I dressed well and introduced myself as the pirate in his videos, and asked him to take them down. I really wanted those videos off the net. And also, I wanted to look at Casey, and listen to his voice, and try to get inside him. I did. What I saw was goodness and innocence and love. Of Mae. I saw the pain in him, his worry for her. In your article you said that after watching John surf Rockpile, you were going to *be* John. You were twelve years old then and you knew exactly what you wanted. When you were seventeen, you gave yourself to him after Cortes Bank. Well, Mrs. Stonebreaker, I was twenty-seven when I walked out of the Barrel bar, wanting to be Casey. Your son. John's son."

"Nonsense."

Through the sliding door curtain, Jen watches the headlights down on Capistrano. A gust blows the rain against the glass with a sudden *swoosh*.

"Your mouth says that, but your heart knows it is not nonsense at all," says Bette.

"Okay. You love him. Say you're capable of that. There's a lot to love in that young man. But you're also a smuggler, an attempted extortionist, and, I believe—an arsonist. The LA and Laguna investigations are *ongoing*. Monterey 9 will walk. Just a matter of time. And they'll have Jimmy dead to rights."

"Don't confuse me with my father."

"How can't I? You're a criminal, just like him."

"Not like him. Yes, I over-limit while fishing sometimes. No finning. And as far as the humans we traffic, well, we move a lot of them from hell into better lives. We do no business in the sex trade. I feel strongly about that. We know our end users—hospitality, big ag, restaurants like yours. Domingo in the Barrel kitchen was one of ours. The burly little guy with the silver tooth, upper right? MS-13 hacked his brother to death in San Salvador for not paying their street taxes. Guess who was next? We got him into Laguna on a panga in the middle of the night. Ten others, too. I told them about the Barrel because I liked the place. See, we are two sides of this, together, Jen Stonebreaker."

"You, cashing in again."

"I made an honest deal with Domingo and his sisters, and delivered what I promised. You hired an illegal immigrant, and what you pay him is on you, not me."

"You're still a criminal and I don't want my son involved with you."

"Understood, and Casey will decide. That said, shall I get you another check to rebuild the Barrel? You understand it is a gift? No conditions except the plaque in the new Barrel?"

"Get out of my room."

Jen feels Bette prying into her with those dark, difficult-to-read eyes.

"I am planning to leave my family's business," she says. Her voice quavers very slightly and her perfect black brows furrow.

"To be a full-time parasite on my son? Stay away from him."

"I won't stay away for you. Only if he wants me away."

"Fifteen percent?"

"No. We talked about that once. I was overreaching and we agreed it was a bad idea."

"And you say you love him, big money or not?"

Bette gets her purse and heads for the door. Jen follows. Facing each other, Jen looks up into the taller woman's dark brown eyes. Tries to read them for truthfulness, evasion, duplicity. Hope and doubt. A pinch of pride. Sees all of this and more.

"Jen, I want to marry him and have his children. They will be beautiful and will love you if you let them. Wus have strong passions. I'll invite you to the wedding."

"You've told him this?"

"Not with words. Not directly."

"You might be taking your vows in a prison chapel."

Two hours later Jen imagines that she's floating on her back near the roaring Mavericks waves, looking up at tiny stars in a black sky.

In fact she's in her bed, but miles from sleep, her mind about to tick off for the third time, what she will need just a few hours from now when she crosses the harbor to the sea. She's packed two bags of gear in Laguna, and now they're in Brock's Go Dogs Econoline, parked down in the guarded Oceano parking basement, ready for Pillar Point Harbor.

This third mental check is vital in Jen's mind because she can't forget anything, can't overlook even one of all the detailed *things* she'll need to survive Mavericks.

Things in addition to fitness and skill, experience and luck.

Eyes closed but mind working, she's in full contest mode now:

She's got Reno and his workhorse boat, *Amiga,* set to meet her at the launch. A twenty-six-foot fiberglass cruiser is no match for a fifty-foot wave, but Reno's terrific under pressure; *Amiga*'s twin outboards have torque galore, and Reno goes in fast and gets out even faster.

Jen has serviced and trailered her jet ski, doing the work herself, deliberately and slowly, like John taught her, making sure the fuel-oil mix is right, and the filter is clean to prevent stalling, and the gaskets and seals are good, the fuel lines fresh, the screws tight. Her ski is a three-hundred-horsepower Kawasaki two-stroke, fast as a banshee and weighing in at eight hundred pounds. It answers to the name of Thunder—Jen's first dog. Of course, she's got it custom painted orange and black in honor of you know who, and she's made sure it's as bright and polished as a dragster. Took her a while to get the gas off her skin and the grease from under her nails.

Four surfboards for unpredictable conditions: two thruster guns—an eight-two and an eight-eight—and two pintail single fins at seven-six and eight even.

Plus four leashes and a spare. Of course, fins and keys to get the fins on and off—she forgot her fin keys once but luckily John had his. Got quite a look from him for that.

Her five-millimeter wetsuit, so thick it's hard to move in, rash guard, inflation vest, boots, hood and gloves, impact suit for under the wetsuit in case she gets mashed into the rocks, inflation vest CO_2 cartridges, helmet, and wax.

Important details include human fuel: protein bars and boxed energy shakes, sports drinks for salt and sugar and carbs, canned caffeine and more sugar courtesy of Casey's sponsors, bananas, nut clusters, and a handful of Abba-Zabas that, when she chews them after a long session, helps the cold, dense seawater drain from her ears. Sliced roast beef and string cheese wrapped in flour tortillas for lunch—cold but filling.

Next, things you don't want but shouldn't be caught without: first aid kit with plenty of waterproof tape, tourniquets and packing gauze for rock and board gashes, a plastic bottle of isopropyl alcohol, scissors, and a freshly sharpened pocket knife.

Finally, she's packed the sea-glass earrings John gave her for her eighteenth birthday, the day he asked her to go to Cortes Bank with him, where he asked her to surf the world and ride big waves together. And more, a lot more. She still wears them, but they're not made to be worn under a neoprene hood. For trips like this she uses the wooden box they came in, with the same funny-page paper, now softened and faded with age.

All that packed into padded board bags so heavy she'll appreciate Reno's help loading in.

She lays there in the dark, facing the ceiling, feeling the ocean beneath her, trying to shut down her mind.

Impossible.

Towing Casey.

Brock and Mahina.

Her own chances riding Mavericks for the first time in twenty-five years. At fifty feet, or bigger.

And John, always and forever.

36

Sunrise without sun.

Jen powers Thunder from the Pillar Point launch toward the break-water and Mavericks beyond, Casey seated behind her. Brock and Mahina are out ahead of them, a plume of ski spray rising in their widening wake.

The sky above is gunmetal gray, and the water here in the harbor is the same color, but shiny. Up on the bluff the old Air Force tracking station globe presides over the harbor, a World War II relic.

Behind Jen trails the rescue sled. When she speeds past the breakwater into the open ocean, she hears Casey's ritual war-whoop invocation behind her: *"God save us all!"*

The sea is rougher outside the second breakwater. Thunder bucks into the chop, her engine whining with the dips and drops. Jen cuts diagonally to lessen the impact, half of her attention already on the waves that she can see coming in a half a mile northwest. They're very big—thirty-foot faces breaking right—nicely formed and spaced at lazy intervals, crowned by twenty-foot plumes of spray suspended by a light offshore breeze. Jen's last Surfline forecast this morning had the brunt of FreakZilla hitting Mavericks between 10 and 11 A.M., carrying forty-foot waves with sixty-foot faces. Surfers measure waves from the behind, she knows—a Hawaiian tradition—and faces from the front. Two helicopters—a red San Mateo County rescue chopper and a black-and-white ESPN machine—weave high above, awaiting action.

Aboard *Amiga,* Jen helps Casey choose his board. Brock and Mahina are trying to sleep in the little cabin, still pounded by three days at the Flagstaff fire, which claimed two lives. Reno holds his boat steady in the current and swell, chattering away about his new granddaughter, but his eyes keen on the waves, which here at Mavericks are prone to sudden changes of size and shift of direction when they hit the reef below.

Jen watches her son waxing his board—an eight-foot-ten, orange-and-black thruster with three of the five available fins deployed. Casey moves like his father, she thinks, deliberately and calmly, on his knees, pushing the wax block across the deck with one hand, rocking with the swell.

He looks up at her. "Hey, Mom."

"These are good waves, Casey."

"These are beautiful waves."

"Don't try to win this thing on the first one."

"Never. Easy does it."

"You have to make it. Then on the next one you do more."

Jen sounds just like her mother, always the coach.

"You sound like Grandma," Casey notes with a smile.

With his thick yellow hair tousled Casey of course reminds her of John. More than reminds her. *Is* John, in one of those rare, exact genetic handoffs from father to son.

"I'll be there if you need me."

"I know, Mom. I got this."

Sitting on the deck, he zips on his booties, pulls on his hood and gloves. Clamps the leash to his right ankle, takes up his gun, stands, and slips overboard.

Jen climbs down *Amiga*'s folding ladder and onto Thunder, which starts up with a throaty blast of white smoke.

Casey hits the lineup—first heat, six men. Jen joins the other five tow skis, buzzing around like noisy wasps, all keeping well away from the big walls of water marching in. *Pipedream,* the judges' boat, rocks steadily inside, allowing good binocular views of the rides. The ESPN chopper drifts low, while the county rescue copter stays higher for the macro view.

Through the raunchy smoke of the outboards and ten jet skis—four of them for rescue—Jen tows Casey into his first wave.

It's a twenty-five-foot beauty queen with a smooth face, a thick lip, and an inviting right shoulder. Casey drops the rope and Jen makes a quick escape, circling out wide so she can see him.

Casey drops in and makes the bottom turn easily, tucks into the barrel, runs his right hand along the cylinder, then accelerates up to the lip again from where he drives a straight fast line out ahead, then launches his board and himself into the sky and over the mounding wave to safety.

Jen watches with a hitch in her breath and a smile on her face, Thunder rocking under her. She picks up Casey on the lee side of the wave, hears the *boom* of it over her snarling ski. She steadies Thunder while Casey straps his board to the sled and climbs on.

They're back in the lineup a minute later. Casey sits behind her on the ski, for elevation, his still-leashed board stowed for now in the rescue sled.

"Beautiful work back there," she says.

"Perfect tow, Mom, but I need bigger."

"You'll get it."

But, as if a switch has been thrown, the morning goes small. Jen watches the breakers come in, like five-foot Little Leaguers wanting their pictures taken.

"This fully sucks," notes Casey.

But if the Surfline oceanographers and meteorologists and wave prophets are right, Jen thinks, those first sets were just a preview. The main attraction is still to come.

"They're on their way, Case."

"That first one will get me good points, but Tom Tyler's was better."

"Be calm."

"I know, because Dad was always calm. I think Brock got tired in the fire."

"He looks pretty whupped," says Jen.

"But he's got that energy in him, like, when you least expect it."

She sits astride the ski, holding in gentle water, clapping her gloved hands together to break the cold. Watches the men in the lineup, some sitting on their boards and others seated behind their drivers. Even through the ski noise, their voices carry across the water. Occasional nervous laughter—nervous because the sets are only an hour and fifteen minutes for your best five rides. There are ten boats in the water, including *Pipedream*. Plus the four rescue skis, hired by the contest organizers. All bobbing in separate, uneasy syncopation. When the big waves come marching in and towering up, all the watercraft and the people on them look like a tiny village perched at the foot of a moving mountain. We're all so small, Jen has always thought. A band of tiny crazies. "Start Me Up" and "Iron Man" slug it out from boats bobbing at opposite ends of the lineup.

Abruptly, the breeze changes direction and gains force, coming from the northwest now, with the swell. Jen shoots an energy drink and it's kicking in. She angles for view, trying to gauge wave direction and speed, trading observations with her son.

Everybody watches and waits as a couple of nice fifteen-footers lope in and break, breeze lifting spray off their backs. The waves are more temperamental now, the lips pouting and collapsing earlier.

The fifteen-footers become twenty feet, then twenty-five. Like they're just warming up, Jen thinks. She's seen this before on the big open-ocean breaks, where a mid-set wave jumps up much higher than the others, suddenly, and for no apparent reason.

Tom Tyler, the favored nineteen-year-old phenom from Santa Cruz, ditches his tow rope and paddles into a twenty-five-foot wave that lurches to almost forty just as he's trying to launch. Tyler is thick and strong, and Jen watches him dig for all he's worth to catch this wave as it towers up and starts to break over him. Tyler makes a miracle drop—heavy as an anvil, so vertical and fast is his descent—then jams on the brakes with a knee-rattling bottom turn, sprints through the massing whitewater, then races up the face, over the top and out.

Jen and Casey holler for Tyler, and offer up neoprene-muffled applause.

"Big points, Mom."

"Focus on yourself, son. Focus on the job."

Pure Mom again, thinks Jen. At forty-six she knows she'll never outgrow her mother's indomitable will to win.

Jen rocks on her jet ski, well to the side of the Pit, the Cauldron, and the Boneyard—three of the most lethal rock formations at Mavericks. They're impossible to locate precisely until the waves inhale and rise up, suddenly exposing the rocks just a few feet under the cold, clear water. Jen glimpses the Cauldron—an undersea grotto—just before a furious six-foot wall of whitewater crashes over it.

A hideous place. Where John went down.

She glances at Casey, a blade of fear cutting through her.

"He's all around us, Mom."

"He always is."

The waves arrive bunched closer now, eager as bulls entering a ring. Thirty-foot faces, Jen figures, as she watches a local fisherman—Sal Stragola, tall, thick, and barrel-chested—being towed into a wave six times taller than he is. He makes the drop but not the turn, has to surrender to the whitewater, then prone out on his gun. The wave crests and crashes over him with a stout *boom*. Sal broncos along in the wall of suds and sand, clambering his way inside, holding on with all he's got. This bailout will keep him from getting held down by any of the next five waves of the set, which might save his life but will probably cost him the heat, scored by judges on *Pipedream*. Jen sees that Stragola is in water too heavy for a jet ski, so by the time he waits out the set and gets back in the lineup, he'll have lost a waveless twenty minutes.

The next wave is Casey's, a wobbly thirty-footer that puffs out early and leaves him with a frothy short shoulder and an easy exit. No points for this one.

Tom Tyler is towed into a forty-foot wave. No sooner has he dropped the rope when the lip splinters ahead and knocks Tyler off his board, then grabs the boy by the neck from behind and takes him down.

Jen hears the shouts and cries, and joins the jet ski fleet making the big semicircle to water that's safe, but as close as they can get to where Tyler went down.

No sign of him. Her stomach tightens.

Engines whine and blast smoke into the air.

A driver she doesn't know gets in too close to climb over the wall of whitewater, which hurls his ski across the water. He crashes, holds on with both hands as his machine lurches in tight circles, sputtering exhaust and seawater into the air. He manages to climb back on, right the ski, and close in on Tom Tyler, who has surfaced just out of the impact zone, holding on to half his board for flotation.

"No worries!" he yells.

Rene Carrasco gets pitched from a twenty-five-foot wave that jumps suddenly, shaking him off like a flea. Jen sees him dive, his tethered board plopping out in front of him. Carrasco's tow partner circles out after him.

Flip Garrison shreds a clean, thirty-five-footer that barrels over him mid-wave and leaves the man hidden inside the tube for three full seconds—only the tip of his gun showing—before Garrison, crouched, shoots out like a ball from a cannon. Clean exit.

Wave of the day so far, Jen thinks.

Ted Kaiawalu purls on his takeoff and flies, arms out, his board mid-air above him. He lands hard, scrambles, disappearing under six feet of whitewater churning with pieces of driftwood and shreds of kelp.

Jen watches the ESPN helicopter hovering out in front of the impact zone, and the rescue chopper below it—so low its blades whirl just above the breaking waves. Looks like one could jump up and grab it, she thinks. The skis slash and the boats scramble for safer water in the heaving sea.

Over the din: "Outside, Mom!"

Jen guns seaward for the next wave, a lumbering forty-footer. She swerves out and away from the still-forming crest, and onto the rising flank.

From where she looks back at Casey, his rope in both hands, lining up with the forming peak, pointing his big board down for the drop.

At once: the wave stops forward motion, and it's face rises up—fills from below—the same reverse hydrology Jen has seen at Jaws and Cortes Bank, when wave and bottom hold still while the wave swells higher, as if taking a huge breath—the strange stall of time when a big wave decides to become a very big wave.

Casey lets go of the rope and drops in.

Elbow down, Jen flogs the throttle and grinds Thunder far along the rising shoulder, then over it, getting air before landing on the kinder backside sea.

She swings down and around to the edge of the impact zone to see Casey make the drop, body and board vertical, arms out, head cocked calmly, measured and methodical like John would be.

Fifty feet, thinks Jen. Sixty? It's the biggest wave she's seen anyone ride and her son is on it, and she's towed him into it. She's bone-deep scared, for everything that can happen, for everything that *has*.

Casey makes the bottom turn, his legs strong and true as pistons, and the wave breaks top to bottom over him with a concussive finality.

He's gone.

Three seconds. Four. Five.

In Jen's mind, even the jet skis and outboards and helicopters seem to have gone silent, but she isn't thinking about that, she's watching the four-story cement mixer in which Casey's future is being formed, and plotting the best way to get down and around to the impact zone if this wave won't let go of him.

Casey bursts out of the barrel, already aiming for the top of the wave, toward which he climbs with calm deliberation. The wave coughs a cloud of spray after him, as if trying to knock him down, then follows with another.

Jen watches her son bank the lip and hold high for a horizontal glide, then tuck in for a fast run back down the wave face. Fast indeed.

A beautifully carved bottom turn.

Then a graceful, arms-relaxed, palms-out, head-cocked, leaning-back-at-the-waist glide up onto the shoulder. Where Jen feels his joy, and, smiling, watches Casey shoot over the black wave and into the sky, disappearing into the windblown spray on his orange-and-black magic carpet.

Next heat, Jen watches from *Amiga* as Mahina tows Brock into his first wave. It's just after ten—the beginning of Surfline's witching hour for the biggest waves of the swell—and the gray sky is dissolving into sun and blue. The offshores have picked up a little, spangling the water with light and lifting white spray off the incoming waves.

Jen's heart—pounding steadily since the ski ride out some two hours ago—has settled into a calm, steady thump. She's finding that place outside herself, from which she can observe and calculate. Finding her "detachment," as her mother used to say. Clear the mind, she thinks: behold the wave, sense its intent, see the future. Pro-act, as Brock likes to say. She watches the waves staggering in, black and windblown, imagines her attack, her drop, her turn.

Mahina pulls Brock into a forty-foot pyramid that, by all measures, appears to be a perfect wave.

He drops in, board straight as a spear, his body lean and ropey, his head a forest of spiky dark dreads.

Jen watches her son, frankly awed—for the how many hundreds of times—by his instincts, daring, and reflexes.

He carves the bottom turn so deeply it slows him, allowing the smooth-faced monster to swallow him back into its maw, then he snakes down again for another turn.

Jen swears her heart skips a beat.

"Fudge, that's massive," Casey observes. "First wave, man."

From the bottom Brock shoots forty feet back up the face—Jen thinks it takes him about one second—then suddenly banks off the lip, his air-borne body and board so horizontal it seems they have to free-fall, but

Brock mocks gravity, riding the gun down and across the great, ribbed wave.

Which now peels off in a long section so fast that all Brock has to do is draw a straight line. But he doesn't; instead, he works the huge flank with a series of goofy tail pumps, like when he was a kid, eking the last few yards out of a little wave in Laguna.

Then a straight race to the top, up and over the exhausted beast, and out.

"Oh man!" yells Casey. "He's gonna win it with that!"

"Your wave was bigger, Case. Don't count yourself out."

Brock's next two waves are thick and heavy, breaking with a random, hard-to-read violence, but still nothing like Casey's freak giant.

Brock unleashes all his aggression on them, pushing the limits of balance and speed, teasing the monsters with the small-wave precision he mastered as a twelve-year-old.

Jen studies him, feeling her old pre-heat confidence building.

37

The klaxon for the women's heat blares just after noon.

The waves are the biggest of the day—routine forty-five-foot faces—staggering in, deranged and urgent.

There's a brief, bucking huddle around *Pipedream,* during which the contest organizers offer to postpone the women due to wave size. They greet the idea with curses and raised middle fingers.

Jen's up against five surfers she doesn't know, all younger by at least one decade, all ranked in the World Surfing Tour ratings, with much better odds to win, place, and show here at the Monsters of Mavericks. She's a walk-on, a big-wave footnote hanging on by her now ancient reputation. And, of course, John Stonebreaker's long-reaching legend.

She plops overboard, last in the lineup, unties her board from the rescue sled.

"You can do this, Mom," says Casey. "God Himself is going to be there with you. So's Dad. Listen to them."

"Got it, Case," she says, sitting on her board now, lifted by a rising swell. "I like what I'm seeing out there."

"I'll get you where you need to be."

She watches the first woman, Ruby Peralta, drop into a marauding forty-foot face. She free-falls and lands staunchly mid-wave, but digs her rail. With the nose of her board trapped vertically, the wave shrugs forward, flipping Ruby into the air, where she's already swimming as the whitewater plants her.

The four rescue sleds scream in, boiling around the impact zone, their drivers calibrating rescue and disaster. A capsized jet ski is a deadly thing. Jen watches Ruby's board—leash attached—hurtling toward one of the rescue skis. The driver ducks and guns his craft toward Ruby, now aloft in the whitewater, stroking hard, head up, helmet long gone. She lunges for the pausing sled, grabs and hangs on as the driver carves a wide arc away from the zone.

Jen watches her climb onto the sled and raise a fist.

"Oh, Mom, look at this!"

Casey nimbly tows her in, waits for her to drop the rope, then guns Thunder to safety.

Jen's first wave unfolds in front of her. She makes it, glances at the three-story drop in front of her, then focuses on a narrow section of it—the upwelling flank down which she must slice. The world reduced to this. Lets her feet obey her eyes, feels the wild slide of her board as she flies across the face and down, ankles chattering, feet locked in the straps.

The g-force of her bottom turn tries to telescope her legs, but Jen hasn't been carrying iron weights in the Laguna Beach High School swimming pool just for the fun of it. She feels the change of direction shuddering up into her back and shoulders as she leans forward, pivots, and makes the turn into the first section.

Which is already starting to break, high above and well ahead of her, a heavy, black-and-white lip, wavering with menace and ready to pitch.

Terrible news.

She can't outrun it from down here, so she races up the face, banks into its power, crouches, hangs high, and holds on for her life as the barrel takes her.

The sound is like nothing else, a percussive roar she feels in her bones.

Two. Three. Four and . . .

Out she blasts, an orange-and-black comet in a dark sky.

Cranks up and off the lip, down and across, speeds through a long section without Brock's dillydallying shtick, then up the face, over and off.

Midair, Jen reaches out both arms and screams as hard as she can.

No words, no thoughts, just the wail of fear banished, of a soul in joy.

Casey bucks through the chop like a bull rider, and picks her up—his smile like the one he had as a four-year-old, looking at his very own first surfboard in the Castle Rock living room twenty years ago, Christmas day.

Back in the lineup, helmet and hood off, Jen chomps an Abba-Zaba, feeling the warm seawater slowly oozing from her ears.

Casey can't shut up: ". . . you killed it, Mom! I saw the photog boat right out in front of you, so they got some awesome vids and shots. Off that lip, oh man, that was rad! This is, like, the best day of my life."

She watches Phyllis Kaiawalu—Ted's sister—shred a thirty-five-foot face with the grace of a figure skater, and make a clean exit.

Maya Abeliera rides a beautifully formed forty-foot face in a straight, hundred-yard sprint that brings her to the faltering crest that knocks her off her board. Maya dives like a seal and dolphin-kicks herself back into the wave, dropping a shoulder and bodysurfing the slowing giant. Her board trails along behind her, like part of her pod.

Jen watches her surface, where she whoops twice, then yells with the breeze: *"Don't try that at home!"*

Jen's second wave is a thick-necked peak. She barely makes it, rides the elevator down, manages the bottom turn, then goes rocket-woman and zooms up the uprising face as the lip breaks behind her. When she glances back and up, it seems to be snarling.

She works the section back down, sees her exit route as the wave seems to snag on the rocks, climbs fast as she can for the soft spot and launches high for the other side.

She lands with a splat on the heavy black water. It's like wet asphalt, and she hears the crack of her helmet and the wrench of her neck. Gets tangled in the leash for a moment but struggles out and climbs back onto her board and paddles hard for Casey.

Who makes a perilous pickup look easy, Jen climbing onto the rescue sled, reeling up her board with the leash. She looks down into the hideous Cauldron again—why does it keep me coming back, she thinks—then she feels Thunder's power as Casey pulls her away.

They join the lineup, from the relative safety of which Jen sees the next set coming in, a dark, horizon-blotting platoon of killers. It's like they're looking for her. The ten-minute klaxon warning blasts across the water.

"You don't have to ride another one, Mom," says Casey. "You'll get the women's wave of the day, for sure. That's, like, two thousand clams and a cool trophy."

"I want to win the whole thing, Case."

Jen hardly recognizes her own voice. It's not the one she's been speaking in for all these years, the one driven by fear and hung on regret. Right now, with the almost warm sunlight on her face, she feels that she is a different being. She's grown. Evolved. Time to move into the world again, she thinks.

Hasn't felt that way in twenty-five years.

John, that sun feels good, doesn't it?

"You know what Grandma Eve would say about winning," says Casey.

"Yeah—it isn't everything, it's the only thing!"

"Mom, remember why we do this. Or the Breath of Life, as Brock calls Him."

"All metaphor, Casey. I want to *win*. It's just the way I am."

"This set is big, Mom. *Real* big."

Jen watches Odile Bertran, pitched off her board before she can even stand up. The barrel takes her down and the rescue skis scream into action.

"They're huge and fast, Mom. I'm going to put you way high up, so you gotta be fast."

Odile pops up on the edge of the Pit and climbs into her tow partner's sled just as he guns it away, Odile dragged through the exploding whitewater.

Maya Abeliera holds the tow rope, looks down, and lets the charging wave go past her.

Holly Blair makes the wave and carves an impossible bottom turn, only to be crushed by the suddenly collapsing peak. The wave elevators her back up, high, then slams her down again, her board tombstoning on its leash.

Jet skis throw up wakes and exhaust.

Jen watches the photographers' boat rollicking just outside the impact zone, and the two helicopters hovering close together, their blades whirling not twenty feet from a breaking fifty-foot face.

Holly pops up in the whitewater, trapped in its churning fury, whirling and flailing, board trailing, snapped in half. It looks to Jen like she's slugging the water with her fists.

Then, as a voice squawks down, she strokes hard for the red life buoy dangled by the rescue chopper.

"Swim left, Holly! Swim to your left!"

Jen's third and likely final wave of the contest is her biggest. It's the cleanup, nothing behind it but a waveless, heaving ocean.

She nods at Casey, whose expression is uncharacteristically puzzled. Feels Thunder's torque and strength.

Throws the rope and drops onto a galloping, fifty-foot thoroughbred that suddenly raises his great head behind her.

The breeze lifts a white plume but Jen can't look up or back, only down, half-blinded by the spray, letting her feet obey her eyes, trusting her stung vision to take her where she needs to go.

Too vertical and she'll unfasten.

Too horizontal and she'll get pitched.

Two one-way tickets into the impact zone. To the Cauldron, the Pit, or the Boneyard.

She's all in because there is no choice.

Rarely on a drop, the nose of a surfer's gun pops off the surface for a split second—a small rise or a hidden dip—and the speeding board takes a gulp of air. At forty miles an hour, the nose rides up, and the body of the board follows, lifting off and away from the wave until the board is vertical. Physics and velocity push the tail out and away, and the surfer comes off the wave and descends—head down, feet above, and arms out—her board behind her like a cross on which she is crucified upside down.

Which is Jen Stonebreaker, an orange-and-black figure falling head-first into the violent whiteout of the impact zone.

The county helicopter lowers for her, Holly Blair safely aboard and the life buoy still dangling. The rescue skis all go banshee toward Jen, with Casey, Brock, and Mahina out ahead of them already.

The wave drives Jen to the bottom, mashing her against the reef, the tonnage of water holding her down. She clamps her hands over the rocks to keep from being dragged, feels the pull of the leash on her ankle as the wave takes her board toward the surface.

Lifting Jen off the rocks, and into the fury of whitewater.

Rag-dolled and tumbling, eyes closed, she pulls three of her inflation-vest pull tags. Nothing happens. Yanks the fourth, and feels the loop come off in her hand.

Is this my sentence for John?

Her terror peaks and tries to flood out of her, but it can't get out. She's got it trapped in there and she feels the nerve-curdling fingers of panic up high in her throat.

She's got breath left, but can't believe so much of it is gone after only a few seconds. The cold weight of the water, and ten feet of pressure here near the bottom, are wringing the air right out of her.

And the wave won't let her go. Like it knows there's no backup wave behind it. Like it's going to eat her here and now. Like Jen belongs to it and it alone.

She thinks she's facing shore. Pulls herself along by the rocks, but the wave lifts her feet and flips her over, then presses down hard again. She's pinned on her back, eyes open now to the dim underwater twilight of Mavericks, while sharp white flashes shoot through her vision. Her leash goes slack.

She rights herself, the wave shoving her head against a boulder. The rocks around her creak and scrape. She feels the spined urchins and limpets slicing through her hood. Clamps the rocks again, draws her knees to her chest, and pushes off with all her might.

Then the whitewater claims her again, rushing fast.

Toward land, one quarter mile away.

She's dizzy now from lack of oxygen and near panic. Not sure what's up or down, really, just clawing her way toward her next breath.

Breaks the surface and swills the miracle of air—which turns out not to be air at all, but a mouthful of brine that scalds her throat and sinuses and lungs.

And turns her world white, as the ocean folds her under, splayed across the reef, faceup again.

God help . . .

Breath of . . .

She struggles over and gets her feet under her again.

Takes hours, while the rocks creak and scrape.

Jen takes a breath—it's reflex and she can't fight it—and shoves off for the surface. Reaches up and pulls her outstretched arms down as hard as she can. Then again. She has to make that bright white light. Has to get the air that's in it.

But she's not going up; she's tumbling again, pounded by the rocks. Hears them laughing.

Thinks:

John, Casey, Brock . . .

Mom, Dad . . .

Brightwhitelight

Kickagain

Breatheagain

Kick!

Then sudden black, and only black.

Casey and Brock are already there, searching the surface, then diving to work the rocks, like crabs, pulling themselves along the bottom, through the half-light, waiting to see their mother somewhere in this hard, dim place.

The wave has passed and the sea heaves around them, smooth and powerful.

The rescue and ESPN choppers clap overhead, and the jet skis rooster-tail through the sea, and the boats pitch awkwardly on the outskirts of the impact zone.

Casey and Brock forage halfway between the Pit and the Cauldron with the help of an eastward, post-set current where she went in, buried by the breaking wave.

They search through a sheltered grotto, bits of seaweed and broken kelp swirling, a finning rockfish backing deeper into its cave. Gravel rises from the bottom in a small tornado.

Eyes alert, Mahina waits on her jet ski, Thunder tethered to her rescue sled.

Casey, big and strong and eight feet underwater now, pulls himself along the floor of this dark world, squinting for a sign of her. An occasional ray of sun penetrates. He's looking for the orange of her wetsuit, or a glimmer of her helmet, maybe, or a zipper, or the yellow pull handle on her inflator, or the pale luminosity of her face.

Brock crabs along six feet to Casey's right, hoping for something soft against his gloves, a flicker of color in the near dark, the bump of her body against his. The smaller rocks click and pop around him. Mahina's jet ski irritably idles above.

Even this close, they can barely make each other out. Three times they surface together for breath, then submerge again: the Stonebreaker twins, born seconds apart one afternoon, twenty-four years ago, now searching for the woman who gave them life.

Then, there she is, right in front of them.

Suspended in the gloom, arms and legs spread like a skydiver, helmet gone and hair lilting in the current.

She is looking at them very calmly. But does she see?

Casey gets under her left arm, and Brock under her right, and they bear her from the water to the rescue sled.

Eyes closed and not moving or breathing, but a distant pulse.

Casey does chest compressions in the rocking sea, and talks to her.

Brock breathes for her, and gently pats her cold white cheeks.

Mahina chants in her native language, words that sound welcoming and hopeful.

Casey, as he pushes and pauses: "Mom, come back. Like, be here."

Brock, between breaths: "We gotcha, we gotcha."

Mahina: *"Aia 'oe ma 'ane'i. Kakou. Kakou."*

Casey: "Ah come on, Mom! *Mom!*"

Brock: "Breath of life! Coming in!"

Then a brutal silence as the living assess the dying.

Broken by Jen, who full-body spasms and blows a storm of seawater into the air.

And another.

And again.

She's still spitting up and moaning as they get her into the helicopter rescue basket, and the deputy latches the gate.

38

The next evening Jen attends the Monsters of Mavericks awards dinner in the Oceano Bar and Grill.

Her bruises and cuts pulse dully, her neck aches, and her wheelchair is cold steel. Can't quite get warm. Her right eardrum is broken, but no bones. A miracle, they said. Her balance is way off when she's standing or getting out of the chair. She's still a bit hazy on what happened, but the doctors in San Francisco say her traumatic, short-term memory loss will probably return. Bed rest. Set your alarm or have someone wake you up once every hour. Oxycodone if you need it. You're one tough woman, Jen—*you're* the Monster of Mavericks.

She picks at the rice and teriyaki chicken, half listens to the MC— actor Robin McKenna from the streaming drama *Legends of the Wave*. She's in a short silver dress with a bow across her breasts, looks like a present to be opened. There's a huge screen behind her, vivid with film and video:

Stupendous waves that look even bigger through telephoto lenses.

Off-the-lips, barrel burials, bottom turns.

Wipeouts.

The old seventies *Five Summer Stories* music plays beneath the amplified *boom* of the waves.

"Let's start off with the awards that hurt!" Robin McKenna announces. "But we have happy endings here! The women's worst wipeout—no surprise—goes to Jen Stonebreaker!"

Casey, his reef-scraped forehead almost hidden under his thick yellow hair, wheels her to the stage but there's no ramp so Robin McKenna slinks down the steps and hands Jen an acrylic-and-gold-look trophy shaped like a wave. Her wipeout unfolds in slow motion on the screen. A ripple of cold numbness wobbles through her. She watches it intently, with little recall of the event.

The actor pecks Jen with a brief kiss, plants a longer one on Casey, then offers Jen the microphone and a white envelope with blue foil trim.

Jen waves away the mike and takes the envelope; Casey turns her chair around and Jen smiles to the cheering audience.

"There's five hundred dollars in that envelope, Jen," says Robin. "And some fantastic shops right across the alley. And an open bar 'til midnight! Enjoy! Wow, we're glad you're still here!"

Back at the table Jen lets her vision drift from Casey and Brock and Mahina, to her mother and father, Pastor Mike and Marilyn, and Bette Wu.

They look different to her. She's never seen them in this way before, never been stolen from them, then returned. Plucked from their world, then drop-shipped back.

Casey's to her left; she touches his face. Brock to her right, likewise.

Funny how they're all looking at me the same way right now, she thinks. Eve Byrne wipes her eyes, and Jen's tough, good-hearted former police chief dad sets a hand over his wife's far shoulder and squeezes. Looks at Jen as if he's the happiest man in the world.

She settles on Bette Wu's pale face. Gets a small smile, no teeth, just a cupid upturn of her lips. Bette's wearing the same seafoam-green leather pantsuit that Jen noted the first time she saw her, in the Barrel bar with her pirate crew, trying to get Casey's attention. Funny, Jen thinks, how easily that moment comes to mind—weeks old—when wiping out on a fifty-foot wave face just yesterday is only a dark, gloomy snippet.

"... the worst men's wipeout goes to Tom Tyler ... we're all real stoked to have you with us, Tommy!"

Jen watches nineteen-year-old Tom Tyler bounce up to the stage in his plaid flannels, shearling boots, and red sequined tails, throwing punches like a boxer. Blond hair to his shoulders. He's about the cutest boy she's ever seen, right behind her own. Wants to adopt him.

The next time Jen looks for Bette, she's not there. Then Jen feels a hand on her shoulder and hears Bette's voice behind her. Jen tries to turn to her but her pain-frozen neck won't let her.

"I know you hate me but I'm happy you're still alive," Bette says. "That wave will haunt my dreams."

"Mine, too."

The MC asks the next winners to stay put until all the awards have been announced. Starts to read from an Oceano bar napkin, holding it close:

Ruby Kaiawalu and Tom Tyler get best rides.

The crowd goes bonkers. Someone raises a beer pitcher to his mouth but drops it. Explodes when it hits the floor. Shrieks. Rene Carrasco slides through the glassy beer in his Ugg boots, arms out, knees bent.

Flip Garrison gets big-wave rookie of the year.

Bonkers again, and loud: *"Flip! Flip! Flip!"*

Maya gets women's first place and the $50,000 that goes with it. Then Ruby Peralta and Connie Arnett.

Jen doesn't podium. Doesn't care. Knows she couldn't have surfed any better, and she had the luck—until the wipeout, at least—well, enough luck to live through it.

She's survived what even her most private dreams had promised would kill her.

Everyone's standing and hooting, bottoms up and shots down. Jen feels like she's in a dazed version of high school again, when she won everything in sight and everybody adored her and she was falling in love with John. Before she grew up. Before their blissful Garden and his terrible end. Happy in this moment, as she was then. Blessed by life and smart enough to know it.

Jen is so lost in her memory she zones through the men's second- and third-place winners, then:

"And now, ladies and gentlemen, girls and dudes, masters and grommets, kooks and locals—it's time for the winner of Monsters of Mavericks men's overall. As you all know, it's based on three waves, judged on points for maneuvers, degrees of difficulty, and style. Style, baby!"

Jen watches Robin take a patient swallow of what looks like a sponsored Pacifico longneck, which brings a horny roar from the crowd.

"Men's overall—Casey Stonebreaker! This year's monster man!"

Casey and Brock each take a wheelchair handle and push Jen through the bodies to the base of the stage again. Mahina and Bette and the moms and dads are already there. The other winners and most of the audience flood in, hamming it up for the cameras, selfies galore, "Wipeout" twanging and thumping loud from the PA.

39

After the awards dinner, Casey and Bette Wu walk the quiet streets to Pillar Point Harbor. It's cold and still, the moon a distant egg in a nest of fog.

They pass Mavericks Surf Company, owned by Jeff Clark, a local who surfed Mavericks for nearly fifteen years before it was "discovered" back in the early nineties. The first guy to really ride it. Alone, because nobody else would dare. Clark is one of Casey's idols, and the coolest of dudes, too. Tight with his dad. Introduced Casey around Half Moon Bay. Took him out at Mavericks when Casey was fourteen, on a medium-wicked, paddle-in day. Warned him that Mavericks has no conscience.

Casey looks through a window at the handsome Clark boards racked along one wall. Simple and clean, no adorning colors. Above the cash register hangs a blown-up photo of their maker, carving a bottom turn on a fifty-foot face.

"You are him now," says Bette.

"No, just me."

"You're better. I've studied all the films and videos. Yours and his."

"He did it first. I just watched and learned."

"You're faster and stronger and more intuitive. A better wave reader. You showed yesterday what you are. You have the royal blood of your mother and father. You are a king. We need to inflate your ego, Casey. We need to make you proud to be the best in the world. Better than Laird. Better than Garrett. Better than all of them."

"I'm only the best for now. Just at Mavericks. But somebody else will be here next year. Maybe looking through this window. I'm chill with that. It's all good."

"More famous. More rich. The best. When they say the best big-wave surfer in the world, ever—it is going to be you."

Casey turns and smiles at her. "That would be pretty choice, Bette."

"It is *your* choice, Mr. Stonebreaker."

She smiles back. She's got a seafoam-green beanie pulled over her ears, and matching duster against the cold. Does a funny little skip, ducks a shoulder under his, and presses an arm to his back. They walk on, passing the rental bikes and paddleboards chained up for the night, and the commercial fishing boats cut into planes and shadows by the dock lights. The bait boat crews are already arriving in this early morning dark. A lanyard pings on a sailboat mast.

"You don't feel so tense when I touch you," says Bette.

"I'm getting used to you. I'm liking on you."

He feels her arm tightening against his back and a gloved hand squeezing his elbow. Feels her head on his shoulder and smells that perfume she wore on Sunset, the one that feels sweet and warm in his lungs, puts his sex drive in gear.

"We will be very good, Casey."

"Totally."

Bette's grip goes tight on his arm as a big silver SUV eases into the harbor from Pillar Point Harbor Boulevard. He senses her attention as she slows their walk.

"What?"

"Nothing."

She rubs his back as if in encouragement, resuming their pace.

"Nothing."

But as the SUV comes toward them, she firmly adjusts their direction away from it and toward the boulevard. Her hand tightens on his arm again.

The Yukon's headlights go off and it comes forward and stops, pointed right at them, fifty feet away. No front plate.

Bette stops.

Casey watches all four doors open and four people get out. In the meek interior light he recognizes two of the shark-finning women from his first brush with *Empress II*—one white, the other Mexican. The other two are Asian women, one big and husky, the other smaller and slender.

"Not in the script," says Bette. "I have to go."

"I'll go with you."

"Back to your room, Casey. I'll call."

"These are pirates."

"I know who they are. This shouldn't take long."

"What shouldn't? What are you going to do? What are *they* going to do?"

Bette walks briskly to the big woman and gives her a brief look before climbing into the middle row of seats.

Casey watches the doors slam, hears the pirates arguing inside. He's thumbing on his video when the Yukon lights blast on, and the vehicle charges right at him. He dives, hits, and rolls.

"Fudge!"

Up on one knee he tries to vid the rear plates but they're blacked out with something, tape, maybe; he can't tell.

So he runs with all his strength for the Yukon, which bumps from the marina onto the empty boulevard, speeding for downtown and the exits from Half Moon Bay.

Casey races down the middle of the empty boulevard after Bette, but in shearling boots and a goose-down tube jacket and the slim-fit Dream Coast jeans he's contracted to wear to all World Surf Federation–sanctioned events, racing isn't easy.

He catches a toe on an orange reflector, goes down, rolls, and is back up again as the Yukon bends south along the beach and out of sight.

He sits in his room, eating the snack basket crackers, the sliding-door curtain open so he can see the Oceano entrance. He's got the little fireplace pegged against the chill.

He thinks about waking up Brock, because Brock's down with the dark side. Like aboard *Empress II* that day, when he handled Jimmy Wu and his pirates like they were kooks. Because Brock is an eighth-dan hapkido black belt. And a volunteer fighter in Ukraine. And a former Riverside County pot grower with violent competitors. And a big-wave surfer, drowned in a three-wave hold-down at Nazaré until Mahina blew the breath of life back into him. Or God did, thinks Casey: there's different ways to look at that.

A loud lowrider rumbles along Capistrano, then a couple of Harleys. No silver Yukon.

Casey takes the elevator up to Bette's room, knocks on her door, and gets the welcome he's expecting: none.

He goes into the ice and vending alcove, where he can see her door, scans the offerings in the machines, gets a two-dollar bag of spicy shelled peanuts. He's always hungry because that's what the ocean does to you, but the day after a big-wave contest he's always fully starved.

The dinner tonight was good but fairly skimpy and you didn't get seconds, so Casey buys more nuts and some Funyuns and a raspberry smoothie.

Watches Bette's door, checks his phone every few minutes, then heads back.

Three minutes after three, and a knock on his door. Pulls it open without checking the peephole.

Bette steps in, holding the beanie to her face.

Bloody everything: hands, seafoam duster, jacket. Splatters on her boots.

She lowers the beanie and looks up at him, eyes roaming his face. Lips puffed up, the upper split. Chin and neck streaked red. Cheeks scraped from blows, eye sockets purpling. Her left eyebrow is cross-cut and meaty at the edges.

Bette hangs her head. Casey holds her gently so as not to hurt her, like when Mae got hit by the car and he set her in his bed. He feels Bette's sobs. Feels love.

And anger. The angriest he's ever been.

"No police," she blubbers through the swollen lips.

"Did you steal the money for Mom's check from Jimmy?"

"No. The check is a forgery. I knew she wouldn't take it. It was just to show her—show everyone—how good a friend I am. To you. This, Jimmy did for joining up with you. For being here with you. For disrespecting family. Me against the other girls."

"I can't believe he would let them do this to you."

She gives Casey a broken look.

"He destroys what he can't own and control," she says. "Always been that way. My mother. My sister. His friends. Anyone he touches."

"Now you."

"This isn't destruction. It's a warning."

He destroys what he cannot own and control, thinks Casey, his mind's eye bright with windblown flames and melting surfboards.

"I know a doctor in Half Moon Bay," he says.

"I make a call first. I want you to hear every word I say."

Bette sits on the couch across from the fire, puts her phone on speaker, and touches a contact with a shaking finger.

Casey sits next to her, sees her bloody fingerprint on the phone screen, hears the quick pickup:

"You have reached Brian Pittman, Laguna PD. Please leave a detailed message. Speak clearly."

Bette holds up the phone so she can look at Casey as she talks.

Casey's anger stirs again, and his pity. Should he have seen this coming? Should he have protected her? Brock would sure as heck have never let this happen.

"Hello, Detective Pittman. This is Bette Wu. You remember me. I am calling to tell you that my father, Jimmy Wu, and his associates hired the arsonists who set the Barrel Restaurant fires and framed Monterey 9. I will tell you all details of how and why this happened. I have recordings. I am an eyewitness."

She thumbs off the call and sets her phone on the coffee table.

For a moment, Casey feels like he's atop a huge Mavericks right, about to drop into the chaos below.

"He'll destroy you now," he says.

She stares at him, a battered woman in a red-smeared seafoam-green ensemble.

Looks down.

"Sorry. So sorry. I did everything I could to talk them out of it. Dad laughed and threatened to disown me for disloyalty. So, I lied to you. Again."

Casey feels betrayed and foolish, but most of all, battered by his failure to protect her, and by the angry sympathy within.

"Let's get you to that doctor," he says, placing a big arm softly across Bette's shoulders, dialing his phone.

He thinks of getting Brock's help here but Brock and Mahina left Half Moon Bay right after the awards dinner, bound for Hurricane Yvette, category three but building, and aimed directly at New Orleans.

40

Looking Back—

WHO WAS JOHN STONEBREAKER AND WHAT WENT WRONG AT MAVERICKS?

BY JEN STONEBREAKER

Part five of a special series for *Surf Tribe Magazine*

After twenty-five years it's time for me to do my job and tell the truth.

The great writer Susan Casey once called Mavericks a portal to the dark side.

She certainly got that right, especially the wave that John caught late in his final heat: a fifty-foot blue-black peak breaking top to bottom, leaving a barrel five times taller than the man trying to ride it.

Onto which I towed John, then sped along and over the shoulder to safety, the rescue sled gliding behind me on its braided nylon rope.

From there I watched him drop into the wave, legs vibrating, feet locked in the straps, like a vertical arrow, John fastened to the pointed, narrow, big-wave gun, headed down *fast,* his arms out for control and balance.

He made the bottom turn, carving deep, leveling off, and backing into the barrel forming over him, raking his fingertips along the cylinder.

In that moment, John was a daredevil in the barrel, somehow managing to look casual within a rifled, two-story tube.

I smiled to myself despite the danger he had chosen.

This is why we do this, I thought. Nothing we'll ever do will match it. Not sex, not love, not being a mother or a father, which I know we will be someday. Not seeing God. Not making money. Nothing but this moment of freedom and velocity, this rush of nature of which we are a part. This mastery of power unimaginable. This pure, terrifying joy.

Then the heavy lip lunged, took John by the back of his neck like a blue-black leopard, and wrenched him off his board.

Leaving him suspended in midair, turning, head down and feet up, his board above, aimed down at him like a spear, its leash wobbling between them.

From my perilous angle—the jet ski rocking hugely on the building crest of the next wave, the rescue sled shifting with its own contrapuntal weight—I watched John vanish into the white avalanche of the kill zone.

I saw my opening, my moment to get there and help him.

But I didn't crank the throttle, because I had something to tell John first.

And I did, firmly:

"I know you betrayed me."

In that fraction of a moment, I hated him.

And in that half second I felt the wave bearing me up, as if I were an offering and I knew that there was no way I could get to him in time. I had missed my moment.

So now you know our secret.

My sons, Casey and Brock, were born just minutes apart, almost nine months later.

As many of you know, last month, Casey won the Monsters of Mavericks contest that killed his dad twenty-five years ago.

It was held during a massive swell, some of the biggest waves ever to hit Half Moon Bay. My boys rode those waves courageously, unpredict-ably, and artfully.

My beautiful boys!

I won worst wipeout on the women's side, mostly because of a huge but handsome wave that took me in and held me close in its beating heart, then launched me into the impact zone like I was a stick. Pushed me under and held me down for a very long time. Lost consciousness. When I awoke I was back on the boat but I didn't know who I was, or where, or how I'd gotten there.

Nietzsche said when you look into the abyss, the abyss also looks into you.

But my fear was gone, because that last wave decided to kill me.

Would have killed me in just a matter of seconds if Casey and Brock and Mahina—Brock's wife—hadn't pulled me out of the rioting Pacific and onto Mahina's jet ski rescue sled. I have no memory of that wave, only of white light followed by black silence.

In which Casey jumped my failing heart, and Brock breathed life into my waterlogged lungs.

Sons.

Heart.

Breath.

Life.

Then onto the rescue chopper and the hospital in San Francisco.

I have one more question for you, John, and for you, my dear readers: Do you forgive me?

Midnight, and Jen stares at that final paragraph, heart beating hard, and a dull knot in her throat. Hits the home key and reads the whole article again.

Here it is, she thinks.

How the world will remember John and me.

Betrayal . . .

A fifty-foot blue-black peak breaking top to bottom . . .

In that fraction of a moment I hated him.

And in that half second . . . I knew there was no way I could get to him in time. I had missed my moment.

She wonders if the world really needs this confession, but she knows that *she* does. It's been three weeks since rising from the almost dead. Her memories are creeping back, and they frighten her but she can face them.

So she saves the story and attaches it to a note to her *Surf Tribe* editor.

Apologizes for taking so long.

Hits send.

Jen spends the next hour walking her dark, autumn-cool beach town. She loves this city, its buildings and streets, its beaches and waves and coves. The boardwalk. The smells of the Pacific and eucalyptus and the restaurants, the smell of the Barrel when it was alive, the smell of the roses up in Heisler Park. Loves the people, the artists, the eccentrics, the homeless huddled in their blankets in the cold retail doorways on Forest Avenue.

Live here; die here in this privileged, charming bubble.

We ride huge waves for the rush of it. And the joy and the danger. We pretty much ignore the rest of the world. We are not superfluous people, but we are highly specialized. We Stonebreakers are the stock of champions, who are, of course, made, not born. We beat fear.

Right now she feels released from her past, although found guilty as charged. By a jury of one: herself.

Freed by her confession, born again by truth.

And Jen hopes—she'd pray if she knew how—that Casey and Brock and her mom and dad and Mike and Marilyn will understand and forgive her for missing the chance to save John's life. If not, well, she's given them a foundation of truth rather than a half-truth.

Jen puts one foot in front of the other as she traverses the sleeping city.

An orange-and-black Corvette howls through the crosswalk at Brooks Street, just ten feet from her.

Jen freezes mid-stride.

Another chance to write a new destiny, she thinks. To do for Casey and Brock what you couldn't do for John.

Keep them alive. Protect and serve.

And do something for yourself, she thinks. Finally. Something for the Jen Stonebreaker drowning in regret and fear for all those many years.

Drown no more.

Ride wild horses again.

41

Belle Becket has her fortune-teller's table set up near the sea wall just south of the Laguna Hotel. The wall has the painting of John Stonebreaker banking off a comically perfect wave at Brooks Street—just a few blocks south of here. For the first time, the painting shows its age to Jen: the gray cement divots, the weakening colors, John's hair fading from yellow to white.

Belle has on the same tie-dye hippie dress she was wearing last month. Her hair is its usual tangled mess, her gray eyes piercing, the racoon makeup lurid.

The November day is sunny and blustery, and the breeze wobbles her sign. Jen notes that Belle has raised her prices. Now the short future forecast is five dollars and the long one ten.

Belle comes around and Jen hugs her gingerly, tries not to breathe. Since almost drowning she dares not hold her breath. Sends a panic through her—her body just won't do it. She breathes in Belle's sharp, wild-gourd scent.

Belle steps back, taking one of Jen's hands in both of hers. Gives Jen an alarmed look.

"I'm sorry about the Barrel! I'm so glad they arrested Jimmy Wu! Good police work."

With a lot of help from Bette, Jen thinks.

"I walk past it every day," says Belle. "The rehab is going faster and faster."

"I got the loan and the builders are good."

"I see a beautiful Barrel there by summer."

"I hope you're right."

"I'm always right. Short or long today?"

Jen has five twenties balled up in the pocket of her jeans. Pushes them into Belle's almost-empty mason jar.

"Long, Belle. Tell me what you see."

"Sit."

Belle moves the shadeless lamp that holds her handwritten grocery-bag sign, then takes Jen's hands and stares at her as Jen closes her eyes.

Then Belle.

"Now I'm underwater with you, Jen. Seeing through you. Feeling what you feel. You are frightened and alone and rolling over a reef. You hit a rock but your helmet stays on."

"It was terrible, Belle. I almost died."

"I read your story."

A long silence. Jen knew that Belle would read her piece. That was one of the reasons she wrote it.

"You push off the rocks for the surface. You break into the light. You gasp for air but the whitewater hits your face and mouth."

Jen concentrates on this. It's another memory that has stolen back into her. It's like seeing it happen for the first time. She feels the terror again, those cold, bony fingers trying to take hold of her.

"Now I see nothing but black," says Belle. "You have stopped seeing."

Black indeed. Thoughtless silence, forever.

But now Jen opens her eyes to the breezy gray light of Laguna. Colliding with death has changed her. She can face the memories of it, and feel the fear—but she can also banish them from her inner eye. Replace them with the bright, living world around her.

"The black can't hold me down anymore, Belle. I can make it. Make it to the surface and breathe."

"It is the euphoria of survival. And congratulations on Casey winning. You must be proud. Your mother, too."

They share a look over Eve Byrne's invincible will to win. Especially for her surf and swim and water polo teams, of which Jen and Belle were once a part.

A long silence.

Belle opens her eyes and folds Jen's hands to the tabletop, palms down. Pulls her tie-dye scarf snug around her neck. Crosses her arms and fixes Jen with a serious look.

"In your article, the New Year's Eve party scene in Laguna Canyon was a real bummer. I could feel your heart breaking when you were in that bathroom."

Jen's imagination arcs back to that night. Over twenty-five years ago, in a flash. She closes her eyes again, lets the memory play.

"I saw and heard you in the words," says Belle. "The people making love in an upstairs bedroom. You recognizing a voice. And a familiar moan. You, hiding in a bathroom and the door is cracked and the light is off. You waiting. John walks past. Moving with purpose. Then Ronna Dean. Your school friend, the singer."

"I wasn't planning on revisiting that today," Jen lies. "It still hurts like the night it happened."

"But why did you write it this way, Jen?"

"What way, Belle? What do you mean?"

Belle's eyes are steel gray and unblinking, framed by the heavy black-and-white makeup. The breeze blows a tangled strand of hair across her forehead.

"You lied," she says. "Right there in *Surf Tribe*."

"Yes, I did."

"You saw *me*. Belle Becket. Not some make-believe Ronna Dean."

Jen stands and walks away from the table. Regards the silver ocean mirroring the gray sky, the tiny waves forming and breaking. Pictures exactly where she'd be if she were just one foot tall on an eight-inch surfboard, riding a little monster like that. She's been doing this for forty years now, since Mom and Dad started taking her to this very beach.

Then she turns and considers the sea wall, where fading John rides a fading wave as a fading sun shines down.

Belle joins her. Stands a good six feet to one side, pushes some sand with a dirty foot.

"I didn't know you knew," she says. "That's how I was able to keep doing this. This thing with you. I wondered but I didn't know. Sure didn't see you when I walked past that bathroom. Did you hate me then?"

"Oh yes."

"Now?"

"Not now."

"No one knows, Jen. And now that you've blamed it on a phantom, nobody's ever going to. But what if someone remembers that party and asks about the singer?"

"I never went to a New Year's Eve party in Laguna Canyon. The one with you and me and John was . . . well, you know where it was."

"The rich old people in Newport. What if your magazine finds out you created a character to cover up a truth?"

"To protect another truth."

"Why all these years? Of this, with me?"

Jen has asked herself this for over twenty years, the anger and the pity fighting inside her like alley cats.

"I saw what happened to you. Your . . . coming apart. I believed some of it was what you did with John. Guilt and maybe shame. And that you felt responsible for what happened to him—in some way. Distracted him, maybe. Confused him. I wanted to help you. Not totally lose a terrific friend, who surfed with me, and made me laugh, and made me happy to be around."

"You pitied the pathetic, filthy crackhead who slept with your husband."

"You weren't that then. You're not that now."

Belle watches her foot in the sand.

"It wasn't John that did me in, Jen. It was my guilt. My greedy heart. It was him drowning up there in the cold. Hundreds of miles away. After that, it was just the pipe, taking over. One puff at a time. Throw in some schnapps. Some bad company."

"More than that one time with John?"

"A few."

"Did you love him?"

"Did I ever. I'd been loving on him since I was twelve, just like you. I lost his baby. Not on purpose. Two months after he died."

Jen has wondered about this, and how she would react. Wondered if there might be someone walking the earth now, about Casey and Brock's age, someone with John's looks and his direct, seeking spirit, maybe Belle Becket's gray eyes, loopy humor, and desire to get high.

"Did he talk about leaving me?"

"No. He was in love with you. But I was . . . present and persistent."

"Fuck, Belle. Such loss. All that for this."

"I'm sorry."

"Me, too."

"Thanks for protecting me and my good reputation," says Belle. "I hope no one puts two and two together, after that article."

"Too many stoned and drunk people at too many New Year's parties. Twenty-five years ago. I think we're safe. Walk, Belle?"

"My jar!"

Belle trudges to her table, stuffs the mason jar money into a tattered bead purse and hikes it over her shoulder. They head north.

"I've gotten lots of emails and letters for that last article," Jen says. "Mostly sympathetic, but some people said he'd be alive if not for me. And I should take full responsibility."

"You did that."

"I thought so."

"What did Casey and Brock say?"

Jen watches a young family, bundled against the cool day, pants hiked above their knees. A boy and a girl run ankles deep in and out of the water, screaming in the breeze. Mom and Dad watch closely.

"Casey said, don't feel bad, Mom, you didn't really hate him. Brock said John would have died whether I'd stopped to curse him or not. They look at me differently, Belle. More curiosity. They're asking more questions about their dad. And me. It's like the article freed us somehow—John and me. Made us more . . . real? The boys' socials have been lighting up with this. Everybody's got an opinion about me."

"I saw Casey last week but we didn't talk. How is he?"

"Tied up with a woman I don't much like. She's using him."

"Let me guess. For his good looks, talent, and sweet heart? And Brock? How is your dark missionary?"

"Driven as always."

"It's so strange that Brock got his grandfather Mike's religious pep, not Casey. Maybe something to do with him almost dying, like his dad did."

"I've thought about that. Casey wants to believe. Brock wants to *be* believed."

"What about you? Since almost drowning?"

"Religious pep? No. None for me. I'm just a protect-and-serve kind of girl—because of Dad."

"Such good boys. Do they still call you Momster behind your back?"

"Face to face now. I take it as a compliment."

The women stop to watch the waves crash in at Rockpile.

"Where we first saw him," says Jen.

"We were lucky, Jen. But John was, too."

Heading back for the fortune-telling table, Belle has a customer waiting. He's a cool-looking surf dude with a board propped in the sand and a leashed Malinois sitting attentively at his feet.

Belle stops and whirls and gives Jen an exaggerated, big-eyed racoon stare. Fusses with her hair.

"How do I look?"

"Convincing."

Jen kisses her cheek.

"I'm still up on Castle Rock in the canyon, Belle, if you ever want to shower or crash awhile."

Not for the first time, Jen takes an awful gut punch at the idea of Belle and John in her bed at home on Castle Rock. Will probably never ask that. The truth may set you free, but right now she doesn't want to be *that* free.

"Careful what you wish for, Jen."

"I mean it."

As if on cue, they both look back at the John painting on the sea wall.

"I'll be seeing you around, Belle."

"You're awesome, Jen. John said that all the time."

42

Late that afternoon Casey and Bette sit in the backyard of his Dodge City cottage on Woodland. Mae lies at their feet under the bistro table near the tangerine tree.

The waning day is clear but cool. Even this far into fall, the tangerine tree blossoms sweetly and the plumeria throws off a spicy scent. The birds-of-paradise stand proudly orange and blue, and the bougainvillea is a purple wall.

He shoots some pictures of the flowers, posts them as a CaseyGram along with a haiku that just popped into his mind:

Bougainvillea bracts
White stars in the middle, like,
A purple riot

Ms. Paige up at Thurston Middle School taught his class the 5–7–5 formula, and Casey really dug how cool the rhythm was, though the best he could get out of seventh-grade English was a C-plus because he was such a slow reader and spent class time sketching waves.

This is the sixth afternoon in a row they've been here. Bette wears

Casey's heavy Navajo-print robe and fleece slippers, as she has all week. That first day back from Mavericks, she slept for twenty-plus hours in the guest room, aided by a space heater and her pain pills. Casey sat bedside, guzzling coffee, waking her up every few hours to Bette's woozy annoyance.

Of these six days, Detective Pittman has been here four long mornings, with his questions and voice recorder and video camera. He's methodical and patient, asking the same questions again and again, checking dates and times, exact locations, exact words spoken, expressions, tones of voice, background, background, and more background.

Casey waits on them like good customers in his bar, checking on their coffees and drinks, making them snacks, eavesdropping. In between Bette's recorded conversations with her father, Mr. Fang, and other principals in King Jim Seafood, Casey overhears "unindicted coconspirator," "plea bargain," "immunity from prosecution," "testimony," and "court time." He also hears Bette tell the detective that she's thinking of "getting as far away from him as I can get when this is over."

"He'll be in prison when this is over," said the detective.

Now in the dimming light Casey considers the stitches in Bette Wu's eyebrow. And the plum-purple bruises around her eyes, fading to orange. The bruises on her cheeks are lighter, too. The two small stitches keeping the edges of her lips aligned as they heal—taken by Casey's surfing doctor friend in Half Moon Bay—should be ready to remove in two days.

They sit side by side to view the sunset. Bette drinks wine through a straw; Casey a virgin version of the Barrel Scorpion, heavy on his seedless tangerine juice, which he uses instead of orange juice. Her phone is on the table and she keeps looking at it.

He refills her glass.

"I like to drink wine more than I used to," she says.

"It's good for you, Pop."

"I love that scene."

They've watched a lot of movies this past week.

"I'll cut back the wine when my face doesn't hurt."

"Hang in there."

"I have a question for you, Casey. I believe that Brock and Mahina and the Go Dogs set our boats on fire. I'm almost certain that you did not. Am I right?"

Casey feels that big ugly surge of confusion/anxiety/stupidity rack his brain as he contemplates his answer. Lie or not? Simple but so . . . complex.

"I didn't set the fires because I didn't think it was right."

Casey studies her eyes, the black pupils set in garnet orange and bruise purple, like the pendant around his neck. It hurts him just to look at them. How do you let them do this to your own girl?

"And I've got a question for you," he says. "How did you frame Monterey 9 for the Barrel?"

She studies him blankly, finally nods. Takes another drink.

"Early morning, after we set the fire, we broke into an Imperial Fresh Seafood Sprinter in their Monterey Park lot. Loaded in some canisters of gasoline, and the cell signal timers, the wires, batteries, everything. And a detailed plot drawing of the Barrel, small x's where the bombs had been planted. Fang placed the anonymous tip to LA police, who patrol Monterey, named two of the Imperial Fresh Seafood pirates we've been fighting with for decades. We'd put the bomb stuff in their garages. The frame might not have been strong enough to fool a good defense, but it was enough for the cops to make the arrests and get them off our backs."

"What about the Sierra Sports Sprinter?"

"Our van. Our people. Forged plates. A Sierra Sports emblem one of our people found in a thrift store."

Casey tries to follow the consequences. Tries to think like Brock would think.

"So, if you hadn't told Detective Pittman about all that, the two framed suspects might have been convicted. And the people who torched the Barrel would be free."

"Yes."

In his mind's eye, he sees the flames lashing the walls of the Barrel, melting the surfboards, eating the paintings and the furnishings and the hardwood floor.

And the *Empress II* boiling over with flames. And *Bushmaster* and *Stallion* and the panga . . .

Which is when Casey admits to himself who set Jimmy Wu's boats on fire.

"Who *are* the real Barrel fire setters?" he asks.

"Fang and Danilo."

Casey tries to reconcile their faces with the security camera video. Can't make firm connections, and wonders how a jury could. Again, it's Bette who can identify them. Convict them.

"You've sacrificed a lot for us. Turned in your father. His business. Your coworkers."

Your face, he thinks.

She shakes her head and looks up at him, a quizzical smile on that battered face.

"And I did it for me, too, Casey."

His heart swelling for her, he takes off his surfboard pendant with the orange Mandarin Spessartite garnet embedded on the deck. It's the orange of his father's famous big-wave gun, and the orange of his mother's hair.

Years ago, he hired the aunt of one of the Barrel waiters to make this pendant. She was a well-known Taxco jewelry maker. Sent her pictures, dozens of them, so she could get the shape of the gun right, especially that wicked narrow tail. This was before he had any money. So he borrowed from his mom against his busboy wages: two thousand dollars, because the Mandarin Spessartite was so rare. It took him a year to pay her back.

Bette eyes it. Casey likes that he can't tell what she's thinking.

Now he stands before her and spreads the heavy silver chain, setting the necklace over Bette Wu's head and onto her fine pale neck.

"Thank you," he says.

She stands and lifts a lock of hair off Casey's forehead, managing a half smile. Softly runs a finger along his reef-cut scab.

Casey gets that funny little jolt he gets when she touches him.

Mae looks up at him like she's felt it, too.

The phone buzzes and Bette checks the caller.

"I've got something for you, too," she says.

Accepts the call and walks out of earshot to the sliding glass door. Then raises a stop-sign palm to Casey, turns, and goes into the house. Mae sits and watches.

Bette talks a thousand times a day, quietly, almost always from somewhere Casey can't quite hear.

Through the slider screen he watches Bette, now heading out the front door. He sidles up to the fence, pokes an opening through the thorny purple bougainvillea, and peers through it as a matte-black Tesla glides to the curb.

Bette gets in, sweeping the belt of his robe inside as she shuts the door.

The car doesn't move.

Casey doesn't like this one bit. Knows that Bette is in no shape physically or mentally to defend herself. What is she doing? She's not running away, is she?

He can't see inside through the blackout window glass.

A moment later she steps out, holding a Tiffany's shopping bag with black tissue paper waving out the top.

He strides back to where he was so she won't catch him spying.

She comes through the house, kneeling a moment to pet Mae's ear.

She gives Casey a pained half smile and sets the bag on the table. Lifts the tissue paper with a magician's flourish and Casey looks inside.

At the neat stacks of twenties bundled with bright yellow rubber bands.

"My eight grand from the sportsbook. For betting on you, mister! Half for you, and I'm going to bank the rest and maybe get myself some new clothes."

"I don't want half. It's yours. Buy the stuff you need!"

Which, Casey knows, as an eyewitness, is quite a lot.

A few nights back, he helped pack up her furnished San Gabriel apartment, and was much surprised to see how little she had: a portable turntable and amp with detachable speakers and some vinyl. Some college textbooks and a few novels, a dated collection of DVDs—mostly Chinese action movies. She had bulk Costco toiletries, health and beauty products, cosmetics. Only a few really sweet rags: the black knit suit with the brass buttons she wore the day she bombed into his house in Dodge City, the white linen outfit she wore on Sunset Boulevard. The seafoam-green leather outfit she'd worn to the Barrel months ago and, later, to the Monsters awards banquet, was by then at the Canyon Cleaners in Laguna, where Mr. Kim had told Casey he'd do his best to remove the bloodstains and restore the leather. Bette had a few hats and pairs of shoes. Some jeans, sweatshirts, and T-shirts. Her ocean-going "pirate couture" as she called it was lost in the *Empress II* fire. As was her pistol, which she confessed to having never once fired. When she stopped a moment to study her framed UCLA diploma—but left it hanging—Casey asked why.

"I didn't quite graduate," she'd told him. "Didn't get the algebra at all, and I liked being a pirate better. That's a fake I had made, just like the check I gave your mother."

Now here in Laguna Canyon with her $8,000 on the table, she sits again and takes a long, slow sip of the wine. Sets a hand on Casey's.

"I've been talking to your studio people," she says. "Introduced myself as a friend and business associate, then called bullshit on their biopic purchase price. Told them this year's winner of the Monsters of Mavericks will not grant an option renewal next month."

"But those guys are cool."

"Yeah, so cool they're going to up the purchase price by four hundred thousand dollars. More important, they've got a writer interested. A-list, Oscar nominee, hot dude—or so they say."

"So if they make it—"

"You get half a million dollars and genuine back end. No Hollywood accounting, I told them."

"That's a lot of money."

"You're the best in the world, Casey. You deserve it."

"You're a good partner."

"When I'm not getting beat up!"

"You look better, Bette. Get the stitches out and let the bruises heal. You'll be pretty again. Extra pretty."

She squeezes his hand. "I'm not pretty now?"

"No, I meant—"

She cuts him off with a soft laugh. "I know what you meant."

Casey's embarrassed, of course. Always ready to say something dumb, he thinks. Should get a trophy for that, too.

She lets go of his hand and takes a sip from the straw, studying him. Beautiful eyes in a wounded face, he thinks. Wonders if he and Brock should beat up Jimmy like his people did to her.

"You'll be all the way pretty again real soon, is what I actually meant."

"You're sweet, Casey."

He thinks of something to say but it sounds stupid, even to him. But, sometimes he can't . . .

"Bette, I like you a *lot*. As much as I like Mae."

Who sits up and looks at him.

Bette reaches out and scratches Mae behind the ears, which she loves. But Bette is looking at Casey.

"We're ready, Casey."

"What for?"

"Let's go inside. I'll show you."

Late that night Casey wanders his little clapboard house in Laguna Canyon, flip-flops around his backyard, checking the closed-for-the-night hibiscus, the abundant sage, the tangerines, and the roses. He's got on his Muhammad Ali robe and a cup of herbal tea in one hand. Bette is hard asleep.

He's taken to this routine since Bette got here, his ears tuned to the cars out on Woodland. Not many this time of night. But he's out here for Bette, because he doesn't trust Jimmy or his people no matter how headed for prison they are. Any guy who'd have his own daughter beat up is capable of a whole lot more than that.

Not on my watch, thinks Casey. I'm dumb but not that dumb.

Finally he knows that he should make the call. It's time. It's past time. It's not in time. Fudge . . . who knows what it is or isn't?

"Yo, bro," Brock answers. "'Sup?"

"I know you burned the boats."

"Had you for a minute, didn't I? Thank you for believing I didn't, at least for a while. You kept me out of jail."

"I wish you hadn't lied to me."

"It was for your own good, Case. I'm not sorry I did."

"I am. Hey, Brock, there's a great big magenta ball out in the Atlantic. They're calling it the Hell Swell. Headed for Nazaré."

"I've been tracking it."

"Interested?"

"I'm in. The mission is broke. I have to win some dough. You?"

"Bette and me are going if it holds."

"You're the man, Case. You're the greatest big-wave surfer in the world."

"Well, for now."

"Everything's just for now, bro. See you tomorrow. It's supposed to rain."

43

By noon, the Breath of Life Thanksgiving Feast has drawn a hundred people to Brock's behemoth cinderblock church in Aguanga.

The day is sullen and gray, with an unusually configured storm expected to hit late in the afternoon: an Alaskan system coming down from the northwest, set to meet an atmospheric river of warm tropical moisture streaming over the California Coast from San Francisco to Mexico. NOAA says the merging fronts are ripe for a bomb cyclone, a sudden drop in atmospheric pressure that can bring extraordinary amounts of rain in a very short time. The atmospheric river will be carrying five times the flow of the Mississippi. Snow above seven thousand feet. Tornados possible along the coast and inland valleys. Very unusual this early in the year. Yet another example of climate change from greenhouse gases, they say. Man-made calamity. The new normal.

Brock's buddies at Surfline are tracking the storm, of course, telling him that it won't hit Aguanga until late afternoon or evening, *but* it's going to be "nuclear." They've nicknamed it the Pineapple Bomb Express.

Brock has flooded his media and the church web page with Thanksgiving Feast invitations to anyone who is "hungry, ready for the breath of life, ready to help those who need help." Roughly a thousand people claimed to be coming. But the enthused "we'll be there" messages from California, Oregon, Texas, Arizona, and Nevada haven't panned out.

He's planned to feed five hundred souls, but more like a fifth of that are here. *The storm,* he thinks. *But shit, if it rains we'll just go inside.*

Where the church stoves and rented kitchen ovens are turning out pots of stews and vegan casseroles of rice, broccoli, cauliflower, and corn; ham and bean soup; chili, both spicy and mild. Go Dogs—some wearing their operational black-and-Day-Glo green T-shirts—serve with long-handled spoons onto outstretched paper plates and bowls, many of them doubled up for quantity.

Outside in the gravel churchyard, Brock, Jen, Juana, and some of the Go Dogs have set up a hundred folding chairs around ten rented tables.

A shuffling crowd of thanksgivers serve themselves from the chafing dishes—carne asada, fried chicken, a tuna casserole, vegan kabobs, and five enormous roasted turkeys carved by Mahina.

There are food trucks semicircled in the churchyard—Teddy the Greek, Taco Motion, Wok On, Curry in a Hurry, Thai Guys—but the lines are short.

Since midmorning, Brock has been watching the vehicles coming into the big dirt parking lot just beyond the churchyard, their windshields and tires caked with dust. And the three-wheelers, travel trailers, and dirt bikes. Bicyclists. And a motorcycle club of old guys on growling Harleys.

Anza Valley locals on foot.

A small multitude of people in:

Jeans and sweatshirts, athletic shoes and work boots.

Cowboy hats and western wear.

Bright sports merch: MLB, NFL, NBA, FIFA.

Dickies and flannels.

A family in faux deerskin tops, moccasins, and feathered headbands.

A family dressed as pilgrims.

My motley congregation, thinks Brock.

From his surfboard pulpit—set up on a raised stage facing the churchyard audience and food trucks—Brock looks on with minor satisfaction. Maybe closer to two hundred people, but still, his best crowd ever. He and the Dogs can take the leftovers down to the San Diego homeless shelters. It's taken a good hunk of money to finance all this—the Random Access Foundation declining to sponsor a Thanksgiving extravaganza—citing the tech downturn and early European mistreatment of indigenous New World peoples.

But that's what money is for, he thinks: to feed the hungry, serve the poor.

From the pulpit he waves to Mahina, shooting video from a ladder in the churchyard, surrounded by the still growing crowd. Waves to Jen and Casey and Bette Wu, standing near the ladder. It's the closest he's seen his mother and Bette get. Mae, at Casey's feet, of course. And both sets of grandparents: Pastor Mike and Marilyn Stonebreaker; Don and Eve Byrne.

Brock almost feels happiness. Feels it trying to shoulder its way past his native anger and his urgent need to act. His need to take off on a huge fast wave, to fight with his fists, to kick whatever ass needs kicking. To protect and serve, in his own heavy, dutiful, crusading, Brock Stonebreaker kind of way.

He feels something like peace right now. A foreign thing. Barely recognizes it. Surprises him.

Brock briefly welcomes and addresses his possibly two-hundred-plus guests. His PA system is good but many of the people only momentarily look up from their heaping plates, nod in Brock's direction, then resume their conversations, raising plastic forks and spoons.

"Eat and be thankful!" he concludes. "And when you're ready, go out and help the people of this world. They need you. Breath of life, baby—breathe it in and breathe it out!"

He windmills a chord of air guitar, looking out to his flock, who clap and cheer a little.

Which is when four whining black-and-yellow dune buggies—American flags flying—slide to sudden stops at the churchyard's edge.

Dust rises and engines sputter out, and the Breath of Life compound goes quiet.

All eyes on big Kasper Aamon and his passenger, dismounting first. Followed by six others—one man and one woman per buggy.

Brock's heart upshifts into a higher gear, his nerves bristling as he stares at the yellow-and-black bumblebees. He's furious at himself for allowing this to happen again. Could have posted guards. But he didn't expect Aamon to invade a Thanksgiving celebration. Brock feels that eager, pre-engagement hyperfocus he felt in Bakhmut, Ukraine.

Aamon ambles through the churchyard, leading his Right Fighters militia—all heavily armed, all in Right Fight trucker hats and black windbreakers with "RF" in tall yellow letters on the backs.

Aamon is strapped with what looks to Brock like a homemade flamethrower: two red canisters strapped to his back and hose-linked to a dual-handled gun holstered on his side. Kasper's shaved face is still slightly swollen from Brock's knockout hook.

Mae greets him, tail wagging; Aamon gives her a disgusted glance.

The food truck people scramble and close down fast. Curry in a Hurry is first to crunch out of the lot and onto the road.

Kasper and his troopers fan out and wend around the tables, toward Brock. Some with their phones up, shooting video.

Brock watches from his scaffold as they approach. Feels the crackle of violence in the air. Feels his control vanishing, and a terrible fate pressing down on them from the heavy gray sky above.

Many of the celebrants drift away from the parking lot, uncertain and probably afraid, some headed for the church, others for their trailers, hidden in the arroyo nearby. Some stay where they are, staring, defiant or maybe just confused—Brock can't figure which. He's got a pistol fixed to the back of the pulpit surfboard, one of several just-in-case guns he once hid in his pot grows. Pulls it free and kneels behind the surfboard, jamming the gun into the waistband of his cargo pants. Then rises, pulling his bongo-drum-and-hula-girl Hawaiian shirt over it.

Casey, Jen, and Juana hustle for the church. Brock's grandparents and three Go Dogs follow. Mahina barrels through the crowd and joins Brock on the stage, where Kasper and the Right Fighters now stop twenty feet short.

"Why bring a flamethrower to a rain storm?" Brock asks.

"Those forecasts are never right. Man-made this. Man-made that. Man-made bullshit."

"You're not welcome here anymore, Kasper. Leave, or I'll call the police."

Kasper Aamon raises his big head, sniffs the air.

"Food smells good," he says. His voice strains through his clenched jaws.

"I have to hand it to you, Kasper. You can take a punch."

"I'll attack first next time, and you'll see how it feels to get cold-cocked. I saw you put the gun in your waistband, by the way."

Brock nods, gets a thought. More than a thought: an idea that floats in on Aamon's air of violence, mixing with the smells of the food trucks.

"Why exactly are you here?"

"Let's just say we're here to shoot video for the Riverside County Sheriffs. To help them close this slum down. We've done our due diligence with the clerk's office. You got no permits for those ratty homemade septic tanks. You got no current registration for half of those trailers. You got no legal camping facilities, which means these tent people can't be living here—county rules, check 'em. Your electrical isn't to code, the well is old and illegal, the propane tanks are rusted and dangerous. You house filthy illegals here. You got women fornicating and giving birth in unsanitary conditions. Venereal disease. A crummy clinic and not even a nurse. You're behind on the property tax. You got no handicapped access anywhere. You don't even have any hydrants in case of fire. Very dangerous, Brother Brock—no fire prep."

Brock nods, looking down from the scaffold, considering the flamethrower. "That's bullshit. Nobody's given birth here. We have a nurse in the clinic, full-time."

"Abortionist?"

"No. So at least get your facts straight."

"You're housing third-world breeders, Brock. Fleas, lice, and a free ride in America."

Four Go Dogs march from the church, squaring off with Aamon and his crew not twenty feet away. One carries a carbine pointed at the sky, the other an AR knock-off. Four more Dogs come in from the parking lot. They draw and kneel, guns pointed at the dirt.

Brock senses the violence to come as he watches most of the last of his Thanksgiving congregants hurry past the Right Fight dune buggies, down the dirt road toward the highway, parents carrying children, a woman in a wheelchair that skids and slides as the big man pushing it tries to get up some speed.

He knows he should have prevented this. Knows his belief that Kasper Aamon would stop short of an armed invasion was wishful thinking. Born of some ancient idea that men could change, better themselves, pass on the breath of life instead of the breath of death. Born of holy men like Jesus and Pastor Mike.

Not surprisingly to Brock, he feels fully energized by his long odds here. By the notion that he can nudge Kasper and his Right Fighters off course.

Surprise and redirect them.

Show them they can change.

Even if just a little.

"Kasper, you hungry?"

Mahina gives Brock a disappointed scowl, then climbs down the stage stairs and stalks toward the church.

Brock hops offstage, sticks the landing. Hears his canvas slip-ons hit the gravel, then the metallic clicks and clacks of safeties going off and rounds being chambered. His scalp tingles and he notes the exact location of his gun, and he feels that cool surge of adrenaline that he gets taking off on a big wave, a surge that washes his vision clear and makes him feel strong enough to fly.

Aamon stares at him silently. Looks like he's expecting Brock to leap ten feet and punch him again. He turns to his fighters on either side. Some nod, others shake their heads.

"Gentlemen," says Brock. "Please be seated. I'll be right back."

He hustles into the chapel and the door clunks shut.

Two minutes later he's back, with a heaping plate of food in each hand. He offers a plate to Kasper, who looks at him, then to his fighters, knowing he'll have to take one hand off the flamethrower to accept it.

Which he does. Standing there with a flamethrower in one hand and a plate of turkey in the other, Kasper looks like a grizzly confounded by a bear-proof dumpster. He's just not sure what to do. So he cautiously sets the plate on the nearest table and takes a full grip on the flame-thrower handle again.

Mahina comes from the church, big plates of food on one arm, and her pistol-grip shotgun slung over one shoulder. Gives Brock a look that assures him she's doing this for him, against her better judgment. Thus the shotgun. In her loose hibiscus-print muumuu she looks to Brock—not for the first time—like some island goddess of war.

She's a genius, Brock thinks. A scary genius.

Next Casey comes from the chapel with two big doubled-up paper plates of chow in each hand, and two more balanced on one forearm, his years of serving food in the Barrel coming in handy here.

Holds out an offering to one of the Right Fighters, a stout woman in a Right Fight trucker's hat and a blond ponytail coming through the back.

She rests her carbine over one shoulder, then Casey places a platter in her right hand.

"Have a seat," says Casey.

"I'll stand."

"Cool, totally."

Casey gets two refusals, then one more taker who holsters his pistol to take a plate.

Bette gets one taker, offers her second plate to another Right Fighter.

"Who's the China girl?" Aamon asks Brock.

"A friend of my brother's," he says, noting the calm resentment on Bette's face.

"Hmpf. Covid and communism."

Casey looks Aamon's way as he passes off another Thanksgiving plate. This time to a heavyset man with short red curls sprouting from under his trucker's hat.

"Much obliged," he says.

"Aloha."

Jen and Juana come out next, each with one hand on a rope-handled plastic tub of sports drinks and sodas. Heft it onto a table with a rattle of ice cubes.

The Stonebreakers carry water.

The Byrnes bring beer.

Aamon tries to sit but the backpack flamethrower won't let him. He straightens and shrugs off the backpack, carries it and the gun to the wall of the church, and props them under the awning.

Hefting himself into his wobbly folding chair, he gives Brock a look.

"I've broken bread with demons before," he says. "Helps me measure what I'm up against."

He glances at his plate, then looks again at Brock. "Just now getting to where I can chew regular."

44

Brock goes to the church wall, draws his sidearm from beneath his Hawaiian shirt, and sets it near the flamethrower.

Comes back and sits across from Kasper Aamon, leaning back and crossing his arms.

No words between Brock and Kasper as they watch the Go Dogs and the Right Fighters crunch off and lean their long guns against the wall. Carefully set their holstered handguns on the ground. Go Dogs guns on one side of the flamethrower; Right Fight's on the other.

They return to their tables and sit.

Time passes in a muted, near silence. Eyes watch them from the thick manzanita. Children's laughter comes through the open windows of the chapel. The Kupchiks and their son bring plates of food to one of the far tables. They wave. Brock notes how much better the boy looks, his respiratory infection handled pro bono by an Anza Valley doctor. They've decided to stay awhile rather than head off to Tulsa.

Brock sees that some of the Breath of Life parishioners have crept back from their trailers; some of the earlier guests have left their cars and reappeared for the Thanksgiving feast.

Brock spots two drones easing in low from the north—Riverside

Sheriffs is his guess, sent in response to the 911 calls no doubt called in by his frightened congregation.

Kasper Aamon takes a long look at them, too, then turns to Brock.

"So your brother won the surfing contest," he says, trying to saw off a bite of white meat with the tiny plastic knife. Which snaps in half. Kasper leans left a little, almost tipping over his chair, then deploys a big hunting knife to cut the turkey. "I watched on ESPN 3. Drank beer through a straw."

"Mom won best wipeout. That's her down at the end."

Aamon calls to Jen: "I saw your wipeout! You're weird people to do stuff like that just for fun!"

Jen lifts an energy drink to him. "It's in our blood!"

Another wordless pause, suddenly broken by the rough clatter of two helicopters descending from the south. Brock sees the green-and-white of Border Patrol, and the black-and-white of the sheriffs.

The drones close in, buzzing like big mosquitoes.

Then Kasper to Brock: "What it comes down to is, we don't have much to say to each other. We have different beliefs, different convictions."

"Yeah, well, people can change, too."

"Don't give me some shit about agreeing to disagree. We believe in different gods, too. And that's where I draw the line."

Brock nods. "Try this: the only god I believe in is the Breath of Life."

"No. The first rule is: there's only one."

"You don't know that, Kasper. You can't."

"I'm absolutely positive."

Brock shrugs. "Look around you. Your god could use some help. That's what we do. Help."

Aamon gives Brock a long look, something like amusement on his face.

"So, just one question, Brother Brock. What's with the hair? You trying to be a Black guy or something?"

"I like it this way. Feels right."

"Hmpf."

The drones vanish into the blue. The helicopters spiral down in a loose helix to hover like tremendous dragonflies over a pond. Sand swirls, plates and cups jump into the air. Some of the celebrants hold their hats.

Brock stands, raises both hands and flips them off. Aamon next, then the Go Dogs and the Right Fighters. Raised fingers and drowned-out "fuck-yous!" Most of the others have their faces down now, holding on to their hats, protecting their eyes. Mae barks and wags her tail, her voice hardly audible against the whirlybirds.

Children spill from the church. One of the boys points a yellow squirt gun at the choppers, and another launches a rubber-tipped arrow from a tiny bow. A girl has a small Dalmatian puppy by its middle, legs paddling air, hugging it to her chest.

Brock foresees a terrible massacre about to unfold, remembers all the cops who've mistaken cell phones for guns, kiddie toys for the real thing.

He and Mahina start toward them, but the swift kids are almost to their table by then. Mahina sits back down and shelters the girl and her puppy on her spacious lap. Brock snatches away the boys' weapons and plops them into the rickety folding chairs.

The helicopters nose in closer, their mechanized roar lowering over him. Brock can hardly see through the blowing sand and dust.

Then, the choppers suddenly rise, back off from each other, and bank away into the sky.

Their terrifying voices fade, then vanish. Like a storm switched off, thinks Brock. Or a killer swell at Mavericks retreating to the deep.

As the dust settles, he looks to the Right Fighters and the Go Dogs—some still flipping off the government warships, some smiling, but none moving toward their guns under the awning.

He takes the puppy from Mahina's lap.

Even with the adrenaline coursing through him, Brock has never felt this exhausted in his life—not from fire or flood or being rag-dolled across reefs by monstrous waves all over the planet.

But he feels the breath of life in him, going out and coming in.

Kasper Aamon is looking at him. "Want to join us, Stonebreaker? Fight for the right stuff? You just saw your government at work for you."

"You're a hypocrite, Aamon. You want to rat out my church to the government you say you hate. It's their power you crave. We'll never join you. We like the people you hate."

Brock reaches out and one-hands the puppy across the table and into Kasper Aamon's big paws. Another wordless moment as the Dalmatian licks Aamon's broken jaw.

Kasper sets the dog on his lap.

"Stonebreaker," he says, gesturing with both hands to the churchyard and the people. "Are you willing to die for what you believe?"

"Yes, but I'd rather die in my sleep."

Aamon considers the pup, petting its head as he gives Brock an assessing glare. "First you break my jaw. Now you try to break my will to hate you. With food? You think we're your Thanksgiving savages? Quaint. But I'll admit I'm finding it difficult to hate you personally. Much as I hate the people you harbor here in this fine country. Which does not belong to them. So, thanks for the grub. We'll say our good-byes now, and get to shooting that video we need to shut down this heathen slum."

A hawk keens high up in the heavy dark sky. Scrub jays bicker on the aluminum roof of the church. Faint music from the trailers.

Pastor Mike stands. "First, I'd like to offer up a prayer of thanks."

Brock is still standing from the puppy pass-off.

"I'll say the prayer, Grandpop," he says.

"Go then, Brock."

Mike sits and Brock looks to the people. Absorbs their attention and bows his head, loc spikes raised like antennae. His voice is rough and resonant:

"Breath of life,

Hear our voices,

We breathe you in, and breathe you out,

Breath of life,
Give us life,
Give us the strength to love. Hallelujah and amen."

Jen opens her dust-stung eyes at "Hear our voices" and watches Brock—her smaller, darker, more passionate, less happy twin son. Her mutineer. Her prophet. Her fearless big-wave rider. *He always wanted to be believed,* she thinks. Watches him here, believing himself.

Then she looks at Casey, sitting with his head bowed, hands folded, blond forelock forward, unflappable Mae dozing between his feet. Casey: her gentle, loving boy, now man. Her born believer. The most beautiful wave rider she's ever seen, his father and brother included. *I don't love that woman beside him,* Jen thinks. *I could try.*

Casey takes Bette's hand. Feels that familiar jolt when he touches her. They trade glances and he squeezes her hand and listens to Brock asking the Breath of Life for peace. Casey smiles at that: Brock's never had peace for more than a minute at a time in his life. Not your karma, brah. Never seen a wave you couldn't ride, a fire you wouldn't fight, a flood you wouldn't paddle your kayak over, a man you couldn't whup. Including me. But, like, peace?

He toes off one sheepskin moccasin, rubs a knobby foot along Mae's soft Labrador flank.

Smiles at "Hallelujah and amen," thinking: epic prayer, bro. You dropped right into that monster. You own it.

Mae likes Casey's warm foot, raises her head and squints up at him, then thumps back down into a favorite dream, on Casey's boat, going fast, watching the birds dive into a patch of white water in a green ocean. Loud noise and the boat bumping. No words for all this, only memories.

Suddenly, raindrops come roaring down, big as blueberries, densely packed and hitting hard.

The children and the innocent pour into the big cinderblock building.

The Go Dogs and the Right Fighters scramble to the wall and collect their arms.

The Go Dogs follow the children into the church, and the Right Fighters trot through the deluge for their yellow-and-black dune buggies.

Standing in the open doorway of the chapel, Brock watches the buggies splash down the gravel road, American flags swaying soggily, clouds of exhaust heavy in the rain. He watches Kasper Aamon's vehicle bounce off the main road and into a sandy wash that leads to the trailers.

Followed by the Right Fighters, buggy engines whining.

He can't believe Kasper is doing this.

But he's not surprised one bit, either.

"Enough of this shit," Brock mutters to himself.

His duty is to the people who have come here for sanctuary, not to change the minds of those who are here to hurt them.

He collects Dane Brockman, Javier Frias, and Keyshawn Quadra, and eight more of his most capable Go Dogs. Eleven of them—his almost dirty dozen.

He fixes Mahina with a hard look, but she's already slung her combat shotgun over her shoulder and she barges past him into the rain like he's not there.

Make that twelve, he thinks: Breath of Life, get us through this hour.

He's got them outnumbered.

Brock directs half his Go Dogs to the eastern narrows of the wash, then he and Mahina and five others lope through the rain toward the western bend.

He figures that the Right Fighters are headed for the trailer encampment that lies on the higher ground edging the wash, where they'll shoot their pics and vids, then circle back to the church and the outbuildings, and his home.

And after that? Time for Kasper's flamethrower?

The rain has lessened and the wind slants it sideways.

Brock can see the yellow-and-black dune buggies through the dense manzanita, and the first row of trailers huddled in the rain. There are lights on in some of them, movement behind the curtains, dogs barking from behind raised cinderblocks.

He shoulders into the sharp, stout bushes, breaking his way to the wash, Mahina and his Dogs behind him.

He sees bear-like Kasper out ahead of the others, already on the far side, the gun of his flamethrower holstered to his hip, a video camera held up, shooting the trailers.

Behind Aamon, two of his dune buggies are mired in the runoff, big tires sunk into the mud, the drivers trying to gun them back to shore, raising rooster tails of mud high into the air.

Drenched Brock watches the other three Right Fighters—two men and women—slipping and sloshing along the bank toward the trailers.

Behind them Brock sees Dane, Javier, Keyshawn, and three more Dogs in measured pursuit, weapons drawn, gaining.

Watches as Kasper lets the camera dangle around his neck, takes up the dual-gripped gun and fires a stream of orange-blue flame against the nearest trailer.

Disbelief joins fury in Brock's combustive heart.

The flame hits the aluminum and sizzles out in the rain, so Aamon shoots another sword of fire but again, the rain drowns it to nothing.

Brock and Mahina ford the wash, feet spread, swaying with the current, guns trained on Kasper, five Go Dogs just behind them.

And, Brock sees, another six Dogs closing in on the far bank.

"Kasper!" screams Brock. "You are not allowed to do this!"

Kasper gives him an almost placid look, then fires another jet of fire against the blackened trailer from which Brock now sees the Jones family—Gloria, Burt, and two daughters—burst from the little front door and run into brush, followed by a small white pit bull, stubby legs already half covered with mud.

The rain picks up again now, heavy, windblown and warm.

Brock slogs on, into the smell of gasoline.

Aamon wheels and throws a comet of flame toward Brock, but the homemade weapon doesn't have much range, and the fire crashes and smokes out in the rushing brown water.

"And you are not allowed to break my jaw and found a nation of filthy heathens!" roars Kasper. "I have the Constitution to enforce."

"Drop the gun, Kasper!"

Kasper fires a weakening stream of flame toward Brock but again it falls into the water and sizzles out. Which lets Brock check his flank, where he sees Dane, Javier, and Keyshawn—guns drawn—surrounding Right Fighters, some with their arms raised and others on their knees, breathing heavily.

Kasper rounds the Jones trailer and aims the flamethrower at the door, slamming open and shut in the wind.

Brock is clambering on all fours up the collapsing bank of the wash when he sees Burt Jones crash through the brittlebush and tackle Aamon from behind.

Brock is on them fast, trying to pull skinny Burt off Aamon, but Burt holds fast to the red cylinders and together they drag Kasper out of the trailer and into the warm downpour.

Big Kasper rolls over and tries to shoot Brock in the face but the newly bent and creased barrel pours smoking orange-black lava down his arm and Kasper Aamon howls in agony that dwarfs even the roar of the storm.

Brock snatches the gun away, pulls bellowing Aamon to the bank and into the rushing flood.

Watches as the big man flails into the deeper middle current, arms clubbing away, his screams high-pitched and terrified. He's already gulping air.

Running along the treacherous bank beside him, Brock thinks: I can do nothing but watch, and let Kasper die. Or jump in and save his sorry ass to fight his right fight another day, and another, and another.

Or maybe change?

Atone?

Forgive?

Generally just get his shit together?

He slides down the embankment, dives flat in, and breaststrokes downstream, the muddy floodwater tumbling Aamon out ahead of him.

Brock snags the backpack flamethrower with one hand, side-stroking at an angle and scissor-kicking hard. Finally rises and drags his cursed, gasping enemy toward the near bank.

SEVEN MONTHS LATER

45

This evening, Casey and Jen sit side by side at the Barrel bar, Mae napping at their feet.

They're tracking the five wall-mounted big screens tuned to network and cable news. The summer light burnishes the room in a warm orange glow.

Their restaurant is rebuilt and remodeled and set for a gala reopening next week, on the Fourth of July.

Tonight's get-together is just family and a few friends.

Casey goes through the bar-top lift door, mixes up two more Arnold Palmers, sets them up, and sits again next to his mother.

The new Barrel is a nearly literal version of the old place: same windows and white walls, same walnut hardwood floors streaked with blond, and island-looking teak furniture, same surfing videos playing nonstop when news and sports aren't on.

Same bronze John Stonebreaker standing in the lobby with one arm on his surfboard and his optimistic, wave-tuned expression which, technically, is focused on the cars creeping along Coast Highway a few yards in front of him rather than the waves breaking along the Laguna shoreline just a few hundred feet behind him.

The damaged big-wave gun surfboards have been restored and refinished and rehung.

The ruined ones have been replaced by equally authentic boards happily donated by the Stonebreaker family's many well-wishers in the surfing "community."

Duke Kahanamoku's redwood twelve-footer, ridden at Sunset Beach, circa 1915.

One of Jeff Clark's classic plain-wrap guns for Mavericks, shaped by Clark in 1999.

A fresh Laird Hamilton ridden at Jaws.

A Maya Gabeira from Todos Santos and a Mike Parsons ridden on Cortes Bank just last winter.

A Garrett McNamara from Nazaré.

A Kevin Naughton ridden in Ireland, prominently positioned because Kevin's been a Laguna friend and mentor since Jen was a girl.

Jen has replaced the burnt-up tiki torches with black wrought-iron wall sconces that give the restaurant a candle-lit, slightly old-world touch.

The local news snippet that Laguna Beach detective Pittman tipped them about earlier today hits CNN first:

In which a reporter from the Orange County Superior Courthouse announces that "colorful" LA seafood distributor Jimmy "King" Wu has been sentenced to serve six years in prison and pay $2 million in restitution for last year's arson fire that gutted the popular Barrel Restaurant in Laguna Beach. She says Wu had attempted to buy the restaurant but was rebuffed by its longtime owner. Wu then ordered the arson as retribution, attempting to blame business competitors for the blaze. The reporter then quotes the Barrel owner, Jen Stonebreaker, saying she's satisfied with the sentence and will reopen her restaurant next week, on the Fourth of July.

"You look great on TV, Mom."

I looked great a long time ago, she thinks, aware again, as always, of how strenuously she clings to her past, her gone best years, when John was alive and the world belonged to them.

"Thank you, Casey," she says. "I'm feeling better now. After the Monsters. And the fear. And the confession I wrote."

"It's good to tell the truth and move on," says Casey. "You're only forty-seven."

They watch similar clips on NBC and Fox, Casey turning often to the lobby windows through which he can see people drifting by, some stopping to press their hands and faces to the glass, checking out the restaurant about to rise from its ashes.

"How goes your movie?" Jen asks.

"They're editing now. The winter footage was fantastic. Oh, man— Nazaré and Cortes Bank were supernatural. All the scientists are saying climate change is making bigger waves. Some of those things at Nazaré were scary."

"HBO Max, right?"

"But we're the producers and we've got creative control. Some. There's going to be lots of you and Dad in it. They want to call it *Desperation Reef.*"

Jen nods and Casey waits. The eight-hundred-pound gorilla is still in the room whenever Casey's various business ventures come up.

"Bette's done good on your contracts and projects," says Jen.

"Thanks, Mom. She works hard at it."

"How about her towing skills?"

"She's good. Not as good as you. We practice a lot."

"But you haven't tried her out in big waves yet."

"It's the usual slow summer for big waves. But there's a nice south swell coming in tomorrow at the River Jetty. Five to seven feet, says Surfline."

Another awkward beat. "I wish you liked her better, Mom."

"I know you're together a lot."

"I want to invite her to something like this. You know, maybe next time."

"I know. I also know that both of you better watch your butts when Jimmy gets out of prison. Hell, watch your butts now, for that matter."

"His pirates pretty much jumped ship."

"But it's Bette who nailed him. Just saying."

Through the front door glass Casey sees Grandpa Don and Grandma Eve coming up the steps to the entrance, first to arrive. They wear their summer clothes—shorts and sandals and bright Aloha shirts. Behind them are Mike and Marilyn Stonebreaker—Mike in his white preacher's suit and Marilyn in a long, peach-colored dress, her hair up, wayfarers on.

A moment later, Brock and Mahina, and Juana and Dane from the Breath of Life Church.

Mae has moved to the lobby, where she stands wagging her tail, as if she's wanting to seat them.

Casey hops off the barstool and heads for the door.

46

The Santa Ana River Jetty up in Newport is a glassy eight feet the next morning, an unseasonal south swell of warm water and beautifully shaped waves.

Casey watches the perfect A-frames marching in, growing to full height, their bodies windlessly smooth, the white spray of the peaks finally breaking, dividing the waves into left and right shoulders that rise invitingly.

It's first light as Bette idles her jet ski—a three-hundred-horsepower Kawasaki two-stroke she's named Wanda, after her sister in New York. The 850-pound beast was endorsed by Jen, who ordered her to service it and check every line, valve, and injector, and all connections, before towing her son into big surf.

Casey sits snugly behind her in his half-john wetsuit, arms around Bette's middle, his surfboard and tow line behind them on the rescue sled.

"Set me up on that last left," he says, over the idling gurgle of the jet ski. He smells her hair and feels her warm ear on his cold nose, hugs her big strong body.

"You got it," she says, half turned so he can hear.

Bobbing a safe distance in front of, and away from, the incoming waves,

Casey watches that third left taking shape outside. It's the clean-up wave of the set, the last, and the biggest local wave he's seen this spring or summer. He squeezes Bette's middle again, pulling himself up against her, comforted and thrilled by the seaworthy strength and beauty that he can feel even through her wetsuit.

We're like pirates in arms, he thinks, letting go of her and sliding into the ocean, stroking back to the rescue sled and his tow rope and board.

A moment later, Bette turns and catches his right-hand shaka sign, the one Brock can't stand, then she eases her machine into a brisk trot and picks her way along and behind the breaking wave. She sidles west, parallel as the wave rises in front of her, gunning Wanda faster now toward the peaking crest. She feels the weight of Casey behind her.

Loves the power of the ski, the power of her own strong body in control of all those horses. Like Casey's.

Swerves ahead and around the cresting wave, then speeds along the left-breaking shoulder. When she feels Casey drop the tow rope she looks back to make *sure* he's dropped it, then opens up the ski and blasts up the steepening face of the breaker and over it, into the sky, engine screaming, Bette getting off this wave as fast as she can so Casey, behind her, can inherit it.

She crashes down into the smooth dark water, cuts hard left, safely behind the wave now, and sees the back of Casey's yellow head cutting along in front of the breaking lip, the rest of him a faint speeding shadow in a wall of blue-green water. Same yellow head she watched so intently in the Barrel bar not quite a year ago when she dressed her best and tried to catch his eye but he never once looked over.

Casey trims along the shoulder, ducks into a quick clean tube, lets it spit him back out to carve the face. Up and down and up and down, what a joyful wave she is, proud but generous and truly, fully stoke-worthy.

Shoots across this living animal, traces a hand along her flank, dips to the bottom and shoots back to the top, where he launches his board.

Flies high, bending into free fall, arms spread and eyes on the gray-blue sky.

ACKNOWLEDGMENTS

My introduction to the literature of surfing was the hundreds of *Surfer* magazines I read and reread as an adolescent. I didn't just read *Surfer*; I memorized it. I loved the sassy writing, the exotic datelines, hip lingo, and its single-minded passion for riding waves. That writing, and of course the photographs, drove me to hours in high school classes, ignoring the teachers, while sketching romanticized waves in my notebooks. It drove me to Newport Beach where I began my own short wave-riding career, bodysurfing 15th Street—a stout beach break with hollow tubes—makeable with nothing but Birdwell Beach Britches and a pair of Duck Feet.

That said, much of the recent nonfiction surf lit is, in my opinion, even better, especially with regards to big-wave surfing and tow-in surfing, which changed the sport dramatically.

These books informed, delighted, and often thrilled me:

The Wave by Susan Casey

Maverick's: The Story of Big-Wave Surfing by Matt Warshaw

Barbarian Days: A Surfing Life by William Finnegan (winner of the Pulitzer Prize)

Ghost Wave: The Discovery of Cortes Bank and the Biggest Wave on Earth by Chris Dixon

Caught Inside: A Surfer's Year on the California Coast by Daniel Duane

Women on Waves by Jim Kempton

"Surf noir" is a literary subgenre that I've enjoyed since Kem Nunn's wonderful *Tapping the Source* pretty much put surf noir on the map. His *Tijuana Straits* and *The Dogs of Winter* are wonderful, too.

Don Winslow's novellas *Sunset* and *Paradise*—part of *Broken*—are powerful stories, steeped in surfing life and death.

Thank you, writers, you inspire.

Thank you, waves, you seduce and sometimes terrify.

Thank you, champion agents, Mark and Robert Gottlieb of Trident Media Group, and my wise and exacting editor at Forge, Kristin Sevick, for helping me make the paddle out and the drop into *Desperation Reef*.

And thank you, Rita, for life, love, and laughter.

ABOUT THE AUTHOR

Rita Parker

T. JEFFERSON PARKER is the author of numerous novels and short stories, the winner of three Edgar Awards, and the recipient of a Los Angeles Times Book Prize for best mystery. Before becoming a full-time novelist, he was an award-winning reporter. He lives in Fallbrook, California, and can be found at tjeffersonparker.com.